The Ingenue

Also by

RACHEL KAPELKE-DALE

The Ballerinas

Graduates in Wonderland:
The International Misadventures of Two (Almost) Adults
(with Jessica Pan)

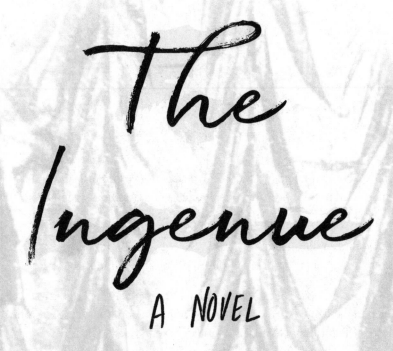

The Ingenue

A NOVEL

RACHEL KAPELKE-DALE

ST. MARTIN'S PRESS
NEW YORK

First published in the United States by St. Martin's Press, an imprint of St. Martin's Publishing Group

THE INGENUE. Copyright © 2022 by Rachel Kapelke-Dale. All rights reserved. Printed in the United States of America. For information, address St. Martin's Publishing Group, 120 Broadway, New York, NY 10271.

www.stmartins.com

Designed by Devan Norman

Library of Congress Cataloging-in-Publication Data is available upon request.

ISBN 978-1-250-83456-0 (hardcover)
ISBN 978-1-250-83457-7 (ebook)

Our books may be purchased in bulk for promotional, educational, or business use. Please contact your local bookseller or the Macmillan Corporate and Premium Sales Department at 1-800-221-7945, extension 5442, or by email at MacmillanSpecialMarkets@macmillan.com.

First Edition: 2022

10 9 8 7 6 5 4 3 2 1

For my father,
Steve Kapelke,

and my mother,
Kathleen Dale

Find what you love and let it kill you.

—ATTRIBUTED TO CHARLES BUKOWSKI

The
Ingenue

Prologue

NOBODY KNOWS WHERE THE ELVES CAME FROM. In lieu of gargoyles, that pair of fairy-tale creatures has framed the doorway of the Harper mansion for as long as anyone can remember. Kneeling mischievously, their pointed ears sticking out from their stocking caps, they lie in wait. Watching the births and the deaths, the parties and the funerals, the beginnings and the endings. But who, every Harper for generations has asked, put them there?

When Georg and Emilia Harfenist had come over from the newly united Germany in 1871 (*ein Kaiser*, Emilia used to say—*bah!*), Georg was as pleased to shed the superstitions of his native land as he was to shed his name: they were now Harpers, and they didn't believe in fairy tales. There was a practicality to America, a straightforwardness to it that suited him. You worked and you saved money; you used that money to buy land; that land was yours, and on it you could build a house for your family. Or, in his case, a mansion out of his wife's Gothic dreams. Peaks and spires, towers and libraries, all perched on a cliff's edge above Lake Michigan, with a view of the wild and wilding waters.

It couldn't have been Georg who chose the elves. The plaster vines and roses curling around the ceiling of the foyer were as far as Georg would go in terms of whimsy. The Brothers Grimm, the Schwarzwald, the fairies, and, yes, the elves, too—they were a superstitious nightmare from which the grimly Lutheran Georg had awoken. Anyway, the timing was wrong. The elves themselves are a paler gray than the house itself. They haven't seen the same number of Wisconsin winters, haven't lived through the same sweltering Milwaukee summers as the rest of the house, which has deepened over time into charcoal, disappearing into the surrounding trees on dark nights.

Georg did set up his cream-bricked brewery downtown, and he did make the beer that made Milwaukee famous (and made the highways, when they came, redolent with the sweet-sickly smell of gasoline-tinged hops), and in turn, he made his fortune. Their fortune. But he hadn't made any elves.

Who, then?

The Harpers multiplied slowly, like a fairy-tale curse: precisely one male heir each generation. And the men, without exception, were an ambitious and dour lot, just as the women they married had an inevitable whimsy that would have gotten poorer women sent straight to the asylum.

So yes, one of the wives could have done it. Which, though, would have dared?

Had Constance put them there sometime during the Depression? Unlikely. Constance was vaguely related to the Rockefellers, and it had been hammered into her from birth: unnecessary public displays of wealth were how you got guillotined. Besides, the family had been in such dire straits by that point that they'd sold off the brewery to a conglomerate. (Freddie had a few qualms about getting rid of his grandfather's legacy but consoled himself that the house was legacy enough. The house, and the money from the sale that should have lasted them a century or more.) There wasn't anything extra to spend on bizarre masonry.

Constance was fanciful enough for the elves, though, and fancy was what the house excelled at. Constance found this out the hard way when she tried to join the war effort a bit later, plowing up the back gardens and planting beets and carrots and potatoes. Though her Victory garden never grew, the hydrangeas and peonies flourished. Despite its founder's intentions, the Elf House was never any good at producing anything practical. Beautiful, it could do.

To tell the truth, Evie was the most likely suspect. In 1950, Evelyn Harper was the first woman born into the family for four generations, inheriting all of Constance's playfulness and all of Frederick's ambition. It was certainly in Evie's nature to have put the elves there. But she did not own the house until her father's death in 1982, and by then the elves were a long-established fact. They peer from the margins of the 1942 photograph of Freddie in his uniform, about to embark on a brave journey

overseas. They peek over the edges of photos documenting Evie's graduation, her Daughters of the American Revolution induction, her wedding.
No, the elves predate Evie by a long time.

Sometime after the unification of Germany, sometime before World
War II. Nobody knows where the elves came from, but the elves are sitting there still. They are sitting there now. Perched on either side of the
Elf House's oaken door, watching the family pass under their motionless
eyes. Though the family is not called Harper anymore. Her 1974 marriage turned Evelyn Harper into Evelyn Kreis.

And, anyway, Evelyn Kreis is dead.

Her husband stops in the February cold, his hand paused on the open
car door. The last weeks have etched themselves onto his face, acid into
stone. A round face, a wing of silver hair above, a Cary Grant dimple in
the chin recently twisted just out of familiarity. A pleasant face turned
uncanny by grief.

At the sound of the piano, though, a twitch of the forehead, and the
sunbursts at the sides of his almond eyes lift. Evelyn Harper Kreis is dead,
but there is music in her house. And now the house will sing once again.

"Hello, the house," the man calls, pulling the oak door closed behind
him. At his feet, a silver-and-white husky, more than halfway to a wolf,
wriggles in decidedly unwolflike ecstasy. A palm on the pup's head—

"I'm *playing*." Her voice is a low, annoyed buzz from the conservatory,
but it makes him smile.

The man looks at the dog. A conspiratorial whisper: "Should we go
bug your sister, then?"

She's crescendoing as they approach the arched oak entryway, her
corn-silk head weaving back and forth behind the piano.

"*Danse Macabre?*"

She nods, turning a page without looking up at him. "The Horowitz
arrangement."

"It's nice," he says, and she does look up at this, the two of them shar-
ing a smile, though her hands keep going. The music is disturbing, discordant. *Nice* is the very last thing it is.

Above them, a dull thump. Another. Each one like a sack of flour being flung against the floor.

The dog's ears prick up.

"What the hell—"

"Oh," she says, her hands dancing madly over the keys. "That's just Patrick."

"Patrick?"

"Yeah," she says, scanning the page in front of her as the notes twist, turn wild. "He's locked up in the attic. It's stupid," she says, stopping to flex her fingers. The silence rings through the room as she looks at him with his own blue eyes. "But I kind of hoped he'd be dead by now."

Outside, the elves wait. Frozen in time.

Chapter 1

"Oh, wonderful! Yes, let's never grow up. We'll have adventures and seek treasure and hunt pirates and—"

Peter Pan looked a little uncomfortable.

"Ah. Well, you see, I didn't exactly mean you, Wendy."

Wendy frowned. "Then what did you mean?"

Peter laced his fingers together, refusing to meet her eyes. "Someone will have to cook and clean and generally look after things around camp, you know. And we thought—"

Wendy stared at him in disgust. "You want me to be your mother? No way. I'm ten." She stood up and beckoned to the fairy. "Come on, Tinker Bell. Let's you and me never grow up together."

—*Fairy Tales for Little Feminists:*
Wendy and the Lost Girls, Evelyn Harper Kreis

December 1991

SASKIA WAS NINE. EVEN AT A RUN, IT TOOK HER more than twenty minutes to check every room in the Elf House, but her mother wasn't anywhere to be found. Saskia had even checked the guest rooms, the semi-haunted spaces with their sheeted furniture like ghosts, where Evie almost never went and where Sas ventured only when she was trying to scare herself. She sometimes thought that the souls of her mother's ancestors who had lived here were lying among the ancient oak bedsteads and bookshelves, just waiting for their chance to rise up and tell her what she was doing wrong.

It was not unusual for her mother to disappear for extended periods. In general, Saskia's parents treated her less like a kid and more like a miniature adult. At parties, with other parents, her mother always said that the best thing to do with children was to let them come up, not to make them grow up. Like Saskia was a blade of grass or a dandelion.

So Saskia was used to being alone in the big house. And though she didn't mind the echoing solitude, Lexi had bribed her with the twin temptations of a trip down to Downer followed by a sleepover. She loved their sleepovers, which were filled with ghost stories they'd cribbed from the bone-curdling *Scary Stories to Tell in the Dark* series. Neither of them was technically allowed to read it, but that didn't stop them. Nor did it stop their attempts to put what they'd learned into practice: summoning Bloody Mary, primarily, though Lex had a Ouija board that had been known to make an appearance.

But as much as Sas loved their sleepovers, she loved Downer more. Downer, the Main Street of Milwaukee's East Side. Saint Nicholas had left her $10, and the bill was burning a hole in her pocket. She never had money. And $10 could buy any number of things on Downer: the popcorn truck sold dime candy in jars, Soaps & Scents had eighty-five-cent tea lights, Paperworks offered its stickers at a nickel a square. She could get eleven candles or 250 squares of stickers with her $10 bill, if she wanted them.

All she needed was to tell her mother, but Evie was nowhere to be found. There was only one place left to look. But the simple truth?

Sas was scared to go into the studio.

For decades, her mother's subject had been women's hands: the hands of famous artists, scientists, writers, actresses; the hands of washerwomen and seamstresses and mothers. She photographed them, she drew them, she was obsessed. The overall effect of going into her studio was like going into the woods, all those fingers like branches pinned on the wall. Like they were reaching out to grab you.

Saskia pulled on her snow boots with a sigh. Johann snuffled at her side, and she held the door open for him, letting him sprint out into the piles of snow. The snow went up almost to her knees, and she was tall for her age; everyone was always telling her. She wasn't sure how true this was. She was Saskia-sized, that was all.

The studio was actually an old caretaker's cottage that Evie had claimed for her own, a five-minute walk from the back door to the edge of the property. Surrounded by the northern pine copse, the cottage had had almost no sun reach its windows until last fall, when Evie had taken out the chain saw and cleared a gap in the trees herself.

Now, the afternoon sun slanted in the wide picture window, illuminating the gold of Evie's head as she bent down over her drawings. Saskia liked to see her this way; it was the only time her mother's expression ever resembled her own at the piano or her father's at the cello.

At the door, she hesitated. Hesitated to break her mother's concentration, hesitated to enter the forest of hands.

She gently brushed her knuckles against the door.

"What?"

"What are you doing?" Saskia asked, sidling up to the desk. The reaching fingers on the walls had disappeared, replaced by a strange parade of figures . . . not girls, exactly, their bodies were slightly too elegant for that. But not women, either: their eyes were wide, shining.

"A new project. What do you think?" Evie leaned back in her chair, a stick of charcoal still in hand as she crossed her arms.

Saskia tried to live up to the question, to the respect that it implied.

"They're pretty."

"Hmmm."

She leaned closer. "They're . . . they're interesting. Mom, what are they? Who are they?"

Her mother set the charcoal down on the table, swiveled without rising to the electric kettle on the filing cabinet, and flicked it on.

"You really don't see?"

Saskia looked again. The portraits lacked context, just bodies on blank white pages. But they wore old-fashioned dresses. Like—

"Are they from fairy tales?" she asked.

Evie swiveled back around as the kettle started to grumble. "Bingo!" she cried, pointing a finger at Saskia. "Well done, Sas. Yes. I've decided it's time to put these old drafting skills to some real use."

Evie taught drawing and illustration at the university, then came home and drew late into the night, until there was only the little orange circle of her desk lamp for light. Saskia could feel her mother itching to get back to work yet didn't want to puncture the bubble of praise, wanting to remain as long as possible in its orb.

"Fairy tales," she said again, bending over the sketches as if to study them.

"*Fairy Tales for Little Feminists*," her mother corrected. "Good title, isn't it?"

Saskia looked at the princesses. They weren't Disney inspired, they were too elongated and sophisticated for that. She hated Disney anyway, everything except *The Aristocats*. Still. There was something more to her mother's pictures, even she could tell. Something in the languid brushstrokes, in the blending of the colors.

Something more—and something strange.

Her mother, watching her face, laughed.

"Come out with it," she said.

"Well, aren't you going to get bored?"

"Why would I get bored?" Her mother looked genuinely perplexed.

Saskia swallowed. "I don't. They're all so—same-y. Aren't they? Don't the princesses all kind of . . . look alike?"

Evie's eyes grew as round as whole notes.

"That's part of the fascination. All those princesses, all those witches, all those dead mothers . . ."

Saskia winced.

"Well, you need a good dead mother to set any princess off on her quest!" Evie cried, palms to the ceiling. "Any mother worth her salt would have stopped each and every one of these girls before she even got a foot out the door."

"But why do you want to tell stories that have already been told?" Saskia said.

"Ah. Because there's something new in them every time. And it's only the sameness that helps us to see that."

Saskia watched her mother for a minute before admitting defeat. "I don't get it."

A knowing smile. "You will. Hey—what did you want, anyway?"

"Oh!" she said. "Can I sleep over at Lexi's?" It was a perfunctory question—Lexi's mom, Georgia, was one of her mother's best friends, and the family lived next door.

But her mother, glancing for a millisecond back to the princesses on her table, had a funny expression on her face. Something tense under the relaxed looseness of her smile.

"Of course."

"Yeah?"

"Of course, you *could*," Evie said tentatively, and sighed. "I'm just nostalgic, I guess. The way you used to sit at the piano. We could just park you there for days."

"I already . . . I already practiced, though. Besides, Mrs. Hauser's sick," Saskia said, picking through the words carefully.

Evie's head went up and down, like her sharp chin was being pulled by a puppeteer up in the ceiling.

"Sure," she said finally. "Well, you're going to do what you're going to do."

Back in the Elf House, Saskia stood frozen in the foyer for a minute. Two. Three.

Finally, she sat down on the staircase to pull her bright yellow boots off. And after padding in her socks back to the piano, she began to warm her hands up once again.

January 2020

IN SASKIA KREIS'S LIFE, ONLY THREE THINGS EVER made her special: piano, the Elf House, and Patrick. Three things are a whole lot more than most people get, but it is hard to feel gratitude now. Hard to feel it as she stands at the gates to the Elf House in the Milwaukee midwinter, bare hands against the Victorian iron, for the first time in two years.

She's known for a long time that things with her mother weren't right, haven't been since she quit Juilliard. But she didn't realize they were like this. Didn't realize that they'd degenerated to the point where her mother wouldn't tell her about the fast-moving disease that was eating her alive.

Didn't realize that her mother wanted the news of her death to hit her like a house collapsing over her head.

It gnaws at her stomach, empty and bitter. Evelyn Kreis had seen something in her daughter that disturbed her, that made her withdraw.

Saskia doesn't know what it is. But that judgment—or rather, the fear of that judgment and its accompanying dismissal—has kept Saskia away from her childhood home for two years, ever since she lost her job. She couldn't face disappointing her mother one more time. And her mother's failure to tell her, to say: *I'm dying*? To say: *Please, come back home*?

It means that Saskia was right to stay away.

Three things made her special, and one—no, two of them are here in Milwaukee. The Elf House and Patrick. She'll see him again; tomorrow, she'll see him again. Two years since their last encounter. The thought makes her insides swoop and soar like the seagulls playing over the lake. What will he think of her, the way she is now?

The first thing that made her special has long been lost to history. Saskia Kreis used to be the next great American pianist. An ingenue, a wunderkind, a virtuoso. She'd had her first public concert at seven, her first recording at fifteen. But something—her talent? her desire? nobody knew for sure, though a handful of obscure internet forums speculated—had tapered out by the time she was eighteen. A promising future at Juilliard was cut off after only one semester, and Saskia had transferred to NYU, where she'd studied computer science (*Computers!* Evie had cried) and electrical engineering, graduating to a career as a mediocre coder.

Thing number two still exists. It is, in fact, more present than ever: Saskia Kreis is the heiress who will inherit the Harper mansion, the Elf House. Fourteen thousand square feet and thirteen bedrooms, full of fanciful plasterwork and custom woodwork, antique furniture and oversize oil paintings. Two acres of gardens and orchards stretching to cliffs, with a sandy beach below. Owing to a bizarre clause in her great-grandfather's will that all subsequent Harpers repeated in their own, the house has to go to the next direct descendant in Georg Harper's line. So it will skip over her father (though she'll let him stay there, obviously—that's never been a question) and land directly in her lap. That beautiful old house.

But even now, she's remembering it rather than viewing it. Just as she has for these past two years. Because you can't see the Elf House itself from the street. Passersby see only the gates, the lane of pines behind them twisting off somewhere toward the lake. You have to follow the gentle curve of the private road before it comes into view. Slate gray, with only a few details saving it from outright harshness. The pointed arches of the garrets, the stained-glass windows, the lacelike wrought iron lining the balconies. And, of course, the elves. A lovely house, a prime example of Milwaukee's Germanic heritage. But the only time the public sees it is on the historical society's annual garden tours of the East Side.

She sighs and opens the gates, feet crunching too loudly through the snow-covered gravel as she makes her way through the trees. As she comes closer to the Elf House; as the East Side fades away.

A *good place to raise kids*. That's what residents always say about Milwaukee's East Side. The sprawling Gothic and Tudor and Italianate mansions on the lake ceding to the properly contained Victorian single-families near the redbrick, leafy university. Beaches and boulevards, bookstores and barbecues. Lake Park delineating the limits of the neighborhood (it was designed by Olmsted, who designed Central Park—a fact the well-educated residents all know and occasionally trot out). Canopies of 150-year-old trees joining hands over side streets filled with kids on bikes.

After the grim necessity of the airport, the ramshackle houses and dirty piles of snow lining the freeway, the East Side feels like a fairy-tale village to Saskia. You'd think that two years away might give her an idealized image of her hometown. But here, in the richest part of the city, the image and the reality are one. It's either wreaths and garlands, gingerbread houses lined with lights, or soft blue skies over sandy cliffside beaches that could be—and are—Instagram worthy, no filter required. Yup. A *good place to raise kids*.

But it has been years since Saskia Kreis was a kid to be raised, and the Uber driver, seeing her address, had rolled his eyes, though he hadn't realized she was watching. A rich bitch. He hadn't realized it's her dead mother's AmEx in her Apple Pay, slyly input by the older woman on her trip to New York the previous spring. Saskia had had no idea it would be Evie's last trip there. Had Evie known?

She turns and there: there it is.

In the darkening light, the Gothic gables of the Elf House give off their own pearly-gray luster. There's still something about the sheer expanse of the house that takes her breath away: the heavy stone arching with an unlikely grace toward the sky. Rows and rows of diamond-paned windows, bay windows, window seats. From the outside, you'd think the house was made for a bunch of Peeping Toms. Is that a shadow, flickering behind the living room curtains? But the house does that, too, the roaring winter fires in its dozen fireplaces creating their own ghosts.

As she climbs the steps, Saskia catches sight of the elves. Perched between her and the sky, the two floodlit stone creatures grimace back down at her. She hasn't had this rush of fear (of what, that they'll spring to life?) since she was a child, and she whirls back around, looking at the land surrounding her. Taking comfort in its elegance, its solidity. The dirty snow coating the city is untouched here, frosting the expansive lawn with fondant perfection. The lake is invisible beyond the cliff at the back of the house, but palpable all the same in the faint roar of the waves, the cawing of the hardy, ever-present seagulls.

It is the same. It has always been the same.

How do people buy houses? she'd asked her mother once she was old enough that money started to have meaning. Eight or nine and she was absorbing common figures for salaries and real estate listings, and the numbers didn't seem to align. If you had a job that paid $30,000 a year, and even the cheapest house cost over a hundred grand, how on earth were you supposed to get one?

They wait for their parents to die, her mother had said. Breezily enough that Saskia hadn't thought too hard about it; not breezily enough to be joking.

Little had she known. Except, of course, that her mother *had* known that this day would come. That someday, Saskia would be back here, ready to stand as next in line.

Evie had known. For the past six months, Evie had known. Ignoring Saskia's calls, responding by text, by email. And Saskia, each time, feeling a small scratch of relief. She's paying for it now; each scratch has come back to claw at her face. *Your mother couldn't stand you. You were less than nothing to her.*

She closes her eyes.

The third thing: Saskia Kreis had once been adored. She had been Patrick's whole world, and he had been hers, from the time she was fourteen until she'd left for college. She would have stayed—would have *done anything for him,* as teenage Saskia had earnestly said, all wide eyes and unpunctured hope. But he hadn't let her. Had insisted that she go. And it broke her heart, and it broke all over again each time she saw him in passing at one of the Harper Christmas parties that were still called "Harper" more than a quarter century after anyone living in the house had borne the name.

Two years since they last saw each other at a Harper Christmas party, but nineteen since their last real conversation, his call breaking through the tangled cell networks into post-9/11 New York. *Are you all right?* Nineteen since he'd touched her with that probing tenderness. Nineteen since he'd let her go, set her free into the wild world, like the Cat Stevens song they'd both loved.

She's vibrating with it, the desire to see him again. To tell him everything, to say: *This is what my mother did. But it wasn't my fault, was it?* To have him tell her that she is blameless, that she is perfect, that she is free.

But the fantasy won't hold for more than a few seconds. She keeps running up against it: What will he think of her now?

Because the truth is that Saskia Kreis was *almost* a lot of things, but now she is scraped bare inside like an artichoke, like somebody's been at her with their teeth. She is thirty-seven years old. Her piano money is gone. She hasn't had a real job in two years. Her boyfriend is married to somebody else. Her best friend is a lady from the boxing gym who would be very surprised to hear herself described in those terms.

She never said any of that to her mother.

She *can't* say any of that to her mother. Anymore.

And yes, she's mad about it. Saskia has known for a long time that a person can host multitudes, but she's never felt anything like this combination of emotions, now, standing on the steps of the Elf House. Grief like a free fall. Rage like one of the mythical Furies. Desire, nostalgia, fear, curiosity . . .

These emotions are all she has right now, in this moment before she sees her father again. Her world is full of absent people.

She grabs her phone, starts texting.

You went pretty hard on me at the gym yesterday. I think you might have broken a rib.

In a few seconds, Gina types back: *Toughen up, snowflake. I barely touched you.*

She wishes she were at Gleason's, sparring with Gina now. Barring that—

Wish you were here, she starts to type. But that's not the kind of friendship they have, and she deletes it. Goes to check the messages from James that pinged onto her phone the second she landed.

Did you get in OK? Wish I could be at the meeting with you.

A code. A stupid, easily breakable code. He's lucky that his wife trusts him; any idiot who'd actually read their messages would have cracked it by now. She stares at her phone, hands shaking from the cold. She sends a thumbs-up emoji as a new message comes in.

I'm so sorry about your mom. Tell me if there's anything I can do.

But what does he think he can do? He can't even admit he knows her.

She doesn't feel guilty at the excitement ringing through her like a bell at the thought of seeing Patrick again. Saskia doesn't feel guilty about much but, beyond that, she's not in love with James. She's never let herself think too hard about what the attraction is, beyond the fact of his hands. His beautiful hands, calloused and strong, shaping beautiful wood to craft beautiful furniture that beautiful people put in their homes. All that beauty aside, James is a bit stupid. She doesn't mean it in an elitist way, he makes more money than she ever will and, besides, she's sure there are smart carpenters out there. He's just not one of them.

She's stalling. And she shouldn't have to think about him right now— wasn't that the only possible upside of this? Of the whole horrible, screaming mess of this post-mother life that she's now been thrust into? The howling loss, the suddenness of it, the disease's work complete hours before her father's phone call came. It feels like that kids' game, Operation— Saskia's fine as long as she avoids that part of her brain. But the second she remembers, the sensor buzzes, aggressive as a scream.

The only upside: a fresh start. Without her mother hovering at her shoulder, watching.

Saskia Kreis has never had a fresh start in her life.

Without her mother's judgment, without the rolled eyes and slammed doors that have characterized their relationship since she quit Juilliard. Without the eternal hope that Saskia would once again sit down at the piano and begin to play.

After years of wishing her parents knew the truth of her life, the possibility of coming clean feels almost startling in its likelihood, its proximity. She can't tell her mother anything, anymore; but she could bridge the gap, repair things, with her father. She can break through the skin of distant affection that's characterized their relationship for as long as she can remember. Because the truth is that she should be mad at him, too; she should be furious that he'd been a conspirator in hiding her mother's diagnosis—Creutzfeldt-Jakob disease, as rare and cruel as a witch's curse—from her these past few months. But she doesn't trust him enough to get really mad at him. She's furious at her mother, furious and a little scared about what it says about her that she hadn't been told. But toward her father, she feels just a little sigh of regretful understanding. *Oh, well. That's Dad.*

So yes, she could tell her father. Tell him everything.

She could say: *Dad, I lost my job two years ago. And I just couldn't give you guys another reason to be ashamed of me.*

Say: *I'm not a team player. That's what they say when, actually, you slept with the married boss and now he wants to get rid of you. The grown-up version of* doesn't play well with others, *the commentary I've been getting my whole life.*

Say: *My contest winnings are all gone. I'm writing SAT questions at fifteen bucks a pop.*

She can say it. She can tell him.

But the floodlights blast on again, the doorknob with its metal vines twists and, in a panic, she glances up at the elves. Their faces scrunched in knowing judgment.

She's not going to say it.

This house has secrets built into its skin. It was never the place for truth.

As the door opens, she's still looking up at the elves, but her father's looking at her, and she pulls the sleeves of her coat down over her knuckles before he can see the bruises.

She meets his eyes.

And despite the last two years, despite the last thirty-seven. Despite herself.

Saskia thinks: home.

The place where she is known. The place where there is at least one special thing about her still. The place where, once again, she can be the person she thinks she is, the person she wants to be. Where she can be Saskia Kreis.

It was one of the hardest lessons of growing up: the failure of the world to take her at her own estimation.

In the meantime, what's one more performance? What's one more game of pretend?

She can do that much for him. And it makes her feel good, the decision. For the first time in a long time.

It feels almost like hope.

Chapter 2

"Come here," Mama Bear said to Goldilocks. "Let's talk a minute, girl to girl." She gestured at the kitchen table, and Goldilocks flopped down ungraciously.

"You," Mama Bear said, "desperately need a lesson in respecting other people's boundaries."

Goldilocks stared at her for a moment, her mouth falling open.

"Does that come as a surprise to you?" Mama Bear asked.

"No—no," Goldilocks said. "It's just—I thought you were going to eat me."

—*FAIRY TALES FOR LITTLE FEMINISTS:*
GOLDILOCKS AND THE THREE BEARS, EVELYN HARPER KREIS

September 1992

SASKIA WAS NINE, AND SHE DIDN'T WANT A NEW piano teacher. But, as her mother pointed out, she didn't pay for her own lessons, either, and so she had no choice. Apparently, she'd met this woman before, at Christmas parties and performances, but Saskia had never differentiated Carrie Driver from the great mass of her parents' colleagues.

Inside Studio 9B, in the same university building as her mother's office, Saskia studied Carrie, her cloud of warm brown curls, her warm brown eyes. Carrie smiled pleasantly, waiting for her to speak. No adult had ever done this for Saskia.

"Mom says you're going to be my new piano teacher."

"If you'll let me." Carrie bent forward in her chair, nodded at Sas to sit down beside her.

"I already have a piano teacher."

"Yeah, your mom said. Anne Hauser?"

Saskia nodded, thinking of Mrs. Hauser's short, fat fingers guiding her on the keyboard. Mrs. Hauser didn't teach at the university; Mrs. Hauser taught in her own living room, which smelled like lemons and where the sun filtered into interesting patterns on the pale green carpet. Compared to Mrs. Hauser, this woman was very young. She couldn't possibly know very much.

"She's been my teacher since I was three." A test of a sort; other musicians often balked at the idea of a child starting so young. But Carrie just nodded.

"You must be very close to her."

Saskia raised her eyebrows, but Carrie wasn't being mean.

"Well, look. Teachers are like tools, and they can help us get to different levels in our playing. I've also had to leave teachers that I've loved before. Now, personally, I think I'd be a good tool for you at this point in your career. But I agree, we should figure out if I'm the best person to help you do that, just the two of us. So, tell me. What do you want right now?"

The air seemed to whoosh around Saskia's ears. Her career. Her teachers. Her decision.

She hesitated only a second.

"I want to be the best pianist who ever played."

And Carrie's face didn't show any sign of amusement. She knew it was possible, as well as Saskia did.

"So, then. Tell me. What else do you need to know before you can make the decision about who the best teacher is for you right now?"

Saskia hesitated, her bravado wavering. But Carrie's steady, grown-up gaze emboldened her, and she spit it out.

"Play for me."

Carrie got up and without a word went to the Steinway across the room. A beat and then loud music, good and loud. Saskia didn't know the piece, but it sounded like Liszt. She was dying to get a better glimpse of Carrie's hands—and since she'd already been kind of incredibly rude, she might as well do what she wanted, go and be a little bit ruder—so she approached the piano from the side and watched in fascination as Carrie brought the music to its conclusion with a satisfyingly booming chord, then lowered her hands into her lap.

Saskia had never seen anyone's hands moving so fast. Saskia had been better than Mrs. Hauser for at least the past three years, possibly four. The other kids she knew who played were resounding amateurs.

"You're better than me," Saskia said, breathless in the resounding silence.

Carrie smiled, a dimple appearing.

"So, do I have the job?" she asked, pivoting around to face Saskia fully.

"Oh yeah," Saskia said.

January 2020

WITH HER FATHER'S ARMS AROUND HER, THE Elf House feels the same as it did two years ago. It is almost the same. The arched ceiling of the foyer like a cathedral, wooden beams curving to a single point at the center from which a brass chandelier descends. On entering for the first time, people always stop, taken aback by the size of the room, the sheer scale of it. But Patrick never had—and it always baffled her.

Saskia waits for her father to pull away first.

And he does, after a long moment, and she stands with her hands on his shoulders, searching his face. He turned seventy last year, which still sends a lightning bolt of fear through her. But his eyes and skin are clear, his hair a softly shining silver, his runner's muscles as powerful as ever. He may be seventy, but he still has the easy elegance of the movie stars he'd grown up watching.

And yet—he's just one person, alone in this enormous house.

The silence feels thick around them. Maybe it's those dark oak panels, hung with mediocre oil paintings of earlier Harpers (*You know, Mom,* she'd said at thirteen, *I don't think these are very good.* Evie had laughed, harder than Saskia had anticipated. *Maybe not, kid. But they're tradition*) that stifle the noise. Maybe it's the thick Oriental carpets, the big blue-and-purple one layered beneath the smaller red-and-gold ones. Or maybe it's just that the carvings, the roses and vines that trim the ceiling, running their way around to the heavy oak banister lining the massive staircase, don't make for ideal acoustics.

With a start, Saskia realizes that the grandmother clock has stopped. Maybe that's all the emptiness is, the lack of the familiar ticking.

A Harper tradition, the clock had belonged to her mother's mother's mother, a great-grandmother that Saskia never met. The hands are fixed at 3:00, with the mermaid half emerging from the waves. Saskia steps away from her father to wind it, letting the metronome of its movement set her heart straight as she syncs it with her cell phone clock: 7:00 P.M. The mermaid floats along, grows legs. In five hours, the hands will again round midnight and she'll dissolve into sea foam. Evie had loved that peculiar blending of the "Little Mermaid" and "Cinderella." Maybe that had even been where her obsession with fairy tales began.

Wolfie stands at her feet, wagging his curlicue of a tail. Like a spirit guide in one of her mother's books, ready to take her through the world of the dead.

"I'll just drop my things upstairs," she says to her father, who is looking at her expectantly. She knows they have things to talk about; she also knows that he is grieving as much as she is, even if Evie's death weren't nearly as much of a shock to him. But she's not ready to acknowledge his grief. She's not ready to have that conversation just yet.

"Go upstairs?" she says instead, to Wolfie. He pushes past her thighs, bounding up the grande dame of the staircase. At the landing, before the turn, he pauses and waits for her to catch up, his fur tinged supernatural by the security lights coming through the deep blue-and-gold stained-glass window. Ten feet wide, it's in a triptych, scrolls and diamonds converging into the family crest the Harper ancestors had invented: a wolf and a lamb curled up together.

A memory from the last time she climbed these steps whispers to her. A too-familiar voice with an unfamiliar tone, cutting through the Harpers' 2018 Christmas party.

Saskia, this is Tim Kempner. The thrill it had sent through her, even as alarms started wailing in her mind. There was a part of her that believed that maybe this time she hadn't chosen the wrong guy. Maybe this time she'd gotten away with it. *I want to advise you that I have Tom Delaney with Human Resources with me on the line.*

And the alarms became sirens.

I'm afraid we're going to have to let you go.

And her own voice, childish and thin, almost fluty: *Why?*

An unfamiliar man, warning: *Tim—*

I'm afraid that's all I can say. I want to thank you for—

But the not knowing was intolerable.

For fucking you behind your wife's back?

A sharp intake of breath, she couldn't tell from whom. But what was HR going to do to the CEO, after all? They were there to protect Tim, not her.

And his voice, again, infuriatingly corporate. *For not being a team player, if you must know.*

HR, one more time: *Tim—*

But Saskia, climbing away from the din of the party, had already hung up.

Now, Wolfie is waiting impatiently at the top of the staircase. Behind him is another window seat, surrounded by bookshelves; Emilia Harper, beloved wife of Georg, had loved her books. It's why the house had both a study and a library—the study was for him, the library, she'd always said, for her. Or so legend had it.

She'd sat there, that night, and eventually, Patrick had found her. He had never sought her out at the parties before, not since they'd broken up, not since their shared secret had dissolved into the past. And how her heartbeat had sped up as he scanned her face.

You're mad.

How well he knew her, still, after all those years. She'd forced a smile.

My girlfriend, Chloe—his fingers hovering in front of her cheeks, not touching—*her face gets just like this when she's mad.*

That was the moment when she'd known: she couldn't go on like this. She couldn't keep circling the past, making the same mistakes and hoping for a new outcome. And she couldn't give Patrick another reason to pity her.

I'm fine, she'd chirped. The first lie she'd ever told him.

But maybe not the last. She hasn't decided, yet, what she'll say tomorrow. Hasn't decided how much to admit. Can she trust him? After the first major disaster of her life, he'd come white-knighting in, ready to rescue her. She had turned him away then, but it would be nice, she thinks—it would be nice to be able to trust somebody like that again.

Wolfie nudges her hot, damp hand and she rubs his head, follows him as he branches off to the right, down Saskia's hallway. He knows, he remembers. Her parents' room is down the other hall, the west hall, but the east is hers. His tail bobs in a question mark as he trots confidently down to the far end, to Saskia's childhood bedroom.

She hasn't prepared herself for the rush of memories that seeing the room will bring back. Because this room has always been her mother's more than anyone's. Once upon a time, Evie had decorated the room for the kind of girl Saskia should have been, rather than the girl she is. Was. White canopy bed, pale purple armchair, antique dressing table. Saskia doesn't wear makeup; the only thing she'd ever used that table for was her keyboard, now hidden under a dust cover. Evie had always refused to put it in storage: *What if you want it?* she'd said. *Just to play around with, just to tinker.* And so it had sat waiting for almost two decades in perpetual anticipation. For Saskia to come back, to come home, once again.

Saskia turns the iron doorknob and flips the lights on, the chandelier sparking to life. But as she blinks the light away, the emptiness of the room snakes around her, sneaky as a breakup when you thought you were just getting coffee. Her keyboard is gone. Her books are gone. The fluffy rug is gone, too. The only thing that remains is the furniture, all of it covered in sheets except for, ironically, the bed. The bed is stripped bare, with neatly folded linens in a pile at the foot.

Saskia steps back, breathless.

Her mother had believed she'd never come home again.

Her mother had *prepared* for it.

All of Saskia's things are gone, but the art still hangs on the walls: framed illustrations from her mother's books, interspersed with those violins. *The haunted violins,* teenage Saskia had called them. Her great-grandfather on her father's side had been a celebrated luthier back in Hamburg, though she's unsure how much of his fame was real and how much was simply family lore. God knows the Kreises didn't have the kind of money the Harpers did, though surely a quality violin cost a fair amount in those days; good instruments always do. But only two generations removed and Mike had grown up working class across town, while the Harpers' beer fortune had given them—well, all of this.

Regardless, when Saskia's great-grandfather died, he'd left behind a series of seven violins in various stages of completion. More than a century later, Evie had strung them up with lavender ribbon on her daughter's walls. Even though the music hadn't come from her side of the family, she'd embraced it with religious fervor. Saskia also used to love this reminder of her musical heritage. It wasn't until later that the violins became a nagging, whining reminder: her personal history is one of *almosts*.

Why are they still there, while the rest of her childhood has been erased?

Saskia was going to come home, eventually. She'd planned (vaguely, one day, maybe) to admit what had happened; to say, *Mom, I got fired. Yes, from computers.* Who the hell had her mother been to decide all of this? To decide that she'd never come home again and that she didn't need to know—not about her empty room, not about the disease, not about anything, not anymore.

The enormity of the anger washes over her, and Saskia squeezes her fists, leans into the pain throbbing from her knuckles. It's too much to process, too much to absorb, for the two weeks she's planned to be at home. Yes, she could have taken more time off from the test prep agency; but she's a contractor and it would be unpaid, and she can't afford eighty hours of mourning. As it is, she'll be squeezing SAT questions in between the memorial service and the reception, between closing credit cards and opening safe-deposit boxes, between will readings and what she imagines will be endless piles of paperwork.

She does the math as she catches her breath, lets it soothe her. Numbers always do. Rent is due in a week: $1,900. At $15 each, that's 127 questions, with a few bucks left over for a coffee. About fifteen minutes per question (she's gotten fast over the years), about thirty-two hours of work. Translated from the math back to the abstract, back to *work*, though, the process sends anxiety shooting through her as she flies across the hall to the servants' staircase, thuds downstairs to the kitchen.

"Dad," she calls, like she had when she was a teenager. "My room—"

But she cuts herself off as she comes around the corner, sees him paused at the marble-topped table, Scrabble board set up and his hands folded patiently before him. The small shaded lamp hanging over his head is the only light in the enormous dark kitchen, a scene like the Hopper paintings her mother loved.

Alone.

"Yeah, I forgot—" Mike says, and shakes his head. "Grab a glass," he says, nodding at the Baccarat glass he's left on the counter for her, from her parents' fifteenth anniversary, and she sees that he's opened one of the Napa reds he and Evie got on their last California trip. "Sit down."

She has to fight to keep her hands from shaking, but she pours, she sits. Wolfie curls up at her feet.

Mike makes a face, almost a grimace, but softer. "Your mother had hoped to talk to you about this herself, but the end came—faster than either of us ever thought. Eight months, the doctors said. But in the end, it was more like six."

"You said," and her voice falls dull between them. "On the phone."

"Yeah. She didn't— This disease, Sas, the utter *indignity* of it—"

Saskia sees the sagging beneath her father's eyes. The slowness of his fingers. *You can choose to be right, or you can choose to be kind,* the NYU therapist had said to her more than a decade ago. It had made her laugh. No true Harper would ever choose the latter.

She shakes her head and reaches for the bag of letters. Jiggles it in the palm of her hand. Picks a tile: A. He does the same, like a reflex: H. She pulls her seven letters. It's been two years since she played, but she remembers.

"I was going to come home," she says, surprised by the hoarseness of her voice.

Mike stares at his letters. "But how were we to know that?" he replies after a long moment. A long moment that says: *Easy enough to say that now.*

"Even so, you couldn't have left my things where they were? What harm were they doing?" She can't bring herself to blame her mother. Not aloud, not to him.

His eyes flick up to her as she plays. EMPTY.

"Okay, cards on the table," he says, and his voice is louder, as though he's trying to make it belong to someone else. "This house—it's too much for just one person. It's too much for two people, to tell the truth. It wasn't built for that. It wasn't built for us."

She swallows. A two-year absence—an associate's degree in missing the Elf House—and it still rises up around her like a judgmental grandmother, wrapping its arms around her, all fourteen thousand square feet of it. Love it or hate it, it's still *theirs*. Always has been.

"It's the Harper house," she says. "It was literally built for us."

He makes that face again, the half grimace. "For some time your mother and I had talked about selling the place. We'd even started thinking of it as our retirement plan of sorts. In fact, around Easter—oh, about eighteen months ago—we even consulted with a few real estate agents. That's when Evie decided to pack up your room."

Goose bumps have risen on her arms, beneath her sweatshirt. The Elf House with no Harpers. The Elf House without her. It's so far from how she'd imagined the next act of her life—

"Mom wanted to sell?" The fire inside her is dry and quiet, but it gains momentum, spurting high. "Mom was always going on and on about how this place was her *legacy*. Her *heritage*. Mom wanted to— No. No! Are you kidding? I mean, I get that it's a lot to keep up with. But, Dad . . ."

He just looks at her until she quiets down, an implied, preemptive forgiveness in his expression. The forgiveness that lets her know just how awful she's being. She sighs like a shudder.

"Saskia, a lot happened in the time you've been away. People change. Times change."

"I mean . . ." She wrinkles her forehead. "Yeah, okay. But you guys came out to see me—not to mention the phone, email—you'd think she could have *mentioned*—"

"Honestly?" he says. "Honestly, I don't think she thought you'd care."

She snaps back in her chair, as though she's been slapped. He goes on.

"Anyway, when your mother got sick, our plans changed. We started talking a lot about her legacy."

"What, like the books?"

He swallows. Lays his tiles down. PEATY.

"The books. Her students. And the Elf House. She wanted this to become a place where students could come and practice their art. *To become more themselves*, she said—" And he breaks into a small smile, a smile Saskia can't bring herself to share. "So, she started talking with some friends at the university about selling it to them. Using it as a home for their pre-college arts programs."

It pinches somewhere deep in her chest, despite herself. She knows he's making reasonable points. But this house was supposed to be hers someday. Just as it was her mother's legacy, it was supposed to be Saskia's. Other girls dreamed of weddings and babies, but not Saskia; no matter how much of a mess of her life she's made in New York, she has always taken comfort in the image of herself Miss Havisham–ing it up as she and the Elf House aged together. It was always meant to be here, waiting for her.

"Is that what you want?" she asks, low.

He gives her a weak smile. "I've never been attached to the house. Too much of a Gothic monstrosity for my taste. But beyond that, yeah—I'd like to retire at some point before the Symphony makes me. I have the beginnings of arthritis here—" He holds up his left hand, contracts it into a claw with a little laugh. "Not ideal for a cellist. And this house— goddamn. The amount of work. I'm not sure you can even imagine."

She bends forward. "So tell me."

"I mean, we've always had to put about seventy-five grand a year into the estate just to keep it from falling down, and the city charges another fifty in property tax. Over the years, it ate up every penny of your mother's inheritance, and then it started to eat into the *Little Feminists* money."

Saskia is nodding, though she doesn't agree with his premise. Wouldn't anything be worth it? Wasn't that the point of the Harpers—to act as caretakers of this magical, dark place?

Her father fixes his gaze carefully on her eyes. "It's a good time to sell, Sas. The market's great right now. And the costs, if we didn't get out now— We found out last fall that the foundation's shot, and that's another hundred grand right there. And the cliffs, you know, erosion's always been an issue—"

"So, she didn't leave me the house," she says, her selfish voice booming too loud in the empty kitchen. At her feet, Wolfie stirs with a groan. "That's what you're trying to tell me. That she didn't want me to have it?"

"That's the opposite of what I'm trying to tell you, kiddo," Mike says, gentle. "I'm saying, she did everything she could *for years* so that you could have it. But she was only human, after all—"

His voice cuts out and she blinks hot eyes down to stare at her tiles.

She's got nothing. The fucking Z, she's got that.

But—maybe not. You play the board, in Scrabble. You don't play your tiles.

If she can get that Z down on a triple letter—

She takes a breath and lays down LAZY on the open triple letter, getting rid of it. As she pulls away, her father reaches for her hand, ready to squeeze—but his palm paused above her knuckles, he freezes.

"Your hands, Sas. Good God."

She looks at them. She'd let her sleeves slide down her wrist, and yes, there they are: the black-and-purple bruises. She thinks they're kind of pretty.

"Oh—yeah. I started boxing. About a year ago?" Her voice lilts in the upspeak he's always teased her about. She clears her throat. "I'm pretty good—"

But he hasn't looked away. "But your *hands.*"

A *musician's hands are their livelihood.* How often had Saskia heard that as a child, her mother thrusting mittens into her tiny palms?

But she's free from all that, now. Free from the piano. Free from *computers.* Free from her mother's judgment. And, apparently, free from this place.

But if this is freedom—if this is her clean slate—then why does she feel so trapped?

"Fine," she says, not looking up. "Fine, yeah, okay. You can't work forever. The place is a money pit. I get it."

He lets the pads of his fingers brush tenderly against the hurt places before squeezing her hand once, then releasing.

They play the rest of the game in silence, the empty house echoing around them. The whole time, Saskia tries to reimagine the house, no longer hers. No longer theirs. No longer anything to do with them.

But it's impossible.

It's her mother's house. It's always been her mother's house. She permeates every oak panel, every gothically arched doorframe, every leaded window. Her paintings are scattered through it, her weird feminist brand of German expressionism coloring the walls; her books line the shelves, her Jane Austen and *Jane Eyre*; and when they play music again (will they ever play music again?), it will be played for her as well as for themselves.

Her mother is there still.

She'll be there forever, Saskia thinks. As she watches her father; as she loses the game.

Chapter 3

"So, what do you like to do when you're not ruling?" the Little Mermaid asked as the Prince swirled her around the dance floor. Every step was like knives, but she wasn't complaining; that, after all, was the bargain she had made.

The Prince smiled at her with his handsome face. "Oh. You know. Things."

"Things," the Little Mermaid said. "Things like . . ."

"The usual. Hunting. Fishing. Carousing."

"Fishing?"

"Yes," the Prince said, his vacant eyes lighting up. "Do you enjoy it?"

The Little Mermaid sighed and pulled away. What a stupidly rotten deal. Maybe there was still time to get her fins back.

—*Fairy Tales for Little Feminists:*
The Little Mermaid, Evelyn Harper Kreis

November 1992

SASKIA WAS TEN. AT SCHWARTZ'S, THE BOOKSHOP on Downer, *Rapunzel* was unavoidable. When her parents had discussed the book signing with her, she'd imagined it was limited to the kids' section, the section she'd been confined to her whole life. But the podium was placed in the middle of the adult section, and the entire store—not just the kids' part—had been fairy-fied. Cardboard cutouts littered the aisles of chairs: a tower, a witch, a crown. Instead of streamers, realistic blond braids were strung from the ceiling. Too realistic, Sas thought with a shudder.

Her father was technically supposed to be looking after her, but her father was chatting with some neighbors who'd come by, so when Saskia spotted Lexi, she was able to mime gagging without getting caught. Lexi giggled so hard she snorted; when Saskia looked up at Aunt Georgia, she saw that her godmother was grinning, too.

Saskia had been to her mother's gallery openings before. Her mother stuck her in a childish dress and Mary Janes, gave her a cup of sparkling cider, and let her wander around the room being charming to adults while she spoke in low, serious tones about her *work*. Saskia had imagined that the signing would be like an opening, which it kind of was. But it was also worse. Because her mother was reading from the book. She was talking in front of people. She was answering questions.

The book wasn't long, and her mother read the whole thing. Parts of it made the adults laugh (other than her and Lex, there were only adults here, she wasn't sure why), and Saskia laughed along with them, though she didn't get the jokes. It was a kid's book, right? She should have gotten the jokes. But the question-and-answer section was even worse. She didn't even understand the *questions*. Second-wave feminism? Exclusionary politics?

It wasn't until the very end that she felt a part of it. An older woman, blue-gray hair in tight curls, stood up.

"I can't help noticing that you've brought your daughter along tonight," she said in soft tones.

Evie nodded. "Yes, that's right. Saskia, stand up."

Saskia slowly got to her feet. In the front row next to her, her father gave her a nudge so she'd turn around to face the rest of the audience. She raised an unwilling hand to wave.

"Yes, and I couldn't help noticing the resemblance—"

And now they were all staring at Saskia's face, back and forth between her and the enormous book cover next to her mother. She frowned. The only thing she and Rapunzel had in common was that they were blond. That was literally it.

"And I just wanted to know how your daughter feels about that."

The room pivoted from Evie's anxious face to Saskia.

"How . . . I . . ."

"Do you like the princess? Do you feel connected to her?" The older woman was staring intently at Saskia, waiting for her answer.

Saskia frowned. "No way. I'm too old for princesses."

"Is that right?" the woman said mildly.

A wicked grin broke across Saskia's face. "Yeah, it is. If you must know, I prefer ghosts."

January 2020

IN THE MORNING, SASKIA IS LISTLESS IN HER black shift and black tights. She runs her fingers over the record of her height that her mother kept on the closet door. *Saskia in 1992. Saskia in 1989.* Looking at the descending pencil marks, she thinks: The Saskias are like Russian nesting dolls. They're all still here. She thinks: This must be what it's like to be a ghost.

Downstairs, she's unable to ignore the fact that the memorial is starting. The gravel crunches as guests pull into the driveway, and there are chattering voices outside the windows. She'll join them in a minute. She will. She needs to look at them. Needs to know who knew before she did that her own mother was dying.

But first, she finds herself in the conservatory again.

The Steinway. That piano—God, she'd loved that piano so fucking much. The one thing in the house that was hers alone. It hadn't been the piano she'd learned on; she'd taught herself on the old Baldwin back when she was three. Still, she has the sudden urge to press down on the first key children usually learn. Middle C.

The sound rings through the room and she gasps.

Her mother had kept the piano in tune.

Between the cold of the house and the humidity of the climate, this piano goes out of tune every few months. Evie had hated the sounds that the tuner produced, the clang and the clamor of the discordant notes as he aligned the hammers, as he made everything sound crisp and new again.

But still she'd done it. All these years.

Saskia grabs her coat, slides on her shoes. She can do this. She can do this for her mother.

Still, she waits for a gap in the stream of guests before she sneaks down the beach path, alone and undisturbed. It's times like these that she longs for someone at her side, a partner. Not anyone specific, certainly not James. Just someone she could count on to shoulder half of the burden.

Invoice incoming, she texts James. In their code, it originally meant: *Thinking of you.* But he knows what today is. He knows what she's going through. He'll get that she means, *I miss you.*

Great meeting last Thursday, he texts back.

Or maybe not. She shakes him out of her head, forces herself down to the beach.

Back when Saskia still played—when she was old enough to have a rudimentary grasp of mortality, but young enough that the ego accompanying her talent was still charming—she thought she'd discovered the meaning of life. Of her life, at least. The point was music; she was doing music with her life. You could draw other conclusions from that, if you had to, about how her talent was adding beauty to the world, about the inherent value in being an artist, but Saskia never did. She had one life, and she was living it like she was singing a song without end.

How stupid. To believe that anything would last forever.

Saskia is supposed to be standing with her father, welcoming the mourners, but as she watches figures make their way down the sandy cliff path, she realizes that nothing in her life has prepared her for this moment. The people coming today will be family and close friends, and yet the thing bringing them together is the same thing that's separating them. Evelyn Kreis's erasure from their lives is in no way the same thing as her mother's erasure from Saskia's. They may have lost a colleague or a customer, someone with funny stories about her students, someone with whom to share neighborhood gossip. Saskia, though? Saskia has lost the person reminding her to get a flu shot each fall. The person who snuck a gag gift into her Christmas stocking every year. The person who slipped inappropriate sexual anecdotes into conversations after one glass of wine too many.

There's nothing Saskia can say to them and there's nothing they can say to her.

Saskia wraps her arms around her body, stares out at the lake, focuses on the pulsing bass line of the waves. Maybe there's more than nothingness at the end of life: after all, there's music in the water. Maybe.

The only people already there are colleagues from the university art department. Wind snapping her hair around her eyes, she scans their faces. Louise, Barry, Danielle.

No Patrick. Yet.

Who knew? The question pounds at her like percussion.

The contingent from the Symphony, her father's coworkers, are looking as stunned as the professors as they arrive. Yes, she thinks, yes, we are all going to die, and nobody knows when. Yes, even you. A single young man—well, probably about her age—looks at her with a probing gaze, takes a step forward. She squints through the wind, and he takes an immediate step back. Something in his face is familiar, but she can't place him. A former student of her mother's?

Enough people have turned up so that there's a critical mass talking among themselves. The general conversation is on the *suddenness* of it all, the *shock* of it all. Saskia's solitary figure isn't so noticeable anymore, and she exhales, surprised by the shakiness of her breath. And then her father is beside her and the ceremony begins, and Patrick hasn't shown up at all.

Today's service marks one more memory for Saskia on the palimpsest that is their beach: the only one that will ever count from now on. Written in permanent marker over the barbecues and bonfires and dawn swims. It's blessedly short: her father didn't want to talk, so Saskia reads T. S. Eliot, "The Dry Salvages": . . . *you are the music / While the music lasts.* Her voice is drowned out by the wind, and she's glad that nobody can hear how it cracks and swoops. They invite the mourners to share stories. Louise recalls Evie's first day at UWM, how she'd come barreling into the staff meeting with a ten-point plan for department success; Georgia talks about Evie as a girl, all drawings and protests and plans for the future; Margie from the choir breaks into "Amazing Grace" unprompted.

There's no body. The cremation process takes weeks, Mike had said last night. He'd held off until he could talk to Saskia in person, as the doctors wanted to know if the body should be autopsied, the extraordinarily rare prion disease confirmed, so that Saskia could be tested for it herself. She'd considered it for a fleeting second, imagining life with that death sentence hanging over her. To wonder if each memory lapse or sleepless night meant that the end was near, as it had for her mother. Without any foolproof diagnostic test to confirm the presence of the disease until after you died, you'd become a mystery that you'd never be able to solve. No; there could be nothing worse. A burden, to know the means of your death. But, anyway, her mother is not yet ashes. Her mother is currently—is—

She makes herself look back up at the people. At the living people still surrounding her.

She makes herself ask, again: Who knew?

Georgia. Her godmother, Georgia, Evie's best friend, is the only one among them with the same expression as Mike: tight, resigned. But not surprised. Saskia feels the flame of rage rising up in her chest even as her godmother tilts her head, even as she smiles at her, soft and sad.

When it's over, the youngish guy moves toward her.

"Saskia," he says, his hazel-green eyes gazing into hers. He rests his hands on her shoulders and her stomach swoops. She knows that face.

"Josh . . . Josh *Asher*?" she says. "Oh my God. How the hell are you?" She winces at the sound of her own voice. It's her Milwaukee voice, her friendly voice, but it sounds strange, like syrup poured over a bloody steak.

He shifts his weight, grins. "I'm good! I mean, I'm sorry, you know. I'm so sorry for your loss. And I'm sorry . . . that I'm being so weird! It's been a long time."

She nods, wind whipping her hair over her face.

"Since high school, yeah. Josh," she says. "Don't get me wrong. Good to see you and all of that. But what are you doing here?"

It's his turn to wince. "Sorry—I know, it's strange—but I'm actually your mother's executor."

"No, Mom's lawyer is Paul." Her gaze darts to the man in the heavy black coat who is standing beside her father at the base of the footpath as the guests make their way up to the house. Paul Fairchild and his dull, impeccable diction, his dull, impeccable Laphroaig, and his shoes with their dull, impeccable shine have been fixtures in her life for as long as—well, for as long as the house has. And before Paul, her family had somebody like Paul: a great line of Pauls going back to 1871 and the unification of the German empire that had sent the Harfenists to Milwaukee, turned them into the Harpers that, in their turn, turned out the beer that made Milwaukee famous. Some of it, anyway. Which had turned into the Harpers' fortune, which had turned into this house.

"No, of course. That is, Paul wrote out her will, but it's customary to name a separate executor. I'm a partner at Fairchild and Locke—well, a non-equity partner—and, given my history with your family—"

"Look." She touches his arm. "I'm sorry, Josh. It's just a rough day. A really fucking rough day. Mom always said that every good fairy tale begins with a dead mother, but she never really covered what that would actually be like—" She is trying to make a joke, but her choking voice gives her away. She doesn't know what it is about him that's making her talk like this.

He looks haunted.

"Yeah, I get that. I just— Shit, Sas." Nobody in high school had ever called her that. "I need to talk to your father. With a certain . . . urgency."

Topics flash through her mind like multiple-choice answers: property rights, cliff erosion, book royalties. The house has stood for 129 years; it's not going anywhere. The cliffs *are* eroding, but that couldn't possibly be described as urgent. Royalties to *Fairy Tales for Little Feminists*—that's most likely of all.

"Oh, okay. Come on, then," she says, shuffling her sand-laden feet away from the water's edge. "Were you having trouble finding him? I think he's over—"

"Yeah, no," he says, and the wind whips up so strong that it almost erases his voice as it carries the sound back over the waves. "It's just— You should probably be there for this."

SHE FELT PATRICK'S ABSENCE DOWN AT THE beach, but now, kicking the cold sand out of her shoes and elbowing her way into the warm crowd, it's nearly pulsing at her: he's not there. Not there to judge her, not there to save her. Just not there. His flashing gaze gliding around the room, catching on this person or that one, evaluating them. Landing on hers, holding it just a second too long, in remembrance of what once was.

But there are many people who are not here. He's not the only one. There's Carrie, who traded in her Symphony job for a better one down in Miami. Sheila, on sabbatical in Spain. Neither of them had been able to get to Milwaukee on such short notice.

For a second, the room seems filled with the ghosts of people she'd once loved. But then Josh's dress shoes make a scuffing noise behind her, wet sand on their soles scratching the parquet, and they yank her back to the unavoidable present.

Mike stands steady and sad at the archway between the living room and the dining room. Knowing Josh will follow, Saskia slices through the small crowd that has gathered around him. Her father's skin seems closer to the bone than it did twenty-four hours ago.

"Dad? Remember Josh Asher? From high school? He needs to talk to you. It's important."

"Josh. Hi," her father says, and she turns to find Josh at her shoulder. He sticks out a hand.

"I'm sorry for your loss, sir. If I could just speak to you and Sas—Saskia a moment. In private."

She watches her father process this request.

"Sure," her father says, and his voice is loose, cool, though his muscles seem coiled tight. "Let's talk in the office."

Josh waits for him to take the lead. At the office's oak doors, her father stops her.

"I can handle this, honey," he says.

"It's okay, Dad. I can—I can—"

His thin lips turn up. "I know you can. But you don't have to. Just take care of everyone out here, okay? I can't imagine this'll take long."

The doors close before she can work up an appropriately convincing objection. After all, it's a relief, knowing that he will listen to whatever Josh has to say for the both of them, knowing he'll immediately provide the kind of wise, thoughtful response it would take her ten beats or more to come up with. Anyway, she can hear through the doors easily; the oak is thick, but the study has a strange echo-chamber quality to it that always drove her mother crazy. *I can't take any more Elgar today, Mike. Practice in the conservatory, work in the study. That's what it's for.*

And him: *Music is my work.*

But he knows she will try to hear through the door, and he's put on a record, Rachmaninoff's Étude-Tableau in E-flat Minor. She looks across the hall, through the entryway to the conservatory. Like the foyer, the library, and the study, it is lined in dark wooden panels that she'd tapped ceaselessly as a child, searching in vain for a hidden passage. At the very back, the window seat takes up the entire wall. When she'd played there, the light would come through the leaded glass in a way that made everything feel sepia tinged, preemptively nostalgic.

A blond figure slides through the doorway from the dining room, and Saskia's heart stops. It's Lexi the Influencer (she always thinks of Lexi's job with a capital I), her phone held steady at the end of her hand. Up from Chicago for the funeral.

Lexi perches at the edge of the window seat, holding her arm higher. Lips pouting slightly, eyes big. Framed perfectly by the tiny diamonds of the windowpanes, lit lovely by the faint gray pulse of the day.

"Oh, honey!" Georgia swoops in to kiss Saskia's cheek, covering it in the tacky texture of her lipstick. "Oh, are you just wrecked?"

"Hey, Georgia." She rubs her cheek, trying to get the greasepaint off. This has never offended her godmother. "Could you get your daughter to stop posing in the conservatory at my mother's funeral?" She could do it herself, she guesses, but there's nothing like a mother's bite. And there's something about the thought of talking to Lexi—

Georgia whirls around, a growl at the back of her throat.

"Alexis Palmer!" she cries, and Saskia has to swallow a laugh as Lexi jumps. She's the same age as Saskia, but you never lose that reflex at the sound of your mother's angry voice. As Lexi skitters over, Georgia turns back to her goddaughter.

"It doesn't feel real. It still just doesn't feel real. I keep picking up the phone to call her. Every day of our lives, we talked. Every single day since we *could* talk. We even tried to string tin cans between the houses, when we were little, but we couldn't find wire that was long enough—"

Lexi arrives at Saskia's side in a cloud of citrus perfume. She has a different face than she used to, Lex. But she's still everything Saskia is not. Yes, they're both blond only daughters who grew up on Lake Drive, but the similarities end there. Lexi has wavy hair, coming in darker at the roots now, so thick her neck must ache from holding her head up. Saskia's hair has always been flat, fine, and pale as corn silk. Lexi's chest has an enviable roundness, whereas Saskia can count each of her ribs as easily as she could when she was a child. Lexi's skin is full and plump still—but that, Saskia thinks, probably has more to do with nurture than nature. If she's anything like her mother, she already has enough bovine toxin and filler in there to kill a small horse.

"Sas," Lexi says, and grabs her former friend. "Oh my God, it was so fast, I'm going to miss her so much—"

Saskia extricates herself. She follows Lexi on Instagram, of course, but she has her muted; Lexi has a tendency to be too much. Saskia normally likes this in people, she knows that she herself is too much, but Lexi's too much is a different kind, a kind that rubs Sas the wrong way.

"But you look so good," Lexi says, meaning that she looks terrible. "And I've missed you so much," Lexi says, meaning that she could happily have gone the rest of her life without seeing Saskia. "Can we get a coffee while you're home?" meaning that she has no intention of hanging out with Saskia, not in this lifetime.

Saskia feels her godmother's eyes on her, though; Georgia's silence is uncanny.

"Yeah, of course."

"There's so much to catch up on," Lexi says, eyes going wide. "You remember Mr. Lepinsky?"

"Um." She remembers he's a teacher, but that's as far as her memory goes. "Was he the one who said I didn't play well with others?"

"Ha! Wasn't that every teacher?" Lexi says, her giggles joining with her mother's as she shows her perfectly capped teeth. Saskia notes the two that used to overlap at the bottom. "No, silly. Eighth-grade math. He got married to Melissa Hargrove, can you believe it? She was, like, younger than us, even."

"Mmmm, no."

"Lexi," Georgia murmurs. Lexi holds up her hands.

"I'm so sorry, I forgot where we—I forgot. But coffee sometime this week?"

"Or dinner," Georgia says. "We could do dinner, all together. Your dad, too."

But before they can set a date, before the women can whip out their phones and scan their calendars, there's the crash of crystal from inside the study. Saskia rushes in.

Her father is bent with both palms on the edge of the built-in book-shelves, head dropped to his chest. One of the Lalique bookends, one of the swans, has been pulled from the bookshelves and lies in pieces, covering and surrounding the desk. Saskia runs over the broken shards to him, rests a hand on his back.

"Daddy?"

She bends down, searching his face. Ever since she was little, their eyes have matched: dark blue, almost black. If eyes were the window to the soul, she'd figured, his and hers were the same.

But that was before she grew up into the person she's become.

He waits until she backs away, then shakily pulls himself upright.

"It's the will." Josh's voice, thin and reedy, comes from by the fireplace. Saskia whirls around to glare at him. *Of course it's the will, jackass.*

"It's Patrick," her father says, choking out the name.

Her voice is somehow calm despite her thundering heart. "Yeah, I noticed that he didn't come. I can't believe it, but then again, he's always been—"

"No," her father says, and shakes his head sharply. "No. I mean, Patrick's one of her beneficiaries, Sas. The house— She left the house to him."

"I HAVE TO GET BACK TO THE PARTY," HER FATHER keeps saying. "Someone has to look after the guests. I have to get back to the party." The third time he says it, Josh's warm eyes land on Saskia's, and she swallows.

"Dad. It's not a party, okay? It's a memorial, and I think people will get it," she finally says, gently.

"No, we can—we can do this later. I have to get back to—to the guests," he says. He cracks open the door, and Georgia is quickly at his side.

The door closes behind him, and Saskia hurls the second swan at the desk. The sound of the crystal shattering against the still-playing music soothes her as she swings around to Josh.

"What do we do to stop this?"

His horrified, symmetrical face crinkles in shock, then concern.

"You can challenge the will, of course. You're her daughter, you have standing. She actually—I didn't get to this, with your father, but—she actually named you the executor of her literary estate. So, Saskia, you'll get the royalties from *Little Feminists*—"

The princesses. Those fucking princesses.

But they're a problem for later.

"Okay," she cuts him off. "Let's challenge the will. How fast can we do that?"

"Well, I just delivered the will to the court and filed a petition for its administration. They have ten days to set the date for the hearing, which is usually just a routine authentication of the will. It's usually a non-event, but if you wanted to—"

"Can they do it faster?"

"They might do it faster," he says. "And in the meantime, you can get your own lawyer to file an objection and petition to set it aside."

She frowns.

"You can't do that for me?"

The lines between his eyebrows look like brackets.

"I'm really sorry—I really am—but that's where I'm not going to be very useful to you," he says. "See, as your mother's executor, I'm her lawyer. I can't be yours."

"So be her lawyer, then. She must have been coerced into this. I promise you, this is not what she wanted. Let's challenge it."

He sets a hand on the desk. She's surprised to see he's shaking, almost imperceptibly. She makes an impatient noise from the back of her throat.

"That's not really how it works. Think of me as representing your mother's wishes as expressed in the will. My job is to execute them, not challenge them. You'll need to get another lawyer for that."

He blinks, and she thrusts a hand toward the door. "Go get one, then! Get Paul, get whoever. The whole firm's here, you should be able to find someone."

He grimaces.

"Paul wrote the will, so he's not uninvolved. Really, you'd be better off getting someone from a different firm—"

Saskia takes a deep breath, closes her eyes.

"I'm going to leave," she says. "And you're going to take five minutes, and you're going to write down the name of some lawyer who can help me, and you're going to leave it on the desk"—she points—"right there. You will come out, and then I'll come in and call whoever you've given me. Got it?"

His face seems to flicker; he's wrestling with something. She doesn't care.

"Okay," he says eventually.

Her nod is so slight it's like a ripple of wind over the water. She shuts off the music. And then she leaves him there, alone, and goes back to the party.

Chapter 4

Knowing that her life depended on it—but knowing, too, that story-telling was her calling, her vocation, the one thing she had been put on this planet to do—Scheherazade sat down and began to tell the King a tale.

—*FAIRY TALES FOR LITTLE FEMINISTS:*
SCHEHERAZADE'S 1,001 STORIES, EVELYN HARPER KREIS

December 1993

SASKIA WAS ELEVEN, BUT EVIE STILL FORCED HER to put on a velvet dress, a hair bow, and Mary Janes for the Christmas party. As at every other party they'd ever had, she had been asked to play the piano. The guests had started out all gathered around her: forty, fifty of them crowded into the conservatory, the hallway, under the archway leading to the living room.

Now, she was alone.

She couldn't figure out what had gone wrong. She had been playing the same things she always played: she started out with the Christmas carols to get the audience warmed up. She'd use that just as a hook, then plunge them deeper into her repertoire—the Liszt, the Ravel, the Stravinsky. The pieces that—so she was told—showcased her talent.

But she had barely started the Liszt when slowly, like waves breaking on the beach at the beginning of a storm, conversation began at the back of the room.

Her playing, the thing that once kept people enraptured, had become something normal. Something average.

From the hallway, she could overhear her father telling the story of how he and her mother met. Hadn't everyone they knew already heard that story? Evie had a bunch of paintings mounted in the senior show at the art institute—Michael's friend, the first violinist, had dragged him to see her boyfriend's work—and he'd fallen in love with Evie's *Self-Portrait: Hands*. Before he'd seen her face, before he'd known anything about her. He'd loved her hands.

Saskia rolled her eyes and paged through her music. She might as well please herself, since nobody else was listening. Except for maybe Aunt Greta—Edmund's wife, who'd come tumbling down the front stairs a century ago and snapped her neck. Saskia and Lexi had recently graduated from generic ghost stories to focus on their own particular ones instead, and Sas found the recitation of her ghosts reassuring: Emilia, Rosemary, Constance, Greta, Annabelle.

The polonaise, then. She smashed her hands down with pleasure. It wasn't Christmasy. It wasn't even particularly pretty, not at the beginning. The polonaise was all about the making of music from a jumble. The kind of sweaty, whirling chaos the party would turn into in a few hours, once they broke into the really good liquor.

"Hey, prodigy."

She shook her head. No interruptions. No small talk. She was playing.

And, to his credit, Mr. Kintner didn't try again. Also to his credit, he didn't leave. He leaned instead against the inside of the arch, tumbler of whiskey in hand, one foot twisted over the other in a relaxed, attentive posture she didn't appreciate until she'd finished, speeding along into the swing of the piece, proudly concluding with the final chords.

"Let me see 'em."

She blinked up at him.

"Your hands," he said with a laugh.

She held them up.

"Hmmm . . ." He squinted at them, stepping around her to study them from all angles. "Not quite Horowitz yet." Vladimir Horowitz and his infamously huge hands; of course not. Almost nobody had hands like his. Though Saskia secretly thought that she might, someday. Someday when she grew up.

She smirked. "But mine are still better than most grown-ups' already."

She didn't know much about Mr. Kintner, only that he was one of her mother's fellow professors in the art department. That reference to

Horowitz's hands was probably the only thing he knew about music. Hoarded like a dragon's treasure for the moment when he was forced to make conversation with her.

"Better than almost anybody's, I'd imagine," he said, downing the rest of his whiskey, the ice clicking against his teeth. "And getting better all the time."

But before she could think of a response, he was already gone.

January 2020

SHE'S BEEN HOME FOR LESS THAN TWENTY-FOUR hours and she's already wandering the halls of the Elf House like Lady fucking Macbeth. Up and down, not bothering to turn on the lights even as the sun sets into a midwinter gloaming. The William Morris wallpaper pulses around her like a panic attack, the wallpaper that's been there since before her mother was born, little birds stealing strawberries for over a century.

Saskia stops to touch one. Runs her fingers along its beak.

In just two days, she's lost both her mother and her future.

How much she's going to miss those birds.

She turns into the Gold Room. It has not been gold in one hundred years or more. As long as she has known it, it's simply been a half-empty space with sheets over the abandoned furniture. The only remnant of its name are the floral brass sconces, tarnished now, dusty, on either side of the ghost-bed.

The house is choking her, yet she longs for it with a dull ache even as she's standing in it.

In the glow of dusk, the windows give off a Technicolor blue light. She presses her hands against the old glass, rattling it in its pane. Exhales around them, watches the shape her breath makes.

A flicker of orange catches her eye. Her father has lit the fire in the pit and is sitting there, fists shoved into his bulky L.L.Bean coat as he stares into the flames. He looks so alone, so bereft; she feels twin lashes within her, the simultaneous urge to comfort him and to confront him.

She digs out an old puffy jacket and some boots from the back of the hall closet. It's incredibly dusty, half an inch gathered on the baseboards; they were her mother's particular bête noire, those baseboards.

Even from the closet, she can smell the wood burning: it's the Christmas tree. That pine was always so distinct in the weeks after the holiday, burning in every fireplace in the house through January. The tang of it, the wild and rough scent.

Outside, Saskia brushes the snow off of the bench across from her dad and sits down. He doesn't look up.

"Why did she do it? Did she really hate me that much?"

Mike still stares into the flames. "You know, Sas—I don't think it was about you at all."

Shame and anger battle for dominance as Saskia struggles to find something to say in response. But her father keeps talking. "I think she did it to ensure her legacy. She and Patrick—you know he's the director of development over at the university now?" Of course she knows. She's followed him at a distance for years, this tender bruised spot on the apple of her heart. "They discussed what she wanted to do with everything. After . . . after. Now."

She nods at her father, wanting him to continue, desperate for an explanation to latch on to. "Like I was saying, her idea was to create an arts center for underprivileged children, his was to restart the pre-college programs with some strategic funding. They'd been talking about it for a couple of years, ever since their pre-college program got cut. And at the end of the day . . . well, it was all getting so complicated, the paperwork and the appraisals and the real estate agents, not to mention her diagnosis and appointments with different specialists. So she must have wanted to simplify things. Not spend her last days tied up in logistics. Patrick can make sure the house goes where she wanted it to go. That's my best guess."

She's frowning by the time he finishes, but his gaze is back in the middle distance, staring into the flames.

"But why—Dad, she didn't give us any options for selling it, she's not giving the right of first refusal to the university. She—" Saskia can't help her voice breaking, even as she barrels on. "She *gave* the house away. You said it was your retirement plan. And she just donated it outright and didn't tell either of us?"

His cheeks puff out and he bends his head forward. "Yeah, kid. I know. And that—I don't know what that's about. There's too much— It's all just a lot. Maybe that part was only a mistake."

"A mistake! I mean, I know Mom was sick, but that is taking careless-ness to an extreme. Wasn't she thinking about us at all? Wasn't she—"

"Saskia!" The tone is sharp, painfully sharp, one she's never heard from her father before. His eyes burn at her. "You will not talk about your mother like that. You don't know what she was like in her last days. If she was even partway down the path to where . . . to where . . ." She had, for just a moment, forgotten what her mother's last few months would have been like, the months after the will; the involuntary movements, the speech impairment, the vision loss and rapidly deteriorating memory. The fight for breath as the pneumonia took over; the wondering if she'd be granted the reprieve of a coma. Or could she still wonder, at that point? Had she still been lucid enough to know what was happening to her?

Saskia hopes so. She hopes not. She doesn't know what she hopes.

The shame makes her glow, makes her skin pulse sick. It's a long mo-ment before Mike speaks again. "When did that kid say she wrote the will?"

He didn't. But she saw it, she remembers. "Early last July."

He nods. "She started getting tested early last June, after the insomnia and the blurred vision got really bad. But it wasn't until she had the MRI, to rule out other neurological conditions, that we got the diagnosis. June twenty-eighth. My mother's birthday."

"Do you really think it was a mistake?" The words rote, routine. The question real.

Mike's fists drive further into his coat.

"Maybe," he says finally. "Either that or she did the math and thought we'd be fine on our own. The books do well, you know. You'll be set up for a good few years with those royalties—"

Saskia has no idea what the royalties look like these days, but she knows now isn't the time to ask for specifics. Besides, the fucking princesses are not the point. The Elf House is the point.

"—and I'll have my pension and Social Security. Without the house to keep up . . . well, I'd be fine, financially. I can live simply. So maybe it wasn't a mistake, maybe it was her wanting to give something to the larger world, maybe it was . . ." She can't tell if he's too choked up to go on or just out of ideas, but she waits a long moment for the end of that sentence. It isn't forthcoming.

"I think we need to talk to a lawyer. Just to understand our options. And—I think we need to talk to Patrick," she says quietly.

Across from her, her father's head turns from side to side, silver gold in the firelight.

"I don't want to bring a lawyer into this, Sas," he says with a sigh. "I really don't. The expense of it. The aggression— Patrick may be able to explain everything, you know. Clear this all up. And if there's no explanation . . . well, he's a decent guy, from everything I know. He may just be willing to relinquish his claim."

"I can talk to him," she says, her heartbeat pounding in her throat. "If there's anything to your theory, he'll be able to explain it. And then, at least, we won't be so in the dark."

Staring into the flames, her father doesn't respond.

"But I really think we should see a lawyer, too, Dad. See Josh's lawyer. Because I'm not sure it's entirely legal," she continues. "After all, isn't part of the house yours? Or maybe one of the older Harpers' wills would have some precedence, with that clause about it going just to a Harper—"

Mike shakes his head, eyes still on the flames. "Her father's will ensured that it stayed in Evie's name only; I was never added to the deed. The house has to belong to a Harper, but it also has to belong *just* to a Harper. It was more of an expressed wish than a trust or anything like that, but the Harpers always abided by it. It's your mother's property. I did toss in a bit of my salary for the repairs over the years. But that's at most ten percent of the value. Maybe less."

"See? It's so ridiculously complicated. We *do* need a lawyer. But, Dad," she says, and takes a deep breath. The idea glitters, too tempting not to say. "Let's just say it wasn't a mistake. Let's say that she did want to give the house to Patrick, as a representative for the university. There's really no way we could buy him out?"

His silver eyebrows furrow, and his expression is disbelieving. "With what money, Sas? I'd be surprised if we have ten thousand in the checking accounts, combined, and the last appraisal of the property put it at two-point-nine million. We had to plunge into the retirement fund for the roof last year, the boiler the year before. Your mother let her life insurance lapse after you left home. Besides, you have no idea what a house like this costs to keep up."

Seventy-five thousand dollars a year, give or take, with around fifty in property taxes. He told her last night. But Saskia knows that's not really what he means. He means she has no idea, because she hasn't been here. She has no idea, because she walked away and stayed away, a long time ago.

But hadn't her mother done the same? Ever since Juilliard, ever since Saskia's failure to meet, let alone exceed, expectations, her mother had been floating away from her. Saskia already has so little to cling to. The house is all she has left.

"I just—I can't imagine a future without the house. I always thought it would be there to come back to—" Saskia's voice cracks and trails off.

"And yet," Mike says quietly, "and yet you never did bother coming back, Sas." There's a long pause. "You know what I think?" he says finally. "I think the future, this transition . . . no matter whether we end up selling the house or having to give it away. Just being *without* it, being able to breathe: it'll be like when you quit piano. Not what we envisioned, maybe, but a new phase of life with its own rewards. Do you remember what you told me when you left Juilliard?"

She shakes her head. She doesn't remember which lie she told to whom anymore.

"*It might be fun to just be a person,* you said." He laughs, and she grins. "Well?" he says. "Was it?"

She can hear the lake crashing onto the shore in the distance between their voices. The faint cawing of insomniac seagulls.

"Not as much as I'd been led to believe," she says finally.

He tilts his head, cheekbones shaded devilish by the fire. "Ah. But you carry the music with you still."

As he stares at her expectantly, she wonders: What kind of life does he imagine she has?

And how far is it from her reality?

"Dad," she says, and she can't make herself look at him. "Dad, I lost my job."

"Oh, Sas. What happened?"

She can't make herself say: *My gut is really messed up where men are concerned, and I fucked my way out of it.*

Neither, though, can she bring herself to lie.

"It was complicated," she says, feeling the scorch of the flames against her cheeks.

"You'll find something else. That programming degree— They'll be lining up for you."

"I . . . I'm trying some other things right now."

"Engineering, then?"

Saskia turns back to the flames. "I only had a minor in electrical engineering, Dad, and that was a million years ago. It's about as valuable as my other minor in piano studies, and you *know* that was just a bone they threw me for the Juilliard coursework. I actually—I actually lost the job awhile ago. And I've started writing math questions for standardized tests—you know, the SAT, things like that. It pays pretty well," she lies. "And it gives me time for my boxing."

"I hate that you box," he says, low. "It worries me."

"I'm safe," she says, though her knuckles contradict her; badly wrapped hands, done too quickly. She bunches up her sleeves over her hands. "I'm pretty dangerous myself, once I'm in the ring. But it's not like I can afford to go pro anytime soon, I can barely afford a trainer once a week as it is, and that's where the danger really is. Anyways, don't worry about me. Let's just fix this. What do we do next?"

He sighs, puts his gloved hands onto his knees. "All right. You want to know what we do? Here's what we do. We talk to Patrick, we see if he knows why it was a gift. And worst-case scenario . . . Well, I know it's not what you planned for, but I've been getting used to the idea of letting this place go. And I do think you'll come to see that having this giant old house to keep up would have weighed you down, held you back. Maybe this is for the best. Maybe—"

Saskia interrupts. "I'll email the lawyer tonight. And then I'll go see Patrick. He owes us an explanation."

For a second, their eyes burn into each other's, identical across the flames.

"Are you sure that's a good idea? Talking to him alone?"

Saskia looks away. "I'm a boxer now, remember?" she says mildly. "Trust me. I can take care of myself."

Chapter 5

Despite all the warnings—maybe because of them—Pandora found herself reaching for the clasp. And she realized: she didn't care whether what she found inside was good or bad. She didn't particularly care if it would lead her to salvation or ruin. All she cared about was knowing.

—*Fairy Tales for Little Feminists: Pandora's Box*, Evelyn Harper Kreis

June 1994

SASKIA WAS ELEVEN. SHE WAS OFF ON HER FIRST TOUR: New York, followed by Chicago, finishing off in Los Angeles. *A mini-tour for a mini-pianist*, her agent, Ron, had said with a wink and a grin. Saskia had nothing but contempt for the man and his hair gel, but *he's the best*, Evie said. *Ron is very, very good.*

Her mother did many things for Saskia, but not housework; never housework. She would cook precisely 3.5 dinners a week. She would pay for the cleaning service to come twice a week, once for the upstairs and once for the downstairs (the *Little Feminists* were doing well). Saskia just left her bed unmade, her room uncleaned, which was how it stayed until the cleaners fixed it up. And in the meantime, Evie would measure Saskia for her uniform once a year, and she'd pick out both everyday and performance clothes from the Neiman Marcus catalog. But when it came to packing—

"It's your tour," she'd said, eyebrows furrowed. "Besides, Sas, you're eleven years old. You know where the suitcases are."

She didn't know, actually. But she was too ashamed to admit that, so she'd stumbled up the grimy steps to the tower on her side of the Elf

House, only to find that apart from a graveyard of old toys and a pile of mattresses, they didn't actually store anything up there under the exposed rafters. A second foray, into the matching tower on her parents' side, had landed her the creamy leather luggage with her mother's maiden-name initials, EJH, embossed on them in gold.

And finally, she was packed. Finally, they were on their way to Mitchell International Airport, on the way to the next step in Saskia's career.

As usual, the three of them rode quietly in the car. After a moment, Mike flipped on NPR, making Saskia roll her eyes. She'd have preferred classical, of course; if not classical, then silence. But Mike's addiction to the news was a tic she and her mother had long since accepted.

And in an update to the Tonya Harding case, the United States Figure Skating Association has revoked her national title after her guilty plea three months ago for conspiracy to hinder prosecution. In addition to the revocation of her title, Harding is banned from competing in USFSA competitions for life.

The newscaster, a woman with a sharp voice, went on, going over what was apparently old news to everyone but Saskia: a competitor, an unhinged boyfriend, a rival injured—

They were on the freeway before Evie realized that Saskia was sobbing in the back seat.

"For heaven's sake," her mother said, twisting around to smooth Saskia's hair away from her hot face. "What is it?"

"Tonya—Harding—" Saskia cried.

She couldn't see her mother's expression through her own tears. They were coming out of her in great gulping sobs; she couldn't remember the last time she'd cried like this. She was famous for her stoicism, even among the famously even-keeled Harpers. Though the Kreises could hold their own: her father was still staring straight ahead into the traffic from the driver's seat.

"The ice-skater?" said her mother, extricating a tissue from her purse, pressing it to Sas's face.

"She got ba—banned—" Saskia gulped.

"Well, yes, honey, but she did break that other skater's knee."

"But she didn't even do it!" Saskia cried. "She didn't. They just said, weren't you listening—it was just some guy. Just some guy who did it, it wasn't even he—her—and they took her title away and now she can't ever skate again."

"Darling. What's she to you? You don't even know her."

Saskia paused at that, letting the salt run into her mouth. It tasted surprisingly good.

"I don't know," she said finally, with a gasp for breath. "It's—it's just—all she knows how to do. It's what she's worked for her entire life. And she's the best in the world. And I think . . . Aren't we a little bit the same? Don't you think I'm that way, too?"

Evie crinkled her nose so small and so fast that it almost twitched, like a rabbit's.

"Don't ever say that," she said with an exaggerated shudder. "That tacky woman."

Saskia ducked her head down, annoyance finally puncturing that strange bubble of tears. She couldn't understand what had come over her. But as it happened, she ended up getting her first period later that day, halfway between Mitchell International and JFK.

January 2020

IF YOU ARE THE RIGHT KIND OF PERSON, DOWNTOWN Milwaukee in winter is a magical place. A *Christmas Carol* at the Pabst Theater and fairy lights trimming the Pabst Mansion; *The Nutcracker* at the Marcus Center; skating rinks and frozen rivers; cocktails overlooking the snow-laced city from the Pfister Hotel; the glowing orb atop the old gas building that predicts tomorrow's weather and is only ever half right. And brick, cream brick everywhere, the bricks that made Milwaukee famous supporting the structures that let you slip, still, into its past: the taverns with their beer gardens, the gymnasiums, the mostly defunct breweries.

Saskia had half hoped that Tara Fernwood's law firm would be in one of the renovated mansions lining Prospect, where the East Side trails off, embarrassed, into downtown, but it is not: it is properly downtown, a downtown she has rarely had to traverse. Not the one filled with mid-winter bus depots, not the one with cocktail waitresses still forced to wear four-inch heels. A Milwaukee, instead, made of glass and steel, of brief-cases and business lunches.

In the elevator to the eleventh floor, two lawyers join the Kreises. Women in skirt suits and pearls. Beneath Evie's camel-hair coat, Saskia is suddenly very aware of the moth holes in the sleeve of her raspberry cashmere sweater, the one her mother bought her twenty years ago. Aware of the winter slush drying in a white shoreline a few inches up her skinny jeans. It's like the flaws in her clothes are part of her, she can feel them *in* as well as *on* her body.

Mike was not raised on the East Side. He was raised on the West Side, out by the stadium, but you'd never know it from the navy overcoat trailing elegantly from his shoulders, the crisp blue shirt and crisp blue jeans tailored beneath it. Whatever her mother did or didn't have, Saskia thinks, you had to give her this: she knew all about the protective cover-ings of good taste.

Mike catches her eye and winks.

He winks. After the horror of her mother's illness and death, the vio-lence of the will—after the unfair, mistaken wrongness of it all, there he is, still. Saskia's father, the good guy, *How can I help you, ma'am?* And that resilience is enough to propel her through reception and into the glass box where they will meet Tara Fernwood, where water bottles and a tray of cookies are displayed in front of a floor-to-ceiling window that looks out onto the icy winter lake.

It's only a second before Tara enters the conference room in a cluster of color, all kelly-green dress and huge Liv Tyler eyes. As she sticks out her hand, her dress shifts and a tattoo on the lawyer's chest peeks out.

A revolver. And coming from it, the words *Happiness is a warm gun.*

If Saskia believed in friends, Tara Fernwood would be under immedi-ate consideration.

When Saskia was in first grade, Mrs. Tanner asked each student to write a paragraph about their best friend. Pale head bent down, Saskia had focused hard, made her choice. The dexterity of her hands, the fine motor skills three years of piano had already given her, meant that she was better than her classmates at forming the letters, though she was never any good at finding the words. She raised her eager hand and was the first to be picked. She'll never forget the laughter—the bubbling, boiling laughter—as she'd read out her work.

My best friend is my mom.

Her world was her parents, Carrie, and Georgia and Lexi; later, it expanded to include Patrick. She hadn't seen the need for anyone else. *Don't you like any of the girls in your group?* her mother had asked, over and over again. But the pianists in her group class weren't her friends; they weren't even her competition. They were just easily outpaced peers for whom she felt nothing but a vague contempt. Well, contempt and a slight confusion. Why weren't they better? They should have been better.

Finally, when she turned ten, Carrie managed to convince her parents that there was nobody in Saskia's league in the city, likely the entire Midwest, most probably the country, and those three-hour Saturday sessions would be better spent one-on-one.

Later, at NYU, there had been a handful of girls she'd gone with to movies, loft parties, shows. But she'd quit playing by then, and how could she ever have explained to them who she actually was? Her self, her core. The women stayed vaguely in touch over the years, Saskia's envy of them thudding more faintly with each passing month, each filtered Instagram post. Coffee dates, wine bars, trips to the Hudson Valley—what was the point? To have an audience for their mediocre lives? She doesn't need that. She's not even interested in her own mediocre life, she can't imagine anyone else would be.

She's a lone wolf, her father used to say when he thought she couldn't hear them. *Don't worry, Evie. I was the same way.*

But her father's solitude was never the same thing, and she's never known why.

Tara watches her notice the tattoo just at the moment Saskia's gaze swivels to her father. Not his sort of thing, *at all.* He even hates the elephant gun her grandfather kept to shoot big game, has consigned it to the deep recesses of the attic. But he's sitting, placidly polite, with one of the yellow legal pads and a pen from the center of the table pulled in front of him.

He's not her mother; he's always been able to accept things as they come to him. If Evie judged, Mike perceived. Perfect Myers-Briggs opposites.

Tara grins at them.

"Sorry," she says, gesturing at the tattoo. "It's so overheated in here in the winter, I had to take off my sweater. Normally I'd never—"

"No, it's cool," Saskia says, and smiles.

Happiness is a warm gun.

Tara Fernwood, she thinks, you are exactly the kind of person I need.

"So, look," Tara says, flopping down next to Saskia as she tucks a strand of her silky dark hair behind her ear. "I've gone over the will, and I'm not sure I completely understand what you were saying in your email. About it being a mistake."

Saskia looks at her father, but he has his pleasant, public face on. She swallows.

"Oh. Well, basically, Mom was thinking about selling the house to the university. We get that leaving it to, uh, Patrick, could have made things easier. But . . ."

"We never talked about giving the house away," Mike says easily. "She always meant to sell it. My wife inherited a sizable family property as a young woman. We had recently discussed selling the house to UWM for an arts center, but she made a mistake in revising her will and left it to the VP of development instead. That's all."

"Yeah," Tara says, her eyes skittering over the documents in front of her. "The bequest does seem . . . generous. But I think the first thing we need to do is to clear up this idea that there was a mistake. There are two witnesses, both of them Fairchild lawyers, and a medical certificate from Dr. Ferdia. No judge in the state is going to overturn the will on those grounds."

Something in Saskia's stomach recoils, draws back into her body.

"Look . . ." Mike's smooth tenor rolls in. "I get that legally, it may not have been a mistake. But I can see circumstances under which Evie might have been influenced—maybe not maliciously, I'm not saying that . . . but definitely influenced."

Saskia doesn't miss the flare of Tara's eyes, but she says nothing. If she's waiting for the Kreises to keep talking, to inadvertently reveal more than they intended to, she's got the wrong family. Mike and Saskia stare back at her in silence: Mike's, mild. Saskia's, throbbing.

"Exactly," Tara finally says. "Really, your only legal option for overturning this is to show that Kintner exhibited undue influence in the writing of the will."

For the first time Saskia wonders: Is it possible that Evie *meant* to leave the house to Patrick? The question snakes feverishly over her skin: cold on the surface, burning underneath. She tries to recall her mother's relationship with Patrick in recent years, the hotshot up-and-comer in the art department. But later, as chair of that department, he'd become Evie's advocate—not to mention a deft handler of local artists' widows. Enough to become director, then vice president, of development for the university. *Grave robber*, Evie had called him affectionately.

No. He was a trusted colleague, but not a close friend. More than an acquaintance, less than a kindred spirit. Enough to merit an invitation to the Kreises' annual Christmas party, not enough to be left a $2.9 million house.

"The only option?" she says.

"The only legal option." Tara raises a shoulder. "It's either prove undue influence or buy out your share."

"Our share?" Saskia asks, at the same time her father asks:

"My share?"

Tara turns to Mike first. "Assuming you've paid for upkeep on the house over the years?" Mike snorts, and Saskia knows what he's thinking: that house is nothing but upkeep. "Well, half of what you spent is owed to you. So say, a hundred grand, two hundred, of the house's appraised value—that's yours. If you can find the rest—"

"Ms. Fernwood," Mike says, and Saskia's back goes stiff. Is he about to do the *not a wealthy man* speech? He is. "I'm a musician. I'm not a wealthy man. The house belonged to my wife, and the bulk of her family money ran out several generations ago. So the idea that I have two-point-something million stashed away is a nonstarter."

Tara nods. "Undue influence, then. That's all you've got. Proving that this Patrick Kintner manipulated your wife—"

Saskia's running cold.

"Say more about that," she says before she can stop herself. Another situation in which she has to be the bitch, the money-grubbing daughter going against her mother's wishes. Because, after all: What if these had been her mother's wishes? What if this really had been what Evie wanted?

That's not something she can think about right now.

A nod of Tara's sleek black head. "Undue influence is pretty difficult to prove. That's not me trying to put you off. Except, honestly, if you can be put off, you should be."

Saskia raises her eyebrows.

"There are two ways we could go about proving it, and I'd want to try both. For the first, there are four things we would need to establish." Tara ticks off her fingers. "Susceptibility, opportunity, disposition, coveted result. Now, her susceptibility is probably the easiest to argue. A woman receives a shocking diagnosis, she has a lot to grapple with. And this was written—what, two weeks after the diagnosis?" Mike is frozen, so Saskia nods. "Opportunity. Did she spend any time alone with Kintner last summer?"

Mike clears his throat. "She taught her last course over the summer months before taking a sabbatical this year. Illustration. She and Patrick used to meet up for lunch a few times a month when she was on campus."

Tara nods. "The coveted result, we have right here," tapping a finger atop the will. "But what you'd really need to dig for is disposition to influence. What could he have done to make her agree to leave him the house?"

Saskia's stomach is roiling. Isn't *that* the question. Mike's face has drawn in on itself, looks grim.

"What's the second way?" she says faintly.

"We'd need to show that there was a confidential relationship between your mother and Kintner. Not just vague, occasional lunches, but specific meetings in the months leading up to the writing of the will. Do you have her phone? Her calendar?"

Mike nods, then clears his throat again. "Yes."

"Good. We'd have to prove that there were suspicious circumstances around the making of the will. To show why it's weird that she left the house to him."

Saskia feels herself sit up straighter, the way she used to in her music theory classes when she was the only one who knew the answer.

"It *is* weird. The Harper wills—" she says. "It's tradition that the house always be left to someone in the Harper line. And only to them. That's why Dad's name isn't on the deed—"

"Good," Tara says, and Sas feels a warmth in her chest that she hasn't felt for years. "Very good. This also plays into the *coveted result* part of the earlier standard. It's a red flag that . . . well, as the statute puts it, *the testator has excluded a natural object of his bounty.*" Mike snorts at the byzantine language, but Sas is transfixed. "And you'd have to establish the closeness of the family, of course."

Suddenly, Saskia's face feels very dry. She gnaws the edge of her lip.

"What does that—" Her voice sounds like a croak. Tara smiles reassuringly.

"Don't worry. For most people, that's the easiest thing to prove. Cards, emails, telephone records. Just to prove that it's strange that Evelyn would give the house to someone else—and specifically not to you"—nodding at Saskia—"since, as you said, according to tradition you'd be the logical next person in line to receive it."

Saskia nods woodenly, like a marionette. All the blood in her body seems to have pooled at the base of her stomach.

"Visits?" she says suddenly. "Mom and Dad came to visit me in New York a few times a year, to . . ." To see Evie's agent and editor, primarily. But did the court need to know that? Couldn't they polish over all of that, as they had among themselves, and say: these were *family* visits?

Tara smiles. "Yes, that's good. When was she last there?"

Saskia casts back in her mind. "May," she says. What symptoms had her mother been experiencing, with her diagnosis a month away? She'd seemed so normal, so *Mom.* But then, how hard would it have been, in those early stages, to keep up a Mom-mask for two hours over a handful of dinners? To plaster a smile on and insist on another cup of coffee when she was so dizzy she couldn't stand, to return to the hotel and stare up at the ceiling as the malfunctioning proteins in her brain built a barrier between her and sleep? Saskia can almost hear it, the midtown night noise so far from her own Brooklyn apartment. Had that been why Evie had insisted on the St. Regis, despite Saskia's protests about the travel time, the distance? To literally create space?

She should have been a better daughter.

"And did anything unusual happen on that trip?"

Saskia is shaking her head *no* as the blood starts pouring out of her nose. She'd thought the nosebleeds would stop when she quit playing, but they never had.

"It's okay," she says over and over again as Tara fusses, presses a Kleenex to her face. "Just—" She waves her free hand. "Keep going."

"That's when the insomnia got really bad," Mike says in a low voice. "New York. She kept blaming the time difference, but it's only an hour—I don't think I saw her sleep for the first three days."

In Saskia's mouth, the blood tastes like metal.

"Okay," Tara says and, to her credit, she plunges merrily along. "I think it'd be in your best interest to start building documentation. You know, just in case. So, over the next few days, I want you to look over Evelyn's records and send me anything—and I do mean *anything*—that might have some bearing on the case."

The blood is slowing now. Knowing it's all over her face, smeared in rusty drying tracks, Saskia removes the tissue.

Tara doesn't miss a beat. "See if you can find any correspondence between Evelyn and Kintner. Emails, call records. Almost everything about estate cases is circumstantial, given that . . ." She trails off, but the unspoken words are still there. That the main witness is dead.

"I don't know that we'll find anything suspicious," Mike's voice cuts in smoothly. "Kintner's a fairly decent guy, as I understand it. Done a hell of a lot for that school."

"But say we do," Saskia says. "What happens next?"

Tara nods. "Well, if you did, you have a fairly strong case. As far as these things go. I really only need to prove three of the four elements of that first test, so even if you can't prove disposition . . . I mean, it would be better if you could. But, basically, we'll work together to create an affidavit spelling everything out in minute detail. I can start with what we've discussed here today and email it to you with further questions," she says to Sas, who gives another marionette nod. "We'll file a written objection to admitting the will into probate and a petition to set aside the will and distribute assets according to intestate rules. Basically, to give everything to her next of kin."

Mike jots this down on the legal pad in front of him as Saskia squints at the lawyer.

"How long will it take?" she says.

"The court will fix a probate hearing date sometime this week. I'd imagine the hearing will be set for a few weeks out. Clear your schedules—you'll need to be there."

More scribbling from Mike.

"And the house?" Her voice is so quiet she's not sure, at first, if Tara heard. "How long can we stay at the house?"

Across the table, her father's hand stops still.

"Until probate proceedings are closed."

Saskia shakes her head. College never prepared her for this language. Tara's face softens.

"Until the end of all the trials," she says.

But Mike's holding up his hand. "Let's not get ahead of ourselves," he says. "It could be that there's a perfectly reasonable explanation for all of this. It seems unlikely, but this *could* be what your mother wanted." And Sas starts at the realization that he's talking to her, her alone. "I think it'd just be better all around if we approached Patrick first. Just to see what he has to say. I'm sure he doesn't want to be any trouble."

The idea of her father and Patrick in the same room. Alone together.

Tara hesitates.

"I wouldn't, if I were you," she says firmly. "There's just too much that could go wrong."

Blood trickling down her throat, Saskia sits up straight to plaster a grin on her smeared face. When her voice comes out again, it's Milwaukee broad.

"Don't worry," she says. "We'll be good."

THEY'RE WAITING FOR THE ELEVATOR BACK DOWN-stairs when Mike grabs Saskia's wrist. She recoils, laughing slightly as she yanks her hand back; he's grinning.

"That infernal *tapping*," he says.

"Tapping?"

He lets his fingertips fall to his thigh, where he starts playing a non-sense song as though on an invisible keyboard.

"You've been doing it all day. Since you came home, actually. Is it nerves? Or something to do with—" He gestures to her bruises.

"Sas—kia?"

She whips around, gratitude cool through her veins, at the sound of her name.

"Josh!" She smiles wide, her heart thumping in her ears as she pulls her coat closer over her ratty sweater.

But his smile is hesitant, and she remembers: she was really awful to him at the memorial service, truly awful. "It's good to see you! What . . . are you up to?"

"Josh," her father says with a nod. The elevator doors open. "I'll just meet you downstairs, Sas."

"Oh—okay." She's turning back and forth between the two men in a daze, settling finally on Josh as the doors clink closed. "You aren't here for our meeting with Tara, are you? We just finished."

He shakes his head. "Another meeting. My job. It's all meetings."

Josh is staring at her hands. Against her thigh, her fingers are tapping out—what is that? The Saint-Saëns. *Carnival of the Animals.* She forces herself to hold still, though her mind insists, like a tic, on playing out the full piece before letting her rest. She hasn't played it since she was seven or eight, but there it lives still, in the electrical wiring of her brain. Like all that garbage does.

She shakes out her wrist.

Josh tries again. "So, how'd it go? Get anything useful?"

Only that it's become exceedingly clear to her that she has to go see the man who broke her heart when she was eighteen and ask him to please explain why her mother left him their house.

"Well," she says. "I mean. Maybe. Kind of."

"Sorry that this is so complicated for you guys. Well, look, I'd better—" Nodding in the direction of the conference rooms.

"Right, right. Well. It was—" She's already turning to go; she's had enough strange revelations for one day.

"Hey, have you heard about the new show down at the art museum?"

"No," she says warily. "Why?"

"No, never mind, I just—"

Oh. Is he . . . asking her on a date? She doesn't know any of this stuff, her only dates the past two decades have been random bar hookups and Tinder house calls and James's regular irregularity. She's kind of surprised anybody still does ask for a date in person; for a moment, she finds his bravery overwhelming.

"But I'd love to see it," she says. "With you."

His face cracks into a smile.

"Are you free Monday?" he says. "The firm is a sponsor, so we get tickets to the opening night. Would you be my plus-one?"

They agree to meet at the museum at 6:00 P.M. Well, she thinks in the elevator, at least she has a friend. Or something. A date, or something. Even if it's awful, it might, at least, make her father happy. *Look, Dad. Look at my perfectly balanced, normal life. Look how well-adjusted I am.*

Besides, she doesn't think it will be awful.

But then again—how would she even know?

Chapter 6

"Let me get this straight," Penelope said. "You want me to sit here and wait while you go see the world?"

Odysseus tilted his head, confused.

"That's right," he said.

Penelope shook her head.

"No freaking way," she said. "I'm coming, too."

—*Fairy Tales for Little Feminists: Penelope and Odysseus*, Evelyn Harper Kreis

June 1994

SASKIA WAS ELEVEN. SHE HAD FOUND HER UNDER-wear spotted with blood somewhere between Mitchell International and JFK, and she had gotten a tampon from her mother, but she had not known how to put the tampon in and so for the rest of the day it had chafed against her, half in and half out. Reminding her, as they made their way to the hotel, that she had now been relegated to the realm of bodies.

Saskia hated the realm of bodies. It was her first trip to New York, after all; there were things to see, ideas to have, streets to walk that had been trod by her heroes. And after they settled into the hotel, after she found a sanitary napkin in the bathroom, she'd spent an afternoon once more in the realm of the mind, watching the city with glittering eyes: the carriage horses outside Central Park, the instruments and weapons collections at the Met, the noise and the clamor of it all.

Her father was at his ebullient best. He'd spent years here, at Juilliard, and if the city had changed since then, he didn't seem to care. But Saskia struggled to enjoy any of it. She couldn't escape the sense that her body was leaking, that everybody would know, that she couldn't stop it. The sense that she was no longer who she had been just a day earlier: that the dry, odorless, smooth little girl was morphing into a monster, a monster with fluids and smells and rough edges. That everything that had once made her special could eventually morph into something—else. Something mundane and mediocre.

Her mother seemed to be as on edge as she was. Before they returned to the hotel, she took Saskia by the hand and led her to a bench in Central Park.

"Do you know what a privilege it is to be here?"

"I guess."

"You guess, or you know? Because, Saskia, you don't have to do this."

"Really?"

"Of course not. We could go home right now. You don't have to perform anymore, not if you don't want to."

Saskia couldn't process it. Who was she, away from the piano?

An eleven-year-old girl. Who wanted to be an eleven-year-old girl?

What would her life look like, without the music, without the specialness, without everything that made Saskia, Saskia? It would mean slumber parties at other girls' houses, the parties she'd been refusing since she was six because of her early morning Saturday lessons. What did they talk about, at those parties? Boys? She really had no idea.

She tried to picture herself without music. How would her parents introduce her to their friends? She imagined disappearing into the background. She felt certain she would fade away, become nothing at all.

"No. I can't. I can't ever stop playing."

Evie squeezed her hand.

"You're so special. You're such a special girl. Come on. We'll be late for NYU."

"NY—"

"The university. The tests." Evie's voice was light, deliberately so. Saskia could hear the strain in it.

"I have to take a test?"

Evie's laughter, like a bell.

"No, honey. They just want to look at your brain. They want to see how you compare to other kids your age. And to grown-up musicians. That's all. No passing or failing."

"Oh." Saskia got to her feet.

"Just—don't tell your dad about it, okay?"

Saskia met her mother's eyes. Shaded, squinting.

She nodded.

She never did see the results.

January 2020

YOU WORK SO HARD TO GET STRONG, AND THEN you go home. And the memories, the histories, start seeping into your shell, like acetone into nail polish, and before you know it, there you are: soft as before.

Saskia can't stand it. They were silent all the way home. And silence has a funny way of ringing through the Elf House, silence that calls attention to itself. Silence like noise. It hasn't even been two days and here she is, trapped again. An animal with her paw in a metal claw. The second they return from the law firm, the second her father pulls the ancient Saab into the garage, she darts out, heading briskly over the gravel to the backyard.

"Gotta make a call."

The wind screams, swirls her hair around her shoulders, her ears, as she approaches the empty firepit. She pulls out her phone with frozen fingers.

Have a second to talk?

She tosses the remains of the Christmas tree woodpile into the metal abyss, fumbles with the starter match as she waits for the reply.

The fire bursts into life just as the reply comes, orange and red against the blue-purple late afternoon sky.

Why are you asking permission? Just call me, you fucking Millennial. It's their running joke, the five years separating them: Gina a baby Gen X'er, Saskia an elder Millennial.

But even though Gina was very clearly just at her phone, it rings six times before she picks up.

"You do and you die," Gina bellows into the phone. "Hey, Sas, what's up."

"I do what and I die?"

Sigh. "Not you. Jocelyn. Turns fucking fourteen on Tuesday—can you believe it? But she's *grounded until then*," turning away from the speaker in, presumably, Jocelyn's direction. "My mom always used to say, 'I hope you have a daughter *exactly. Like. You.*' Never realized she meant it as a curse."

Yeah, Sas tries to say, but it comes out as a garbled choke, a mix between a laugh and a sob.

"Oh, fuck—I didn't mean that, I wasn't—"

"No, don't worry," Sas says, catching her voice. "Sounds like something my mother would have said, herself."

She wants Gina to give her some wisdom, something that will save her. Gina does that sometimes, though you can never guarantee when. *I just wanted to hit something, you know?* Saskia had said to her, over drinks after their first spar, as they shared their boxing origin stories. But Gina, who'd been at this a lot longer, had just stared blankly, then squinted her dark eyes. *Hasn't anyone ever told you? Boxing's not about hitting, hon. It's about not getting hit.*

She's heard it a million times since then, but that first day, the saying had resonated through her body like a punch. She wants Gina to say something cool like that.

"I fucking hate you!" a girl calls in the background.

"What the hell else is new?" Gina shrieks. Then, softer: "How are things there?"

"A fucking mess." But it sounds too dire and, honestly, Saskia's *fucking mess* is nothing like Gina's. Gina's fucking mess is when Bobby doesn't send child support three months in a row. Gina's fucking mess is when the boyfriend before him, the one who'd made her say *never fucking again* and take up boxing, starts calling at 4:00 A.M. "But it was always going to be a fucking mess."

"Yeah," Gina says. "It's so weird, when your mom dies. God, I remember.

It was like falling into an alternate universe. Like a sci-fi show or something, where just one thing about your life is different, but it changes everything."

The fire pops, and Sas jumps.

"Yeah," she says, her heart catching in her throat. "Yeah, it is exactly like that."

"Don't you—don't you dare open that door— Look, Sas, I'm sorry to cut you off, but I've got to go. But tell me if there's anything I can do, okay? Like, really tell me."

"Yeah," Saskia says. "Yeah, of course."

They hang up without saying goodbye. They've never said goodbye, they're not that kind of women. When they're done, they're done.

Gina's hollers still ringing in her ears, Saskia goes in to start dinner.

DINNER IS A DIFFERENT KIND OF SILENCE, THOUGH. Mike is refusing to discuss the possibility of establishing undue influence, of doing anything beyond simply asking Patrick to renounce the will. And the more she thinks about it, the less certain Saskia is that Patrick is the kind of man to do such a thing. Who *would* renounce a will like that? A priest, maybe? But even priests weren't the men she'd been raised to believe they were, were they, and besides—the ones that actually were holy could still find some use for $3 million.

And that's if it was even a mistake in the first place.

Later, after Mike has gone to bed, Saskia slides her boots and coat on and makes her way out back. Past the firepit, its embers still glowing rosy orange. Through the winter remains of her grandmother's floral border, the rosebushes covered with little jackets her mother would have put on them back in October. As she pads over the snow, there are places where the evening's frost has already hardened into a thick glaze of ice, supporting her weight; others where it's still fine and loose as powder and her foot plunges straight down to the frozen grass. If it were one or the other, she could move smoothly, but as it is, she's a strange figure, limping her way to the carriage house studio.

The orchard, then: the raspberry bushes at the edges, surrounding the cherry trees, the pears, the apples. All of it too sour to eat, good enough only for pies, and Evie would never have baked a pie. The lake air warms

the trees in winter, cools them in summer. They're stark now, black and white as the old films her dad loves to watch on TCM, ebony and ivory against the fluorescent navy sky. In summer, it's so colorful with fruit that it looks like an impressionist painting. What will happen this year? Saskia imagines the fruit falling, rotting soft and mealy into the ground, nobody left to pick it.

It's too much house. That's what Evie always said, looking at the monthly statement from the cleaners. Saskia had always rolled her eyes. *My heart bleeds.* In Bed-Stuy, she has four hundred square feet, and she doesn't even own it. But maybe it is too much house. Too much land. Too much history.

She can almost smell the fructose fermenting, overripe into the soil.

She should turn on her phone flashlight, but she can't bring herself to: the moon is full, the shadows are long, and her mother would have loved the whole scene so much, would have painted it. But in Evie's version, Saskia would wear a medieval dress with bell sleeves, would have a wolf at her side.

Saskia flicks on the light and stands in the doorway of her mother's studio, sketches on the bulletin board fluttering in the breeze from the door. Here is the missing color from the world outside: smudges of blue and green and ocher pastels, mugs full of rainbow markers, colored pencils worn down to nubs. All these materials for creating, belonging to an artist who will never create again. Saskia can almost hear the free-range fairy tales floating around. This was where they'd flowed from her mother's brain; this was where their silly magic had happened.

There they are, all twenty-six of her books, lined up in a perfect row on the shelf to her left. More color, more life. Chronologically arranged, they create a rainbow: the deep crimson of *Rapunzel* fading to the burnt sienna of *Cinderella* into the yellow of *The Twelve Dancing Princesses*— always her favorite.

Saskia closes her eyes.

Have as many adventures as you can.

Don't look for a knight. Look for a sword.

Be who you are, and people will love you.

This was the code threaded through the books. This was the code that had made them so popular. Evie's heroines were annoyingly, improbably outspoken; annoyingly, improbably self-sufficient. But they always—annoyingly, improbably—won.

In all of Saskia's life, she'd found only one thing in those books that had been truly useful in the real world. Only one thing that carried as much power in the real world as it did in fairyland.

Being the best was all that mattered.

Saskia has known for a long time that the books don't contain universal truths so much as they contain an alternate universe created in direct opposition to the one in which Evie had been raised, her restrictive childhood and adolescence: Episcopal church, Daughters of the American Revolution, white dresses, and mandatory piano lessons; implied and enforced chastity as a young woman, followed by marriage and its implied and enforced monogamy. Going to art school in Chicago had been her greatest rebellion.

Art school. In Chicago.

She's being unfair. She knows she is. What did Saskia want from her mother? Not to have tried to make a better world? She'd never promised to have all the answers. The books presented a vision, that was all.

She fights back the instinct to punch a wall. Love, hate, nostalgia, whimsy, frustration—there are so many feelings, and none of them make any sense with any of the others. She wants the cleanness of a one-two punch, a one-two punch she can take: jab, cross. It's all of this strange shit coming out of nowhere, the uppercut, the left hook, that's throwing her off.

The perfect jab. A clean sonata. A beautiful line of computer code—

She sits down at her mother's computer, wakes it up.

There's a password, which she cracks in less than thirty seconds: Wolfie1974, the dog and the year Evie was married. And then a cluttered desktop, an unsurprisingly cluttered desktop, cluttered as her mother's mind. Her eyes dance over the icons. Photos of the dog titled only with strings of numbers. Scans of illustrations from the most recent book, *Scheherazade*, which had raised a minor Twitter scandal back in 2015 (*Surely the storyteller wasn't meant to be white?*). In retrospect, Evie had been lucky—it hadn't made nearly as much noise as it would have today. Folders scattered willy-nilly through everything else.

Saskia crosses her fingers that her mother set up Outlook. At the bottom of the screen, she clicks the icon and holds her breath.

Evie's Gmail forwards here. Perfect.

Since Evie's death, only spam has come through. There's not much from the previous few weeks, either, since the pneumonia hit. But back at the beginning of December, there are dozens of emails between Evie and Jody, her publisher, with Ellen, her agent, copied. Mike had sent them the same notification he'd sent to UWM, so they'd stopped emailing— but Sas reads the last email, from December 15, with growing anxiety. *I know how difficult it must be to write right now. Yes, we can talk about another extension on* Persephone and Demeter *beyond the initial February 1 deadline. Would three months—*

For a moment, the deluded hope of the exchange winds her like a fist to the throat. There wouldn't be a February 1, for her mother. She'd never live to see it.

But in the meantime: the book.

Fuck. Someone's going to have to deal with that. Saskia vaguely remembers her mother talking about the book, though she herself had been fixated on the fact that it was a book for adults rather than children. She'd never gotten over thinking of her mother as primarily an illustrator and had more or less assumed that Evie would never finish the adult book. But from the emails, it sounds like the book's almost done.

Almost, but not quite.

Sas searches the computer for the manuscript, finds five different versions. She opens the one with the suffix FINAL_final_2, weighing in at eighty thousand words and change. Great, something she can do: she'll skim it tonight, make sure it's finished enough, send it on its way. Pass GO, collect $200. She forwards it to her own account.

Next.

The royalty statements for *Little Feminists*. Still bringing in nearly a hundred grand a year, she sees with some shock. Who'd have thought that that second-wave feminist claptrap would still be so popular? And, scanning through the uploaded statements from the past decade, she sees that it's gotten only more popular as the years have gone on. It's all of that girlboss feminism, Saskia decides, with its similarly reductive rallying cries. And since she'll be the one to benefit—it washes over her, the relief, like a wave. She could give up her job. She could. In all of the chaos surrounding the house itself, it somehow got lost on her: her mother has (accidentally?) set her free.

A search of the in-box for Patrick's name turns up nothing but overly excited newsletters from the development office she's *sure* he didn't write. (*What's new at UWM in 2020? What* isn't *new?!*)

Saskia sighs and clicks the FINANCES folder on the desktop. A copy of the last quarter's taxes, Evie declaring a healthy $45,000 income for the last three months of 2019. Christ, that *Persephone* book must have gotten a far bigger advance than the *Feminists* had—and after the *Scheherazade* debacle, too. But there's only a couple thousand in the account. Where'd all that money go?

She opens a folder saved just as HOUSE. And shivers as she sees the saved email thread between her mother and Patrick from early last July.

Attached, please find a copy of the signed and witnessed will as drafted by Fairchild & Locke. I trust it will meet with your approval.

She frowns at the curtness of the email, at the formality. Furrowing deeper as she reads Patrick's response:

Excellently done. Thank you. I'll be by tomorrow evening.

And Evie:

Make it Thursday; Mike will be in Toronto.

Well, there's the fucking confidential relationship all right. Saskia forwards the email to herself, then directly to Tara from her phone. His approval. His visiting the house when her father was out of town. Why? Why was any of it necessary?

But wasn't that Tara's job, to figure it out? It's her job to gather evidence, as much as she can. Saskia plunges on, into the innards of her mother's hard drive.

Receipts, saved for deductions she couldn't take (the Kreises paid the alternate minimum tax), Sas skims over. Back, back—

And her gaze catches on a document Evie had entitled simply "FIX THIS."

2019 City of Milwaukee Combined Property Tax Payment Coupon.

WARNING: If the first installment payment is not paid by the due date, the installment option is lost. The total tax becomes delinquent and is subject to interest and penalty charges.

Monthly Installment Payment Due: February through July 2019: 15,483.98.
Monthly Installment Payment Due: August, September, and October
2019: 14,335.25.

What?

Over a hundred and fifty grand in property taxes due.

What? No.

But another two hours at the computer digging through emails and bank records (password saved on the computer, thank God) say *yes*. It looks like Evie finally made a payment of thirty-something grand in April—just after signing the contract for *Persephone*—but that meant that they still owed $120,000 to the city of Milwaukee. And for the rest of the year, the accounts didn't have more than $15,000 in them for more than a few days. Each royalty check had plunged into the account and immediately been torn apart: a roofer here, a contractor there, the energy company—good *Lord*, what they'd paid for heating, especially as the months got colder. The bills pushed up into four figures a month as the year went on.

So even Evie's book money hadn't been enough to ward off the rest: a tax warrant, a lien on the house—a lien on the *Elf House*.

She's punching numbers into her phone faster than she ever has in her life.

"Tara Fernwood."

"Tara, it's Saskia Kreis. Sorry to be calling so late. I just forwarded you—"

"Yeah, it's fascinating. Excellent work."

"Thanks. Good. What do you know about tax law?"

A low, rolling laugh.

"More than I ever wanted to. What's up?"

"There's a property tax lien on the house. A hundred and twenty thousand. Who pays it?" She hadn't realized how much it worried her until she feels the pounding of her heartbeat in her ears.

"The beneficiary," Tara says. "Liens belong to properties, not people."

"Thanks. I'm finding more stuff. I'll keep sending it—"

Her finger's hovering over the disconnect button when Tara cuts in.

"Send the documents on the lien over to me, too. Just in case."

After the call ends, Saskia collapses back in the chair, shaking slightly with the cold, trying to make sense of what she is seeing. Her mother couldn't afford to keep the house, that was unavoidably clear. So she'd decided to sell it. Then she'd changed her mind, decided to use it in another way.

But what other way? What had she gotten in return from Patrick?

Saskia shuts her burning eyes. Enough. Enough for tonight. She'll give Patrick a call in the morning—though her skin seems to shrink against her body as she imagines him picking up. She'll email him, then. She'll do something.

Saskia's trembling has turned to shivering. She shakes her legs out, feet prickling as the blood rushes back into them, turns to go. She grabs her phone from the table and flicks the lights off. She makes her way back through the snow, climbs up the stairs and into bed.

Beneath the canopy, she opens her mother's manuscript, scrolling down past the title page. Saskia can't really remember exactly what happened to Persephone—something with the Underworld? Or a pomegranate? But she's halted before she begins by the first words.

For my daughter.

Three words: a hand on her neck, pressing down on her windpipe. A gift from beyond the grave. Take a house, leave a story. No money, plenty of mystery. Some of this, not enough of that—

She barely makes it through the first lines.

Once upon a time, the goddess Demeter had a daughter. Persephone was a golden girl, a dream, a delight.

Moments like this—where the past hollows her out—this is why James is useful. Knowing that she can steal into a different life for just a moment. Knowing that she can call for him and he'll be there—maybe not exactly when she wants, maybe not exactly how she wants, but still, at least she can count on a broad expanse of muscle and bone holding her. The comfort of him: solidity without the risk.

She checks her messages.

Thinking about you today.

Thinking about you, too, she writes back before she can stop herself. An emoji would have been just as good.

But he doesn't belong to her, he's never belonged to her, and her phone doesn't ping a reply. He's with his wife, of course. He has nothing for Saskia. There are never any good endings to these stories, and she'd known that before she started the affair. The man goes back to his wife, recommitted and penitent, and there you were, still stuck in your own story, still on your own.

She downs two Xanax, but she can't relax. She can lie here staring up at the canopy, or she can get up and read her mother's book. It is for her, after all.

Like a reflex, like muscle memory, Saskia slips out of her room, around the corner to her tower door. Up the winding staircase in slippered feet, fuzzy blanket wrapped around her shoulders.

The Elf House has two towers, though they line up so precisely from the driveway that you can't tell there's more than one. Without windows, they're all but uninhabitable. The west tower, on her parents' side, they use as an attic. The east tower has traditionally been empty except for a damp pile of old mattresses and some random boxes. The doors at the end of the hallways look like all the other doors. Behind them, though, are winding spiral staircases two stories high, carrying the traveler into a different world: round mansard spaces, peaked ceilings like witches' hats.

She's always thought of the one at the end of her hallway as her own tower, which is what her mother had called it: *Saskia's tower*. For Mike, it was *Saskia's attic*; to a real estate agent, it might have been *the secondary loft*. Really, it's not much of anything. When she was little, they'd started finishing and soundproofing it, with the goal of adding value to the house and giving Saskia her own studio in the meantime. But there was the conservatory downstairs, no window to crane a piano in, and they never would have sold the house. In the end, a refurbishment would only have increased their exorbitant property taxes, which—as Saskia is now keenly aware—were high enough.

Even today, the attic is still paused in its pathway to whatever it might have been: the semi-bathroom in the corner, a working toilet and a non-working sink hidden behind a half wall. The ancient, puffy pink insulation, never to be plastered over. The soundproofing material visible in the gaps between the floorboards.

She stands still at the top of the stairs for a moment, listening to the thump of her heart. Emptiness. She's surrounded by emptiness.

At the far end of the space, her old CD player, covered with a fine layer of dust, splattered here and there with paint. She thought she'd thrown it out years ago; it had broken, played each disc on never-ending loops. The only way to stop it was to dig your fingernails below the still-spinning disk and pry it out, watch as it flew across the room. The CD case next to it has her own face on it: an image Evie had taken of Saskia at fifteen in the birch copse behind the house, midwinter, simmering and seething at the camera.

In the corner, that same ancient pile of mattresses: her father's doing, definitely. He hadn't grown up with money, had taken on his own parents' Depression-era mindset of scarcity. So now there are five queen-size mattresses, so cold they'd feel almost soggy to the touch, propped on top of each other in the corner. All they need is a princess. Though the huge pile of boxes surrounding them does take away from the effect somewhat. She rifles through a few of them but finds only her old school uniform, saddle shoes, trophies.

Her trophies weren't the apocryphal *participation trophies* people said kids these days received. She'd never gotten a trophy for participating in something, and if she had, she wouldn't have taken it. She can't think why anyone her age would. Like their parents had ever emphasized participation. That generation—they'd prized only greatness. Showing up, if that's all you were going to do, meant less than nothing, meant being only the background noise that the winner drowned out.

Saskia sits down on the mattresses with her phone.

And she reads.

She reads it all.

A thin plot, if she's being honest. It could have been summarized in less than a page, though her mother had of course written much more than that. Persephone, beloved daughter, was stolen from the world, taken belowground by Hades. Her mother, the goddess of the harvest, Demeter, searched the world for her. Eventually, she blackmailed the other gods into helping her make Hades return Persephone to the Earth. But Persephone, having eaten pomegranate seeds in the Underworld, had failed to read the small print; she was trapped there forever.

Saskia hovers over the first chapter for a long time. Here is Persephone's story of her life before the abduction, told as she'd never seen it before.

Persephone is always painted as the consummate damsel, stolen away. But here, in these pages, is a new kind of goddess; an Evelyn Harper Kreis kind of goddess. She talks back to her mother. She is unwittingly rude to the servants, though she apologizes later. She is not particularly likable, though she's not unlikable, per se; she's a teenager, that's all.

The abduction, then, to which Evie's Persephone is a more than willing participant. Hades is daring, charming. Funny, even. And if he has to trick her a little to get her down into the Underworld . . . well, it's not the same as carrying her off, is it? It's not the same thing as kidnapping her.

It's too much, somehow, and Saskia can't pinpoint why. The only thing she needs to know is whether the thing is finished, after all. And so she's skimming, scrolling through the rest, when a section of Demeter's story catches her eye. Demeter, imagining Persephone's capture.

Hades had picked her daughter up like a sack of grain, stolen her from her friends picking flowers in the field. He had stolen her away, carried her like a child, and taken her here, into the dark. Into the dark, through the labyrinth of memories and pain, and now, alone in the cavern of her dark room in his dark kingdom, as Demeter imagined it, Persephone felt her stomach rumble. Tears came to her eyes. How much more indignity was she expected to take?

A mother's projections of her innocent, victimized daughter. When really, the daughter had been anything but. Had been half-complicit in her own abduction. Had been full of the hubris and sarcasm of youth.

Would Demeter realize the difference between the daughter she had and the daughter she thought she had?

But the manuscript stops soon after that.

Saskia wishes her mother had written the ending. Not only so that she could turn in the file and get the delivery payment her mother would have been owed, but because she genuinely wants to know. She can't even remember the proper conclusion of the myth.

Sas Googles it. Apparently, they reached a compromise, the abductor and the mother: most of the time, Persephone was with her mother on Earth. But three months of the year, Hades took his due, claimed his bride once more. Hence Demeter's passive-aggressive neglect of the crops; hence the chill in the air; hence winter.

Saskia knows instinctively that Evelyn Kreis would not have been satisfied with this version of events. But how would her mother have ended it?

With Persephone saving herself. With making Hades suffer. All those books have their princess triumphing in delight before living happily ever after.

Saskia knows she *could* slap an Evie-ending on it.

But clearly, this Persephone was no princess. Hades, no prince charming.

And besides, the question for Saskia has always been: *What about* after *happily ever after?* For her, each and every one of her mother's stories has the same unwritten ending, the same ending after the ending. Because what happens to a princess who renounced her crown to have adventures, once those adventures end?

She's just some girl, that's all. Out in the world alone.

Chapter 7

And as Cinderella went off to complete her first marathon, Cinderella's stepsisters stared at their bloody feet: the one missing her heel, the other with a single stump where just a few days before there had been toes.

"You know," the elder said, turning to the younger, "I think we might have some seriously warped priorities."

—FAIRY TALES FOR LITTLE FEMINISTS:
CINDERELLA, EVELYN HARPER KREIS

September 1995

SASKIA WAS TWELVE. SHE AND LEXI HAD BEEN promoted to the middle of the bus: a relatively safe position. Far enough from the driver for coolness, far enough from the back to avoid the older kids' taunts. But the middle had its own threats, and Saskia still knew enough to be wary when a girl's face peeked up over the back of the seat in front of them.

"So, you're, like, really good at the piano?" Becca Talbot's voice was almost a bray. Saskia couldn't fathom what it was that made her so popular. Could people not *hear* her?

She raised her eyebrows and pointed to her headphones, looked out the window.

But Becca Talbot was even louder than Rachmaninoff as she swiveled her head to Lexi.

"So, like, she actually *does* think she's better than everyone else."

But Lexi just looked away. Lexi was loyal to Saskia, but she would have liked to be Becca Talbot: with her swimming pool, her Nintendo, her two rich parents battling to win her love.

Saskia took her headphones off with exaggerated slowness and a sigh.

Becca's face broke into a watermelon-smile of delight.

"So, how good are you?"

Better than you've ever been at anything. Better than you will ever be at anything. But she could feel Lex, still, tense as a cello string beside her.

"I'm good," she said. Hating how defensive her attempt at humility sounded.

"I guess you'd have to be. You play, what, like a million hours a day?"

Faces were turning to them. The other kids liked to see Becca go in for the kill. But, more than that, they liked to see her play with her victims first.

Saskia was nobody's victim.

"Six. More on the weekends."

Fake bafflement.

"How do you have time for anything else? Have you ever even, like, kissed a boy?"

"Of course she has," Lexi chirped indignantly. It was all Saskia could do to keep from gaping at her. Lexi had, this past summer at the Maine camp that her father insisted on sending her to. And she knew that the upper schoolers parked outside the armory to make out.

But Saskia?

This new requirement, the social demand for romance, had been like an itchy tag at the back of Saskia's neck since seventh grade started a few weeks ago. She practiced the piano religiously, obsessively. She got decent grades. She even had a friend. She'd been doing everything right, or right enough, until this past year. Now, the requirement that boys find her attractive, on top of everything else, seemed very unfair. How could you even control what somebody *else* liked?

Becca gave a little snort. "Sure she has." She turned back, but not before murmuring: "I bet you're not even that good at piano."

"She's so good you wouldn't be able to understand it," a voice came from across the aisle. It was one of the boys from the other seventh-grade class. "She's so good that it would go right over your head. You wouldn't even *know* what you didn't know."

Even as Saskia's face reddened, Becca had already flipped back around with a snort, thumping against the fake leather seat with an exaggerated push of her weight that made the seat back buckle out against Saskia's knees. Saskia raised her leg sharply in return, resulting in a muffled yelp from the other side.

Saskia whipped around, wanting to show him, this guy—what was his name?—her gratitude, but after a second of staring at him meaningfully, she dropped her gaze.

She'd probably gotten it wrong. She must have gotten it wrong.

January 2020

PATRICK RETURNS HER EMAIL QUICKLY, CONFIRMING their meeting Friday afternoon. But Sas can't dwell on that for too long. As it turns out, Evie wrote her own obituary; Saskia finds it on her mother's desktop as she searches through the various calendars for Patrick appointments—spotting them, finally, dotted through Evie's Google Calendar for June 2019. But as she's forwarding the screen-shots to Tara, another folder catches her eye: FOR AFTER. There's only one document in there, and Saskia clicks it open with trepidation. But it's brief.

It is with great regret that we announce the passing of Evelyn Harper Kreis of Milwaukee, on _____, at the age of _____ years.

The only child of Constance and Frederick, Evelyn leaves behind a husband, Michael, and a beloved daughter, Saskia.

Bestselling author of the Fairy Tales for Little Feminists *series, Ms. Kreis was also a renowned photographer and illustrator. A tenured professor in the Art and Design Department at the University of*

Wisconsin–Milwaukee, focusing on drawing, Ms. Kreis twice received the university's award for outstanding teaching. Evelyn was a woman of many passions, including gardening, opera, and literature.

A memorial service will be held _____. In lieu of flowers, please send donations to the Creutzfeldt-Jakob Disease Foundation.

Tonight, they're eating their dinner of memorial leftovers in the den. Her father's skin looks paper-thin in the firelight; she can see all sorts of purple-blue veins, arteries, beneath the surface. She takes a deep breath. *Into the ring, Sas.*

"I, uh, I'm going to see Patrick on Friday."

And his eyes pause on her, uncannily still over his soggy sandwich.

"Are you sure I shouldn't be there?" Not the same as: *Do you want me to come?*

Does it seem strange, to him, that she wants to see Patrick alone? Or is she finally coming off as responsible, the kind of daughter who follows through on things, who can be trusted? She presses her lips together, shakes her head, forces confidence and lightness into her voice. "I can do it. It's better coming from me, he'll see me as more of a . . . mediator." She's lying, can't he tell she's lying? She barrels ahead. "Also, I found— this—" She can't think of a suitable introduction, so she just passes her phone over with the obituary pulled up.

Her father reads it, face a mask.

"Did you write this?" he asks, handing the phone back to her.

"No. I found it on Mom's computer," she says again.

He nods.

"Do you want to add anything?" she asks.

He shakes his head so slightly she almost misses it.

"Can you send it to the *Journal Sentinel*, kiddo? And maybe the *Times*?"

"Sure," she says, starting her search for email addresses. As she sends them, he turns on the news. This was never what the Kreises did, eating in front of the television, and in no world was it a *Harper* habit, but it's better than chilled silence. She wishes she knew how to read her father's moods better. The truth was, she'd never had to—that was her mother's domain. When it came to raising Saskia, her father had always been the capable and calm adult in the room, never the parent whose feelings she had to manage. At least, never before.

Saskia shovels the rest of her sandwich into her mouth. *Mess here, not sure when I'll be back,* she texts to James. It's after eight in New York, which means she's texting beyond their agreed-upon hours, and she's not bothering to use any of their coded language, but fuck it. That's his problem.

Then, Georgia. When institutions failed you, when you ran up against walls, what did you do? You turned to other women. The princesses have taught her that much. She taps out: *Let's grab lunch, just the two of us?* Within seconds, her godmother shoots back a series of emojis. Saskia interprets them as hungry, hug, yum, fire. Georgia has always had what Saskia thinks of (very uncoolly, she's sure) as *a way with the youths.* She's the only one of her parents' friends she's ever been able to stand. None of the endless *What do you want to be when you grow up?* that she got from everyone else. What did she want to be? She was already being it. Who the fuck were they, now that they *were* grown up?

Saskia sets her phone down. For a moment, the plaid couches, the threadbare velvet cushions, the snoring dog curled tight at her feet—she feels wrapped up in the warm embrace of the Elf House, as the fire casts flickering light onto the paneled walls.

Five generations of Harpers. All of the women—Emilia, Rosemary, Constance, Evelyn, Saskia—marrying into the name or inheriting it, but they are all, somehow, still here.

When she dies, she thinks, she wants to come back as a ghost that haunts the fireplaces, twisting flames into clues about who she was. *Saskia Kreis. Prodigy. Heiress.* And then, perhaps, she could finally say the third thing that had made her special, whispering it into eternity.

Beloved of Patrick.

In the meantime, their names beat on in the background like a drum. *Emilia, Rosemary, Constance, Evelyn, Saskia.*

This is their house. Theirs. Always has been, always will be.

WHEN SASKIA WAS GROWING UP, BARTOLOTTA'S Lake Park Bistro had been one of a small handful of Milwaukee restaurants where you could spend more than $100 on lunch. That hasn't been the case for a decade or more, prices rising ever higher around the city, but Georgia suggested it and Saskia's too proud to refuse. It's a restaurant full of memories for her: after-concert dinners, celebrations, her first sip of champagne. And nothing, not a single linen tablecloth, has changed, she thinks as she weaves under the hanging chandeliers, following the waiter to her godmother. Only she has. Saskia, and the cost of a Cobb salad.

Georgia has picked a table looking out over the water, and Saskia feels her blood whooshing in time with the waves. For a second, she resents it, resents it all: the expensive restaurant, the inescapable lake, the Elf House weighing like physical bricks on her shoulders.

She kisses her godmother's cheeks with a smile.

"Aunt Georgie," she starts once they've ordered.

"Yeah, kid." Georgia has this showbiz cadence to her speech, even though she's never left Wisconsin, which used to drive Saskia nuts. It seems more endearing, now.

But Saskia has to hold firm if she's going to get the information she needs. She looks into the older woman's eyes.

"You knew," she says, and it's not a question.

Georgia blinks away, startled, looking out over the frozen lake.

"About the disease?" she says finally, weakly. "Sure. I knew." But before Saskia can say anything, she's turned fierce and garrulous, mouth running fast as she twists back to the table. "I couldn't not know. We talked every day of our lives from the time we could talk. You think I'd miss something like that? But, honey"—and she grabs Saskia's hands with her own, which are cold and bony—"if you think I didn't want to tell you, you're dead wrong. The fights we had over it! You're long since grown up, after all, and I kept saying to her, 'What if you misjudge that final window, to say goodbye?'"

Saskia starts as Georgia pauses. So, her mother had planned to tell her. Eventually. But she had failed to realize how quickly things were deteriorating. The same failure that had allowed her to renegotiate a ninety-day extension on her manuscript submission in mid-December, when she wouldn't survive January.

"If it's any comfort," Georgia says, her voice turning slower, rougher, as she blinks away again, "I would give anything not to have had to see her the way she was, in those last days. Not telling you— Don't you see, Sas, that it's the best thing she could have done? It was a gift."

Before Saskia can reply, the waiter cuts her off, trotting over with Georgia's rare steak, Saskia's Cobb salad. They pull their hands apart.

And Saskia, for one, is grateful. She feels like she's just been doused with a bucket of water.

"Thank you," she murmurs, smoothing the already smooth napkin over her lap. "But, Aunt Georgie, I've been wondering. Was she being funny about anything, last year?" She rolls her eyes at her own vagueness. "The house. Did she talk to you about selling it, about giving it away?"

Georgia's plucked, arched brows draw together. "Oh, kid. I mean, we never talked about it, not exactly, but it's one of those things you just know. It was unsustainable, keeping it. But I think it broke her heart, a little. The idea of selling. All that history." She picks out a french fry and swallows it. "I'm glad she didn't have to be the one to decide to let it go."

Saskia tries to make her voice light, but it just comes out strangled. So when it came to the will, Georgia knew nothing. So even other women couldn't save you, sometimes. "No?" she says.

Georgia shakes her helmet of a bob, starts sawing her meat into tiny bits. "When we were little—we were like you and Lex, you know, two only daughters—we used to talk about how we'd rule the East Side, grand dames in our side-by-side mansions. Christ, she was obsessed with that place." She pops a cube of the rare steak into her mouth. "But, I mean, if your house is anything like mine, you must be paying a *fortune* in upkeep. We did chat about that." She shrugs. "Are you asking whether she would have been okay with you selling? Is that it? Are you thinking of putting it on the market?"

Saskia opens her mouth but can't bring herself to speak.

She could tell the truth, of course. But there's something about the situation that she knows doesn't reflect well on her as a daughter. Evelyn left the house to some acquaintance? Or, best-case scenario: Her mother donated the house to the university? And Saskia didn't know any of this? Well, *why not*, Saskia?

"What would you do if you needed a ton of cash for your house?" Saskia asks instead. Might as well answer Georgia's question with a question; her godmother does it enough herself. And Georgia doesn't mind, her eyes dancing to the ceiling.

"Oh, Christ. What *haven't* we done. Reverse mortgage, home equity line of credit . . . there's plenty of money to borrow if you have assets, darling. And of course, we do have the assets. It's not about that, it's about whether you want to pay the cost." *The cost.* Georgia's reveling in the mystery, of the vague dramatic utterings, and Saskia doesn't begrudge her the theatrics. But she does make up her mind to go straight to the bank afterward.

And then that hand, again. Reaching out from across the table, grabbing at her. She lets it happen.

"You know, I was so envious of your mother growing up—next to the Elf House, ours is just . . . well." Saskia keeps her face studiously blank. Georgia's house doesn't have a name; it was built sometime in the 1920s, a good fifty years after the Elf House, though on Harper property that they'd sold off around the time the brewery folded. And while the Elf House is all stately gray stone, Georgia's is an Italianate palace with fountains, with orange terra-cotta roof tiles. It looks perfectly ridiculous when it snows. "We used to play the best games of hide-and-seek in there. Did you know that one time, Evie had to hide one of her boyfriends in the dumbwaiter?" Saskia shakes her head. "Well! She heard Mr. Harper coming home. And her father was *scary*. And this is before the sexual revolution went mainstream, of course—oh, he would have murdered her if he'd found out about her Pill!" Georgia blinks at her a little absently.

"The dumbwaiter . . ." Saskia prompts.

"Oh! And she has Bob . . ." Georgia laughs. "She has Bob up in her room. And she's absolutely *frantic*. She tells him to hide in the dumbwaiter and goes downstairs to greet her father. But Bob—cute boy, Bob, not the brightest. Bob climbs down *the laundry chute* instead! Escaped through the basement."

Saskia laughs. "To be fair—"

"Oh, I know, they're right next to each other. And that house, with everything so dark and windy . . . it's amazing he didn't get trapped between walls or something. Or in a secret passageway. We looked so hard for a secret passageway when we were young, but I'll tell you what—" She holds up a finger. "If anyone could find one and get trapped in there, it would be Bob Robinson!"

"Wait, Mom dated someone called *Robert Robinson?*"

Georgia rolls her eyes. "Well. That's why he went by *Bob,* you see?"

As Georgia prattles on, Saskia realizes how far they've gotten from what she needs. You can't dance around things with Georgia. She'll answer any question you ask, but her monologues will never contain the information you need, because she's not really listening.

You just have to fucking say it.

"Aunt Georgie," she says, "what do you know about Mom's will?"

"Nothing, babe." Her godmother pops a french fry into her mouth, red brown with the juices from her rare steak. "Why? Did she leave me something?"

"I . . . No."

Georgia scans her with those round eyes. "I always did like that silver Queen Anne tea set," she says.

The responses rise quick and thick in Saskia's throat. She takes a deep breath and forces herself to go on. "She left . . . she left kind of a weird bequest to Patrick Kintner."

"Who's Patrick Kinder?" Georgia says.

How to answer that question? "Kintner. A colleague from the university."

Georgia scrunches up her face, shakes her head. "Oh, wait. Is he the Fox?"

In another context, Saskia might have laughed at the antiquated compliment.

"I always thought he looked more like a lion," she says.

Georgia laughs with a little snort. "No, I mean—Christ, the man's sexy, if it's the guy I'm thinking of. Dark hair, about six feet?" Saskia nods. "Yeah, Jake and I used to call him the Fox. Because he has this weird way of kind of . . . slinking around. Looking right at you like he's thinking about how to get through you." She gives an exaggerated shiver. "Honestly, sexy or not, he's always given me the fucking creeps."

Saskia has to look away, at the waves beating against the shore.

"What did Evie leave him?" Georgia asks, bending forward.

"Oh. It's nothing. Anyway, come by the house sometime this weekend," Saskia says, clearing her throat. "I'll make sure you get that tea set."

AFTER LUNCH, SASKIA DRIVES TO THE BANK, WHERE she waits for an hour before the Kreises' banker, Jeffrey, is free to talk with her. It takes him another hour to finally convince her that a mortgage for the kind of money she needs would cost about $7,000 a month. And even with the *Little Feminists* money, even if she pretended she was going to keep her current job, Saskia won't pull in anything like the $250,000 a year the bank would need to see for that kind of loan.

She offers an alternate solution. With her father's salary, though, if he were to cosign—

Is Jeffrey blushing? Surely bankers don't blush.

"It's our policy not to give out a mortgage to anyone who will be over the age of seventy-five when the term ends. And your father—"

She holds up her hand. She doesn't need it said: the reminder that one day, one day maybe not that long from now, he, too, will die.

Jeffrey does offer her a boon, a single boon: a mortgage for the expenses, the foundation, the cliffs. It comes out to $500,000 for thirty years, in her name, at $2,500 a month. Given that the lien is part of it, it's incredibly generous. All the same, she has him recalculate at $600,000. They'd need to win the probate case for that to work, and Tara doesn't come cheap. And, as Tara warned them, the whole thing could take months, if not years.

For $600,000: $2,900 a month. She could afford it, and she's approved. A zing of hope like a laser beam cutting through her.

But she has to say no, for the moment. Has to tell the banker that her hands are tied until the court decides the house is theirs.

As she leaves, her phone pings with a message from Tara: the probate hearing's scheduled for February 20, a month out. She'll have to change her ticket, have to stay longer. The heaviness of the Elf House is descending back upon her before she's even pulled out of the bank's parking lot.

And it's all she can think of as she drives. What good is it, to have everything in the world tossed in your lap, if it doesn't allow you to keep the one thing that you want?

Chapter 8

"But what difference does it make what I look like?" the beautiful swan, who had just moments before been an ugly duckling, asked.

"It's not that it matters, exactly—" the ducks stuttered, looking awkwardly down at the ground.

"No, it doesn't. Society's beauty standards have messed you up. What makes one duckling any prettier than any other duckling, any-way?" The swan paused, looking each and every one of her siblings in the eye. "I'll tell you what. It's nothing to do with who any of us are on the inside. It's all about who the humans want to eat."

—*Fairy Tales for Little Feminists:*
The Intelligent Duckling, Evelyn Harper Kreis

January 1996

SASKIA WAS THIRTEEN.

"'Born one month after the death of infamous virtuoso Glenn Gould,'" Mike read from the program, then looked up in disgust. Evie refused to catch his eye, and he resorted to staring at her in the lighted mirrors of the guest artist's dressing room. "Evie. It's *ridiculous*."

Evie tugged a little too sharply on the brush, and Saskia pulled away with a snarl.

"She's already a prodigy. Isn't that enough? You don't have to make her into the reincarnation of a dead genius—"

"Oh, Mike," Evie said, twisting around to open the dry-cleaning bag. "You know how these things are. They asked for a biography, but what they really want is a story—and, besides, what else is there to say? She's thirteen!" She pulled out a full-skirted white dress.

Saskia made a face. "Is that what I'm wearing?"

I am not putting a child in a ball gown, Evie had declared to Mike and Carrie at dinner when they'd planned it all. *It would be* very silly *to put a child in a* ball gown. Saskia reached out a hand to the gauzy fabric, at the blue ribbon running around the low waist. It would fall to just below her knees, the sash sticking out behind her in a bow.

"Mom, I'm going to look like a ghost!" Saskia cried.

"Well, you love ghosts," Evie said absently, jimmying the fabric off of the hanger.

"Mom!"

"Saskia, you were the one who wouldn't go to the store with me to try the dresses on. You were the one who insisted that I should just order it for you."

They stared at each other, Saskia's dark eyes on Evie's pale ones, turning hard like sea glass now that she was mad.

And Evie threw up her hands. "I know, I can't do anything right. I'm the bad guy, I'm the villain here. But if I didn't buy the dress, Saskia, you would not have a dress. And"—whirling around to Mike—"if I didn't write the program notes, Mike, there would be no program notes." Saskia looked down as her mother's heels ticked away, but she couldn't miss the slam, how the door seemed to vibrate on its hinges for seconds afterward.

And then her father's hands clamped down on her shoulders, warm and solid and calloused where he held the cello, held his bow. It was wonderful having him here. He lived in a separate world from Saskia, she thought sometimes. His evening performances, his weekend matinees; their lives touched only at very specific points, her concerts among them.

You waltz in and out of her life, and I'm sorry, Mike, but we can't both be the fun parent, she'd heard her mother spit a few weeks ago, when she hadn't realized Sas could hear her.

And her father: *Yeah, but honey, I'm just so fun—*

And her mother's giggles, and Saskia had turned up the volume on her Mozart.

"Look, Sas," Mike said, leaning back against the counter. "It doesn't matter what you wear. You know how they're always making us dress up in our tuxedos for our concerts. You think I like being strangled half to death by my own bow tie?"

Despite herself, she smiled.

"The only important thing is that you have fun, yeah?" he said.

Saskia raised her pale eyebrows.

"What's the most fun piece you're playing tonight?" he asked.

"The Mazurka. Fifty-six, one," she said, her eyes widening. "I have to fake the elevenths," splitting into a grin, then hesitating. Did they have the same kind of thing in cello? She wasn't sure. "For the really big reaches, when I have to hit two notes really far apart at the same time. I have to use two hands for most of them, but Carrie says nobody will be able to tell."

Mike nodded, face grave. "Then think about that," he said. "Think about the fake elevenths. How you'll be the only one who knows they're not real. Well. You, me, and Carrie. Those elevenths—those elevenths are what matter. The dress? The dress is just a costume."

"Yeah," Saskia said. "Yeah, okay."

Minutes later, dress on, she slipped her hand into her father's and they walked to the stage, Evie just a few paces behind. The three of them stood poised behind the curtains, poised as the announcement came on, poised as the applause rippled over, around, through them, and then—

"Have fun, kiddo," Mike whispered. "Remember the elevenths."

And Saskia dropped his hand and walked out onto the stage alone.

There was nothing like the pride of performing. She'd never been able to put it into words, she wasn't sure even her father understood: the full warmth she got in her chest as the audience's eyes widened, as they sat back in delight to watch her play. Look what is possible. Look what this child can do. Look what I can do.

If you didn't know anything about piano, you'd think only the fingers were important, but it wasn't true. She moved, swayed, twisted from her back, her shoulders, her hips, her elbows. It was part of her performance, part of how she experienced the music.

Offstage, Carrie had her doing a series of push-ups and sit-ups every day to strengthen those muscles, in addition to the Hanon exercises for her hands. Onstage, the dance of her fingers across the slick ivory keys, the heat and shine of the spotlight, the invisible spectators seeing every movement, hearing every note—

It was like nothing else in the world.

It was like flying.

And then the applause. It sounded like rain pounding down when she was especially good. Building and building, soaking her, pounding down around her.

And its final, inevitable, break.

January 2020

THE UNIVERSITY'S WINTER IVY HAS GONE THREAD-bare against the red brick. How often has Saskia sat in this same parking lot, in this same car? A hundred times, at least. It is half a mile from the bank, another half mile to the house, distances she'd never consider driving in New York, if driving were even an option for her there. Yet here she is, pulling into the parking space that is still her mother's, even though Evelyn Kreis will never park here again.

It would have been too cold to walk: the cold has clasped on to the city like one of those slap bracelets from when she was little, tightly banded, refusing to let go. Two degrees, but with a windchill that's much lower. Something about the cold feels different here than it does in New York, where you're never too far from a coffee shop or a subway station or a bodega, blasting heat as soon as you walk through the door.

At least she doesn't have to go to the arts building. She has a thousand memories in the arts building. The leafy patterns the trees left on her mother's wall. The posters pinned up haphazardly in Patrick's office. Her legs wrapped around him in the red light of the darkroom. But today's all about administration. And the administration building—she can't remember ever being here before, down these black-and-white marble halls.

And then, there: *Patrick Kintner, Vice President of Development.*

Saskia pauses, reaching with vertiginous guilt into her pocket for her phone. She turns on a Voice Memo, hesitating only a moment before sliding it back into her pocket. She doesn't owe him anything at all, anymore. She *doesn't*, she tells herself fiercely.

The door is open, and Saskia is momentarily surprised at how well the outer office would have met her mother's exacting standards: plush

Oriental rugs, wood-paneled walls, maps of the campus from a century ago in gilt frames.

"Can I help you?" the twentysomething receptionist chirps from behind the desk. "Work-study? Something—else?"

None of her business, Saskia reminds herself. Not anymore.

"Yes, hi. I'm—"

The inner door opens.

"Saskia Kreis," says Patrick.

Her name has always sounded like a knife when he says it. For at least seventeen years after they broke up, he still attended Kreis family functions. He and Evie were coffees-on-campus buddies, and the end of a relationship with her daughter—the end of a *secret* relationship with her daughter, one that Evie had never known about—was not going to stop that. And so for seventeen years, Sas had waved too cheerfully at Christmas parties, had let herself linger afterward in the faint glow of longing. Their interactions had always been polite, even pleasant (at least, from the outside). Always brief.

Patrick. The one who got away.

(Technically, *she* was the one who got away. But he'd been the one to make her go.)

Now, it's been two years since she's seen him. Not so much in the scheme of their history. Not so little, either. His hazel eyes, so warm they seem almost golden in some lights, have a few more crinkles around the edges. He turned sixty in August, and his mane is full silver now; it suits him.

He approaches her, setting a hand on her forearm, kissing her cheek. And whatever anger she's directed at herself for loving him, for the intensity of it, the feverishness of it, dissipates as she looks into his eyes. As she feels his body brush against hers: *ah, yes.* She remembers. And she forgives herself.

He tugs slightly at her forearm. "Come in, come in."

Something strange about his skin on hers, and it takes her until she's collapsed into the faded leather armchair in front of his mahogany desk to identify it.

"No calluses," she says, nodding at his hands. "Haven't you been out on the water?"

Perched on the corner of his desk, he flips his large hands over to study the palms. Looks up with a grin, a wink. "It's January, Sas. Nobody in their right mind sails in January in *Wisconsin*."

She has to laugh at that. At herself.

"But in the summer, you can't get me on dry land. The new boat, *The Ingenue Two*—she's got a motor. Makes the going way easier. Not like the last one. You remember?"

"Oh, my God!" she cries. "I'd totally forgotten."

"An hour, hour and a half out into the lake and the wind just dies—"

"And there we were. Just floating."

Silence. Both of them remembering what they did with that time, alone on the lake. Before the wind rose again.

"And look at you now," she says.

He stands, holding his hands out at his sides. "Look at me! Some ending for a bohemian, hey? Shove me in a suit, corral me till five P.M."

He had never seemed like an institution kind of guy. But his charm, his ease with the wealthy . . . he was always completely in his element at the Christmas parties. On some fundamental level, this new role fits him down to his bones.

"How are you liking it?" she asks.

"Oh . . ." He stretches his legs, turns to look out one of the two huge windows arching behind his desk. That gravitas. He's like an actor playing a dead president. "I'm not sure it's a question of *liking* it. It was time for me to grow up. Set something aside for the future."

It's as good a segue as she'll get. She takes a deep breath, tries to fight the blush rising on her cheeks as she considers what she's about to say.

"Look, I don't mean to make this weird. But has Josh Asher been in touch with you about my mother's—"

Before she's even finished her sentence, he's holding up a packet of papers from the glossy surface of his desk. Papers that look a whole lot like her mother's will.

She nods. "My dad and I—" But she can't finish her thought. He's coming closer to her, sitting on the arm of the leather chair next to her, and his proximity, the dark stubble, the smell of pine and clay; it's overwhelming.

When he speaks, his voice is low, gentle. "It must have come as quite a surprise to you."

She shifts in her chair, trying to maintain some distance. "Yeah, it did. We can't help— Well, the thing is, Patrick, we couldn't help wondering—"

His head drifts, ever so slightly to the side. "If it was a mistake? If she meant to do it?"

She breathes deep, from her sternum. "Yeah."

"No."

"No, it was a mistake?"

"No, it wasn't a mistake."

She squints her eyes shut. "Start over."

He laughs, gently. Seats himself properly in the chair, angled toward her.

"Your mother and I had both been thinking a lot about legacies. About what we'd leave behind when we're gone." She tries to breathe around the tightening of her throat, tries to keep listening. "And over the past year or so, we began work on a project that means a lot to both of us. An arts center for the pre-college kids."

She's fighting it, but the guilt is inescapable. How bad a daughter she'd been, how bad a person. Her mother had never even broached the subject with her. She hadn't even heard her mother's voice in three . . . four months, she corrects herself. She'd tried to call at Thanksgiving, had ended up with an apologetic email from her parents about how they'd been with Georgia. She'd tried again at Christmas, and her mother had texted a reply hours later: they had been watching *It's a Wonderful Life; it's too late now, catch up next week?* But next week had come and gone, and finally, two weeks later, Saskia had been about to call home herself when her father's name lit up her cell phone and everything she knew about her life changed.

But she can't think about that now. She needs to stay focused.

"Why the pre-college programs?"

"Well, we haven't had an art and design pre-college course since 2012, did you know that?" She shakes her head. "The costs were just getting too high. We tried to make up for it about a decade ago by raising the price. Twelve hundred dollars for a six-week program. But then the *Journal Sentinel* came after us, and it was the final nail in the coffin. Well. They went after all the pre-college programs, really, but they singled us out—art and design—for the cost."

She frowns. "I mean, it costs what it costs, right?"

"Saskia—" And he laughs. "Ever the innocent. Think about it, who can afford a twelve-hundred-dollar summer program in *the arts* for their kids, particularly in Milwaukee? White parents. You know that we're consistently named one of the most segregated cities in America? All of that redlining. Anyway, the journalist did his research and found that while the school accepts around seventy-five percent of undergraduate applicants, that number jumped up to ninety-five percent for those who'd attended one of our pre-college programs. Basically, only the rich kids could afford our summer programs, and then the rich kids got rewarded with almost guaranteed college acceptance. We couldn't keep the program going after that. We couldn't afford to reinforce the idea that our admissions are rigged."

Evie had never said a word. Saskia thinks about the calls she used to have with her mother. Dumping out the mundane details of her own life, the dinner she'd cooked, the run she'd gone on, all the while avoiding anything actually meaningful: the men, her work, her boxing. For the first time, she realizes that Evie must have been doing the same thing.

She never knew any of this.

"Okay," she says, twisting her hands together. "Fine. But if Mom really wanted to help underprivileged kids, couldn't she just have made a donation? Started the Evelyn Kreis scholarship program or something?"

His face is kind, though there's a hint of incredulity sneaking in. "Saskia. Of course, she'd have loved to endow a scholarship in her name. But . . . with what money?" he says, his lightly admonishing tone reigniting the burning sensation in her chest.

Of course. She closes her eyes for a second, trying to will the blood out of her face again. But she fails this time, feels it pulsing through her cheeks as Patrick goes on. "Look. The thing about these programs, unlike English or econ, is that they actually require studio space and materials, in addition to classrooms. Finite resources. And our undergrads and faculty need to access those over the summer, as well. When I was head of the department, art and design flourished under my leadership. We attracted more students, more great teachers. But the facilities didn't grow accordingly. We're working with the same space as we were twenty years ago."

"So . . . the Elf House," Saskia says dully as the puzzle pieces slide into place.

He nods. "The Elf House."

"But . . ." She takes a deep breath; somehow, she already feels defeated. "Why wouldn't she have first tried selling it to the university?"

"Sas, look. It's a beautiful house. It's a historic house. But to spend three million dollars on it, only to invest more funds to actually convert it to the kind of facility your mother and I wanted? It was always a tricky proposition. And, given my insight into the development arm of the university, I increasingly felt that there was a high risk that if the sale went through—and that was still a big *if*—the university would use it for a new president's house. You've seen the current place?"

She shrugs; she knows she's been there for some university function or another, but not in decades. And she probably hadn't been paying that much attention in the first place.

"We don't refuse gifts," he says firmly. "We take everything that comes our way. But if she tried to sell the house to us, she faced the possibility that one, we wouldn't buy it and two, she would essentially forfeit the right to have any say in how it was used. As a gift, and as a gift channeled through me, she could be much more involved. And beyond that . . ." A pause as his fingers brush over the polished surface of the desk, wiping away an imaginary smudge. "Your mother . . . she was a very sick woman at the end, Sas. And I think she just wanted to spend her last days doing things she loved, rather than being buried in paperwork."

So there it was: even Patrick had known her mother was ill. Of course, Evie would have wanted to spend her time with her hands in the dirt, pulling up weeds. To sit on the sofa with her eyes closed, *La Traviata* on the ancient record player. To hole up in the cottage, finishing her book.

How many conversations with her mother had Patrick *had*, to work all of this out? More than one. Probably half a dozen or more. All of that time, Saskia had been prancing through New York, oblivious; all of that time, her mother had been here. With him. Telling him what to do once she died.

Saskia watches his open face, his patient eyes. She nods.

But he's waiting for more from her, face open in bright anticipation. She gathers her thoughts.

"I just wish I'd known," she says.

"I think," he says carefully, like a harpsichordist picking out the delicate notes, "I think that she worried it would upset you. I know she tried to bring up some of the details with your father, and the reaction wasn't . . . what she'd hoped for."

Saskia can't imagine what that would look like. As long as she's been alive, Mike has acquiesced to Evie's wishes. Been the mild-mannered squire in the background.

It's hovering between them, ready to be plucked out of the air. And she has to ask; she can't stop herself. She doesn't really want to know; she has to know.

"Patrick," she says, and her voice has gone hoarse, "did my mother know about us?"

But he meets her question with his steady, lighthouse gaze.

"No," he says, and his tone is final. "Never." The word resonates through the room.

Her hands have gone shaky. But Saskia can't avoid it: Evie had known she was dying. She had known, and she had orchestrated this. With Patrick, who knows what she'd wanted. Knows it far better than Saskia herself ever could. Suddenly, her fight for the Elf House no longer seems like such a noble quest. It makes her feel like a tabloid cliché. The overlooked former heiress, fighting against a worthy cause to get her grubby hands on a dead parent's money.

And yet—that's not entirely who she is. It's all so complicated. It's all just ever so slightly . . . off. Something doesn't make sense, but she can't identify it, other than the diffuse, floating cloud of wrongness surrounding them. She follows his eyes down to her knee, where her fingers are tapping something out. It takes her a minute to put a name to the notes. *Requiem.* Of course. Her subconscious is so freaking predictable.

And Patrick. His words, his body, his scent, and his mind; she's too ready to believe the best in him. She forces herself into the adversarial position again. Makes herself say it.

Her stomach twisting, she unfolds her legs. Feet on the floor, down to earth. "All talk of legacies aside, there's still the matter of my dad. He was planning to retire in a year or two. And I just can't imagine that they didn't discuss this, that he wouldn't hear her out, before she'd make that significant of a decision. I don't suppose there's any way . . ." Saskia had thought about it in the car on the way over, what she had to offer. It wasn't much. "Maybe the programs could use the outbuildings, or a wing of the house, for a period of time? While my father continued to live there? And we could maybe talk about donating it in a few years. If we could just stay there for the duration of my father's lifetime . . ."

But Patrick's face is almost mournful, and she can't stand the sound of her own voice begging. He takes her hand in his: the bruises and cuts of a boxer against the smooth perfection of a sailor's palms in winter.

"Sas, you know I'd do almost anything for you." She tries to keep his gaze while still breathing fully, but both aren't possible, and her breath comes out short, choked. "But I owe this to Evie. To the community, to the students, but most of all to her. Especially now that she's gone. It's what she wanted, Sas. It is."

Her mother could have told Saskia at any time. Saskia would have dealt with it. Would have come home, come back to her. But she chose not to.

And then, as Saskia swims alone in the abyss of her contrition—how does he manage it?—the conversation shifts back to pleasantries, to nothingness, to cheek kisses and goodbyes and promises of coffee. Her legs feel light and trembly, full of helium, as she makes her way back down the halls and out the front door, and it's only when she's sitting in her car again that she thinks: *Wait a minute.*

The taxes. The lien. The not insignificant details she'd forgotten to mention.

Her mother was keenly aware of the back taxes due on the house when she changed the will in July. They didn't make any sense as part of a gift, only as part of a sale. Who'd want a gift that would cost you more than a hundred grand upon receipt? What institution would want to take on that burden?

Beyond that, Patrick himself doesn't make sense to her. She can see him more clearly, now that he's not right in front of her. Because what is he *really* doing in that formal office, in that obsequious role? His *growing up*, his *settling down*. No matter how good he is at making people give up more than they'd bargained for—something about *him* still doesn't add up.

Why the hell is he there?

BACK AT THE HOUSE, SHE CAN'T SIT STILL WITH THE silence in her head. Saskia plans her weekend: a five-mile run and thirty minutes with the jump rope. She's been letting her conditioning fade; she's letting her body go; she can't spar while she's home, but she could, should, keep up her fitness levels.

The idea of finding a temporary boxing gym for next week, for the next few weeks—hell, the idea of being a woman in a Midwestern club—makes her shudder. And a run sounds good, it sounds clarifying. She's dying to go past the lighthouse, for one thing. The North Point Lighthouse, still functioning after a century or more, keeping the ships from thrusting themselves against the rough shore. A loop through the park, down by the beach, winding back up St. Mary's Hill, past the water tower; that should give her a good five miles. A tour through the monuments of her life.

It's a reflex, reaching into the mailbox and bringing in the day's letters. The envelope on top is from the county treasurer's office. Labeled FINAL NOTICE OPEN IMMEDIATELY in block red letters. The regret washes over her again. She can't believe she didn't mention it to Patrick: the $120,000 that he, or the school, would need to pay. Does he know?

And the lien—she'd been so caught up in memories of her mother, on imagining the conversations that had been taking place without her, that she'd forgotten. In retrospect, even thirty minutes later, their conversation has already blurred into a haze in her mind. She is no longer sure exactly what Patrick said. Only that he'd left her faintly nostalgic and comforted, saddened and resigned—with just the slightest tinge of suspicion.

But Saskia Kreis's middle name might as well be *slightest tinge of suspicion*, and she's learned she can't trust that feeling. She tears open the notice—*30 days before legal proceedings*—and her heart's going off like hoofbeats at a racetrack. Thirty days and the government takes the house? It's too undignified to even consider. How the hell would they ever get it back *then*?

"Where's Dad?" she asks Wolfie as she goes into the house. It's the system of finding each other that the Kreises have used for decades, far more reliable than the ancient intercoms. And Wolfie, preemptively proud of himself, wags his tail all the way to the study, where she pats him on the head, praises him.

Mike is sitting behind his behemoth of a desk, sorting through piles of papers like some Dickensian villain. He looks up quickly, then looks up again to smile at his daughter.

"Hey, kiddo. What've you been up to?"

She crosses the room, Wolfie peeling off halfway to jump into a brocade armchair, and hands him the final notice without saying a word. He looks at it for a second before tossing it onto a pile of papers a foot high.

She waits for him to say something. To say, *Oh, we took care of this.* To say, *Ach, this stupid mistake, it's cost me so much time.* But there's just silence, and she lets her eyes wander around the room. Beneath the black wrought-iron radiator, a spider's spun silver webs, thick as cloth. She winces.

"When's the last time the cleaning team came in?" she asks.

Mike's face, loosening into despair, tells her immediately that it was the wrong question.

"Kid. Do you have any idea how much it costs to clean a place like this?"

Saskia grimaces. "My friend Gina cleans. She makes fifteen an hour—"

"We paid seven fifty a week. Up until last year."

"Oh." Her voice small.

"You have seven hundred and fifty dollars a week to spare?" But his tone isn't mean, just teasing. "Does the SAT pay you that much?"

She rolls her eyes. "Fifteen bucks a question," she says. "But I'll keep it, thanks very much. Maybe I'll just get the vacuum out every now and again."

He laughs, the suddenness of it startling her.

"What?"

"I'll give you fifteen bucks right now if you can tell me where the vacuum is."

A beat. She makes a face.

"Well, it's a big house," she says, and his laughter is warm, almost distracting her from the matter at hand. "Dad, seriously, though. We've got thirty days to pay the overdue property taxes. And then they'll start legal proceedings against *us*—"

"Honey," he says, "I've got it under control."

She throws up her hands. "But you obviously don't! Thirty days, Dad! Less than a month!"

He looks up at the ceiling, then slowly lowers his eyes to hers.

"We got some advice from Paul last year. The county almost never forecloses on non-mortgage liens, kid. And your mother was working out a payment plan—I know she made a big payment sometime last year—so, yes, I'll take care of it. Really."

She can tell by the firmness in his tone that she's supposed to drop it. But there's too much, it's too knotted a web, for just one person to work out alone.

"Listen, Dad. I've been going through Mom's papers, trying to organize some stuff for Tara. They're a fucking mess. The lien, the foundation, the cliffs . . . I mean, yeah, she got a chunk of money for her new book last year, but the book—it's not even done. So, I dropped by the bank today, and Jeffrey says we could get a mortgage on the house, cover some of the expenses that way—"

"Saskia," he says, and his voice is exhausted, if gentle. "Sas, you really need to disabuse yourself of this kind of magical thinking. Your mother would not want you to saddle yourself with decades of debt just to keep this place going. Even if we get to keep the house for now, we won't get to *keep* the house. We'll just be keeping it to sell it."

She's screwed up her face, tight against his words. He smiles at her expression.

"I know. But it's not such a bad thing, three million dollars."

"But Dad . . . the *Elf House*—" And her face flushes as her voice breaks. When was the last time she cried in front of him? Not since she was a child.

"Sweetie. What are you realistically going to do with a place like this? What would any single person ever need all of this space for? You're telling me, in all honesty—all magical thinking aside—you wouldn't rather have half the estate? You wouldn't rather take the one-and-a-half-million? And in time, a bit more?"

And for a second, she lets herself imagine it.

She imagines letting the Elf House go.

A million and a half dollars, and a hundred grand a year—for at least the next few years, she figures—on the royalties. She could pick up and move anywhere, anywhere in the world. She could buy her own place. She could get a dog, her own dog. Buy daily private sessions with world-class coaches; take her boxing to the next level. Visit her favorite cities, Vienna and Moscow, see more of the world, but fresh this time, unfiltered—

She shakes herself out of her fractured thoughts with the memory of Patrick's face.

"It's all moot," she says, her voice rough. "I mean, yes, of course. I see the appeal. But it's all moot unless we can actually get the house. And, Dad, I'm not sure that we can. I went to see Patrick today."

He leans back at that, crossing his muscular cellist's arms in front of his chest.

"It was all very pleasant. But he says that, apparently, he and Mom had been discussing turning the house into an arts center. And he seems to think that she left the house to him, rather than to the university, just to make things—easier? I guess at the beginning, she thought about selling it, but then once she got sick, she wanted to make sure it was used for what she wanted it used for? And so she decided to donate it outright."

His eyes narrow as his jaw tenses.

"Her plan—*our* plan—was to *sell* it to the university. Always."

Saskia shakes her head. "Not according to Patrick. Not by the end. Or . . . the beginning of the end, I guess. Not by last July. He also said . . ." And she pauses, not sure if she should broach it. She doesn't want to shame her father, but she has to get it all out there, if they're going to get to the bottom of this. "He also says that she tried to talk to you about this new plan, and you didn't . . . react well."

And then she waits.

Finally, her father exhales and swivels away. "I don't think that's right. But to be honest, I wasn't . . . I wasn't always the person I wanted to be. Those last few months." He makes a disgusted sound from the back of his throat. "She was always trying to bring up the will, but I shut her down. I thought it was important to keep a positive mindset, at first. And then . . . I guess I just wanted her to enjoy the time she had left, not to have to think about that stuff." His eyes flicker to the side. "My memory's been . . . well. Everything has felt very slippery these last few months. I have to read back through my journals, see what I can piece together. I should probably go talk to him myself, just to make sure."

"Dad—" she says. But then triumph breaks like a wave, washing over her panic as she remembers. "Actually, you don't have to. I recorded it. Here, I'll just AirDrop it to your phone—"

But she pauses just before hitting *send*. What exactly had they reminisced about? What would their conversation give away? She pretends it's sent, sliding her phone back into her pocket. He has too much paperwork to deal with, he'll forget. And in the meantime, she'll listen to it again, edit out anything incriminating.

Anything incriminating for *her*.

Still, as she leaves the room, she feels the sword dangling over her head, suspended by a filament as fine as one of her mother's hairs.

Thirty days.

Chapter 9

But there was more to life than being obedient. And the moment the twelve princesses set foot on the dance floor, they felt a creative fire take hold of them that was like nothing they'd ever known before. They couldn't leap like this in the castle, couldn't shake like this in the throne room. Beyond the pleasure the sisters felt in the dancing itself, there was, too, great joy in seeing the satisfaction on each other's faces.

—*Fairy Tales for Little Feminists: The Twelve Dancing Princesses*, Evelyn Harper Kreis

January 1996

SASKIA WAS THIRTEEN, AND THE AUDIENCE WAS clapping, and she was trotting offstage, smiling until her face was as sore as her fingers, and it was only then that she realized something was caked around her nose. Not the makeup Evie had patted onto her face before the concert. Saskia reached up a fingernail and scratched, staring at the rust-colored powder that came off under her fingernails.

"Did I get a nosebleed?" she asked her father.

"Look down, sweetheart. . . ." And she saw that the entire front of her dress was painted red. She'd had no idea it was happening: when she was performing, all she felt was the music.

"Oh, honey, let's get you cleaned up!" Evie trotted over, a wet wipe in her hand, but Saskia wriggled out of her grip to wave at the group of people behind her, taking the wipe with her and cleaning off her own face. Aunt Georgia and Lexi, some of Evie's professor friends, a cluster of Symphony musicians who hadn't been needed for the performance.

"You were marvelous!" Georgia cried, clutching Saskia's upper arms, keeping her bloody body from pressing against her own immaculate cream suit.

"You were so good," Lexi said shyly, emerging halfway from her mother's side. It was always weird, seeing Lexi at performances; they never knew what to say in front of the grown-ups. She was in a headband, too, though her blue dress, dotted with little golden flowers, was way more the kind of thing that Saskia would have wanted to wear herself. Lexi and her perfect wardrobe, Lexi and her relaxed mother, Lexi and her peaceful, charmed, storybook life.

But then again—how could it be storybook? Things had to happen for there to be stories. And nothing ever happened to Lexi.

Lexi, Saskia thought, had no idea what it was like to be surrounded by all of this. Lexi had no idea what it felt like when that thunder, that applause, came for you. Came after you. The roar of grown-ups impressed by what you were capable of. The feeling that you were part of the real world, the actual world, where things mattered, where you mattered.

Was it possible that she actually felt bad for Lexi?

"Here," Lexi said, and handed Saskia the bouquet of white roses. For years, Lexi and Georgia had brought her American Girl dolls instead of flowers at performances. But Saskia had them all now and was getting too old for them, anyway. Besides, she'd never known exactly what she was supposed to do with them. Dress them up?

"Saskia!" Evie called, flapping her fingers so Saskia knew to come quickly. "Saskia, come say hi to everyone."

"Sorry," Saskia said with a grimace at Lexi, and ran over, thrusting the flowers into her mother's arms as she turned to the adults. "Thank you so much for coming."

"Oh, you were wonderful," cried one woman from the college. Saskia knew she'd seen her before, but she couldn't remember her name. "The Chopin was just—"

"You are one very talented little girl," boomed a man with a gray mustache. Louis, she thought—yes, he was the Symphony percussionist, yes, she knew him.

And just as quickly, the talk rose around her again—they didn't really need her there for it, and that was okay, she was happy just to be present, to listen, to grab at little snippets of conversation as they floated around her. *The next Argerich—the charisma of her—*

She felt his eyes on her before she knew where the gaze was coming from. She turned; he stood half in shadow, apart from the crowd. Mr. Kintner. Patrick. Staring at her face. At her hair. At the blood spattered across her perfect white dress.

"Well," he said. "You little Viking."

January 2020

IT'S A STRANGE FEELING, DRIVING DOWN TO meet Josh at the art museum Monday evening. Not just being back in Milwaukee, not just in reclaiming this stage for her life, but also in dating someone else here. Saskia had only ever dated Patrick in Milwaukee. She'd only ever been his.

Does everybody's first love imprint on them this way? she wonders, pulling into the parking lot across the street from the museum. Does everyone get the sense that their first love is the *true* love of their life? That dating anybody else, no matter how long afterward, is akin to cheating? And yet she cherishes this kind of tortured thinking, she holds on to it tightly. It is shame and agony, and she treasures it. Because it's still the truth, isn't it? She was his, once. And it had made her special.

Josh waits for her at the entrance to the museum, its white bones rising up around him in the dark. She remembers when Calatrava first released his plans for it; Evie had been delighted at the wings, how they moved in the wind like a seagull's. Saskia feels very much like her mother tonight; she's wearing one of Evie's black dresses and a pair of her earrings, 1960s-style pale blue orbs on her ears the color of her mother's eyes. If she'd had to rely entirely on her own closet, she would have had to show up wearing either yoga pants or the dress she'd worn to the memorial service. And as strange as it felt to smear her mother's red lipstick over her lips, Saskia feels like a grown-up—or at least like a child's image of adulthood come to life.

Josh, meanwhile, is still in a suit and tie from the office, tickets in hand.

"So, what's the show?"

Josh points to the placard on the wall in front of them. *Capturing Cream City: Milwaukee Photographers, 1970–present.*

Saskia's heartbeat goes irregular. She tries to swallow with a dry mouth. After a moment, she attempts a smile.

"Is that . . . okay?" Josh asks.

When Saskia goes to museums, she goes to the Met, she goes to the Museum of Natural History. She doesn't go to MoMA or the New Museum. Doesn't go to the countless contemporary galleries scattered across the city. Nowhere she might see Patrick's work or work that might remind her of Patrick.

"Oh. Yeah. It's just, with Mom teaching at the university—a lot of these guys were her friends, you know—"

"We don't have to go. We could just go get a drink or something. Some dinner—"

She shakes her head.

"No, it'll be fun," she says, and takes a glass of wine from a circulating waiter. "Let's do it."

Cutting through the vaulted, open gallery, she tries to scan ahead, tries to see if she can spot his work. But the photographs all look the same from far away, masses of black and white.

They wander around together. She stops in front of a series of the Pabst Mansion, not unlike the Elf House. Old Milwaukee, built on beer money.

"Elephant in the room," Josh says.

She smiles. "More like Elf House in the room."

"For what it's worth, I'm sorry. It's a beautiful house. It always seemed like the kind of place a girl like you should live."

"Josh Asher," she says, raising her glass to him, "you had one hell of a crush on me."

He raises his in return. "As did everyone with half a brain."

"Excuse me?"

He tilts his head, looking at her. "Oh, we were all in love with you. I think it's . . ." He pauses, lets her hang. "It's that nobody's happy in high school. Nobody. And there you were, not needing anything from anyone. You just seemed to float above it all. It was like—nothing could touch you. There was so much power in that. It was very attractive."

Before she can reply, a group of older couples comes up beside them. Saskia moves on to the next series of photos: the lake, a rite of passage for these photographers. There's so much lake.

"You must have been one intense kid," she says, not looking at him.

Josh is studying her, she can feel his gaze.

"Maybe that's why Evie chose me as executor," he finally says. "She saw the similarities between us."

The similarities? Josh is a good person, a kind person, an open person. Their senior class president. Saskia is all scar tissue and defense mechanisms and hasn't been in touch with a single person from the University School since the day she collected her diploma. Whatever the reason her mother picked Josh, it definitely wasn't because of their similarities. "Why'd you go into estates, anyway? And why here?"

"I couldn't stomach most types of law by the time I graduated. Corporate litigation, malpractice, all that shit. It seemed like the best non-evil option."

She narrows her eyes. "Immigration. Public interest. Human rights."

"The best non-evil, non-soul-crushing option," he amends, and she concedes with a nod. "And people worry about their families and need lawyers to help take care of them. That's also why Milwaukee, by the way. My mom was sick."

Saskia notes the past tense. Before she can say anything, Josh adds, "She died two years ago."

She worries that he might try to force a bond over this before she realizes: he doesn't have to. She can feel the absences, his mother and hers, in the space between them. She sees in his warm eyes that he does, too.

But then they move on to the next series and she stops thinking entirely.

Before she can even break down what she's seeing, before she can even start to parse the photos in front of her, her brain goes into fight-or-flight mode, screaming: *Help.*

It's her.

Saskia is face-to-face with herself.

For a moment, she stands in fascination. Wide black-and-white eyes. Teenage limbs twisted around a fire escape—the fire escape that descended from his living room windows into the trees. The paleness of her skin against the dark of the evening; the shadows of a leafy tree branch cast dark across her neck.

The girl frozen in this photo has no idea. She doesn't yet know how the possibility of someday finding herself on some museum wall will haunt her for decades to come.

For a moment, she is just able to marvel at her own unremembered beauty. The unfinished, almost raw quality of her bare teenage arms in summer. Not yet muscled, never been in the ring. The insouciant rise of her shoulder from the cotton scarf wrapped around her body. The trust in her eyes.

"Oh, shit," Josh says at her side. And the spell is broken.

And Saskia is flattened. She is as two-dimensional as the image before her. Her throat has collapsed, she can't speak; she needs someone to blow air into her lungs like she's a first-aid dummy.

Her wide, panicked eyes meet Josh's, and he wraps his hands around hers.

"Do you want to go?" he says, glancing back at the wall label almost reflexively. "Patrick Kintner— Fuck."

She follows his eyes. *Saskia: A Portrait of Midwestern Adolescence, 1999.*

"Sixteen," she says low, to herself.

"Sixteen?" Josh says.

She shakes her head. "Or seventeen—no, sixteen. My birthday is in November—this is summer—"

"You were a baby."

"He was a friend of my mother's." And the world falls into place around her, dropping like a stage set. And suddenly she is not sixteen anymore, suddenly she is thirty-seven. Suddenly she is not on the fire escape, feeling the warm breeze stroke her skin; suddenly she is in the drafty open space of the art museum.

Suddenly, she is not with Patrick.

"Do you want to go?"

"No, I want—to see—" She can barely get the words out, she's already sliding over to the portrait to the right, the silvery-blond hair glinting at her out of the corner of her eye. She is ready. She is ready to see herself, to see more of herself. Desperate to see the specter that has haunted Patrick all of these years, as he himself has haunted her.

And yet.

Kelly: A Portrait of Midwestern Adolescence, 1991.

Saskia catches her breath.

This girl. This girl on the beach.

This *other* girl.

She takes a step away from the photograph. But how much worse it is once she does. Because there's another. And another. There was another girl. And several more besides her, too. All young, all blond, all in black-and-white. All in late adolescence, though various features—black eyeliner here, a tattoo there—make it harder to pinpoint ages more precisely. Only one other name, in addition to Kelly: Julia. The other images are named after the places where they were taken: *Bradford Beach, June 2003.*

But she keeps coming back to Kelly. *Kelly, 1991.*

In a group of twelve, there's only one of Saskia, so she studies Kelly's series like she's going to be tested on it, she studies it like it's a map of a distant location she needs to learn by heart. Some of the places are public (beach, mall), some not (car, couch). A catalog of the places she'd been with him. Their catalogue raisonné.

Because she knows these places like the back of her hand. She knows them, but she knows more than that, too.

She knows the look of love in Kelly's eyes.

And she doesn't understand much about art, but she can feel it, too: the love pulsing at Kelly from the other side of the camera.

It's so familiar.

She hates this girl, suddenly and irrationally, with a rage swelling up inside her like a thunderstorm. She hates this girl, this girl whom he'd loved as he'd loved her. She hates her more than she hates any of the other ones, except maybe Julia. Because there is one picture of Saskia, but how many of Kelly? Five—six. She hates this girl until the date pops up before her eyes again, 1991, and she realizes that this girl is now a full-blown middle-aged woman.

This woman has a good ten years on her; she came before Sas, not after. Somehow, it's a balm.

But the others. The tenderness, the excitement. The joy, in all of their eyes, no matter the expression. Some came before her, but plenty of others came after her, scattered through the 1990s and early 2000s.

She is in the middle.

She was just another girl.

It takes her a long minute to notice that Josh is no longer beside her.

She whirls around the room, looking, but the room is full of tall men wearing crisp white shirts. When Josh appears again, striding jauntily toward her, she feels like she's been yanked back from the edge of a panic attack. She is in no position to be on a date right now. There's something smoldering in her, an anger she doesn't know how to hold. She wants to call the curator. She wants to call the director of the museum. She wants to go back through her memories and cast them through the lens of this new information.

"Look, Josh, it was nice of you to invite me here, but I'm just exhausted, it's been such a weird few weeks. Could we rain-check the rest of the night?"

"Sure," he says, and his voice is gentle. "Sure, it must be—a lot."

"It's just, I'm tired all the time these days. And I should check on my dad."

"Of course," he says.

Exiting through the gift shop, she hesitates just a minute before palming a postcard of the fire escape portrait. It's not like she doesn't have the $1.25, it's that she won't pay for work that feels like it belongs to her.

"This was great," she says again, too chirpily in the hellish orange lighting of the parking structure.

"Are you sure you're okay—"

"Yes, I'm fine."

He grasps her hand. "Saskia, that postcard—should we maybe go back and just drop a couple bucks on the counter? I know, it must be so strange, but the museum is a nonprofit, and it's a work event, and I just feel . . . don't you think?"

She stares at him.

"What postcard?" she says.

SASKIA SPENDS THE NIGHT IN AN INSOMNIAC stupor, staring at the postcard grasped between pale-knuckled hands. The bruises are fading, erasing the evidence of her time in the ring. She can't see her teenage hands in the photo, but she's sure that they must have been plumper, once. She can see the sinews now, the places where the skin goes slack between her knuckles. She thinks about all of the things those hands have done.

She pulls her heavy limbs out of bed, goes to the fireplace. Takes down the most finished, though still unfinished, violin from the mantel and pushes the postcard through the waving, carved holes to the empty space below. If only it were something she could burn and be done with. If only it were just one thing that she could forget and not this infinitely replicable image that will now dot refrigerators and bulletin boards all over the city.

She gets up without ever really having slept and drags herself down to the kitchen table. There, her father has left a black gift bag, ribbon tying the handles together. He did this sometimes; he used to do this, before a big performance, after a big test: the surprise present. Saskia plunges her hands into the bag, pulling out the item inside, a round metal container.

An urn. Etched onto it: *Evelyn Harper Kreis, 1950–2020.*

"Holy *shit—*" she cries, and her father steps through the threshold just as she drops the urn onto the ground, as the last trace of Evelyn Harper Kreis's body scatters all over the kitchen floor.

For a moment, she and her father just look at each other.

"Dad, I'm so sorry," Sas says. "I just—it's just so *gruesome.*"

Her father doesn't meet her eyes.

She swallows. "Why did you leave it at my place? You put it there like it was a gift."

"Did I?" He looks nauseated. "I didn't mean to. Just meant to set it down. I thought we could call Georgia. She and Lexi could come by—"

"Yeah," Saskia says before he can finish. She can't bear to hear it said: they'll have a private ceremony, and they'll consign her mother to the waves. After everything, after all of it. This final goodbye is too much.

Evie would have hated fitting into a sleek black shopping bag. How much that would have galled her. Maybe not as much as being swept up into the dustpan, though. By the time Saskia has finished cleaning, her hands are coated in the remnants of her mother.

Is this the sum of a life? Saskia thinks later as the four of them stand on the beach. Not just any life, either. A good life. An incredible one. At the end of the day, here they are, her mother coming out of the urn in undignified lumps. Falling to the lacy shoreline; but the wind is against them and the ashes blow back onto the beach, mixing pale gray into the sand, among the rocks.

And still, all Saskia can think is: Kelly. Julia.

Is this what jealousy feels like? She had never been jealous. Had been so goddamn certain of her specialness, of her uniqueness, while they were together. Why else would he risk it, a relationship with a teenager? Why else would he have put everything on the line?

But it hadn't been everything, had it? Because back then, people would have *frowned upon* what they were, sure. But would he have lost his job? Would he have actually lost anything that mattered to him?

She's not sure.

She's grateful, as the ashes float to the water, as they dissolve, that nobody is talking. Lexi shoves her cold hand into Sas's, making her start; but it's not entirely unpleasant, and she holds on tight. And yet she is still not fully there. It's not the insufferable meaninglessness of this ritual—it might be almost holy, if she could make herself focus on her mother for thirty seconds instead of this constant pulsing:

Kelly. Julia.

It hadn't been just them, either. It had been five girls. Or six. So interchangeable, she can't even tell how many, she lost track even as they were staring back at her from the gallery wall. All of them blond, all of them gangly, all of them in that in-between space, somewhere between childhood and adulthood.

Lexi drops her hand as Mike comes back toward them, as he wraps his arm around Sas's shoulder. As Georgia gabbles on and on about Evie's hair; ah, well, let her. It's a miracle she was quiet for so long. As they start to head back up to the house, and in the space between the names in her head, Saskia's own voice starts to emerge.

Asking: Is it truly jealousy she feels?

Or is it something else?

Chapter 10

She was a second away from telling him all about her journey, just as he'd requested. But as Little Red Riding Hood looked at the Wolf, she remembered something that her grandmother always told her.

"Wait a minute," she said. "I don't have to smile and be nice to strange men."

"But I'm not a man," the Wolf growled.

Little Red Riding Hood: "Well, you're male, anyhow. In my book, that's pretty much the same."

And then she karate-chopped him in the neck and went on her way.

—*Fairy Tales for Little Feminists:*
Little Red Riding Hood, Evelyn Harper Kreis

August 1996

SASKIA WAS THIRTEEN, AND THE END OF SUMMER was on the horizon. The light was already falling fast in the evening, and that Friday, it was already dark enough that she could see Lexi's flashlight signaling from the cliffs an hour or so after dinner. The sky was streaked with scarlet and purple, on the opposite side of the Earth from the rapidly sinking sun, and Saskia ran out under it to meet her friend.

This year, Lexi would not be attending University School. When Jake left Georgia a few months earlier he'd promised enough child support to cover tuition. But the money hadn't materialized, and he was impossible to track down, so Lexi was starting at Shorewood High School instead. She was only five months older than Saskia, had always been a year ahead in school, but now she'd be going to a high school—a public high school—and Saskia was afraid of what it would do to them. It seemed so far from where she was now.

Lexi was waiting between their houses, by the beach path: half hidden from the view of her parents and Aunt Georgia by the circle of three willows, like sisters lowering their hair. As she approached, Saskia could see that Lexi's full cheeks were wet, shining in the almost-dark.

"I can't believe I have to go to Shorewood," Lexi said, collapsing into Saskia's arms. Her hand was shaking as she offered Saskia a bottle of Coke.

Saskia shook her head. "I have lessons early. I'll never sleep."

Tears brimmed in Lexi's eyes, but she still somehow managed to roll them.

"I put in an antidote against the caffeine."

Saskia took a careful sip, letting the spiky liquid coat the inside of her mouth.

"Rum?"

"Malibu."

"Your mom's going to notice."

"Mom doesn't notice anything lately." Lexi's wet face seemed to glow blue in the half-light. "You know what she bought me to wear on my first day?"

Saskia scanned back, thinking about the clothes she'd seen Lexi in recently. "Old Navy?" she said finally.

"Yeah."

"What's wrong with—"

"It's really fucking lame!" Lexi's voice broke. "Everyone else is going to be in Abercrombie, I just know it. It's so stupid, I spent so many years hating that stupid uniform at the University School, and now I'd give anything for it, I really would."

Saskia scrambled for something to say. "They can't *all* be in Abercrombie." She tried to remember how much the jeans her mother had bought her there had cost; Mike had made a fuss about it when he saw the credit card statement.

"All the important ones will be. We're so fucking poor, and all she has to do is sell that house. And she'll never do it."

Saskia swallowed. Lexi's house was smaller and not as old as hers, but grander, like an Italian palace. It had to be worth at least a million; theirs was. That was all she knew about it, other than that her parents thought it was an eyesore but that she was never, ever, to repeat this to Georgia or Lexi.

"Have you . . . talked to her? Not about the jeans, but about . . . like, everything else?"

Lexi pulled her knees under her chin. "She wouldn't get it."

"And, what about . . . your dad?"

"He's useless." Lexi put her face down to her knees and started to sob. Saskia set a hand tentatively on her back.

The rod returned to Lexi's spine; she sat up straight. With the back of her hands, she brushed her tears away. Saskia imagined she could see them flying like diamonds into the dark.

"You're so—fucking—lucky," Lexi said, and Saskia was so caught up in the sound of her friend trying out the swear, at the tentative wobble of her voice, that it took her a minute to realize the meaning of the sentence as a whole.

"Lucky?"

"Not to feel things. Not to care."

Saskia felt something inside her recoil. How was it that no matter what she said to other people, they always turned it back around on her? She had just been trying to help.

She looked out over the dark lake, swinging her leg. Took another sip of the Coke.

"I feel things," she said finally, softly. "I care."

"Yeah, but not like—not like us, you know? You're like—you're like a grown-up."

"But I'm not, I'm just . . . me." She pictured the rum swooshing through her veins, crystallizing around her brain. "Look, I've got like"—*a ton*, she almost said—"a pair or two of Abercrombie jeans if you want them. Size two?"

Lexi's eyes glowed. "Are you serious?"

"Sure." She had six or seven pairs, actually; the bottom drawer of her dresser had gotten hard to close, and she'd taken a few of them up to the tower for extra storage. She only ever wore them on the weekends, after all, and she didn't really care about clothes.

Lexi hopped to her feet. "Can we get them now?"

"Sure." She let her friend pull her up, Lexi's moist palm in her dry one.

"See," Lexi said, wrapping her arm around Saskia's waist as they headed back to the house, Coke bottle nestled in the roots of the tree still behind them, "I knew you weren't real. Not a real teenager, anyway."

"Oh, no? Then what am I?"

"I don't know," Lexi said as Saskia steered her around to the side door, avoiding the kitchen. "Something else."

She wasn't sure that taking Lexi up to her attic, the attic full of the scraps of her young life, would do anything to disprove this idea. But as Saskia searched through the boxes, Lexi looked around the tower with wide eyes. Eventually she climbed on top of the mattresses to jump, giggling the whole time. She didn't come down until Saskia came back with a pile of jeans, just as the wall beside them gave a sharp creak, leading to shrieks—and then more giggles.

"Do you think Emilia's ghost is up here?" Lex whispered loudly.

"Definitely," Saskia said firmly. "Emilia, and probably Cecilia, too. They're a family tradition, you know."

January 2020

THE PHOTOGRAPHY CURATOR, GARY TOWERS, WAS eager to see Saskia. Surprisingly eager; unnervingly eager. Her email went out at 10:52 the night of the museum reception, and by 11:30, there was a response waiting, complete with an invitation to lunch the next day. It sends a shiver up her hands, through her arms. How many *Saskias* can he have heard of? He must know who she is. From the photos in the exhibition alone, he must know.

Saskia hadn't wanted to meet at a restaurant—like she's going to spend money on any of this shit?—but Gary had been insistent. She wasn't thrilled with the location of the restaurant he picked, either. Cathedral Square, the netherworld between the lake and downtown. She'd have preferred Bartolotta's or Beans & Barley; she didn't care about the fanciness so much as the familiarity.

But the gastropub, when she enters, has a dated mid-1990s decor that immediately comforts her. Saskia loves the 1990s. Sometimes, when she feels very lonely, she puts on early episodes of *Frasier* and *Friends*, shows she'd never watched when they were actually on the air, just to see the sets, the clothing.

What was it about that decade? She'd felt protected, back then. When she thinks of her childhood, she thinks first of the cocoon of the Elf House and then of Bill Clinton. During the period she'd grown up in, history seemed like something that had already happened. The world had been discovered, and their task was to act as caretakers of this tamed and precious thing. Of course, she knows very well *now* that it had not been a safe or happy time for many, many others. But rather than rupturing the bubble of her own memories, this knowledge has somehow gilded them, hardened and preserved them. She's always known she was lucky, but it took some experience of the world to see just how lucky she was.

And today, her luck holds out. She was worried about spotting Gary, but a round-faced, white-haired man with tortoiseshell glasses hops to his feet as she enters.

What does she look like, to him? He must have given her teenage portrait more than a cursory glance, to have included it in the show; he must be reconciling teenage Saskia with the woman standing before him. She forces herself to smile and reach out her hand.

"Saskia Kreis," he says, holding out a hand. She takes it, soft and warm in her own. She's taller than he is by an inch or two. Men tend not to like that. "I'd know you anywhere."

She feels her cheeks heating as she sits down. She's acutely aware that he is a professional, that she has not had anything like a real job in years. It makes her feel like she's playacting at adulthood. "It's nice to meet you."

His eyes almost twinkle as he studies her face. She tries to think of who he reminds her of but flounders.

"I was so very sorry to hear about your mother."

"Oh, you knew my—"

The ice water being poured clinks against her glass, splatters her forearm.

Gary's turning up his hands, pink palms to the ceiling. "By reputation, of course. We met in passing at events over the years. A great loss to the art community. And to . . . Well. A great loss."

The waitress, all shiny black hair and overly made-up face, is back, asking if they've taken a look at the wine list. The question surprises Saskia: Do people still order drinks at lunch? It's so 1960s.

But with a wink at her (asexual—fuck, she hopes it's asexual), Gary orders the second most expensive bottle of white on the menu. An alcoholic? God, she hopes he's an alcoholic. But after they make small talk about the weather (*So erratic! Well, climate change*), the waitress brings the bottle and he sniffs the cork and swishes the wine around in the glass and does all of the annoying things that have always been dating deal breakers for Sas. Then he raises his glass:

"To Evelyn Harper Kreis."

She couldn't have been more surprised if he'd slapped her. Raising a robotic arm:

"To . . . well, to Mom."

She processes the implications as the waitress takes their orders. Why the restaurant, why the wine? This is not simple good manners. This is not even romantic.

Does he want Evie's drawings and photos? Is that it?

It clicks: of course.

This is *development* work.

Oh, fuck. She's got the art museum's Patrick.

"I'm really sorry," she says. "But to be clear, I'm not here about my mother's work."

He tilts his head to the side. *Santa.* That's who he reminds her of.

"Is it promised somewhere else?"

She blinks. "Well, no. I'm not sure . . . You want the princesses? Like, the sketches?"

Gary laughs, showing even white teeth. "Not exactly. No, my pet project is building up our collection of Midwestern artists. I'm particularly interested in your mother's early work. The hands, and especially the photos. Though I'd bet you anything that Sheila would be grateful for the drawings, and for the princess sketches, too. But her photographs of hands, those are what particularly interest me. There's such a—a wholesome sort of feminism to that series. It's fascinating."

Wholesome feminism. An oxymoron, Saskia thinks, or it should be. The revolution will not be wholesome.

"That's interesting," she says. "But really, that's not why I'm here. Kind of the opposite, actually. I came to talk about the current show."

"Oh! We're quite pleased with it, yes. You have to get down to the museum while it's up. I can comp you a ticket—"

"No," she says, louder than she meant to. "No, I saw it last night. One of the lawyers at Fairchild and Locke invited me to the opening." She pauses to take a drink of water, ice cubes banging against her teeth. But Gary is waiting, waiting for her to go on. "It's really something," she says finally.

"Yes, isn't it? We're so proud to be showing off local photographers like this. There's such an artistic community in Milwaukee, and yet outsiders rarely know—"

"Hmm, yes," she says. God, he could probably go on like this all day, if she let him. But: *Soft*, she reminds herself. *Softer.* "I was fascinated by the juxtaposition of images. I'd love to hear about how you put it together."

The waitress sets their food in front of them: her club sandwich, his steak sandwich. Room service food.

His Santa face cracks open into a broad smile. "Well, I'm not sure how much you want to hear. It came out of a brainstorming session that Sheila and I had last spring. Sorry. That's Sheila Neach, our curator of modern and contemporary art."

But Saskia knows Sheila Neach. Has known her since she taught museum studies at UWM with Evie, decades ago. She grasps her sandwich tightly, rips off a bite with her teeth.

"Of course," she says after she's swallowed. "Sheila's an old family friend. Well, acquaintance."

"Of course," he says, and she wonders if he's mocking her with that echo. "I'd forgotten—but of course, Sheila was gone for the second half of the year. Off in Spain, gathering some Picassos."

"So you selected the works alone?" She has to wait until he finishes chewing his bite of the enormous steak sandwich.

"No. We selected the artists we wanted to showcase together, and then we asked each of them to submit portfolios for the show. I think we ended up hanging what they submitted, almost without exception. We wanted it to truly be a snapshot of Milwaukee artists as they see themselves." He hesitates over his sandwich, fingers paused, and sets them back in his lap without picking it up. "Cards on the table, Miss Kreis. Is this about Patrick Kintner?"

She makes herself keep her own hands in her lap; they're too shaky to be trusted on the table right now.

"I wasn't thrilled," she starts slowly, editing herself as she goes. "I wasn't thrilled to see my portrait hanging there."

He flinches fleetingly before his face becomes open, earnest once again. "I'm sorry to hear that."

"Is there . . . is there a process by which I could request it be taken down?"

Another wince, but he holds this one longer, until it becomes a grimace. "I'm awfully sorry. I truly am. But the show's catalog has been published. We have tour dates set—it'll be off to Chicago, then San Diego in the spring." As though she should be excited about that. "May I ask why it bothers you, though?"

She's shaking her head before she realizes what she's doing. "No. I . . . no, it's just, I don't know. It seems like someone should have asked permission, gotten a waiver . . ."

"Ah—" And he holds up a finger as he takes another bite of his sandwich, making her wait, again, while he chews. "But you see, it's not being used commercially. In art, the use of another's image is protected by the artist's First Amendment right to expression."

She looks at his expression. There's a hardening, the slipping on of a mask beneath the Santa face.

What he's really saying is, *You better not sue.* What he's really saying is, *You have no right.* She debates bringing up the postcards—$1.25, that's still commercial, isn't it?—but sees immediately. That's not the path to take.

"And what about my rights?" she says quietly.

"If I can be frank, Miss Kreis," Gary says, bending forward over knitted-together hands. "I would think most people would be flattered to be in such a show. To be photographed by such a talent. To have been chosen—"

And he goes on, but all of the blood has leaked out of her face. It's the same argument she used to make to herself. The same language she used to justify their relationship to herself. Before she'd realized. Before the show had made her see. Patrick hadn't loved her despite her age. He'd loved her because of it.

"I'm sorry," she says, getting onto shaky legs. "I can't. I can't, with this, right now. The way you—" She stops her fumble through her purse, stares at him. "There were five or six young girls up on that wall, Gary. So, the question I'd be asking myself, if I were you, is just how he chose us. What else he did to us." She finds her wallet, drops two twenties on the table. It's the last of her cash, but she can't owe him anything. "Tell me one more thing. Whose idea was it to include Patrick in the show in the first place? Surely you owe me that much," she says, her voice fierce as she sees him hesitate.

He holds up his hands. "Hey, I have no problem telling you that. It was all Sheila. And she just got back yesterday, if you have any *further* questions." He picks up his sandwich. "Delightful to meet you. Do let me know what you decide to do with your mother's collection, won't you?"

And as she stands there staring at him in bafflement, he tears off another piece of meat.

FURY IS RUNNING SHALLOW BENEATH HER SKIN, misplaced though it may be. Of course, Sheila had wanted Patrick in the show. Any retrospective of Milwaukee photographers from the last fifty years would have to include him. And Sheila couldn't have known what he'd submit, could she? She might have been thinking about his widely published (and highly acclaimed) AIDS portraits, not the never-exhibited portraits of teenage girls.

And yet.

And yet. Saskia finds herself whirling the Saab into a skidding U-turn just in front of the Wisconsin Conservatory of Music, doubling back toward the museum. It takes her only a few minutes and some helpful directions from a docent to find the administrative offices. Only a minute more to pinpoint Sheila.

Sheila Neach. *Dr.* Sheila Neach, a title she rightfully insists upon. In Saskia's mind, Sheila has blurred almost entirely into Georgia, though she isn't like Georgia in most ways. Sheila is tall while Georgia is short, highly educated while Georgia had dropped out of college at the first opportunity.

Sheila has always, as far as Saskia knows, been extremely committed to her career, while Georgia has only occasionally dabbled in real estate. Still, there's something similar in how they carry themselves. A hard iron core beneath the layers of funky scarves and fuchsia lipstick. A certain brassiness that Saskia has always appreciated.

She doesn't appreciate it now, though. Not as Sheila holds a finger up at her, telling her to wait in the hallway. Not as the elegant twenty-somethings in the contemporary art office pretend not to see her hovering awkwardly in the doorway. Not as they pretend not to recognize her.

Finally, Sheila turns. Saskia last saw her at the Christmas party two years ago, and Sheila hasn't changed a jot. She has the same Kennedy-esque good looks: broad boned, freckled, her auburn hair a wavy halo around her face. *The kind of woman for whom the term* handsome *was coined,* Evie had said after meeting her, when Sas was eleven or twelve.

"Saskia," Sheila says with a sigh. "Sorry about that. What can I do for you?"

But Saskia's gaze has drifted over the curator's shoulder to a bulletin board. Where, yes, her teenage self drapes over a fire escape, shrunk down to a handy three-by-five postcard.

She raises her eyebrows. "I need to talk to you."

Sheila follows her eyeline to the postcard, nods sharply. "Meet me in the café in five minutes."

The café is institutional, flexible wooden chairs and round tables facing the water. Saskia gets a black coffee, mostly to have something to hold in her ice-cold hands. She hears Sheila's heels clicking through the vaulted space, and she does not bother turning to greet her.

Sheila sits down, sighing again like this visit is both anticipated and inconvenient.

"Spain must have been nice," Saskia says, not bothering to keep the accusatory note out of her voice.

"Spain was very nice," Sheila says, hard brown eyes unflinching. "But I was sorry to miss the memorial, you know. It's a great loss to us all, your mother's death. I only heard about her illness after the fact."

True or not true? Sheila's shellacked exterior makes it impossible to know. Saskia gives a sharp nod.

"Your friendship meant a lot to her." It was a phrase Saskia had over-heard someone use as she cut through the crowd at the memorial service, and she is pleased to have it come in handy now. "Anyway. What were you doing in Spain?"

Sheila breaks into a mischievous grin. "Collecting Picassos for an up-coming show."

"I thought we were done with Picasso?" Saskia says, though she's par-roting the remark. It was something she'd heard from James, who'd heard it on a Netflix comedy special—that #MeToo had come for Picasso and his particular brand of misogyny, his obsession with underage girls.

Sheila rolls her eyes dramatically. "Oh, honestly. If you want to know the truth, I'd love to do a whole show just on canceled men. Put some Gauguin in there, some Chuck Close. For Christ's sake, has *nobody* read their Barthes?" She waits, but Saskia just blinks. "'The Death of the Artist'?"

Saskia shakes her head. "I studied computer science and electrical en-gineering."

"Anyway, I'm going on. It's not like you came here to talk about critical theory."

"No. I came here to talk about Patrick Kintner."

It can't be a surprise. Sheila saw her eyeing the postcard; she had to have suspected that Saskia would have *opinions*. And yet Sheila's face goes through a shifting rainbow of change: from bleached-out white to mottled purple to red.

"He's an important artist," she says finally, almost indignantly. "And a very important local one. Who knows where he'd be now if UWM hadn't shunted him into admin after all of those accusations a few years ago. . . . Oh, you didn't know?"

Now it is Saskia's turn to look surprised, and Sheila laughs, short, through her nose. "Yeah, that's why he got moved into development. They couldn't prove a goddamn thing, but all the same. The provost chose to put him in something *less student facing*. That spells death for an artist, that loss of free time. Absolute death." Saskia is overwhelmed by the im-plications of what Sheila is saying, even as she realizes that somewhere deep inside, she'd already suspected exactly this. But Sheila barrels on, lost in her own monologue. In that way, she is definitely like Georgia.

"You have to realize," Saskia interrupts measuredly, "that it came as a bit of a shock to find myself face-to-face with . . . myself."

And the relief in Sheila's eyes, as the line of her mouth relaxes.

"Well, *honey*! I figured your mother would have told you about *that*." But her bravado is undercut slightly as she reaches the end of her sentence, remembers that Evie is dead.

"My . . . mother? Saw this picture?"

Sheila studies her for a moment.

"She saw the whole portfolio, hon. She came to lunch the same day I got it from Kintner, last June. I showed it to her, thinking, Oh, she'll be so delighted to see this sweet portrait of Saskia included in our show. But I left her with the portfolio for about five minutes and when I came back . . . oh, I have never seen her so mad—she was spitting, even worse than you are. But it's art!" she cries, her shoulders climbing toward her ears, her eyes going wide. "I told her then and I'm telling you now. It's art, it's history, the public has a right to see it. I'm not here as a mediator, you know. I'm not here as a judge. I'm here—"

"To curate," Saskia says, harsh. "To choose."

"Yes," Sheila says, emphatic. "Yes! And that is my job, and I have been doing it for almost fifty years, and I'll tell you what, there aren't a whole lot of women who can say *that*. It was all men when I got here. And, honey, I'm sorry if you're upset, I really am. But it could have been a whole lot worse, and you only have your—" She cuts herself off, standing up and crossing her arms. "Do you want to know why I wasn't at the funeral, sweetie? It's because your mother wouldn't have wanted me there. She couldn't stand the sight of me after that. But I am a *curator*, it is my job to preserve, to show—"

But it's too much, and Saskia can't process it all, she can't even keep up. Sheila's gibberish is flowing too fast into her mind, with only one product coming out.

"What aren't you telling me?" Saskia finally says.

But Sheila just shakes her head, staring back at her with a quiet rage. "What do you want from me? You Kreises. I swear, I have had enough. You can't sue, they're not commercial, and it's one fucking photograph, Saskia! One picture out of a hundred in the show! And—I can't emphasize this enough—it is not my job. To protect your feelings."

Saskia takes a sip of her cooling coffee with shaky hands as the clicking of Sheila's heels recedes into the depths of the museum. She stares at the water, pale gray today under a chalky sky.

And she wonders: Whose job is it, then?

Chapter 11

Snow White and Rose Red were two sisters, living with their widowed mother, who loved each other very much. Snow White had flaxen hair as yellow as corn, and loved to spend her time indoors, cleaning and cooking and reading. Rose Red had dark hair as black as a raven's wing, and loved to spend her time outside, climbing trees and going on adventures and taming wild animals. Both of the girls' choices were equally valid, for each represented the kind of life that each girl felt was true to her.

—*Fairy Tales for Little Feminists: Snow White and Rose Red*, Evelyn Harper Kreis

June 1997

SASKIA WAS FOURTEEN AND HAD HAD ENOUGH OF what the adults insisted on calling her "peers." Becca Talbot and her ilk were bad enough: moving in a pack, never doing a single interesting thing, spending all of their time just whispering, whispering. But the boys were worse. The snapping bras, the spitballs, the smell; did none of them shower, ever?

The girls were beneath contempt, but the boys felt like another species altogether.

And so, that year, Saskia began to take a secret, fevered pleasure in skipping school for the day, only to spend it in the same building where her mother worked. The logistics had been easy enough to manage: out the door at 7:15, same as ever, to holler at the bus driver: *I'm going down to UWM today.* Her "independent study" at the university, such as it was— Carrie had arranged for her to have free rein of the practice rooms—

would never have been allowed at a public school, and both her guidance counselor and her parents had made her extraordinary privilege perfectly clear, but then again—Saskia wasn't an ordinary girl.

That June, the trees were bursting with green, century-old elms reaching full branches above her head. There was an extra pleasure in going into the building now, when the university's regular spring semester had ended and the summer session hadn't yet started: a sneaking specialness to it, when the students who normally eyed her with suspicion had been banished back to their homes for three months, with only Saskia remaining.

She wanted 10A that day: 10A had a nicely balanced Yamaha. Not as resonant as the best Steinway down at the Conservatory, but with a lighter weight to the keys that would be just right for the Liszt running through her head: *La Campanella*, sparking like fireworks.

But when she got to 10A, some idiot was playing Haydn in there. Badly.

She turned abruptly to make her way back to another studio. And ran smack into a wall of a man. She squinted up into Patrick's face, the taste of metal already tanging on her tongue.

"Oh, fuck," she said, wiping the back of her hand through the blood.

And Patrick pressed a hand to her cheek.

There was nothing condescending or amused about it. Instead, he seemed almost reverent. The strong lines of his face wincing at her.

"Come on," he said. "Let's get you cleaned up."

As he pulled his hand away, she saw blood on his fingers. Her blood on his skin.

"You, too," she said.

Nothing was an inevitability yet. Everything was still possible.

"Don't tell my mom, okay?" she said as she followed him upstairs, to his stairwell-adjacent office, ducking behind him so as to stay out of view from the other rooms.

"No?" he asked, key turning in the lock. It was late spring and there was a chalky, warm smell to the building, something familiar and dry and satisfying.

Evie's office was a riot of papers, of overflowing sketches and textbooks and portfolios from this student and that one. Pencil shavings and charcoal ends and family pictures and ancient coffee mugs with rings of brown dried all gummy on their bottoms. Her windows faced the older redbrick buildings of what had once been Downer College.

But Patrick's office looked out over a cluster of trees, waving their almost obscenely full-leafed branches in relief against the sun. It dappled the room with a shifting slideshow of silhouettes. *Blonde on Blonde*, the Bob Dylan album cover, was framed on the wall. A portrait of a woman's body, muscular and lithe, was propped up on a bookshelf. One of his? No—she squinted to read the signature. Maple something, she wasn't sure. The piles of books that weren't shelved were neatly arranged. Tiny cacti lined the windowsill.

The vibe just felt—young. Like a life Saskia could aspire to, rather than a future that seemed out of reach.

Patrick *was* younger than her parents. Their friendship had been cemented by his friendly work relationship with Evie, by their shared gallerists, by acquaintances they had in common. Despite the age difference, he'd been coming to their annual parties for at least five years now. He couldn't have been more than, what? Forty? Not even. Thirty-five? He'd started in the department five years ago or so. That would be about right.

"Up," he said, pointing to the desk.

"Yes, Doctor," she said, laughing.

He came close to her. Stood between her parted legs. If she moved her thighs a centimeter in, she would have been straddling him. She fought the wheezing that seemed to be trying to come from her throat. Swallowed.

He stared into her face. His eyes were brown, but this close she could see the rings of gold around the centers. Lion eyes, she thought.

"Hold still," he said softly.

January 2020

AS SHE DRIVES HOME, ALL SASKIA CAN THINK ABOUT is a single question: What does she want? She thought it was just the Elf

House she wanted. The Elf House and then that fucking picture taken down.

But the Elf House . . . the choice isn't really between her keeping the house forever or Patrick getting it. It's her keeping it for a time, her keeping it for as long as she can, her holding on to it with bleeding claws; or it's her selling it, living like a queen, like a princess, in luxury, a kind of wealth she hasn't known since she was a child—or it's him. It's Patrick getting it, Patrick laying claim to one of the few things that had ever made her special. And he'd already taken one of them away from her.

And then there's the picture. She's hurt, angry, jealous. Betrayed. And she understands now that even if it gets taken down—which seems less and less likely—she will still feel these things, because it will still exist. She will exist, always now, as one of a *series*.

That afternoon, as Saskia sits in her mother's studio with Wolfie at her feet, watching the fading daylight twitch shadows over the desk, she gets an email from Tara. The draft affidavit is attached. It's good, as far as she can tell; it's in total legalese, but the writing is strong, the facts are there.

It's just that the facts aren't enough. The facts don't add up to much that Sas can see. It's not the full story. It's not even *a* full story.

What is she missing? She reads back over the body of Tara's email.

It is a circumstantial case; the best evidence we have is, of course, linked to the opportunity to influence and the coveted result. But these cases usually are circumstantial, so I'm not too concerned. That said, if you find anything at all that might be relevant, even if you aren't 100% sure how—

That's enough for Sas. She stops reading, finds the online image of herself on the art museum website, sends the link over with a brief summary of her day's meetings.

Relevant, irrelevant? Who is she to say?

She hopes Tara can. She wishes somebody would.

Surely the fact of the picture, displayed without her knowledge or permission, means something.

Tara's email pings back immediately: *Revising*.

She allows herself to picture it: winning the case. Being the Elf House heiress again, if only for a little while, if only until she can sell it. Getting everything. Patrick getting nothing.

And she has to admit, if only to herself: it still isn't enough.

Underneath the anger and betrayal, she feels it as a kind of longing, as a spiraling loss: Patrick as a white knight, Patrick as the good guy. The story she had told herself for so long—she still wants it. She doesn't know what to do, who she is, without it. And now, she can never get that back, and in the meantime, there he is, just out in the world. And the world— people like Sheila, people like the provost at UWM, people like fucking *everyone*—they're all still going around with that image of him as the charming artist. *They* still get to believe in the story.

No. If she doesn't get to believe in that story anymore, neither do they.

It chills her, the thought that she could still have power in this situation. It's a responsibility—and yet it's a freedom, too. To be able to tell everyone: *Here's the real story.* To say: *Oh, but look—he lied.*

To say: I'm *the truth teller. Me.*

And then, that Wicked Witch voice every woman carries, somewhere inside herself: *Who would believe you?*

But people need to know what he did, she thinks.

People need to know who he is.

Kelly. Julia. She hears the names again.

Yes. That's what she'll do. She will gather them together, a band of Furies. And then—the *Journal Sentinel?* Maybe. Maybe *The New Yorker,* why not aim high? Why not begin with the best and see what happens? See what a band of women's voices can do. How far they can go.

How much they can destroy.

She grabs a fresh notebook from the pile on her mother's desk, and she writes their names on the crisp front page.

Kelly. Julia.

And what is she supposed to do, in the meantime? What is she supposed to do as the courts and the banks and the fucking museum and everybody else decides who she is, what she'll get? Her fingers are tapping frantically against the desk—one of Scriabin's sonatas—and she thinks, suddenly calm: numbers.

She can lose herself in the numbers.

And the numbers being money, it's not a pointless exercise; they're the future. Her future.

Gary had wanted Evie's photos, spoke of Sheila wanting her drawings. Well. She doubts the latter part, but Saskia looks her mother up on Artnet all the same. Evie's work has appeared in a number of recent auctions, including one at Sotheby's. Over the past few years, the value of her drawings and her photos has gone up, up: $750, $1,000. Saskia wonders what they'll do next. What is the value of a dead artist? More than an alive one, if Gary is any indication. Maybe artists are like mothers in fairy tales: the true story begins only after their deaths.

The dog grumbles at her feet as she pages through the enormous files of her mother's prints, tries to come up with an estimate for how much they're worth. There are around ninety prints there. Selling at a grand each—but would they? She should have paid more attention to this part of her mother's career. Should have paid more attention to a lot of things.

As the late afternoon sun gilds the studio, she sits in front of an Excel sheet, inputting value after value. All in one place, it doesn't seem like so little. In fact, the abundance is almost overwhelming—though somehow still not enough. Not enough to save the house forever. But already this goal is coming loose in her mind, replaced only by the desire to know what she and her father have. To know that they'll be okay.

She inputs a rough estimate of what the photos are worth. The value of her piano. They can probably get something for the countless sketches and notes for *Little Feminists*, too. Maybe Jody could be talked into releasing new editions of some of the fairy tales, with bonus material from the deceased author's archives? The royalty payments for the next two years, which she estimates based on an average of the past three. The initial installment of the advance for *Persephone and Demeter* went to the property taxes—the sums, $37,500, are identical, and the check went out the same day the advance came in—but there's still three more $37,500 installments to go.

If the book is publishable.

With jittery fingers, she types up a summary of what she's read to Ellen, her mother's agent. She lingers a bit too long on the most recent part she returned to, a part that sticks in her head, a part with that jaunty Evelyn Harper Kreis touch: *When Persephone reaches the Underworld, she's not the compliant, sweet maiden we always read about*, Saskia types. *Instead, she's full of piss and vinegar, mocking Hades, conniving, trying to reason her way out of an unreasonable situation.* At the end, she hesitates for only a moment before typing: *It ends there. Is this in any way publishable as is? I'm attaching the full manuscript here.*

But Ellen, it seems, doesn't need to read the full manuscript, because her phone dings with a new email just five minutes later.

I'm so sorry, Saskia. Your mother wasn't famous enough for an unfinished manuscript to be publishable. We're looking at a return of the initial advance here. Luckily, the publisher paid it out in quarters, so it's not as much as it could have been: $37,500.

Of course, she knows that the publishing house is not a benevolent institution. It's not the government. She gets that. The advance was not an NEA grant, it was not a Guggenheim award (ah, if only she'd been a Guggenheim)—it was given on the basis of a *product* for *sale.*

No product. No sale.

And yet.

$37,500.

The last time Saskia looked at her mother's bank account, there wasn't much more in there than in her own. At this point, the January payment from UWM, her last paycheck from her sabbatical semester, should have come through: about $5,000.

Where the fuck is she supposed to get almost forty grand right now? Sell her piano? Wait for the next round of royalties to come in sometime that summer and give up the right to almost half of them?

She could live for a year on $37,500. She's gotten by on less.

What would the princesses have done?

Written their own endings. Her mother's voice comes into her mind, clear and strong.

And all of a sudden, she knows what to do.

Ellen—thanks for your email. Given the amount of work Mom's already done on the manuscript . . . close to completion . . . finish it myself. I'm not a published writer . . . but grew up immersed in her stories . . . she did name me as manager of her literary estate. With a talented editor . . .

The reply comes back in minutes.

Mothers and daughters . . . process mirroring content . . .

And then the bottom line.

I think I can sell this plan to Jody.

Yes, okay.

How has this happened? Somehow, Saskia thinks, slamming the computer shut with such force that Wolfie jumps awake, her list keeps growing. Somehow her quests keep multiplying. She doesn't just have to save the Elf House. Doesn't just have to find the women, doesn't just have to cancel Patrick. Doesn't just have to save herself.

Now she has to finish a whole motherfucking book, too.

Chapter 12

"Let me get this straight," said the miller's daughter. "You want to tell me what to do with the child I shall bear? You want to tell me what to do with my body?"

Rumpelstiltskin winced. "No, it's not that, I just want—"

But she cut him off. "No, Rumpelstiltskin. You see, I'm pretty sure that capitalist structures have gone to your head. Nothing's worth losing control over my own body." She shook her head. "I shouldn't have lied about being able to spin straw into gold. I see that now. And I am willing to accept the consequences."

And when the morning came, she confessed her falsehood to the King. And the King was so overcome by her honesty and her integrity that he proposed on the spot. They did not have children but instead ended up lavishing affection on their three corgis and spending extensive time abroad, and neither of them ever heard from Rumpelstiltskin again.

—*Fairy Tales for Little Feminists:*
The Miller's Daughter, Evelyn Harper Kreis

June 1997

SASKIA WAS FOURTEEN, AND NONE OF WHAT HAP-pened next was inevitable. She was still just a girl, sitting on top of a professor's desk as he held a damp rag beneath her nose. It felt too awkward to look into his eyes, so she looked beyond him instead, to the framed black-and-white photos clustered on his walls. They were beautiful at first, but shocking once your eyes started to break them down. Emaciated men, dotted with strange, irregular bruises. Men under quilts, men sipping water.

There were so many bodies. She didn't know what she was supposed to say, but she knew from attending her mother's shows that she was supposed to say something.

"Those are intense," was what she finally settled on.

Patrick laughed. "Yeah, well. They're not nearly as decorative as your mom's stuff, that's for sure." She tried to keep her face blank, but confusion must have leaked through all the same. "Pretty. They're not as pretty."

"Oh." She'd never thought of Evie's hand series as pretty, exactly. And the princesses, well, Evie tried to make them look like everyday girls.

"It's a hard line to walk. The collectors who really know their stuff, they don't care about how aesthetically pleasing something is. The grittiness, the intensity—the reality, they want it, they love it. But there aren't many of those around here. Most people just want something that looks nice to hang over their sofas. No offense to your mother, of course."

Patrick was talking to her like she was an adult, and Saskia nodded, pushed her hair back behind her ear. But she wasn't sure why it was bad to make something pretty. People had to look at what was on their walls, after all. That was where they lived their lives.

The curiosity overrode her fear of looking naïve. "It's bad, to be decorative?"

"No," Patrick said slowly, drawing out the word in a way that meant yes. "No. It's just one of the cruelties of the art world. The frivolous rake in the cash, while serious artists— Do you need another rag?" he cut himself off.

She glanced down at the cloth, already soaked through.

"Yeah," she admitted, and he turned back to the sink.

It should have made her angry, his suggestion that her mother wasn't a serious artist. She was a tenured professor, wasn't she? She had gallery shows, didn't she? But each retort fizzled and died on Saskia's tongue.

Because the truth was that she liked what he was saying about her mother, and she liked that he was saying it to her. He was confirming something she'd always suspected: Evie was a glorified amateur, a one-trick pony. They were the real artists, Patrick and Saskia. Their work was pure, uncorrupted.

And they could recognize that in each other, even when the rest of the world could not.

She grabbed the new rag from Patrick, held it to her nose. It smelled of chemicals: like metal, like photographs.

Could he see the pulse in her throat? She could feel it throbbing. Pulled her chin down to try to stop it.

"Uh-uh," he said, a dry finger tapping her chin. "Head back."

She made a face but complied.

"I know," he said with a laugh. "How boring. Tell me about something, then . . . tell me what you're playing right now."

"It wouldn't mean anything to you."

His voice was gentle, insistent. "Tell me anyway."

"Liszt. *La Campanella*," she said. "And then I'll go home to study Ravel's *Gaspard de la Nuit*."

"Study it?"

"Yeah. Sometimes it's easier for me to think about the music when I'm not at the piano. And this one—it's all trembly, wobbly, but there's this really mathematical side to it, too—" She stopped herself. He wasn't a pianist. He didn't care. (Not that other pianists seemed to care much, either; she couldn't understand why.)

"Go on." He set a hand on her knee, and she shook her head, hair falling loose around her shoulders.

"Nah. It's hard to explain."

Her heart thrummed so hard that it seemed impossible that he couldn't hear it, too. There was nowhere for her to look, nowhere to look, nowhere to go.

And, she realized with an electric buzz, she didn't want to go anywhere.

His hand was still holding the rag to her face and, like a reflex, movement without thinking, like the C-major scale. She reached up and covered it with hers.

A shaft of sunlight fell across her face, but she fought to keep her eyes wide, open for him. To see everything he did, everything he was, as the daylight burned through her corneas.

January 2020

SHE WANTS ALLIES. SHE NEEDS ALLIES. ONE VOICE alone yields nothing; one voice alone yields, at most, suspicion. It takes Saskia six days to track down Kelly. Facebook yields nothing. The UWM archives seemed promising, once she'd figured out how to use her mother's password to navigate the labyrinthine system—but though there were numerous Kellys in the art and design program in 1991, further research proved each one to be the wrong Kelly: this one brunette, that one Black.

In the meantime, Saskia is running every morning. In the meantime, she is doing hand exercises, trying to get the stiffness in her fingers to go away. In the meantime, she texts Josh an apology, asks if they can meet up when things are easier. The rapidity of his response calms her. *Of course.*

How you doing? James's message pings through at almost the same moment. She stares at it for a minute, then reaches down deep.

I'm sad. And I'm scared.

Typing it, admitting it, makes her feel better. And when his response finally comes back hours later, a sad-face emoji, it's interesting: she feels almost nothing at all. Because she'd expected nothing from him.

But a part of her wishes she had someone she could expect things from.

Finally, the answer comes to her when she's out on a run.

The pre-college program.

Patrick's baby.

As soon as she gets home, she grabs her laptop, navigates to the UWM administrator portal. And there she is: Kelly Sutherland. Enrolled in the art and design pre-college program, summer 1991.

Once Saskia has a last name, it takes ten minutes to figure out that Kelly is now a kindergarten teacher at Atwater Elementary. Five minutes to drive over there. Thirty minutes to find parking, because Saskia hasn't been in an elementary school since she was *in* elementary school and had forgotten the afternoon pickup frenzy, the way that parents and children somehow found the correct pairings in the great daily mob. She ends up parking up by St. Robert's Church.

The words she plans to say echo through her head like a tune as she walks over the icy sidewalks to the school. *We have to show the world who he really is. We have to band together to be believed.* It's a strange feeling; she's used to having either songs or numbers running through her mind, but this is something else. Is this what it felt like to be a writer? She does sound like her mother in those sentences, she realizes, and scraps them. She'll play it more casual. Play it by ear.

The redbrick building gives off a cozy, almost cottage-y feeling; it exudes baby ducks and Laura Ashley and story time. It implies a childhood Saskia would have liked to have.

It is also surprisingly easy to get into the school. She just walks in the door, then looks at the room directory to see that Miss Sutherland is in room 104. No security guards, none of the restrictions that she'd been taught public schools now employ to keep kids safe. And while a few adults give her passing glances in the hall, they really do just scan her, skip away. She looks like a parent, she realizes, and wants to laugh. She's older than most of the parents here, probably. And God help whatever kind of child she would end up having.

Miss Sutherland's room is surrounded by coat hooks at the level of Saskia's waist. Above them, huge cutout clouds, a sun emerging behind them. Construction paper raindrops, and—

"Can I help you?"

After hours studying her pictures, Saskia would know Kelly anywhere. She recognizes her almond eyes (though they're pale brown, and she'd been imagining them blue), her waves of thick honey-colored hair. But the three-dimensionality of her is somehow a surprise: the scent of rosewater coming off of her in stale waves, a scent Saskia hasn't smelled since Granny Kreis was still alive—

"You're not one of my parents, are you?" Kelly asks with a broad smile. "The kids are all out in the parking lot with the bus monitors, but—"

"Patrick Kintner," Saskia says. She'd meant to phrase it as a question, but she couldn't find the correct words. *Are you Patrick Kintner's ex?* was wrong. *Are you one of Patrick Kintner's victims?*—well, that was wrong, too. What were they?

But ultimately, all that she needed to say was his name. The color starts to drain out of Kelly's face, as though she's fading into one of her photos.

"You'd better come in," she says, and pushes the door fully open with a single, shaking hand.

"Sorry," Saskia says, letting the huge alphabet, the flags of the world, the explosion of color in the room, wrap around her, cushion them. "I'm sorry. I just—Patrick. You used to know him?"

"So, you finally caught him," Kelly says, collapsing into the one adult-size chair in the room. Saskia perches carefully on a child's desk across from her. "I've been wondering, the past few years, if it would ever happen. Are you from the police department, or the university—"

Saskia shakes her head.

"No. No one sent me. I was—" The acid rises in her mouth at the same time as the words. "I don't know what we were. I don't know that there's a good word for it, or any kind of word for it. But whatever we were . . . I think you might have been it, too."

That *too* sticks in her throat.

Kelly sets her head in her hands, runs fingers through her thick hair. She's muttering something; it takes Saskia a moment to make it out.

"I'm sorry," she finally hears. "I'm so, so sorry."

"Why are you— You didn't do anything to me," Saskia says. Why should Kelly pity her? They are the same, aren't they? They are almost the same.

But she's been thinking of Kelly as a victim this past week, after forcing herself away from her initial, jealous conception of the girl as a tempting seductress.

They are the same. But Saskia is not yet ready to be a victim, she's realizing.

And Kelly looks up, meets her gaze. "Didn't I?" she says. "If I'd told anyone. If I'd told a parent, a teacher. Would he have kept going?"

Julia. The unspoken third name. The name that Kelly doesn't even know. It hovers on Saskia's tongue. She, too. Saskia also could have stopped it.

"It was wrong," Saskia says, her voice coming out husky. "It was wrong, what he did to us." And, as she says the words, she realizes: she believes them.

Kelly doesn't say anything.

"And I want to make him pay."

Kelly laughs, dry. "So, what. A court case? It's too late for me. Statute of limitations is up. Yeah," she says to Saskia's surprised expression. "Yeah. My daughter turned fourteen last year. And I just . . . I started remembering. So, I looked into it. And I realized I missed the window of opportunity. I'm too old, the statute of limitations has expired."

Saskia closes her eyes, trying to come up with a brief explanation. To tell Kelly that yes, she wants to bring him to court, but no, it's for a different reason—and the worst thing that will happen to him is that he won't get something he currently doesn't have.

But Kelly doesn't need to know that.

"Not a court case. I mean, maybe we say what we say and the police will go after him, it's happened before. But—what I really want to do is actually say it. Loudly. Publicly. What happened between us. But the thing is—it means so much less, coming from just one person. Because if I say it, if I tell—I want to fucking be believed."

Kelly bites her lip. "Okay. So say we go ahead and talk to a journalist— that *is* what you're suggesting?" Saskia nods, not trusting herself to spew out any more garbled responses. "So, we go to a journalist. We tell our stories. What would that do? What would that possibly accomplish?"

"A whole lot," Saskia says, her eyes flaring. "First of all, I bet you anything they'd throw him out of the university. Maybe take away his pension. Galleries would stop showing his work. The museum would have to take down our fucking photos—"

"Photos?" Kelly's arched brows shoot up. "He still has those photos?" She jumps to her feet, flips around to the whiteboard, and begins erasing furiously. A drawing of a house, a square base and a rectangular roof; and then it's gone.

"You haven't been down to the art museum lately, I take it." Saskia pulls out her phone, pulls up the images from the virtual exhibition. Has to approach Kelly from the side to get her to look at them. The expression on her face is part relief, part something else. Shame.

"Oh. Those. But . . ." She hesitates. "There are much, much worse photos. Of me, at least."

Saskia licks her dry lips. There's no reason to make this any harder than it already is, for either of them. She doesn't think there are other photos of her. She doesn't even remember this one being taken. But she'd remember *that*.

"All the more reason—"

But Kelly's furiously erasing the blank whiteboard still. "I have a kid. I have a job. I don't—I can't—"

Saskia watches the woman convince herself, and there's nothing she can say, because yes. Yes, of course. Not everybody thinks that being right is worth the risk of letting those kinds of photos out into the world. Saskia isn't even sure *she* would think it's worth it, if she were Kelly. If those kinds of photos existed of her.

She watches Kelly's golden hair shaking with the force of her movement, and she realizes. She thought she just wanted an ally. And she does, of course she does; she wants several of them.

But, in coming here, she also wanted to prove something to herself. To hold on to the belief that somehow, she was still the special one. That there was something in her relationship with Patrick that was different, that was loving. That was real.

That was about *her.*

It's a small loss, almost an insignificant one in comparison with the recent earthquakes on the terrain of her life. And yet a tiny, sad part of her watches Kelly, and she knows: in a fundamental way. On a profound level. They are the same.

He made them the same.

She watches Kelly's arm swipe up and down on the board. Saskia grabs her wrist, freezes her. But Kelly still won't look her in the eyes.

"Don't you want to hear him say it?" Saskia asks. "Don't you want to be the one to *force* him to say it?"

"Say what?"

"That what he did . . . that it was wrong."

"But I know what he did was wrong," Kelly says, finally turning toward her, her forehead wrinkling. "I don't need him to tell me that."

Chapter 13

The Prince was climbing up her hair. Ever closer, ever advancing.

Suddenly, Rapunzel felt a chill sweep through her.

She didn't know this man. She didn't know if he was good or bad. She didn't know if he preferred dancing or jousting, swimming or running, tea with milk or with lemon.

The sight of his body mounting her braid filled her with disgust, and before she knew what she was doing, she shook her head, sharply.

She sighed as she watched his screaming body fall.

"Well," she said. "Looks like I'm just going to have to save myself."

—*Fairy Tales for Little Feminists:*
Rapunzel, Evelyn Harper Kreis

June 1997

SASKIA WAS FOURTEEN, AND SHE COULD FEEL Patrick's breath on her face as he stood before her.

"You have wonderful bone structure, you know."

She laughed. "Yeah, people are always complimenting me on my skeleton."

He smiled, but his gaze was probing. His finger drifted to the side of her nose, to the apple of her cheek. "I bet you photograph well."

She could feel her skin warming beneath his touch but couldn't bring herself to duck out of it. Was he going to kiss her? No. But then again, he might. How would she know?

He held a dry cloth to her face, took the bloody ones away, leaving them in a disgusting damp pile in the sink.

"I wonder," he said. "I've been doing a series on contemporary Midwestern adolescence. Would you be interested in taking part?"

He'd returned, was standing close again, and she couldn't figure out if she was supposed to hop off the desk or not. Eventually, she did an awkward half slide, half wriggle, down the side of the desk to avoid pressing her body against his.

"What, in having you take my picture?"

He nodded.

"Not—like that . . . ?" Waving her hand at the skeletal limbs framed on his wall.

"No," he said, laughing. "No, nothing like that. Just you being you, that's all."

"Sure," she said, and immediately worried she sounded too eager. She had no idea how to navigate this situation. How did other girls learn this stuff? "Yeah, whatever."

But Patrick was already crouched over his desk, scribbling furiously on a card.

"Here's the address," he said finally, slipping it into her hand. "Saturday, two thirty?"

She nodded. And throughout her practice that day, she kept it propped up on the music stand beside the score. The words, *PATRICK KINTNER, ART AND DESIGN*, pounding at her with every note.

January 2020

NOT KELLY, THEN. BUT SASKIA HAS TO GET AT LEAST one other woman on her side before she calls a journalist. She has *The New Yorker* reporter's email address written in block letters in her notebook, though she can't bring herself to actually write the email just yet. Maybe Julia, when she finds her, will have the words to describe what they did.

No. Not what *they* did. What he did to them.

And yet the loss has hollowed Saskia out. Made her question everything. She has to stop, to catalog everything she knows now, versus what she thought she knew.

She knows that she loved him. She knows now that he made her believe that.

She knows that he broke up with her. She knows now that she'd grown too old for him.

She knows that he's been the specter haunting her relationships for the past twenty years. She knows now that it wasn't her who was broken.

But she doesn't know what any of this makes her.

Julia is likely another pre-college alum, but Saskia can't bring herself to track her down just yet. She needs a plan, a better plan than she had with Kelly, which was no plan at all. And, in the meantime, it's increasingly apparent that there's more to her Milwaukee life than there is waiting for her back in New York. (WHEN *are you coming home?* James texts. WHEN *are you leaving your wife?* she almost texts back, but stops herself, writes nothing. After all, what if he did it?)

For starters, she has to play hostess.

At six the next day, Saskia takes the gold-leaf china out of the sideboard piece by piece. The dust on it is as thick as her thumb, and she curses, goes to get dish soap and a clean cloth, wiping off each setting before placing it on the dining room table and returning for the next. The set is as old as the house, and they almost never use it. The last time she can remember was when Saskia won some competition and they'd invited Carrie for dinner. It's the gold leaf as much as the provenance of the plates that makes them almost unusable; you can't put them in the dishwasher.

Lexi and Georgia are coming over for dinner. And she thinks that the text that pings her phone a few minutes beforehand must be them—*can we bring anything, we're running late.* But it's Gina.

Jos is gone.

Saskia runs into the butler's pantry out of instinct; it's where their landline used to be. The pane of glass over the family silver section has cracked straight down the middle, while spiderwebs swing freely between the cabinets and the marble counter. This fucking house. Who *could* keep it clean?

"Gina, what the fuck?"

"I'm just . . . Saskia, where *is* she?" Gina's normally placid alto has gone rough around the edges, frayed from crying or screaming or both. "She hasn't been in touch with you, has she?"

"With me? No! If she had, I would've told you right away!" Her blood is rushing through her veins. Bubbling up, boiling.

"It's just when she does this, she usually runs to some friend, some relative . . . and you're about as far away as she could get, which seems to be what she wants right now, and she thinks you're the fucking coolest—"

"Hey. Hey. Hold on. You've got to think straight here, Gina. She's mad because you forbade her to see her boyfriend." Her heartbeat slows to a death march at the realization that nobody ever did this for her. That she hadn't been forbidden from seeing Patrick, much less searched for. Another small, sore spot at the core of her, and she takes a deep breath. "A thousand bucks says she's with him."

"That— Oh, I am going to *murder*—"

Saskia lets Gina go off, though she's confused. Gina should have thought of this. Gina *would* have thought of this, if she were less unhinged right now.

"You have someone who can come by and stay with you?" Sas asks. "Your sister?"

"In Florida. Oh. But I could call Bobby."

"I thought you hated Bobby."

"Oh, yeah. But when I think about what Bobby would do to that kid, the boyfriend—"

The doorbell rings.

"You sure you're going to be okay? Call the police if you don't find her in the next fifteen minutes."

After ending the call, Saskia goes to the foyer, Wolfie at her heels and her father trailing down the stairs. How long will it be before Jocelyn realizes what a good thing her mother is doing, has done? Will she be twenty? Thirty? Will it ever happen?

When she opens the door, the sight of Georgia and Lexi between the elves momentarily stops her heart.

Arm in arm. Mother and daughter.

"Come in, come in!" she cries, and her voice is too loud, too fake, but it's the only one she can muster. They slide their beige coats off—Georgia's camel-hair Diane von Furstenberg, Lexi's J.Crew—and Saskia hangs them in the closet, then bustles them into the living room for drinks.

Thank God Georgia doesn't bring up their lunch date—or the Queen Anne tea set Saskia dropped off the other day. Though that's the last thing Mike would care about.

"How have things been in Chicago, Lex?"

"Cold! Colder even than here. This time of year, I always start looking at Zillow listings in L.A."

Georgia tousles her daughter's hair.

"Don't you dare!"

The microwave beeps and Saskia trots off to the kitchen. Though it had seemed like a total waste of money, Saskia is grateful that her dad suggested takeout from Beans & Barley, as she plates the rosemary chicken, the honey-glazed carrots, and the garlic mashed potatoes in the porcelain serving dishes.

"Dinner's on!" she calls through the archway, trying to pull out the fake Southern, fake homey accent her mother always used for the phrase. It just comes out weirdly British, though, and the three of them blink at her before getting to their feet, drinks in hand.

It had felt too strange to take her mother's place at the foot of the table. Too strange, too, to have her father sit at the head across from nobody. Saskia finally settled on seating the families across from each other. It makes the long table feel cozier, she thinks, standing to pour the good white her father chose.

"It still feels like we should be giving you girls milk," Georgia says with a laugh.

"Yeah, the three glasses a day we grew up with? It's amazing we found room for anything else," Lexi says.

"At least at your house, you always had Nesquik syrup," Saskia adds, trying to join in the boisterousness. "But Mom would never . . . Mom would . . ." She can't even finish the sentence. Nobody will meet her eyes.

"So, Lexi . . ." The mild, resonant boom from Mike. "How are things in advertising?"

"It's not advertising, Uncle Mike," Lexi says. "It's influencing."

Mike pierces a carrot, takes a small bite. "Oh? How's it different?"

Lexi's hazel eyes light up. "Well, influencing is not about spreading awareness. And it's not really about selling." Saskia stifles a snort. "It's about putting a particular product or service in front of a particular audience in an organic way, a way that's meant to speak to them without them realizing they're being spoken to. Curating content."

For a moment, Mike is speechless, and Saskia can feel the gravitational pull of her father's gaze on her.

He used to stand at Evie's dressing table, rolling a jar back and forth in his palms. *Moisturizer,* he'd mutter, rolling his eyes.

Evie, snatching it back: *And what's wrong with* moisturizer?

It's not a word, Evie! It's just a face cream. I hate the goddamn bastardization of the English language at the altar of capitalism.

Evie had laughed, great gales of laughter. Kissed him.

Saskia forces herself to keep looking at Lexi.

"Curating?" Mike finally manages.

"Yep! Content curation."

Georgia's looking at her daughter with smiling eyes, and Saskia doesn't think it's fake. She doesn't know how it's possible, but then again . . . well, it's Georgia.

"And what do you curate?" His voice is polite, but it's got that extrasmooth edge to it. *Don't answer,* Saskia wants to warn Lexi. *It's a trap.* She casts a look at Mike, but he just grins, takes a bite of the chicken.

"Wellness products," Lexi says.

His eyes narrow in a simulacrum of polite confusion.

"Medicine?"

He knows wellness isn't medicine—she isn't sure why he's teasing Lexi this way.

"No, not medicine exactly—I mean, I'm not a doctor! I make sure my followers know that. But, like . . . preventative products people can use to optimize their physical well-being."

Mike opens his mouth to speak and Saskia kicks his shin.

"I know, I know." Georgia's palms are up and she grins at Mike. "It's all Greek to me, too. But I will say, it pays the bills. Rather well, too." She pats her daughter's hand, and Lexi squeezes it, looks back at Mike with a smirk.

"We can't all be heiresses, you know."

Lexi is looking at Mike as she says it, but the comment is directed at Saskia. And despite her mother's muffled "Christ, Lexi—" her smirk remains. Sas just shrugs. Fine, she can be the rich bitch for Lexi, if that's what she needs. She's been enough people's abstract nouns in her life— prodigy, virtuoso, muse. What's the harm in one more?

But Mike is snorting. Then laughing.

"Saskia? An heiress?" Mike squeezes her shoulder before throwing his head back in another laugh.

Lexi's eyes dart around the room, from the chandelier to the china shelves, through the carved arch to the piano.

"Evie left the house to Patrick Kintner. A family friend," Mike says, regaining his composure. Georgia's hand flies to her mouth as Lexi blinks in the news.

"I'm so sorry, it was a terrible joke, I never would have—"

But Mike just shakes his head, smiles softly.

"What are you going to do?" Lexi asks, looking directly at Saskia, and for once, she's utterly guileless.

Saskia feels like a sponge that's been twisted tight.

"I don't know," she says in her voice that is barely a voice at all.

She wants to tell Lexi all of it. About finding herself pinned to the museum wall. Patrick's appointments with Evie last summer. Tara. Kelly. Atwater. But she still doesn't have the whole story, and she's not sure it would make sense to anyone who's not her.

She's not ready to have another person look at her with Sheila's incredulous eyes.

But she does manage a shaky smile at Lex. And is surprised to see her old friend smiling in return.

Before she goes to bed that night, Sas checks her phone and finds a message from Gina: *She was at fucking Bobby's.*

Better than the boyfriend, Saskia writes back.

Barely.

It surprises her, how relieved she feels that Jos wasn't with the boy.

She has a thousand things she could say, none of which Gina would want to hear—Saskia's not a parent, after all—and so she just sends back an emoji wiping sweat from its brow, followed by a heart. Gina sends back poop.

Chapter 14

"It's very simple," said the Sea Witch. "All you have to do to become human is to give up your voice."

The Little Mermaid bit her lip.

"But my voice—" she said. "My voice is how I tell people where my boundaries are. My voice is how I set limits. No. You can take anything you like, but I won't let you take away my voice."

—*Fairy Tales for Little Feminists:*
The Little Mermaid, Evelyn Harper Kreis

June 1997

SASKIA WAS FOURTEEN, AND PATRICK WAS A SONG she couldn't get out of her head. He was the bass line echoing through everything she did for a week. Brushing her teeth, he was there. Doing her homework, he was there. At the piano—he was always, always there.

And on Saturday, she waved goodbye to Carrie and walked the six blocks down Downer to the address of the studio he'd given her. But it was funny, as she checked the note again—the address was actually two blocks south of the commercial strip, it wasn't a professional studio at all. So where was she going?

The address, when she reached it, turned out to be an apartment building. Turn-of-the-century red brick, bracketing a central courtyard. Her whole body was lit up with a kind of buzzing, an excitement and a something else, and her breath was coming out shaky. She did her pre-performance breathing exercises to slow it as she found his name, listened closely to his garbled instructions, and followed them up to the third floor, the top floor. The final door on the left, his door, was already cracked open by the time she reached the top. She knocked anyway, knuckles brushing tentatively against the wood. After all, what if she'd got it wrong? What if it wasn't his?

And then the door swung open and there he was.

He filled up almost the whole frame, he was so tall. After a week of imagining him, there was a hyper-realness to his presence that unnerved her. She'd forgotten about how tan he was, though summer had just begun. About the vague smell of photo chemicals he emitted, sweet and tangy. About the way his eyes disappeared into sunbursts as he smiled.

The way they did then.

"Saskia Kreis," he said, and stepped back to let her pass. "Come in, come in."

The apartment was an extension of his office: the same black-and-white photos, the same type of framed album covers. Though here, the Dylan wasn't *Blonde on Blonde* but instead *The Basement Tapes*. To its side, Creedence Clearwater Revival, Bruce Springsteen, the Rolling Stones.

"You really like old music, huh," she said.

"I mean," he said, laughing in that low growl that sent vibrations through her, "it's not the Spice Girls."

She put all of the acid she could muster into her voice. "Like I would listen to the Spice Girls."

"So what do you listen to?"

He walked into the open kitchen area, and she turned to follow him. Felt stupid standing there all of a sudden and hopped up on a stool. The wicker of the seat cut into the backs of her legs, and she pulled her skin away. But when she set her leg back down, the grooves still pressed, deepening the welts.

"Martha Argerich right now," she said. "She's just put this three-disc album out—nobody does Chopin like her. Nobody. Not even me," she said, and laughed at her own hubris.

But he didn't laugh, though the lines around his eyes appeared. He just looked at her.

"What?" she said, twisting her feet around the stool legs.

He tilted his head as he studied her with those fiery eyes.

"You're not like other girls," he said.

And the spark within her rose, burst into delighted, giggling flames in her chest.

She lifted her eyes to him with a cat grin. "No," she said. "I'm not."

He made her a coffee on his fancy bronze machine, a mocha; she'd only ever had coffee at her parents' dinner parties, and then only drowning in milk and sugar. She took a sip, expecting to hate the bitterness of it, and stared down into the mug when the sweetness coated her tongue instead. An adult drink she enjoyed. Maybe there was space for her in this world.

Maybe she was ready for it.

And then, just when she was vibrating with the caffeine, the camera.

She reached for her bag, but he didn't want her to change clothes, wanted to capture her in her Abercrombie & Fitch. All right. She started to get up, to move toward the light, but he wanted photos of her there, on the stool. All right. He brought her her Discman, had her put on her headphones and listen to the Argerich.

All right.

How many photographs? A hundred. Two. He couldn't possibly need that many of her, and she disliked the feeling of being watched from the side, seeing the brown-and-gold blur only in her peripheral vision, as Martha played in her ears, as she looked down at the faux marble grain of the counter, stared up at the huge blank expanse of the refrigerator.

The body shots done, he approached.

"Should we do some close-ups now?"

Before she'd even nodded, he had one hand on either side of the stool and was twisting her toward him. She couldn't believe how close he was. This close, the only part of him she could really see was his eyes. She could feel the camera bumping between them from the strap around his neck. She could feel his arms still emanating heat on either side of her body. But the only thing she could see was his eyes.

She leaned forward. She kissed him.

She'll never forget that. Not at fourteen. Not ever.

And then she pulled back, stunned at her own daring, and watched his face.

"You're so beautiful," Patrick said.

Saskia was fourteen, and "beautiful" was not a word she had ever heard used to describe herself before. Special, yes. Talented, constantly. Pretty, sometimes; but always in that horrible, condescending tone. *Well. Look how pretty you are.*

There was the word, and then there was him. Him, between her knees, touching her face so gently, so tenderly, as the sun hit her eyes. His were a lion's eyes, his stared back at her, his were looking at her like she was a miracle. Not what she could do. Not what she could play. Just the fact of her.

And so it was not a surprise when he moved, closed the distance between them again. As she heard, then felt, his breath approaching; hot and gentle. It was not a surprise. The surprise was the feel of him against her lips. The questioning, the hesitancy. The softness. The momentary brush, like a butterfly's wings.

She kept her eyes closed for a long time after, the echoes of him reverberating through her skin.

And that day, that day when their lips brushed together for the first time. Then the second time, and the third.

All she could think was: Yes. I'm a person, now.

January 2020

THE MILWAUKEE RIVER RUNS ALONG THE LOWER East Side, dividing the city. It always makes Saskia think of drives out to Granny Kreis's house, before she was six and grandparentless for good. To get to the West Side, they had to drive past the river and through downtown, over the highway with its smell of hops and yeast and gasoline, sweet chemicals nauseating. Back then, the area where Julia's yoga studio now stands had been ramshackle, vacant lots and lower-middle-class homes in disrepair. Decades later, gentrification has crept in: it's all glass and metal condos and gastropubs and river views.

In her bag, Saskia carries a series of articles. What can happen when women band together: the Weinstein case. What happens to a woman on her own: Woody Allen. Even if she doesn't get Julia to come around today, she'll leave them with her. Show her how important it is for them to join voices. To say: *Our lives could have looked so different.*

To say it together.

But, of course, she does not know what Julia's life looks like now. If the yoga studio is anything to go by, it's bright and airy, pale wood and glass letting the winter sunshine in. Its smell, cedar and lavender, is so different from her own gym's disinfectant, and she wonders, suddenly, if maybe Julia is happy. Maybe she won't want to dig up the past, will prefer to let sleeping men lie.

If Saskia's life looked like this, maybe she would, too.

But she has to know.

"Hi!" Saskia says at the front desk. It's her Milwaukee voice again, bright and syrupy, and she tries to calm her register. "I'm looking for Julia Manchin. Is she—"

"Her class should just be finishing up in Studio A," the sleek yoga girl behind the counter says. "You can wait, if you want."

So, Saskia hovers in the hallway, peering through the door to the studio. It's crowded; who are these women who can take an 11:00 A.M. yoga class? Well. Saskia could, actually. If she were that kind of woman.

After the namaste, after the rest of the women roll up their mats and prance away, Saskia reaches out a hand.

"Julia?"

The instructor turns to her with a broad smile.

"Can I talk to you for a moment?"

"Sure, what's up?" Julia leans back against the wall, arms folded over her chest. There's something tightly wound beneath her yogi surface, Saskia can see it in the clutch of her bare toes against the floor.

"It's about Patrick Kintner."

And the tightening of the fingers around the mat—

"Oh my God. Is he okay? Did something . . . did something happen to him? Are you from the police?"

Why do people keep asking her this? In what world does she look like a cop? She's starting to understand why her mother wore makeup.

"No, it's— Can we talk privately?"

Julia leads her tentatively through a door. Saskia vaguely expected it to lead to a staff room of some kind, but they're in the locker room. A nice one, nothing like the bare-bones lockers and benches they have at the boxing gym. Steam creeping from a sauna in the back. Women wrapped in plush towels, body and hair, as they pat their faces with cream in mirrors above piles of high-end soap and vases of fresh flowers.

As the instructor leads her to a bench in the back, Saskia realizes that Julia smells like essential oils, like patchouli and jasmine. Saskia wonders what she's trying to cure herself of.

They sit and look at each other.

"So," Julia says. "Patrick."

"Yeah. I've been going through some things lately, and I . . . I guess I wanted to talk to you about what happened between you and Patrick."

Julia's taut face relaxes in relief, and hope surges in Sas. Is it possible that Julia's just been waiting all of these years for someone to ask her?

"Oh my God," Julia says, and sets a manicured hand on Saskia's arm. "Are you his girlfriend? It was over between us, like, ages ago. You really don't have to worry. We're just friends now."

"Are you still in touch?" The words are out before she realizes she's speaking, and she curses herself. They came from that hard little ball of jealousy she's storing just behind her breastbone. But, she tells herself, this is relevant. She does need to know.

A slim shoulder rises. "A bit. We get coffee every few months. And the two of you . . ."

Saskia's head spins as she tries to take this in. The girl Julia had been—how could adult Julia betray her in this way, staying *friends* with the man? Then again, Saskia had nearly done the same. Trotting into his office, grinning at him. Luxuriating in his smell.

The memory doesn't make it easier to forgive Julia, though. It just makes it harder to forgive herself.

"No. No," Saskia says. "I dated him back in the nineties." That word, *dated*. It's wrong, but what other words are there? None that feel right.

Huge eyes stare at her. Huge and green and blank.

"I was fourteen," Saskia clarifies.

Julia's face breaks into a smile again. She looks just like a child.

"Oh," she says, knowing. Conspiratorial. "So, he was your first love, too."

Even though Saskia thought this herself for years, it still stuns her to hear someone else say it out loud. "I was fourteen," Saskia repeats.

"I was sixteen," Julia offers. She really thinks they're having a different conversation. "God, he was so romantic. You know he named his boat after me?"

Saskia squints, trying to remember. But she would have remembered that. "*The Julia*? Really?"

Julia rolls her eyes. "I mean, he couldn't. Obviously. No, *The Ingenue*. But we both knew. I was so into him. Tore my poor little heart into a million pieces when we broke up."

Saskia knows this version of the story. Saskia told herself this version of the story for about two decades.

Saskia believed this version of the story herself until eleven days ago.

And she pauses, teetering on the cliff's edge between belief and reality. And for a flash, Saskia also can't remember what was wrong with the situation. Hadn't she wanted Patrick? Of course she had. Hadn't he been good to her? Yeah, he'd been a great boyfriend. Or, at least, a good one, she thinks. She didn't know exactly—it's not like she had other points of comparison.

There—that's what was wrong with the situation.

But could she make herself believe it again? Better to be the happily ignorant Julia than the quietly suffering Kelly, after all.

She knows that she can't, not now that she's seen her picture—on the gallery wall, in a rack in the museum gift shop; she's seen her picture and she's seen the others.

And no: she can't ever go back.

Even if she wanted to.

"Julia," Saskia says, low, "that boat's always been called *The Ingenue*."

A crease between Julia's eyebrows. A split second before she shakes her head.

"No," she says firmly. "No."

"It's been called that since at least the late nineties," Saskia says.

"Sorry," Julia says, hand slapping down against her thigh. "But what is it, exactly, that you want?"

It's hard to let it go. The fact of the boat's name, the fact she knows for sure. But how could she prove it? And, even if she could—what would that get her? Julia would just find another reason not to believe her.

"Okay, let's say that it wasn't. Let's say he *did* name it for you. Doesn't that still set off alarm bells? Isn't that a total red flag?" Saskia asks, trying to swallow the bitter taste of the hypothetical she knows to be false, failing. "He obviously had something to hide. He knew he had to hide your relationship. Otherwise it *would* be *The Julia*, wouldn't it?" She wants to go on. Wants to say: *And isn't there something in that word*, Ingenue, *that makes you want to claw at his skin? The erasing of everything else you were into a stock character, an archetype. The removal of individuality, uniqueness, of everything that made you special. Doesn't it hurt?* But Julia's eyes are already rolling upward, her face already folding into a smirk.

"I mean," Julia says, "he's practical, that's all. What if we'd broken up and he had to redo all of the registration and all that stuff. . . ." They sit for a moment in silence, neither knowing anything about boat-naming practices.

What Julia says makes sense, perfect sense, in the story that she's telling herself. Saskia knows, Saskia recognizes it; she's only a millimeter removed from telling herself that same story.

It's the fact that both stories exist that negates them. Julia's story and Saskia's old one—that Patrick loved them despite their age, that they were special, that they were unique. They can't both be true at the same time. They're mutually exclusive.

But she doesn't know how to explain that to Julia. Saskia has the sensation of being back in college, of being forced to do group work with idiots and trying to explain the most basic concepts to them. She was a terrible teacher, could never make them see. Why couldn't they *see*?

"Julia," she says slowly, "we were teenagers. Those weren't consensual relationships; they couldn't be. They were crimes. Take a look at—" She rifles in her bag, shoves the stack of articles into Julia's hands.

But Julia hops to her feet. She sets the papers on the counter across the way and starts finger-combing her hair in the mirror.

"I mean, yes and no. It was and it wasn't. Maybe technically, but it's like . . . come on." Julia pauses for a moment, gaze frozen on Saskia's in the mirror. "What do you want, anyway? Are you, like, planning to sue him?"

What can she say? What could she have told herself to make herself see? She scrolls through her phone quickly, pulling up the art museum page with their portraits that's still open in her browser from the other day with Kelly. She holds it up; Julia blinks at it, blinks away.

"He's a *photographer*. We were subjects. So what? What are you trying to prove?"

Saskia stares at her hand, suspended in midair. She can't believe that someone could see these photos and not know there was something wrong.

But then again—the curators had. The public seemed to.

She has to tell her story. She has to tell it or the indifference will erase her.

"He was a middle-aged man sleeping with teenagers. One after the other after the other. Seducing us. Making us *his*. We *were* his subjects, in more ways than one. Don't you think he should pay for that?"

And Julia's eyes, as she whirls around, have turned hard, though she's smiling tightly.

That gaze, that smile. It hits her in the gut. Saskia recognizes it too clearly from night after night with disappointing men. She thinks of the time spent alone in her apartment staring at her phone, the banter-bordering-on-cruelty that she'd sent to Tim. The code she's developed with James. She thinks about the distance between her and her mother. And she sees: it didn't have to be this way. She never had to feel unloved, unlovable. She never had to feel so alone.

"I—" Julia starts. But Saskia can't let her.

"Why can't you see it, Julia? We weren't his girlfriends. We were his fucking *victims*."

Victims. The second she says the word, she feels its approximate right-ness. She can accept it, now. Who is a victim, after all? Somebody who has had something intolerable done to them. And this frustration. This uselessness. This loneliness, the photographs, the fear in Kelly's eyes, the futility of the fight with this woman: What other word to describe them than *intolerable*?

Victims. If it's not right, it's still the closest thing she has.

And then Julia shoves the articles back into Saskia's bag.

"Sweetie, I don't know what happened between the two of you," she says with a wry smile. "But *I* seduced *him.*"

Chapter 15

"Maybe it was stupid, to sell a cow for magic beans," Jacqui cried. "And, okay, maybe they're not even really magic, I don't know. But there has to be more to life than buying and selling just enough to get by. And the possibility of magic has to be worth something. It is to me, anyway. The belief that there's something more than—" She gestured to the four walls of the cottage she and her mother shared. "Something more than this."

—FAIRY TALES FOR LITTLE FEMINISTS:
JACQUI AND THE BEANSTALK, EVELYN HARPER KREIS

October 1997

SASKIA WAS FOURTEEN, AND SHE HAD BEEN DATING Patrick for four months. Well, seeing him. No, dating him—even if they didn't go out, even if nobody knew about them, she was his and he was hers. What did that make them, except boyfriend and girlfriend? He wasn't a boy, though. Manfriend?

It was easy, at first, to fall into a routine with him. One Wednesday afternoon when she was supposed to be in the practice room and he was supposed to be having office hours, they met up at his place instead. One Sunday when she told her parents she was out with friends, she was with him. Then the next Wednesday. The next Sunday.

They watched old movies, *Casablanca* and *His Girl Friday*, *Breakfast at Tiffany's* and *Manhattan*—films he'd seen a thousand times and she hadn't seen once. They listened to old music, Cat Stevens and Johnny Cash, until she was forced to admit that the lyrics were starting to mean things to her now, too. They looked at the photographs he'd taken of

her, that first day; they took more. He learned that she hated the sound
of motorcycles, that she was utterly fearless in the face of spiders. She
learned that he hated undeserved recognition of kitsch more than anything else in the world, a category that included her mother's artwork
(though he would never have called it *artwork*). They also kissed, a lot—
first on the sofa and then in his bed. It took months for him to start
taking off her clothes. More months for her to start taking his off. He
never asked. He could wait.

And then that particular Wednesday. Skin against skin and him, smiling into her face, smoothing her hair behind her ear, laughing as she
shuddered against him. And she thought: He adores me. She slid a leg
around him and that was that. He was inside her, spreading her open
beneath him, and it hurt a little—then it hurt a lot—and then the look
on his face, the helplessness and the urgency, it was too interesting for
her to want to stop. The adjustments that she made were minor, to avoid
discomfort rather than to get any kind of pleasure. Moving her hips here,
letting herself exhale, breathe deep here.

Then it was over, and she watched his expression, fascinated. The exhaustion on his face. The gratitude as he turned back to her.

"Your turn," he murmured.

His mouth on her neck, he skimmed her nipple with his palm, lighter
than he'd ever touched her, and her breath caught.

"You like that." A statement, not a question. All the better, because in
what world was this a question of like or dislike? It was—it was—

She raised her hips. Once. Then again. And gasped. There were certain ways she was used to her body responding. This, her legs wrapped
around his shoulders, wasn't one of them.

"It feels—funny—"

"Just breathe."

She didn't know what was happening. Only knew the urgency of it,
only knew this growing—this—

"Patrick—I'm—"

She was late getting home that night, past ten (they'd fallen asleep),
and Evie was sitting, waiting up at the kitchen table, as she rummaged in
the refrigerator. Saskia knew it was not good that her mother was waiting
up for her, she knew there was *a talk* coming, and yet she couldn't exactly

make herself care. She was in her body now. In the soreness, in the pain that remained. In the ecstatic memory of—of that. Of them.

"Saskia," Evie said, "where have you been?"

Saskia pulled the lid off of a yogurt. "With my boyfriend, okay? I have a boyfriend." And she spooned the yogurt into her mouth, watched with secret delight as her mother's face went from surprised to calm, controlled. Too controlled.

"Who is he?"

She thought about telling her the truth. Her mother the feminist. Her mother with her body positivity and her discussions about safe sex—

But she couldn't do it.

"Josh," she said instead, imagining one of the gentler boys in her class, with one of the more popular names at University School. *Good luck narrowing that down, Mom.* She tossed the half-eaten yogurt container into the trash, and it was not until she found the Walgreens bag with birth control hanging on her doorknob the next evening that she knew her mother had believed her. A good thing, too; they hadn't used anything. Patrick hadn't offered. And she hadn't known what to ask for.

The next morning, she had felt different: in the soreness mostly, but also in the simultaneous veils of shame and pride that had fallen down over her shoulders overnight. She'd done it, she wasn't a virgin; but she was something else now, and she didn't quite know what that was. She drifted through school, then to her piano lesson. Her playing sounded the same to her, normal, but—

"Enough!" Carrie cried, after making her pound through the Liszt for a third time. "Saskia. Get your head in the game, will you?" Saskia looked up blankly as her teacher ran her fingers through her curls, yanking at her roots, and sighed. "Go home. Get some rest. Let's see how you do tomorrow."

But Saskia wasn't any better the next day, or the one after that. She didn't know why she felt ashamed. She shouldn't have; her mother had never presented sex as anything dirty, never tried to keep her from it. Was it the litany she and her family had fallen into? Every Wednesday, every Sunday, as she went off to see him:

When are we going to meet Josh? Her mother.

Looks like somebody's Joshing around. Her father, of course.

Oh, sometime. Yes, very funny. Her, always, lightly and with no intention of ever following through.

Maybe if she could really have told them, told anyone. If she could
have asked her mother the questions she really had, about what she should
be doing with somebody so much more experienced, with a man she so
desperately wanted to please.

But in the meantime, the secret, and the inexplicable shame of that
secret, sat heavy on her shoulders. She tried to focus on the keys, tried to
focus on her movement, tried to focus on anything and everything that
wasn't his body or her body, but they were the only things in the world to
her now. It wasn't until Carrie smacked the wood of the piano with a flat
palm at her next lesson that Saskia looked up and started to wonder: What
else had she lost, along with her virginity?

January 2020

THE HOUSE FEELS EXTRA HAUNTED TONIGHT.
It's no longer just her mother's absence hanging in the hallway, flickering in and out of mirrors and windows and glass-fronted cabinets. All
of a sudden, it's everyone else. It's Emilia, tracing her fingers along the
wooden bookshelves. It's Rosemary, newlywed at nineteen, huge pale eyes
gazing out onto the lake. It's Grandmother Harper trapped in a body she
could no longer control, glaring from her wheelchair. It's Great-Cousin
Annabelle, who scraped her ankle on a rusty nail and died of lockjaw
three weeks later. It's the nameless faces of women Saskia doesn't know,
hiding behind the birds in the wallpaper. How many Harper lives have
been lived here?

It cannot be Patrick's.

And yet what can she possibly do?

Saskia's encounters with Kelly and Julia hover shamefully just behind
her, like bad Tinder dates. Except worse, because Tinder has an inex-
haustible supply of straight, horny men, while she has . . . what? No more
names. Just a few anonymous faces, anonymous to everyone but their

owners, flashes of blond hair in pictures taken long ago. She tosses the articles she'd so carefully printed out the day before onto the fire. She can't risk her father finding them, and she has no use for them anymore.

She's not going to speak out alone. The only thing worse than all of this happening is all of this happening and nobody believing her. Of opening her in-box to find streams of vitriol spewing out of strangers' mouths. Of becoming like Cassandra, the princess from one of her mother's stories, an ignored prophet.

She can't do it. She can't make herself do it.

Her phone dings, startling her; she'd forgotten the sound was on. Tara, with the revised affidavit. Reminding her again of the hearing date, almost three weeks away, when the court will hear their objections, if they file them in time.

Ah. Now, there's a thought.

She'd dismissed the idea of a legal case against Patrick out of hand at first, thinking only of Tara and her $450-an-hour fees. But she's seen, now, how much money there would be if she were only free of the house: the piano, the sketches and photos, the royalties. Hell, even the furnishings inside the house belong to her and her father, don't they? And if there's anything worth spending money on . . . best to spend it on keeping Patrick out of the Elf House. It's hers: her heritage, hers to sell.

But also, to spend it on justice.

Statutory rape. The term causes her arms to break out in goose bumps, chills her hands. In no world had she ever before imagined that it would apply to her.

Well, it does, Sas, she tells herself harshly. *So, what are you going to do about it?*

Evidence. There's only her, her and her memories. The photo—that's something, though she's pretty sure any court would regard it as circumstantial. Maybe he really *had* been trying to create a portrait of Midwestern adolescence, she imagines some defense attorney—a woman, he'd definitely hire a woman—saying to the jury.

And then she remembers.

She's on her feet, bounding out of the room and up to her tower. There, in a box labeled SAS ELECTRONICS, she finds it.

Her old flip phone.

She somehow kept the charger, thank God, and when it finally powers up with a familiar tinkle of notes, she opens up her voice mail folder, a folder with only one message left in it.

She makes herself dial in.

TUESDAY, SEPTEMBER 11, 2001, a robot voice screams at her.

And then: his voice, his terrified voice.

Darling, I had to reach you—Sas. Oh my God. I can't— Are you okay? Call me as soon as you get this, I can't stop thinking about you. I've been watching the news and all I can think about is you trapped, trying to get out. Call me when you can. I'm here for whatever you need.

And then, a long pause.

And, Sas, I know you've been upset with me, but I need you to believe this. I'll always look back on our time together with love.

The nausea rises deep at the back of her throat, and she thrusts the phone into her pocket.

She has it. She has the evidence, and who knows what more the little Nokia has in store? She'll go through it later, if she can make herself. She'll give it to Tara, if she can't.

She'll give it to Tara either way.

The closeness of the tower is suffocating. She has to get out.

She'll set up an appointment with Tara in the morning.

On shaky legs, heat pounding unbearably under her skin, Saskia descends the stairs, then goes to the end of the hall, to the Blue Room, where the janky heating system has always been extra fallible. It's satisfyingly frigid, icy air filling up the space between the bare floor and the floral pargeting on the ceiling. Furniture hung with sheets, like the rest of the unused rooms. Dust an inch thick in all of them. What would she have done with all of that empty space, here on her own? Nothing, probably. Left it closed up, like her mother had. Maybe she would have rented the rooms on Airbnb, made some money. Hosted residencies for struggling artists.

Her own reflection in the great gold mirror above the bed catches her eye. She's pale on a good day, but phantasmal in the Wisconsin winter light, embossed royal-blue wallpaper surrounding her, the lake through the window behind her. She goes to the window, looking down; the bright rectangle of a cell phone bobs in the dark outside. She pushes the window up.

"Hello?" she calls out.

"Sas?" Lexi's voice. "Hey! You want to come down?"

The familiarity of it—scrambling for her shoes, grabbing the warm-est woolen blanket from her closet to wrap over her puffy coat. It's been twenty years since she's done this, and still she's pounding down the stairs like no time has passed at all.

Her father is in the den, reading glasses on and a huge World War II tome in his lap, Wolfie curled up beside him on the couch. The steadi-ness of him fills her chest with warmth.

"Just going out to see Lex," she calls.

"That's nice, kid. Glad the two of you are friends again."

She's not sure if that's what they are. But she's glad, too.

Normally, they never would have met outdoors in January. In the winter months, they'd hole up in Lexi's room or Saskia's, sometimes in the abandoned stables on the edge of Georgia's property; in later years, in Lexi's car. But it's a warm night, warm for January, at least. With her full winter gear, her blanket, Saskia is almost hot. Her body heat pulses through the layers of clothing as she strides toward the cliff's edge.

Lexi, too, has a plaid blanket around her shoulders. Blue and green, University School colors.

"Want?" She holds out a mug of hot chocolate to Saskia, who takes it, widening her eyes at the taste.

"Oh, shit, that's got a kick. Must be an Evelyn Kreis recipe."

"Finish it," Lexi says, lighting a cigarette. "I shouldn't." She takes a drag and holds it out to Saskia, who hesitates. Smoking was a her and James thing, as it had once been a her and Patrick thing. But, she thinks, taking the damp filter from Lexi, maybe it could be a her and Lexi thing. Again.

"I thought you'd be back in Chicago by now," Saskia says, passing the cigarette over as she realizes how it sounds. "I'm glad you're not," she clarifies.

"Nah, I needed to take some time away." Lexi blows silver-blue smoke out over the beach. "I really do miss your mom."

"I miss her, too." Is it the first time she's said it out loud? "But, God, she was so complicated. Things are such a mess right now. I always wanted your mom, you know." Lexi snorts. "No, I did. I mean, Georgia's got her issues. But at least you always know where you stand. She never would have kept something like a fatal illness from you."

"Yeah," Lexi says with a wince. "I doubt she'd be able to keep it from anyone. But don't be jealous. Where I currently stand? It's about two hundred grand in debt."

"Wait, what?"

"Right?" Lexi takes a drag, grins sideways at Saskia. "Guess I shouldn't have bought so many lattes."

Saskia reaches for the cigarette. "I'm pretty sure it's not the lattes that did it."

"Yeah, no kidding. More like the college loans."

Saskia looks studiously out over the moon-flecked lake. She knows that Georgia had money problems after Jake left, knows more than she should. Knows she's not supposed to know. Saskia is surprised when Lexi goes on, but maybe Mike's revelation the other night seeded the ground. "Why didn't anybody ever tell me to go to community college? *Good debt*, my ass. If Mom had only sold the fucking house . . . but she always has to have a façade. Dad leaves, and it's, *Look at my wonderful new career in real estate!* Always a show, with her."

"I wonder about the two of them," Saskia says.

Lexi frowns. "My mom and dad?"

"Mom and Georgia. How much their life choices were about not wanting to let each other down."

Lexi shrugs. "I think they saw it as the great accomplishments of their lives, keeping these houses in the family. The last of the debutantes, protecting the last of Milwaukee's great beer mansions. You ever see that picture of them in the white dresses at their debut?"

Saskia rolls her eyes. "The one hanging over your staircase or the one hanging over ours?"

"I just . . . I still can't believe she'd do it. Your mom. That she'd give the house away. *Giving* it away?"

"I know," Saskia says, fire and fury lighting her from the inside. "I keep trying to tell people— Selling it, *maybe*."

"Maybe," Lexi repeats.

"But this charity stuff . . . fuck. She had to have her arm twisted practically off to buy a table at the art museum gala every year."

"Fair enough, though," Lexi says, staring ahead. "She was an artist. They should have comped her."

"I mean, yeah."

Lexi flicks the end of the cigarette down to the beach; they watch the tiny light spark against the sand, then go out.

"Are you sad about it?" she asks Saskia. "The house?"

Saskia hesitates. "Want to know a secret?"

"Always."

"I'm not sad. I'm *mad*."

Lexi nods. "So, you're going to fight for it."

Saskia's head bobs. Yes.

"Truth for truth? I'm not going back to Chicago," Lexi says, clasping the blanket close. "I can't afford it anymore. I'm going to stay at home with Mom for a while."

"But you love Chicago," Saskia says, taken aback by Lexi's pronouncement and the burning jealousy it instantly ignites in her. Come home for good. You can do that? That's allowed?

Lexi rolled her eyes. "Love it or not, I'm broke. Besides, I'm Insta old now, and that only works if you have a baby. And I'm about ten thousand steps away from having a baby. So, home it is."

"Maybe," Sas says, trying out the words like a foreign language. "Maybe I'll stay, too. I guess I haven't decided yet."

Lexi tilts her head. "The house—"

"He can pry it out of my cold, dead hands." She meant it as a joke when she started saying it, but she's not laughing.

"Patrick?"

Saskia nods, wordless

"And he was the guy? Back in high school?"

The winter air isn't that cold, but it stings as her eyes widen. "How—"

Lexi shrugs, blanket dropping again. "The look on your face at dinner, when your father said his name. It's the same one you used to get whenever I mentioned your boyfriend." There's a long pause as she swings her legs out over the cliff. "I thought you hated me, then."

"Why would I have hated you?"

A short laugh from Lexi. "For going to public school. No, that's not fair, you're not that much of a snob. I guess . . . I guess, for my dad leaving us? Like you could somehow see whatever it was in us that made him leave."

"Fuck. No, Lexi. It was just . . . it was Patrick and it was piano, but it was never you."

"Yeah, well," Lexi says softly, lighting another cigarette, "I know that now."

"Lex, about Patrick. You can't tell anyone. Not ever."

"I mean, I won't"—she exhales loudly—"but are you sure? I mean, what he did was fucked up. That guy's, like . . . thirty years older than us."

Twenty-three. But who's counting.

"But, no," Lexi goes on. "I won't tell anyone. Until and unless you want me to."

The silence now is uncomfortable, waves beating against the shore in time with her heartbeat. Lexi feels it, too, feebly offers a mom-type question: "So, what else have you been doing with yourself since you've been home?"

"Besides trying to figure out if we can keep the house?" she says. "I've actually been trying to finish Mom's latest book so that it can still be published."

"Princesses?"

"Goddesses, in fact. It's like . . . a grown-up version of the Persephone and Demeter myth."

"No kidding," Lex says.

"Yeah, a contemporary retelling for adults. But I can't figure out how it should end, and I'm trying to rethink it, like Mom would. Right now, Persephone's down in the Underworld, Demeter's searching for her, but it just seems . . . too trite to use the real ending. Too unlike life. And too unlike my mom."

"Do you want to hear some alternate endings?"

"Do you *know* alternate endings?" Saskia asks, surprised.

"One thing I do have is a hundred-and-fifty-thousand-dollar degree in classics from Northwestern. Yeah, I know."

Saskia tries to mute the bafflement in her face.

"Oh," she says lightly. "I'd forgotten your major."

Lexi gently punches her shoulder. "Shut up. You never knew."

Saskia laughs. "Okay, well: I want more than the bargain. More than Hades gets half of Persephone's life."

And Lexi, with an air of authority Saskia has never heard before, says, "You want to send it to me? Maybe we can talk it over. Work on finishing it together. If you want."

To Saskia's surprise, she does. Before she can change her mind, before she can talk herself out of it: "Yes," she says. "Definitely."

Chapter 16

"I cannot thank you enough for discovering where my daughters have been going, and why I am spending an arm and a leg on shoe leather. In return, I shall do as I promised. You may have one of them as your bride."

The Prince turned to the eldest. She was the one with the spark in her eye, a swing in her hips.

But she just stared at him. And when she folded her arms over her chest, he knew her answer was no.

The Prince moved down the line. One after another, each of the daughters responded in turn.

The King balled his hands up into little fists. "Surely one of you has enough sense to see that a single prince is hard enough to come by these days. Let alone twelve of them."

"Don't look at me!" one of the middle daughters cried. "I'm gay!"

"It doesn't matter, because none of us wants to get married," the oldest daughter said. "In fact, we're planning to go onstage."

"On—" the King sputtered.

"Yes." The second-eldest nodded. "As dancers."

The King and the Prince exchanged a glance.

"In that case," the Prince said hesitantly, "I do have contacts at the best theaters throughout the land. Perhaps I could act as their manager?"

The King let out an enormous breath.

"Wonderful," he said. "Just perfect."

"Shall we say . . . twenty percent on gross receipts?"

As her sisters exchanged tentative glances of agreement, the youngest princess stepped forward.

"Hold on," she said. "We're the ones doing all the dancing. Why should you get a cut?"

—*Fairy Tales for Little Feminists:*
The Twelve Dancing Princesses, Evelyn Harper Kreis

November 1997

SASKIA WAS FIFTEEN, AND SHE WAS PLAYING
Rachmaninoff's Piano Concerto no. 3 with the Milwaukee Symphony
Orchestra, rehearsing for the next evening's show. Carrie had carpal
tunnel and had recommended her as a replacement. Poor Carrie. Still,
a bum wrist didn't entirely explain why she'd never sprung to the next
level. As a symphony pianist, she had one of the most prized spots
in the country—and yet no albums. No solo tours. Saskia had heard
Carrie play hundreds of times, and she still didn't understand exactly
what was lacking. The notes were correct. The inflection was there.
The musicality. And yet there was something missing, a spark—

At rehearsal, Saskia was nothing but sparks. Her technique was flagging (her technique had been flagging for some time), but at least the
sparks still came, when the audience was there. And what better audience
than other musicians?

At the end of the pyrotechnics, she put her hands in her lap, fingers
trembling. She was proud; everything that had been missing from her
playing this past year . . . well, she'd left it all out on the stage, hadn't she?
The symphony musicians were on their feet now, applauding her.

She had her coat on before Mike came running down into the audi-
torium.

"Hey, kiddo. Great stuff. You heading out?"

"Yeah." Four missed calls from Patrick; he wasn't used to having her
cancel their Wednesday afternoons. But what was she supposed to have
done? Turn down the chance to play with the Symphony?

"I just—you know, if you stick around—" Her dad was smiling bashfully.

"Do you have a solo?"

He laughed, eyes bright and steady. "Shostakovich fifteen. It's a Russian program. I'm surprised you haven't heard me around the house."

Her mouth felt dry. "Well. It's been busy. And actually"—holding
up her phone, keeping it snapped closed so he couldn't actually see the
screen—"Josh . . ."

"No problem," he said fast. Too fast. "You go see your boyfriend."

She was halfway down the aisle before he called after her. "Nice playing today, Sas."

On opening night, she brought flowers for him and stood close to the stage in the wings as he came to the fore, as he made the cello sing Shostakovich's grinding, heartbreaking notes. As he—

Well, as he got through it.

She watched him, clutching the skirts of her taupe silk gown until the fabric was clammy from her sweating palms. Because that's all he was doing. Getting through it. He wasn't having fun with it. And hadn't he been the one who'd taught her that? That the *play* of playing an instrument was what made everything else worthwhile?

Saskia forced herself to look away from his trembling vibrato, from the sweat on his forehead, out into the audience. How many of those faceless bodies could tell the difference? How many could even tell that his performance was workmanlike, uninspired?

At the end, when she rushed onstage to congratulate him, a few ignorant spectators stood for an unearned ovation. As she hugged him, she thought, I can't believe it; Dad isn't that good. "Wonderful," she murmured, smashing the roses between them. "You were wonderful."

February 2020

THAT SATURDAY, IT'S JUST PAST SEVEN WHEN Saskia wakes. But when she opens the door, she finds Wolfie waiting. As he sees her, he starts whipping circles around her in a frantic dance to get her downstairs. If he were a child, he'd be crossing his legs and hopping up and down. She jogs with him to the back door and lets him outside.

Her father always gets up at six. Why hasn't he let Wolfie out yet?

The house is silent as Wolfie barks at a squirrel. Heartbeat in her fingers, she briefly wonders if her father has died. If she's the last person standing, as she was always going to be in this family.

But from the top of the stairs, she can hear his snores coming gently from the west wing, and her heart relaxes, slides back into place. Although it doesn't seem good that he is still sleeping.

She knocks perfunctorily on the door.

"Dad?" The air is thick, and a lump of blankets mutters and stirs. She approaches the bedside. "Daddy?"

He startles awake. It's only as he pulls himself upright that she realizes: he was sleeping on Evie's side.

"Sorry," she says, taking a step back. "I was just worried. It's after seven and you're usually out the door by six."

He blinks in surprise. "Did you let Wolfie out?"

A barking at the back door.

"Yeah. I'll get him in a minute. I was wondering, though—if maybe you want to go for a run?"

SASKIA AND MIKE HEAD DOWN TO THE TREES, stretching silently where the pine alley begins. It's a beautiful day, more like spring than February, with a bright early-blue sky and a softness to the wind. Wolfie, not yet on his leash, runs between the two of them, turning his head from one to the other.

She looks at her father, and he shows a dimple.

"C'mon, kiddo."

At the gates, he breaks into a light jog. Going easy on her—Wolfie's straining at the leash, suggesting that they usually go much faster—he's testing her out, seeing what kind of shape she's in. She speeds up.

"So, kiddo. Tell me," Mike says.

"Tell you . . ." Her heart's beating faster than it should, this early in the run. Either she's in worse shape than she thought or her body's balking at the world of secrets she's kept from him. At all the hundreds of things she could have told him and never has.

"Your quest."

"Quest?"

That word. Evie had totally brainwashed them.

"With the lawyers."

"Oh! Well, Tara's drafting the affidavit. There's . . ." But she can't bring herself yet to tell him that his adolescent daughter is hanging in the art museum. Time enough for that if Tara says there's enough evidence to move forward. "Anyway, I set up another appointment with her for Friday, just to check in."

"Do I need to be there?"

She has a vision of him storming into the exhibition hall, ripping the portrait off of the wall with his bare hands; she's not sure where it came from. He's always been gentle, her father. Whatever else he has or hasn't been, he's always been that.

"No," she says quickly. "No. We'll get it wrapped up soon enough."

"Well, that's good. The appraiser's coming in two weeks, you know. They have to assess the value of the house and of all of the stuff inside."

"Appraiser?" Her stomach tightens. "But all of the stuff—that's *ours*."

He shoots her a sidelong glance, with a snort of amusement. "Sure. But it's a necessary formality in the whole probate process. Your young suitor Josh has to establish . . . what'd he call it? *Date of death values*."

She gives an exaggerated shudder. "That's pretty grim."

"That's life." They laugh. Because, of course, it isn't. It's the opposite of life.

"And he's not my suitor. We went on one date."

She can feel the shrug in her father's voice as he speaks. "Okay. But he does require a professional valuation of all assets from the day she died, for the official record. I've been sending over mountains of paperwork, but the actual stuff . . ."

"Yeah," she says, thinking about the postcard in the violin, the ancient phone now in the drawer of her bedside table. "I guess. Whatever they've got to do."

She and her father are almost the same height, and their feet hit the ground in unison like a single heartbeat.

"You know, I've been reading back through my journals," her father says. "And I'll tell you what. I don't think your mother ever mentioned donating the house to the university, or Kintner by name. Right up to the end, our conversations were all about ensuring our futures. About making sure we were provided for. *Safe*, she kept saying."

Saskia stops so suddenly she almost pitches forward.

"Seriously?" she says.

"Yes," he says, looking over his shoulder. "Hey. We going to run, or what?"

She catches up, her mind racing.

"But . . . but. Then how did he get her to change the will?"

"We don't know for sure that he did anything," Mike says, but there's a skepticism undercutting his words. "It was early on, when she wrote the will, sure. But the doctors, they said that personality changes, psychological effects, acute distress . . . they're not uncommon. And who knows when those symptoms actually began? The only thing I can know about what she felt is what she told me."

"But she went to the lawyers in July. How was she in July? There's a doctor's certificate affirming that she was competent."

The thumping of their feet echoes between them, the metronome keeping their pace.

"She was competent," he says finally.

"So, Patrick has to have done something. Either that or they were in on something together, and . . ." After seeing that photo of her in Patrick's portfolio, after protesting the exhibition of her daughter to further his career, her mother couldn't have been particularly disposed to a *collaboration*.

"Dad," she says. "Look."

And she tells him.

Not everything, just about the photo. Tells him that she doesn't remember it being taken, that that period of her life, her life back before, is a blur. Tells him about her meeting with Sheila, about Evie having seen his portfolio of adolescent girls.

"Anyway, according to Sheila, Mom was *pissed* at him. She definitely wasn't in the mood to give him any gifts," she finishes, breathless. And then she falls silent, wondering if his own silence indicates belief or disapproval or both; or something in between.

"That mother*fucker*," Mike mutters finally between gritted teeth. "And he won't take it down?"

"I didn't ask him to, I only went the museum route. You know Tara said to stay away—" Her pulse moves to her temples at the hypocrisy. "One meeting with him was enough. And besides, if even the curators can't get it down, what the hell's an artist going to be able to do?"

Their identical strides pound over the icy bridge straddling the ravine.

"I'll tell you this much," Mike says. "There's something wrong with that guy. And he's not getting the motherfucking house, no matter how much I want to get it out of our life. I'd give it to the fucking Scientologists before I let him have it. He's not moving in."

She takes her first deep breath of the run, nearly choking with it. "No," she agrees, "he won't. That house is *ours*."

They turn and start heading up a slight incline. He's side-eyeing her again.

"When's your return flight, again?"

She's been meaning to push that flight back for weeks, now, but has never quite got around to it. Beyond staying with her father. Beyond the probate hearing. New York feels, suddenly, empty. Gina darting home to her daughter after every spar. Drinks with Tessa and Andrea and Annemarie, the college friends she sees the most often, not one of whom has so much as pinged the group chat to see how she is. She has a strong suspicion they've started a new one without her in it. James in her Ikea bed, always in the daytime, always leaving before it's dark. Timed assignations are the only kind she's ever known.

She realizes she can't remember the sound of his voice.

"You okay?"

"Yeah." She's slowed to a walk and puts her hands on her hips. "Lexi's moving back into Georgia's house, did you know?"

"I didn't."

"Yeah." She flips her right foot up into her palm, gasps at the sharp stretch in her quad.

"Kid," her father says gently, "you've always got a place here if you want one."

One second she's stretching, and the next, she feels like she's choking, her vision goes blurry—

Her father wraps his arms around her. He's fleecy as a teddy bear in his winter getup, and he's patting her back.

"I'll sort this mess out if it kills me," he says fiercely. "Get that bastard and that fucking house out of our lives, get us a fresh start, Sas. Don't cry. I'm going to find a way to fix it. I promise. I'm going to take care of things."

She wipes her hot cheeks with the backs of her hands.

"And if you can't? We'll . . . what, live together in a shitty apartment down by the river?"

"Exactly," he agrees. "In a shitty apartment down by the river."

"Dad," she says quietly, unable to meet his eyes, "why didn't Mom tell me?"

And, to his credit, he doesn't pretend to misunderstand her. He doesn't try to change the subject. But the silence as he hesitates is unbearable.

"Georgia said that she meant to call me home at the end. And okay," she says, her voice wobbling into vibrato before she clears her throat. "Okay. But that doesn't make sense, because if she didn't want me to see her sick . . . well, I would have in the end, wouldn't I? I would have seen that anyway?"

Only I didn't. The silent words beat between them.

"Georgia— I'm not sure Georgia ever really understood your mother's choices." He turns away from her, but at a walk. For a split second, she watches his back receding, then joins him. "At least, not in terms of anything but vanity, about wanting to be remembered a certain way. But you're right, she did want you there at the end."

For a moment, there's just the sound of Wolfie's paws clicking against the icy pavement. She waits, but he doesn't go on.

"But then, if not that . . . why the silence?"

His voice, when it comes, is rough. "The silence, Sas? That was for you. She didn't want you to have the same year we had, with each stumble, each dizzy spell, signaling doom. She wanted you to live your life. To do what you were going to do. Without seeing her terrified by hallucinations. Without seeing her forgetting you—"

She has the urge to sprint away as his words break off. And yet she can't; she has to be there. She has to know.

"But in her plan . . . there was always the likelihood that when I came home, at the end, she'd already have forgotten me."

It's a long moment before her father coughs. "I know."

"Or be in a coma."

"I know that, too. I know and I knew, Sas." And his voice is so gentle she wants to die. "You think I didn't realize that her vision of calling you home, then drifting peacefully away like Garbo on a theatrical deathbed . . . you think I didn't realize that it was nothing but magical thinking? Of course I knew. But it was a year full of awful choices. Between more awful and still-awful options. Of course, it was going to get to the point when you had to know, when you had to see her, and when you did, it was going to be nightmarish. Of course it was. I told her that. I did. But

I wasn't going to spend our last months together fighting. Once the pneumonia hit, I told her we had to call you, but she made me swear not to. I don't know if she thought she was going to get better, or if she just hadn't realized what the end would look like. But she asked me to swear. And so," he says, finally lifting his eyes to meet hers, "I swore."

"The end," she says softly. Accident or deliberate decision, that she hadn't been called home? Fate or choice? It burns hard in her: the idea that she will never know.

Her father's voice drifts to her, too casual, in the thin winter air. "We were so lucky it was pneumonia."

"Lucky!"

"Yes, lucky. Because it was fast. Because they could treat the pain. Because she hadn't yet lost all of her speech, and she had moments— moments of knowing me. At the end. She was still there, sometimes. And as far as this disease goes, that's as lucky as you get." In the cold, their breath comes out like steam before them. "It was a year full of fucking awful choices," Mike mutters again, fierce.

They loop back in silence. The two of them together, Wolfie trotting ahead. Her footfall matches her father's, which matches the blood pounding through them.

Chapter 17

"And maybe it's just a joke to you," the Princess said, twirling the pea between her fingertips, "but the fact is that I have very specific sensory issues. And I would never join any family who was so cruel as to exploit them just to confirm that I have some kind of socially constructed 'royal blood.' Thanks, but no thanks."

—*Fairy Tales for Little Feminists:*
The Princess and the Pea, Evelyn Harper Kreis

March 1998

SASKIA WAS FIFTEEN, AND SHE HAD DECIDED NOT to like Italy. For one thing, it was too hot, even in March. There was no air-conditioning, and there were flies everywhere. Beyond that, her phone had lost service somewhere over the Atlantic; her phone was no longer a portal to Patrick.

"Waiting for a call from someone special?" Evie teased on the airplane as Saskia stared at the blank screen. She sighed and flipped it closed.

"Ugh, Mom. No."

"It wouldn't be Josh, would it?"

An out. She'd take it. She sighed again, dramatically.

"You know, Saskia, we do need to meet him one of these days."

Saskia just rolled her eyes, though her heart fluttered up to her throat. "Well, you're not going to meet him in Rome, are you?"

"When we get home, then. Soon. It's been—what, a few months?"

She leaned her head against the window and closed her eyes. When she woke up, they were landing.

She was in Italy for a competition, which of course she won. But after the generic sterility of it—the same screen they had everywhere, shielding her from the judges' view; the same ballet flats she always wore; the same gold medal on the same blue ribbon, she had dozens of them already—her father was waiting for her.

So while Evie was out shopping, Mike led her through the heat-baked streets of Rome. He clamped headphones over her ears to drown out the traffic as they walked to St. Peter's Basilica, as she craned her neck up to try to find the end of the vast dome to the sounds of Verdi. As they walked to the Trevi Fountain, she watched the waters splashing in time to Puccini. As they dangled their legs over the Tiber to Rossini.

Huh. Opera. It was like Patrick's old music—she hadn't thought she'd like it, but it turned out she did.

And the same turned out to be true about Rome.

But even though they were out late that night, Evie was even later coming back to the hotel. It was already dark when she appeared, dragging a gilt mirror in her wake.

"At the—Porta—Portese," she gasped, hoisting the thing onto the luggage rack so that Mike and Saskia could admire its curlicues, the way it glinted dull gold in the light. "Isn't it glorious?"

She didn't think it was so glorious a week later, lugging it onto the plane because it was too fragile to be trusted to a commercial shipper. Finally, a sweaty, red-faced Evie collapsed beside Saskia, sliding the mirror between their seats with a grunt.

"Mom!" Saskia cried. "I'm not going to stare into a mirror for *ten hours straight!*"

And her mother glared at her with an expression Saskia knew better than to fight.

She closed her eyes instead. Slept. And even before she could see land, before the lights of America were underneath her again, her phone was dinging, buzzing, insisting upon itself, and Saskia curled around her phone to view Patrick's missed calls with a quiet, purring delight.

By the time they landed at O'Hare, Rome already felt very far away.

February 2020

BACK HOME, TOGETHER. HOME FOR THE MOMENT.
Together for the moment. It's not enough. Even though he was just out, just joined them on their run, Wolfie's clawing at the back door. She lets him out, watching him dart into the trees, on the scent of a possum or a raccoon—or even just a squirrel, he's not picky. For a moment, she's so overcome with the joy of him that Patrick retreats into the back room of her mind and, watching the dog's silver figure weaving in and out of the oaks, she feels momentarily okay.

You can love a dog like you loved people when you were a child. Without fear. Only this happens for opposite reasons: as a child, you love without the knowledge and thus the threat of death; with a dog, you love *despite* death's ever-presence. Because each dog (except, perhaps, your last dog) will die before you, you can love them fully and accept their coming death fully, both simultaneously. Not *can:* have to. The pairing of these truths forces you into the present tense; and so, in the meantime, joy.

Wolfie trots from the southern copse to the northern, head down like a soldier running through no-man's-land. His paws sink into the increasingly muddy slush and Saskia turns to get a fresh towel from the laundry room.

When he doesn't return, Saskia sighs, slips her coat and boots back on. The grove is thick and deep enough that it feels like a forest from three sides. To the east, the trees thin out and then disappear altogether toward the lake. From the beach, you can see their roots poking through the side of the cliff like the sprouts that come out of potatoes. One May, when her dad was on tour and her mom was in New York, she'd taken Patrick out to the edge to share a bottle of the Malibu she'd insisted he buy her. Trees at their backs, packed earth beneath their legs, the lake crashing beneath their dangling feet. When he kissed her, it tasted like coconut and summer; she could have sworn she smelled sunscreen.

She follows the paw prints in the snow to the carriage house, where Wolfie waits, wagging his tail at the door. She opens it (had she left it unlocked the other night? Wisconsin habits, that false sense of safety, coming back too easily) and lets Wolfie sniff around the studio. She sits on the steps, folding her legs into a pretzel, waiting for him to give up.

The steps.

Somehow, she forgot about the loft space.

There's not much up there. Only Evie's "archives," as she called them. But they were just boxes of old papers; she kept her photographs and drawings in the vertical file downstairs, packed neatly away, dehumidifier running all the time.

Evie's archives. And her safe.

If there's anything her mother wanted to hide—if there's anything at all, it will be there.

The light filters up through the stairwell, but without a fixture up there it's as dark and windowless as the towers. Saskia flicks on her phone's flashlight and crouches down.

She'd figured out the combination long ago, when she was little. Long before she gave a shit about anything that her mother would actually store in there.

11–12–1982.

The black metal door swings open for her birthday.

Her parents' passports on top. An envelope full of hundreds, which she slips into her coat pocket. Files with the deed to the house, their birth certificates, medical records, tax returns.

But.

At the bottom, the very last file has her mother's name on it, in big block letters like a child would write. Or a kidnapper.

Saskia slides the palm-size photos out.

Black-and-white breasts on a headless figure. Small, pale nipples, pear-like curve. But it takes her until the next photo, when she sees the hands lying over her stomach—the lines of them, the grace of them—to realize.

It's her.

No face. Just a torso and the hints of limbs, like the ruins of a classical sculpture.

Until she flips to the next, and there she is: staring at the camera. Posing for him.

There's a whimper. She looks quickly at Wolfie, poking his head into the crawl space, before she realizes, as he licks her cheeks, that the sounds are coming from her.

That she's crying, crying at her own lost image, crying for the girl she was, the woman she has become.

They're small as Walgreens snapshots, though the paper is thicker than you'd get at the drugstore; these are *art*. She runs the fingers of one hand tightly through Wolfie's fur while flipping through the photos with the other. She's still crying in the dark, like when she was little: trembling lips, hot face, tears on the sheeny gloss of the surfaces.

She doesn't remember.

Does she?

She doesn't.

She never would have let him take naked pictures of her. She feels as certain of this as she does about anything. She wasn't that kind of girl, she thinks fiercely, and yet. There they are. And so she was. The angularity of her body, the languidness of her eyes.

She was *looking* at him. Why can't she remember?

Faintly, so faintly, a memory breaks to the surface: telling him to open the camera, expose the film.

She wasn't vain—not about her looks, at least. And he'd come late to the digital transition, she only ever remembers him shooting with film. In what other scenario would she have asked him to ruin his negatives if he hadn't taken pictures she never wanted printed, never wanted to see?

She closes her eyes, trying to grab on to the free-floating memories, to yank them out by their roots.

More faintly still: a heady night, a giddy one. One of their experiments, something with booze, or could he have drugged her drink, roofied her? Would he have had to?

The truth is, no. He could have handed her a roofie straight out, she would have taken it without question. She trusted him, completely.

But does that mean he didn't drug her—or that he did?

The photograph, her teenage face, has become damp under the heat of her palm. She crumples it with a soft moan.

Because it's not over yet, the images keep coming. And here: black-and-white still, but the nipples darker. Here: a body reduced to its torso again, but the breasts rounded, high. Here: a face in profile, and she knows, she knows without having to look too hard. She knows it's Julia.

It's Julia and it's Kelly. It's her and it's them, and it's one or two or ten other girls besides. It is hard, it is too hard, not to compare their bodies to hers. To her teenage self, to her present self. She'd once had the same taut skin they had; she no longer does. She now has muscles they've never dreamed of, her teenage self included.

But that's not a game she wants to play anymore, and she shakes her hands out, as she used to at the piano.

Facts, Saskia. Find the facts.

There are thirty photos. Enough for an exhibition. Exhibition quality, too. Signed.

There are at least five girls. Why does that hurt? Why, after all of this, is that something that hurts?

(Because—her uniqueness still means something to her. Her former uniqueness, her faded uniqueness.)

She flips back to herself with trembling hands. She's lying on a bed. It could be the tower mattresses, but the framing's too close to tell; it could be his bed, too. The bed where he'd driven into her for the first time when she was fourteen, when her body had expanded, been forced into expansion—

She gathers them up, shoves them quickly back into the envelope. It is only when both of her hands are in Wolfie's fur, as she bends to press her face against his rough, grassy body, that she sees that a plastic envelope has fallen out as well.

Shaking fingers guide it open. The negatives.

It feels too real to be real, like she is living in a video game, in a movie. She's had this feeling only once before, on that horrific September day: flash, explosion, flickering of lights, and then the cloud of dust like a wave pounding at Lafayette Street, the people running, powdery white as statues, only they were statues that screamed, statues that floundered, fell. You don't ever forget the sounds.

Today, all is silence but for her breath and the dog's. And yet it is the same feeling. Too stunned to ask questions. Too stunned to move.

"Wolfie!" her father's voice rings from the house. "Wooolf—ie!"

The dog's ears perk; he throws a questioning glance at Saskia. She squeezes him, untangles her hands, and he is out the open door in a gray flash.

She hesitates with the bag of negatives in her hand.

It takes only another minute for her father's voice to call again, as she knew it would.

"Saskia?"

It's not a good name for yelling. It's a good name for hissing, for whispering in the dark. It is a name for shooting at someone like an arrow. She quickly runs down the stairs, propels herself to the door.

"I'm just in the studio! Back in a sec!"

"Okay!"

And she collapses into her mother's chair, which spins wildly in a full circle, another, from the momentum of her weight.

How had she forgotten that he'd taken those photos? But even if she had remembered, she never would have thought he'd print them. She never would have thought he'd risk it.

Child pornography.

The phrase seems so separate from anything that happened between them. And yet here they are: the proof, the pictures.

She reaches back into her memory, and there it is: the sound of the shutter waking her from her teenage sleep, and he's hovering over her with a smile. She imagines the rest: Patrick, alone in the darkroom; sheets of photo paper, blank; chemicals eating away to make the image until her rib cage, her navel, her hip bones, began to emerge. . . .

Forget about why he printed these photos. Why the fuck did her mother have them?

The realization hits Saskia like a left hook. Had she traded her house for her daughter?

She must have.

Saskia has her tower, but Evie had hers, too: the crawl space with the safe, beneath the eaves. And it was where she'd stored her secrets, and it was where she'd hidden this.

The worst thing she'd ever done? Or the best? Saskia doesn't know.

Because, clearly, her mother had done something to obtain the photos—presumably to stop Patrick from showing them. And the negatives, to keep him from printing new ones. But at what cost? At the height of his career, Patrick couldn't have gotten more than ten grand a photo.

The realization of her mother's protection, of her ferocity, breaks over Saskia at the same time as the awful visual: her mother's hands on the images of her daughter's naked body.

Her mother's imaginings of what had led to the photos.

Her mother's vision of his fingers sliding into her, his cum on her belly, the scent of them intermingling until it was impossible to separate him from her, her from him, the teenage prodigy and the darling of the art world.

Her mother's knowledge of what Saskia had done. Of the enormous secret she had kept for decades.

But even if Evie had promised Patrick the house in exchange for the photos—the fundamental unfairness of such an exchange is almost too much to consider. Then again, what else could she have possibly offered Patrick, other than the Elf House? The Harper money was long gone, the debts immersive, all-consuming. The royalties—she could have let *him* manage the literary estate—but Evie never would have left her stories in such dangerous hands. Would he even be capable of understanding, let alone continuing, what she'd been trying to do with her princesses?

No. She wouldn't have entrusted him with the stories. And, anyway, why would Patrick have believed that the royalties would continue at their current rate for more than a couple of years?

Okay, fine: she could have gone to the police, Sas's contradictory mind spits at her. Evie could have called Saskia with that horrible, ominous low voice she'd used when Sas was really in the shit. She could have done so many things that weren't this—

Ah, the other part of her, the better part of her, responds. *But remember: she'd been out of time.*

So: Evie had given Patrick the one thing she had. The one thing he wouldn't refuse.

The cold seeping in from outside the studio is convulsing her body, and she has to go back to the house. Shoving the envelope into one pocket, the negatives into the other, she unwittingly slams the door behind her, fear giving her limbs a new and unexpected power. Inside the house, she bounds up the stairs two at a time.

"Lunch in ten, Sas?" her dad calls.

"Sure!"

She's breathless by the time she reaches her room. Takes two tries with the Firestart to get the logs to catch light. The cracks and pops of the eventual flames burst in her ears as she closes her eyes, imagines the fact of her teenage body crumpling away into nothing.

But she can't bring herself to throw her image into the flames, to watch herself burn.

With steady hands, she grabs a violin from the wall, the same one currently housing her postcard. Crouched before the fire like a goblin, she tests the first picture. Snapshot size, it slides easily into the instrument. There are a lot of them, her body, her body, her body, and then all of the bodies that are almost hers, but not quite; and it takes just a little bending, a little twisting, to get them all in.

But they fit, in the end. Just as she was sure they would.

Chapter 18

But as the door of the candy cottage creaked open, Hansel jumped back in fear.

"A witch!" he cried.

Gretel took one look at the woman and rolled her eyes at her brother, incredulous.

"Shut up, Hansel. Are you kidding me? Witch is just a name ignorant people give to women whose intelligence frightens them. My lady," she said, curtsying to the witch. "May I stay with you a spell and learn the ways of the woods?"

"But—your brother—" the wise woman said, pointing. Gretel turned to see Hansel scampering off into the trees.

"Eh," Gretel said. "Let him go."

—*Fairy Tales for Little Feminists: Gretel and the Witch*, Evelyn Harper Kreis

April 1998

SASKIA WAS FIFTEEN, AND LEXI WAS SIXTEEN AND full of fun. Her dad wasn't good for much, including tuition, but Jake had been good for a brand-new Volvo, shiny and white, for Lexi's birthday.

That Volvo made their year. Saskia, whose attendance numbers had never crawled above 75 percent, let them drop well below 50 as Lexi drove the twenty minutes up from Shorewood, buzzing a missed call onto Saskia's cell and picking her up in the parking lot. *Piano*, Saskia wrote in the attendance ledger.

And then it was anything, it was everything: greasy lunches at Ma

Fischer's, smoky coffees at Fuel, avoiding the gazes of creepy hippies at the Rochambo tearoom. When it was warm enough, it was the beach; when it was cold, it was Bayshore Mall.

It was the life Saskia had never known, and she was starved for it. There were so many moving pieces: her parents, her piano, Carrie, Patrick, and now the escapes with Lexi. She lapped it all up like a grateful dog.

That day, they'd gotten McDonald's at the drive-through and sat on the cliffs at Klode Park. Only a mile or so north of their cliffs, but those were off-limits during the day. Georgia had an erratic habit of popping home between house showings (she'd gotten her Realtor's license last year) and Evie was usually working in the cottage when she wasn't teaching or holding office hours.

"Ugh, I'm going to have to pay for this later at the gym. But worth it," Lexi said, popping another fry into her mouth. Saskia didn't know what to say; she had her father's metabolism, it was hard for her to put on even a pound, but she had already learned this was not something she was supposed to say to other girls. As if they didn't have reason enough to hate her already.

Although—since starting high school, something had shifted. The vaguely annoyed glances from her classmates had morphed into vaguely pitying ones, and she wasn't sure why.

"So, Katie's costume thing. Should we do a couple's costume?" Lexi chattered on.

Saskia hadn't worn a costume since she was eight, the year they'd gone as fairies, but she nodded. "Yeah, okay. But what?"

Lexi's eyes flared. "I got a good idea. Imagine this: blue dress. Black wig. Big white stain—"

Saskia raised her eyebrows. Some movie she hadn't seen? Probably.

"Monica Lewinsky!" Lexi cried.

Saskia couldn't help wincing. She didn't read the papers, but they were left strewn about the kitchen enough that she knew that Monica was young and caught up in some sort of sex scandal with the president.

"And I'll be—what, Bill Clinton?"

"Or a cigar," Lexi said, mouth quivering with laughter. Saskia laughed, too. Saskia did not get it.

"Oh—shit, I'm going to be in San Francisco that weekend," she said, making a face.

"Oh yeah? Piano?" Lexi said, but her voice had taken on a grown-up distancing. Saskia twisted a fry between her fingers, felt the potato go grainy against her skin as it split open. There it was, that pity.

"Yeah."

Was it pity, though? Or was it something else? She couldn't help thinking about the rage that had lashed off Lexi months ago, when she'd first heard of Saskia's boyfriend from, of all people, her mother.

"Are you fucking— A boyfriend, Sas? And I have to hear about it from my motherfucking mother?" Her voice had buzzed like a hive of bees over the tinny telephone line.

And Saskia, cursing herself for not realizing what would happen, that Lexi would find out. Like her mother could keep a secret from Aunt Georgia. Like Aunt Georgia could keep a secret at all.

"I didn't want to jinx it—"

Hard laughter. "I mean, whatever. Josh, Mom said? Is it Josh G. or Josh A.?"

It had taken her a minute to decide. "Josh P.," she'd said finally, liking her lie. Liking the way it filled her mouth.

And the suspicion, the suspicion the adults had never once shown. "Who? I don't know him. New?"

"Ish."

But Lexi wasn't focused on *the Boyfriend*, as she insisted on calling him that day. "I can't believe the amount of school they let you miss," she said instead, rolling her eyes. "It should be illegal."

Saskia made a face. "It probably is. They just don't report it."

"At twenty grand a year? They better not!"

Sas wiped her moist palms against her plaid skirt. "Do you miss it?" she asked quietly.

"No . . ." Lexi said slowly. "It's such a relief not to have Mom so worried about money anymore. But it's so weird to think of you all just going on there without me," she said, digging into the small striped purse against her hip.

"I'm not," Saskia said. "I'm here."

Lexi found what she was looking for, held up an orange Walgreens bottle. "Speaking of Mom," she said.

"Oooh, what is it?" Saskia said.

"Xanax," Lexi said, twisting the cap and tapping out two, palming them over to Sas.

"That's not what the bottle says, it says alprazolam."

"Yeah," Lexi said, eyebrows furrowed. "That's generic Xanax."

"Ohmigod," Saskia said, trying not to choke on the pills as she swallowed them dry (there was something so reassuring about swallowing pills, something so much less druglike than powders or liquids). "So, your mom has, like, mental health problems?"

Lexi tossed three into her mouth, rolled her eyes. "Whose mom doesn't?"

February 2020

AFTER THE PHOTOS, IT'S A FEW DAYS BEFORE SASKIA can do anything but lie in bed, staring at the constellation of pleated fabric on the canopy above her. She feels burned, like her skin is raw; like if she moves too fast, she'll scream with the pain of it. She tells her father that she's come down with something, a stomach bug; he keeps his distance. Day into night, night into day; at moments, she forgets that she isn't actually sick.

And the whole time, shame pulses like sunburn on her skin. Three million dollars. Her mother had given up the money and more—the family history, their legacy, the place where both she and Saskia had taken their first steps—all of it, she was willing to sacrifice to save the reputations of a handful of girls, most of whom she didn't even know. Who on earth would think that was worth it?

Evelyn Kreis, that's who.

The same woman who'd re-created all of those princesses in her own image, who'd imagined a better world. Who'd wanted to save the girls; to save *all* the girls.

Three million dollars.

She repeats the number to herself like a mantra. But she's always found numbers more soothing than mantras. More soothing than pictures, than stories. You say there are three of something, that's a fact. Nobody can argue it.

Three million.

Three million minus the 120,000 in back taxes.

Three million minus the 120, minus another 100,000 for the foundation.

Three million minus, minus, minus . . .

On Tuesday, finally, it becomes too much to take. That night, she dreams of her mother, sitting in the armchair beside Saskia's fireplace. In the dream, Saskia approaches with hesitation, staring wide-eyed at the resurrection. And then, dropping to her knees beside the chair, begins to ask her questions. *Why, Mom? Why all of this? Why—*

But Evie just stares into the fire. And after a moment, she begins reciting her numbers.

Three million, minus . . .

Saskia awakes with frustration throbbing through her. Frustration—and a flicker of hope.

Rolling out of bed, she grabs an old accountant's ledger from her desk. (At his death, her father's father had left hundreds of these things, and the family was still working its way through them fifty years later.) The Montblanc pen Georgia gave her for her college graduation. And she adds up all the costs she can think of, the ones that must be paid, the ones that must be taken care of soon: $750,000.

She pulls out her phone to google the average salary for a VP of development, but it's not enough. About $150,000. At the job for five years . . . no, Patrick couldn't possibly have that much saved. UWM might have accepted the gift, sure, if he'd been able to give it to them outright. But what institution would accept a gift, endow a center, that would cost them three-quarters of a million dollars before they'd even gotten the keys? Not even counting the renovations they'd need to make to create studios, conference rooms, whatever else the center would need. They wouldn't bother turning it into Evie's arts center. They'd sell it without setting foot in it, pocket the two million and change, slide it quietly into their endowment.

She stares at the numbers.

There's no way. There's no way he can do it. Not for himself and not for the school.

A glimmer of hope: the thought of that mortgage, like an oasis in the desert. But it's not, she tells herself. It's a mirage. Because as much as she feels a responsibility to the house—especially now, especially as it is her skin, her eyes, her hair, that were all responsible for its possible loss—as much as she feels that, she craves the freedom its sale will buy for her. For her—and, yes, for her father as well.

It's not going to be theirs for much longer.

But, she swears to herself, flipping through the pages, it's not ever going to be *his*.

SASKIA CONTINUES TO AVOID HER FATHER FOR the rest of the day, darting down to take her lunch plate up to her room, refusing dinner, like she's a petulant teenager again. And as she paces in front of the window, before a darkening sky, she realizes: the only way Evie could have come upon these photographs is if they had been in the portfolio Patrick submitted to Sheila.

That's what Sheila wasn't saying.

The timing works out. Evie saw the photos in June, fought first to get them taken out of the show; received her diagnosis; and finally, offered the house in exchange for the prints and the negatives. Knowing she had only months left. She'd known it, and Patrick had known it, too.

Patrick had counted on it.

The free-floating pain centers in her belly, in her temples. These photos might have been in the *museum*. After her conversations with Sheila and Gary, Saskia has no doubt that they would have happily included them as part of Patrick's portfolio. She runs to her bathroom, vomiting her lunch into the toilet, and kneels on the tiles, sweat seeping from her skin.

It's in her body, the hatred. He's infiltrated her body again, all of these years later. Not with his love, this time. As toxic as that had proved to be, this is a new and different kind of poison.

It's a relief when Mike leaves the house that evening, off to see a friend or run errands or take care of the business of his life that's been so neglected these past few weeks. Before the sounds of the wheels on gravel have subsided, even before the headlights have faded from view, Saskia's darting into the conservatory just as night begins to fall.

And after eighteen years, Saskia Kreis is playing the piano again.

If she were thinking straight, she'd warm up with some scales. If she were thinking straight, she'd start with something simple. But tonight, she can't escape her teenage body, and she's pounding out the *Appassionata* with stiff fingers, with inflexible hands, with a torso that's breathless after only a few bars.

Name your feelings, Saskia, the NYU therapist told her. He always said her name wrong, *Sas* like *ass,* not *Sas* like *cost.*

Embarrassed, she thinks now.

Ashamed.

And furious.

Furious that she hadn't remembered that night of blinking in and out of consciousness. Furious, for some reason, at her mother.

For months, she'd kept those photos. Why had she kept them? Why did Saskia have to see them, to bear witness?

Her mother knew this was coming. This day, this moment. Her mother had protected her, yes, but always knowing that someday Saskia would understand exactly how much.

Why hadn't she told Saskia when she first discovered the photos existed?

The memory of how he'd won her so easily. *You're not like other girls.*

The memory of how she'd leaned in. How she'd kissed him.

The memory of his fingers under her eyes, and the realization that none of her dreams was going to happen, that she'd been imagining things this whole time—

And crawling into his bed and trembling before him in the darkroom, and now her mother, her mother forced to know this side of her—

How much more indignity is she expected to take?

In the moment, the therapist in her head tells her. *What are your senses telling you in the moment?*

In the moment, she looks at her hands. Her hands that had been so battered and bruised when she'd arrived. Healed for days now. Deceptive. Everyone knows the worst bruises are beneath the skin, anyway.

In the moment, she listens to the notes. Without judgment—it's hard for her to do anything without judgment. She focuses on the individual notes. They're like numbers, really. Music and math are so linked; each telling stories of their kind, each breakable into their component parts.

She hits middle C and it rings out so clearly, so purely. And she thinks: Well, at least the math will destroy what he had planned. He won't be able to argue with numbers, at least. He'll have to give up whatever twisted dream he's *really* trying to pursue.

The phone in her pocket buzzes, startling her out of the music. She pulls it out. Josh: *Maybe I'm way out of line here given the way things ended the other night, but I'd love to see you again. Interested in getting dinner sometime?*

The same component parts, just a different arrangement. It's like standing out on the cliffs behind the house, she feels like she's about to jump or back away; some kind of decision is required and it's required *now.*

James—her relationship with James hadn't had those same parts, which maybe accounts for some of the startling indifference she's felt in his absence. A self-protective measure, maybe. But no, she has to give herself more credit than that. Unlike with Tim, unlike with her former boss, with James she'd never made any demands, never even asked him to leave his wife. It hadn't even occurred to her when they were together. She didn't actually want that.

Before moving forward, you have to clear the path.

And James? James is just shitty math.

She stops for a minute and sends him a quick message: *I'm staying in Milwaukee a bit longer. I had a great time with you. I wish it could have been more.*

And she does, she thinks; she does wish it could have been more. But she'd also deliberately chosen a situation that would not give her more. She'd done that on purpose; she'd fucked up the math herself. She needs to remember that she does this, she thinks, as his crying-face emoji comes flying back to her. A crying-face emoji. Good God.

And so that chapter is closed.

She returns to Josh's message, thinking: The price is too high. It'll cost too much.

For starters, the photos. What would he say about the photos? It comes to her too clearly. He'd feel sorry for her. It's not the wrong reaction, necessarily. It's human, it's humane. And yet it's not what she wants. She can keep going, acting like nothing's changed, of course. But she doesn't want to. She doesn't want to perform, with him.

Dinner, she writes back, *in a couple days?*

In a couple days, she'll have formulated a plan. Time heals all wounds, wounds all heels.

And in the meantime, she texts Patrick to arrange a meeting. She has to do it. She has to try. Has to say to him, like she says to Wolfie when he's gnawing on something he shouldn't: *Drop it.*

Only it's the Elf House that Patrick has between his teeth. And no matter what she tells him, she's not so sure he's going to let it go.

The piano is soothing. The piano is soothing, but it's not enough. She wants to punch, to hit. She wants to stare down her opponent, the way she's seen the professional fighters do; she wants to stare at him and have him see the promised revenge in her eyes. She wants to be in the ring, but barring that, she just has to move.

Wolfie hears her steps and is waiting at the door for her, wagging his tail hopefully. She grabs his leash and her mother's house key and the two of them plunge into the underwater emptiness of the winter night. She's walking as fast as she does back in New York, the dog trotting at her heels, and it is only after a few blocks that she realizes where she's leading them.

Down to Downer.

When she was little, it was one of the most interesting places within the radius that her parents' free-range parenting style had established. Its brick storefronts, its cabinets of wonder. But she and Wolfie round the corner and that place is gone. It is hard to believe it ever existed, Saskia thinks, staring at the ATMs lining the ground floor of the parking structure where the popcorn truck used to be. The old street is unrecognizable now; then again, she's avoided this particular block since she was eighteen, so it's not surprising. Patrick's apartment is just up ahead. She pulls the dog along behind her, picking up the pace until they are both running.

The building is the same, if more polished now. Small topiaries line the courtyard walk, dotted with vintage-looking lampposts, lit soft gold in the night. He'd bought his two-bedroom here for $60,000, back in 1992, had paid off the mortgage by the time she'd graduated. She wonders what it's worth now. She's never in her adult life so much as considered owning property beyond the Elf House. To imagine it would have been what her father calls *magical thinking*: With what money would she have made a down payment? What bank would have rated her a good risk?

But they will now.

She stares at his darkened windows. She thinks: the arts center. The *legacy*. All of it. It had been a lie that Patrick was telling. It had maybe even been a lie that Evie told Mike, even at the beginning. She can't prove the latter, but she can sure as hell prove the former. The university never had any intention of using the house as an arts center. Beyond the few exchanges between Evie and Patrick, no official conversations had ever taken place. Because that hadn't been their plan. Not Evie's. Definitely not Patrick's.

That much, she can prove.

And she's sure as fuck going to.

She will get him to admit that he lied about the arts center. She will get him to admit it, and she will record him, and she will present the proof to the court. And, God, are there ever courts in her future. She'll get him to admit it, and then she'll go to Tara and she'll find out what to do with her phone. With the evidence of the abuse—yes, she tells herself ferociously, *abuse*; if you were a victim, it was abuse—and with the photographs. She looks even younger in them than she does in the fire escape photo.

It comes to her with a buzz, like a text: the photos could win the statutory rape case. Beyond the shame, beyond the fear, a tiny ping of victory. But beyond that, something else. The vague sense that even that, even winning—it is not enough for her.

But it's all she has.

With firm fingers, she grabs her phone and types out an email to Gary, not caring how awkwardly things ended at lunch the other day. *I'm going through my mother's estate. Is there any way of dating unsigned prints? Or, barring that, the negatives themselves?*

She's going to get the house back, she thinks, staring at the place where he lives. And then, she's going to send him away forever.

SHE AND WOLFIE WALK HOME SLOWER, ALMOST peaceful in the winter night. The East Side is still; the streets around her don't feel fully alive, somehow. The leftover Christmas lights hurt. Evie was always judgmental about taking them down late. Her mother must have seen some of these same lights, back in December. Back when she was still alive.

Thank fuck she already has her appointment set with Tara for the day after tomorrow. Today, tomorrow, last year, ten years ago: time seems to swirl around her, like she could reach out and pluck a year at random out of midair. If only she could. She wants to grab a moment from last summer, yank it down around her, find her mother, and say: *I understand what you did. But I can't live with your solution.*

Because, unlike you, I have time.

The probate case alone could take months, Tara had warned. Maybe even a year, if discovery went on for a long time. And that was just about a *house*. To prove abuse—to prove child pornography—well, the child pornography spoke for itself, didn't it? But she needs more than the time to find evidence of it, incontestable proof of her age in the photos. She needs the time for it to go to trial as well.

It could take years.

Years during which her teenage body makes its way through evidence files. Years of Patrick's smug, perfect face from the defendant's stand. Years of funneling money into paying Tara's bills as well as the house—

Years that she owes to herself.

It's the only way forward. But she realizes what it means. She realizes what she'll have to do.

The one thing she'd always sworn not to. Coming home before her time; spending the dredges of her youth in the Elf House.

But. In all the times she'd imagined returning to live with her parents, she'd always pictured herself arriving exhausted, defeated. That's not how she feels now. The heartbreak and the horror and the shame and the rage have taken hold inside her, zooming through her veins like liquid gold.

She has a purpose. She has a plan.

She can let herself do this.

Gina, I think I might stay here for good.

She presses *send* before she can second-guess herself, and when her phone rings, she stares at it in surprise.

"Gina?"

"You chickenshit. You think that's how you deliver news?"

"I didn't want to call too late!"

"My daughter's not at home. You think I sleep anymore?"

"Still with Bobby?"

A sigh is all the answer she needs.

"So, you're staying."

"I have to." There's more to say, but Saskia isn't sure she has the words yet.

"I guess it makes sense. Everyone leaves New York, in the end."

"It's not the city, it's just . . . My family. Legal stuff. I'm the only one— I'm the only one . . ." But she doesn't have a good end to that sentence.

"Well, I do get that." There's a long pause. "Fuck, Sas. I'm going to miss you."

"You and Jos have to come visit. Come spend the summer here! It would be good for you both to get some of this fresh Midwestern air."

"What would we do with ourselves in the middle of Wisconsin?" Gina's voice is lighter now. Forgiving.

"Spar with me," Sas says. "Keep me on my toes. You remember how you used to say that boxing's about not getting hit?"

A dry laugh echoes.

"Literally everyone says that."

"No, I know. But I heard it from you first, and it always kind of surprised me. Because you're so aggressive in the ring. I've never seen you pull a single punch, in all of our time together."

She can hear the smile in Gina's voice. "And?"

"And," Saskia says, "I'm going to need that now. For what's coming."

Chapter 19

The Snow Queen sent the mirror shards into the center of Gerda's eye and cast her spell: The worst things you ever believed about yourself are all true.

But to her shock, Gerda just blinked and shook her head.

"I don't believe it," she said. "Your stupid mirror magic doesn't work on me. I never trust mirrors, anyway. My self-worth comes from within."

—*FAIRY TALES FOR LITTLE FEMINISTS:*
THE SNOW QUEEN, EVELYN HARPER KREIS

May 1998

SASKIA WAS FIFTEEN, AND PATRICK WAS RUNNING his fingers along the notches in her spine as the boat rocked gently beneath them. Her parents were in San Francisco for the weekend, and they'd taken advantage of the opportunity for their first spring sail. Now, with *The Ingenue* anchored on the quiet lake waters below the full spring moon, the two of them were tucked into the cozy cabin belowdecks. Saskia fought to keep her eyes open, but Patrick's voice kept calling her back.

"I'm so sorry I couldn't be there for you," he was whispering. "You brave girl."

She didn't know why he was sorry; they both knew why he couldn't have been there, as her parents stood anxious guard around her hospital bed. But it was fine. It had been a dramatic episode, her heartbeat exploding irregularly through her veins as she played the Beethoven *Hammerklavier* onstage at the Marcus Center, lights bursting in fireworks in her vision until finally she'd stood for her bow and collapsed. The day in the hospital afterward had been much more boring, and she had lived on the hope of seeing him striding through the door after visiting hours were over and her parents had left. He lived only a block from St. Mary's, after all. But it was what it was. *Anxiety*, the doctors said. A *panic attack*. Well, okay. It had felt like so much more than that, but it was what they said it was.

And now, remembering, she opened her eyes: she had a bonus for him. She dangled over the side of the bed, rummaging in her purse. Finally, bounty in hand, she held up the translucent orange bottle for his approval.

"Klonopin," she said, as he squinted at the label without admitting that he was squinting.

He wrapped his hand around hers. Her fingers were long, but his were longer. He had the biggest hands, calloused from the darkroom chemicals and the sailboat's ropes.

"Ah. But, babe, I already got us a treat."

He refused to let her get bored with him. *You will, you know.* She wasn't bored, but she was bored by the repeated warning, and so she'd followed along obediently as he introduced first alcohol, then pills into their afternoons and evenings. It wasn't like they were driving anywhere. And it was medicine, what was the problem? Georgia took pills. Saskia had had codeine for some minor dental surgery the year before. It wasn't like she was shooting anything into her veins; it wasn't like she was even snorting anything. It was just swallowing a pill, a pill like a thousand other pills.

And then it felt like flying.

That night, it was a simple white pill. She downed it with her rum and Coke, and then his hand was stroking her again, his lips were on her skin, she was running her fingers through his thick, soft hair.

She woke feeling like she'd emerged from a fever, finding the boat moored in McKinley Marina.

"What the— Fuck! Shit!" She stared at her phone. Eight. Eight in the morning.

Patrick, beside her, stirred, his hand knocking the Canon onto the floor.

Saskia wiggled her jeans on, frantic. "Patrick, this can't happen! Fuck, my parents are already home. I've never— How did we even— I don't remember anything from last night, do you?" She clicked her bra clasp closed and stared at him, naked on his knees, running his fingers over the camera. "Wait, why is your camera out? Did you take pictures—"

Patrick set the camera back on the table, close against the wall. A mischievous grin that made her stomach swirl, drop.

"That pill hit you good, Sassy," he said, crawling over the bed to her. She hated when he called her that, she fucking *hated* it, but she was scanning the floor for her shirt, she needed to get out of here. And then his lips on her neck. "You got a little . . . playful, and you wanted—"

She put her hands on his shoulders, guided him away. "Whatever. Toss them, okay? I've got to run, I'm going to— Fuck!"

But her parents weren't even home when she tiptoed in the side door, breathless and wild-eyed. They didn't come back until much later that night. By then, she was soaking quietly in her claw-footed tub, Chopin on the stereo and bubbles popping into nothingness around her body.

February 2020

DRIVING NORTH OUT OF MILWAUKEE, YOU CAN tell precisely when you cross the city limits. It would be possible even if you were blindfolded. The roads literally change beneath you, the patchwork of potholes and cobbled-together repairs replaced by blissfully uniform asphalt. Saskia rolls her eyes as she passes the WELCOME TO SHOREWOOD sign—decades of white flight from the city allow for a reliably high tax base, which, in turn, allows for up-to-date infrastructure. But with every block Saskia drives from Milwaukee, the buildings gain a superficial polish and lose their history. Still, she appreciates the smoothness, if only on behalf of the Saab's finicky suspension.

Shorewood fades into Whitefish Bay (*White Folk's Bay*, they'd called it in high school—as though they weren't already the whitest high school for miles around themselves) as the neat-edged American flags on the fronts of the houses get bigger, brighter. Saskia drives inland from the lake a few blocks, parks on a side street. There was a spot open right in front of City Market, but she couldn't risk taking it.

She picks up her phone, glancing at her reflection in the rearview mirror. She feels like she's aged a year in the last few days.

But, she thinks, the anger burning down to her bones, I'm still younger than he was the first time he fucked me.

Today's the day that she's going to finish it. To clinch the case. Her mother could never have wanted to give Patrick the house, not really; if she had, she would have told him about the huge financial burdens that came along with it. And when Saskia reveals this to Patrick, he'll have to give up the ghost. He'll have to admit he was lying about his conversations with her dying mother, lying about his intention to use the house for the university's pre-college programs, lying about his commitment to Evelyn Kreis's legacy—lying about it all.

She hesitates over the keypad as an email notification pops up. Gary. She opens it: *Sadly, there's not a lot we can do to date negatives, let alone prints, with any degree of precision. However, there are usually context clues we can use from the images themselves, from your mother's career—*

So she can't establish her age in the photos from anything scientific. She closes her eyes. One thing at a time; that shit can wait.

She pulls Tara's number up on her phone.

"Tara Fernwood."

"Tara. Saskia Kreis."

"Saskia!" The relief is palpable in the lawyer's voice. "Are we good to go with the affidavit?"

"Um. Well, look. I'm bringing in some stuff to our meeting that's going to change the case, I think substantially. I just—"

"Okay, but Saskia?" Tara's voice rises. "The hearing's in two weeks. That's ten business days. The clock started once Josh filed the petition for administration; we had thirty days. Now we have half that. It's a lot harder to contest a will after it's been admitted into probate, and I—"

"I know, I got it," Saskia cuts her off like a teenager reprimanded by her parents. "But it has to be perfect before we file. He gets a written notice once we do, you said?"

"Yeah. But I don't think—"

"What were the four things we needed for the case? Tell me the four things again."

A pause.

"Susceptibility, opportunity, disposition, and coveted result."

"Where are we weakest?"

"Disposition," Tara says after a moment. "We need to prove that Patrick was actually willing to do something wrong, something unfair. Saskia. What's going on?"

But she has what she needed. If she proves he lied about the university's intentions to use the house for an arts center, she'll prove that he had malicious intentions.

"Thanks. See you tomorrow."

She turns on a Voice Memo and climbs out of the car. The quarter for the meter tumbles out of her hands and she watches it fall, stares down at the square of sidewalk beneath her feet. On Milwaukee's East Side, each concrete block is stamped with the year: *City of Milwaukee, 1918. City of Milwaukee, 2004.* But there's no such history imprinted into the sidewalks here.

"Well, look who it is!" For the first time in her life, his cheerful voice disgusts her. He doesn't have the good grace to come five minutes late to let her pick their table, check her hair, brace for the thought of him. Nope, this is Patrick through and through. Eminently in control.

She forces herself to smile as she looks up at him.

How different it is, seeing him now, knowing what she knows. His beaming face, his sun-kissed coloring, his crisp white shirt beneath the heavy wool coat—all of it so attractive to her just a few days ago. All of it revealed to be nothing more than a trap, a trap with which to catch little girls.

It is so strange, walking into the café with him. Two adults, side by side; to the rest of the world, everything must look completely normal, aboveboard.

She's never had that with him before. And yet it's too late to appreciate it, she's beyond feeling anything but alarm at the thought of him by her side.

"Why here?" she asks as he holds the door open for her.

His grin is bashful. "Oh. I was working from home this morning. My place is just down the road."

She feels the blood rising into her cheeks with a prickly itch. How stupid she'd been, standing outside his apartment. Of course he'd moved. Moved out, moved up.

But fuck him and his house. She's here to talk about *her* house. The Elf House.

The Elf House and the money, she tells herself sternly. That's what all. No photographs. The photographs are burning through her bloodstream, taken by this creep, this con, this— But no. Money only. Until then, small talk.

She studies the menu posted above the counter. It's a perfectly nice middle-class street, full of perfectly nice middle-class bungalows. But it's not the nicest part of Whitefish Bay, not bordering the lake or a park or far enough north to have lots of land.

"Gave up on Downer?" she asks after ordering and paying for her fajita wrap.

"Hamburger, rare, and a Coke," he says to the girl at the counter, and turns to Saskia with a wink. "Grew up, more like."

That wink seems to brush against her skin, creeping along her spine. His eyes, the central attraction of his face with their gold sunbursts at the center, the warm brown surrounding them. She glances back at the teenager who took their order, relieved to see that she's already turned around, is already chatting with a coworker. Not staring after Patrick at all.

Strange, she thinks; the jealousy is gone. It's been replaced by this fear, this protective instinct.

He guides her to a table in the corner without making it seem like he's actually guiding her. Stealthy sheepdog. And then he sits, back to the wall like a soldier or a spy, while she's stuck with the chair facing inward, the chair facing him.

Student facing, she thinks.

Patrick props his call number next to hers and opens his hands wide.

"So, what can I do for you?"

She can't look at him, though she feels his eyes on her. His eyes, his camera. She imagines shoving the metal call number apparatus through his eye, so far in it hits the back of his skull.

"This isn't— Not the house again, is it, Sas?"

As though it could be anything else. She pulls the accountant's ledger out of her tote bag, spreading the green-lined pages in front of him.

He follows her finger across the sheet. But she can see, she knows him. He understands nothing.

"Mom was holding out on you," she says finally as the waitress comes and sets their food in front of them, takes their numbers away. She takes a bite out of the fajita wrap, nods in surprise. Spicy. She's not used to spicy food in Wisconsin. With a greasy finger, she points, smudging the paper transparent wherever she touches. "It's a shitty deal. The foundation needs significant repairs before long. Back taxes are overdue. Cliff repair is constant, and it's not going to get better. You're looking at spending around seven hundred and fifty grand before you even set foot in the place, likely more."

She sits back as his eyes dart across the page. *So what do you think of that?* He never did have a head for numbers.

"It seems like something that someone who was making a gift would have told the recipient," she says.

His brows draw together. "Your mother—her illness—"

Saskia shakes her head. "There's a medical certificate. She was still lucid."

He looks up with a boyish grin. "Then I'm sure that she, like me, assumed that the university—"

She makes a face. "Has better ways to spend three-quarters of a million dollars, plus whatever they'd need for renovations. Come on, Patrick. You're telling me that they're going to pour time and effort and cash into this white elephant? They'd sell it off in a heartbeat, and you know it. What's your game, here?"

Backlit by the storefront window behind him, his eyes look pure gold as he narrows them thoughtfully at her. Then he smiles, shakes his head. The silver in his hair is bright, glowing. It would photograph beautifully in black-and-white.

"No game. The possibility that the university would sell it was one of the reasons your mother put it under my care. I can oversee the work, look after the renovations—"

"With what money?" She didn't mean to be so blunt. And yet the hammering of her heartbeat, the adrenaline in her blood like an itch as he resists, pushes her into it.

He raises a broad shoulder. "There are plenty of options. Reverse mortgage. Sell my place, make a few investments—"

"Sell your place and live where? Make a few investments in what? But fine, let's just say that gets you the seven fifty. *Maybe.* How much more to turn it into studio space, to make it actually functional? Just admit it, Patrick. You never wanted it for the arts center. You could do the arts center anywhere, if it's something that the school actually wanted to support. Do it on some property they already own. You don't want the Elf House for Mom's legacy. You just want it for yourself."

She snaps back in her chair, cursing herself. She wasn't supposed to say so much. She was supposed to be subtle, cunning. And look, his reaction—he's grimacing at her brazenness. At her bluntness.

"I appreciate your concern. Can I keep this?" he asks, folding the green paper back in on itself, shutting the ledger. It's halfway under his arm before she closes her mouth, grabs it back. He laughs, exasperated. "*Saskia.* I do appreciate it. I do! And I understand where you're coming from. Really. The loss of your mother was such a shock, and you want to make sure the house is cared for, maintained. But I'm not a bad guy. And I have resources at my disposal, and I'm going to make sure that this all turns out the way your mother and I—the way your mother wanted."

She opens her mouth at that. But he's already turning away, gesturing at the waitress, asking for a to-go box for his burger. Once she'd been the object of his affections, his object, the only object, now she is nothing, now she is—

Saskia does not know what it is in him that always wins.

But whatever it is, it ends with her.

She looks at him with fevered eyes. "Or maybe you're just looking forward to the possibilities of the soundproofed tower. I mean, it's no *Ingenue.* But there's still potential there, I'm sure. Turning it into your own special *studio.* For example."

He stands up.

"You know, honey," he says, and there's a mischievous catch to his voice as it lowers, as he bends down toward her to whisper, "I just don't know where you get these crazy ideas. They're going to ruin you in the end, you know. Better let them go before they destroy you."

No, Saskia thinks, popping the last of the fajita into her mouth as she watches him turn away. No.

The only one who's going to get destroyed is him.

Chapter 20

"And on her sixteenth birthday, she will prick her finger on the spindle of a spinning wheel . . . and die!"

And with that, the evil fairy spun away in a cloud of smoke.

The King leapt to his feet. "No child of mine shall be held hostage to some fairy's whims! Guards! I want every spinning wheel in the palace gathered in the courtyard and burned."

But the Queen held up her hand. "Honey," she said, "think things through. We live in a preindustrial society. What, are we just not going to have new cloth for the next sixteen years? No. No," she repeated thoughtfully, "I think from now, spinning will be an entirely masculine occupation. No women are to be allowed in the same room as those darn contraptions. Just the men." She smiled sunnily at her husband. "Problem solved!"

—*Fairy Tales for Little Feminists: Sleeping Beauty*, Evelyn Harper Kreis

June 1999

SASKIA WAS SIXTEEN, AND WHEN SHE HAD AGREED to attend Lexi's seventeenth birthday party, she hadn't realized that it was a *party* party. She'd always kind of assumed that these kinds of parties, beach and bonfire and beers, didn't happen anywhere but in the movies that she avoided watching if she could help it. But it turned out they did happen; she just hadn't been invited to one before.

She was dressed prettily, little sundress and strappy heels, but even this was wrong, for this kind of party. They weren't playing Top 40, Britney

Spears or *NSYNC, but rather sad and whiny songs by bands she didn't know. They weren't drinking Budweiser or Miller Lite, they were drinking cocktails out of plastic cups, courtesy of Aunt Georgia (*If you're going to drink, I'd rather you do it here*). It was all so different from anything she had anticipated that the familiar beach felt like foreign soil, even as she sank her bare toes into the sand she knew so well.

Saskia could hear her mother: *You'd like the other kids a whole lot more if you judged them a whole lot less.*

Maybe.

But as the fire crackled between them, as it shot sparks up toward the enormous full moon hanging over them, she couldn't think of a single goddamn thing to say. They were talking about music. She could have talked about music! But the only things she could have contributed would have been in a different language from theirs. "Clair de Lune." "Bad Moon Rising." She'd added another dialect to her repertoire over the past two years, thanks to Patrick, but it wouldn't get her anywhere here.

It hit her like a chill wind. Once upon a time, there had been only one thing pulling her away from people like these people. From Lexi, from normal. Just the piano, that was all. But now, there were two.

She looked over her shoulder to the Elf House. In the dark, only her windows were lit: hers and the hallway's lights to lead her back home. With half-drawn curtains, they made the house look like it was smiling at her. And when she turned back to the group, she could sense it still at her back like a benevolent grandmother.

Maybe she was starting to feel the Malibu, after all.

Her hands started picking out "Clair de Lune" on her bare thigh, goose-bumped in the dark. If only she were at home, now, in her room. Pressing down silently on the unplugged keyboard, twisting and contorting her hands as only she could.

Lexi wouldn't notice if she disappeared. Lexi was laughing next to a boy, Lexi was dipping her toes into the lake, letting the water lick and pull back, lick and pull back.

But Saskia had committed to being here. And if there was one thing Saskia had in spades, it was perseverance.

"How you doing?" In the shadows, in the bright flaming light illuminating their faces, the boy next to her was only vaguely familiar.

One of the Joshes, she thought; Josh Asher. Still, she turned to him in gratitude.

"Oh," Saskia said. "I'm okay."

There was a beat, and she realized she should have asked him how he was. Shit. She was always missing things like that.

"You don't look so okay," the boy said. "You look pretty miserable, actually."

"No. No," she said, her voice trailing off.

He smiled and took a sip from his plastic Solo cup. His cheekbones stood out bright against the fire.

"You know one of my favorite things about my mom?" he said. Saskia, startled into attention, shook her head. "She never forces me to stay for things. She always says: 'You're not happy somewhere, you can just go.'" He tilted his cup to the side. "Not that I want you to go. But I'm just saying, it's an option."

"Well," she said. "It's not my parents keeping me here."

And it was his turn to fall silent.

"Full moon tonight," she offered, attempting to keep the conversation going.

He smiled. "Werewolves'll be out."

"Did you believe in that stuff when you were a kid?" she asked. "Fairies, ghosts, werewolves?"

The boy snorted. "Yeah, of course. You?"

"I don't know," she said, twisting her cup between her hands. "I don't think I did. But I wanted to believe, you know?"

He was looking at her, searching her face. "*X-Files*?"

"What?"

"*I want to believe.* Like X-Files?"

"Is that a movie?"

He laughed, short and dry.

"A TV show."

"Oh."

There, always and forever. She had made a choice when she was three years old, and it hadn't even been a choice, she hadn't known she was choosing. But now here she was, having opted out of normal human life, and most of the time it didn't bother her, it really didn't, but—

She didn't have to be there.

"Your mom was right," she said, getting to her feet. "Thanks for the advice, Josh."

And by the time Saskia was back in her room, fire roaring safely in the grate as she picked out the notes to "Clair de Lune" silently on her keyboard, she had already forgotten all about him.

February 2020

OUTSIDE TARA'S OFFICE, ALL THE WEATHER SEEMS to be happening at once. The snow would be considered a blizzard anywhere but Wisconsin. Behind them, over the lake, lightning, the muffled boom of thunder.

Saskia discards her winter clothing with disgust at its wetness, how her mother's wool hat and gloves cling to her skin. Tara hangs them on the coatrack behind the door, watching Saskia with careful eyes.

Because Saskia has been greased with new purpose.

She is here now, she is home, she is ready to see this through. She spent the rest of yesterday finding movers unethical enough to pack up her New York shit without her there, FedExing them the keys, and informing the management company that she's vacating the apartment (she's supposed to give a month's notice, and the February rent she has no intention of paying was due last week, but fuck it, she's in Wisconsin, what are they going to do?).

And now here she is, ready to step into the ring.

You want a clean slate, honey, go ahead and take it.

Holding Tara's gaze the entire time, she sets the picture she chose and the telephone on the desk. It is the picture containing her face: her innocent, loving face, above a taut, angular torso, above the slight curve of her breasts contradicting the sharpness.

Tara's eyes scan it, professional and detached, before landing on the phone.

Saskia nods and grabs it back, fiddling with the buttons until the robot's voice comes on, loud and grainy through the speaker. The robot; and then, him.

TUESDAY, SEPTEMBER 11, 2001. *Darling, I had to reach you—*

When it's over, the two women stand facing each other.

"Patrick?" Tara says, nodding at the telephone.

Saskia nods. She points at the photo. "Patrick," she says, and sets down the rest of the photos she's holding. Julia. Kelly. The others. "They were nearly in the show at the art museum. Instead, Mom traded the house for the prints and the negatives."

Tara closes her bright eyes, then collapses into her desk chair, swinging back and forth as she blows out her cheeks. "*Fuck,*" she says.

Saskia swallows as she sits down.

"Fuck?"

"No—no, no, not *fuck,* just . . . *shit,*" Tara says, and Saskia can't help a smile.

"Is it good for us or bad for us?" she says.

"It's . . . it's more than it seems," Tara says distractedly, and hops to her feet again, pacing in front of the windows, backlit by the lightning storm. "Okay. Let's talk through it. So, in addition to undue influence, you're looking at a lot of other possibilities here. You're looking at possession of child pornography. Production of child pornography. Possibly endangering a minor, things like that. And then there's the other piece."

"The other . . ."

"The statutory . . ." Tara looks at her. "If that's what happened? How old were you?"

"I don't know, I can't date them exactly," Saskia says hoarsely. She doesn't say, *I don't remember him taking the photos.* She doesn't say, *I think he drugged me.* "Younger than in the fire-escape portrait. What does that mean? What does it mean, for him?"

"For the pictures? I'd want a more specific date, if there's any way you can get it. A journal, an email to a friend, anything . . ." Saskia shakes her head, and Tara sighs. "Well. If you were even a day under eighteen—if any of you were—it can be considered child pornography. But it'll likely be complicated. Free speech, First Amendment, art, *I know it when I see it—*" Saskia blinks at the free association, and Tara shakes her head. "I'm sorry. Criminal law isn't my specialty, so you'll need to confirm this with someone who knows for sure. And for the abuse . . . off the top of my head: the statute of limitations varies by the age of the victim. Under thirteen, no statute applies. Between thirteen and sixteen, it's until the victim turns forty-five. Sixteen to eighteen, until the victim's thirty-five. But I'd need to double-check all that."

"If it starts when she's fourteen and it keeps going until she's eighteen?"

"If she's . . . fuck, criminal law class was a long time ago. I think there's a statute of limitations on the multiples. Three years, something like that? But you'll need to talk to the cops. The D.A. Maybe a personal injury lawyer."

Saskia laughs at that, laughs like a bark.

"A personal . . . like an ambulance chaser?"

Tara's gaze is unflinching.

"Like the lawyers who take civil claims to court for you. If you want a civil case. If you want to sue. You could do it with the other girls. The other victims. Makes it harder to deny."

But it's one thing for Saskia to call herself a victim. It's another thing to hear someone else use the label.

She looks at Tara and sees pity in her China-blue eyes. And something in Saskia lashes back, against this woman she genuinely likes. There's something about pity that makes her just a girl who was abused. That makes her just another girl. That makes her just like everyone else, and she can't stand it.

"I don't know about suing," she says. "I don't see why everything has to come down to money, in the end."

"I don't know why, either," Tara says, shrugging. "I only know that it does. But look. Are you going to the cops?"

Saskia imagines tying the rage monster living inside of her to a pole in the basement of her mind, smooths over her expression.

"I don't know. Is that how he goes down for this?"

"If you're not interested in suing, yes, it's the only other way. To get criminal charges brought against him by the state." Tara goes back to her desk, leans forward. "But look, Saskia. If you're going to do it, you've got to do it *now*. Otherwise the cops will wonder why you didn't do it earlier, before we file the affidavit, and it's going to look incredibly fishy."

She swallows. "And . . . if I don't? If I don't do anything?"

The pity again. "Well, it's up to you, of course—"

"No, fuck that. Do you have to tell them if I don't?"

Slowly, Tara shakes her head. "No. I don't have a duty to report. Though I would strongly encourage you—"

"Okay, so what happens if I do go to the cops?" Saskia needs to get out of the laser beam of the lawyer's blue, piteous stare, so she goes to the window, keeping her back to the office. Presses a hand against the chilled glass.

"The abuse would be a class C felony. Forty years, state prison. The pornography is going to be harder to prosecute, as I said. And . . . it's complicated. Mandatory minimums of three years per instance, which can be interpreted as per image that you put forward as evidence. But there are lots of exceptions. You really need a personal injury . . ." A shuffling; Saskia turns to see Tara flipping through a bunch of cards, plucking one out. "Christine Terrare. She's great."

Saskia turns back to the window in time to see a lightning bolt shatter down over the lake. "But you can tell me how this affects the probate case, for one thing."

"Of course, I'm just . . ." There's something she hasn't heard before in the lawyer's voice. Dismay. "I'm just not used to this kind of thing. It's awful. So awful for you, and your father—"

Saskia whips around. "My father doesn't know. Not yet. Not about that," pointing to the photographs on the desk.

Tara's head bobs. Not: *He'll eventually find out.* Not: *Don't you think you should tell him?* But still: that sympathy in her eyes.

"The probate case," Saskia repeats, striding back to her chair. "How would bringing charges against him for—" She's not ready to say the words yet, just waves toward the desk. "What I mean is: Which case takes precedence if he gets charged for the other stuff? There were," she says, Sheila's words ringing in her head, "some other cases at the university brought against him, too. I don't think they went anywhere, though."

"Right. So, those are likely to be seen as prejudicial. Don't worry about them right now—though it's definitely something to share with Christine. More important, the D.A. isn't going to delay bringing charges just because there's a probate case. The judge in our case is likely to stay—to delay—the trial until the criminal cases are resolved."

"How long would those take?"

"Months," Tara says. "Together, years. Now, there's a small possibility that evidence of the criminal cases would be ruled inadmissible in our case, which means no stay would be issued—it wouldn't be considered necessary. But, on the other hand, since you found these while researching the probate case . . . evidence from our case *might* actually be admissible in the criminal case."

Saskia frowns, trying to parse the legalese into normal language. "Okay, so . . . the criminal cases wouldn't help the probate case, but the probate case could help the criminal cases?"

Tara nods. "Again, it's complicated. It has to do with the Rules of Evidence. But basically, in the criminal case, you'd have to testify how you found the photos, how you knew they were taken by Patrick, and all of that. And if you can't establish how you discovered that the child porn crime took place *without* disclosing facts about the probate case, then that info would *have* to be admissible in criminal court. If there were a stay on our trial, and Patrick was convicted of the criminal offenses, it would be up to the judge whether to admit those convictions into evidence. They're highly relevant, in this case, but you never know—"

Saskia makes a frustrated noise at the back of her throat. "Fuck. So it's all super messy, is what you're saying."

"It's basically all up to a judge, is what I'm saying," Tara says, that soft look returning to her eyes. "To decide whether the value of the information supporting our undue influence case outweighs the danger of unfair prejudice to Patrick."

Saskia lets her head fall back so her chin points straight up at the ceiling.

Years of this. She is looking at years and years of thinking about Patrick.

Years and years in which she and her father can stay in the Elf House.

Years and years in which she'll be trapped in the past. Chained up like the monster in her mind.

"Fuck!" she cries, slapping the arm of her chair.

"I'm sorry—I'm so, so—" But Tara cuts herself off as Saskia sits up and looks at her with fierce eyes. The lawyer reaches across the desk with the card: Christine's number. "I can come to the meeting with you, if you want," she says softly.

"I don't know," Saskia says, shoving it into her bag. "I don't know yet what I'm going to do."

Tara nods.

"In the meantime, this is more than enough to establish disposition," Tara says, taking out her phone and snapping pictures. "So that's something. I'll revise the affidavit accordingly."

"Wait," Sas says, an edge of panic in her voice. "Wait. I'm not ready to tell my father—I don't even know—because if we submit these as evidence in our case, won't the police go after him anyway for the criminal stuff? Isn't that possible? And then I have to . . . fuck. It's all just so much. And it's fast as hell, and I'm just—"

Tara's gaze cuts across the desk, and her eyes have turned flame blue against the heavy gray sky behind her.

"Decide soon," Tara says, and it's like acid after cream: the acknowledgment that Saskia is the decider, that *she's* the one who decides.

The pity is gone, and Saskia can finally breathe again.

This is still Saskia's story.

But her heart starts beating like a hummingbird as soon as the lawyer goes on.

"Thirteen days left until the hearing," says Tara.

Chapter 21

Guinevere surveyed the round table, the knights scattered around it, and she smiled her first real smile all day. By the time she'd seen the empty chair, she'd made up her mind.

"No," she said, "no, I don't think I'll be marrying anyone today. But I would very much like to be a part of this."

"But—but the politics of it!" King Arthur sputtered. "What will happen to our kingdoms if we do not marry? You can't forget the politics, my dear."

She looked at him, vaguely condescending.

"Haven't you heard? The personal is political. And this is how I choose to spend my life. Squire," she called. "Fetch me my armor."

—*Fairy Tales for Little Feminists:*
Guinevere, Evelyn Harper Kreis

July 1999

SASKIA WAS SIXTEEN WHEN HER MOTHER DREW the line.

"Saskia, I understand that you're a Scorpio and that you like your privacy. But you've been dating this boy Josh for over a year, and it's past time that your father and I met him. Mike? Isn't that right?"

Her father looked up from the newspaper, like they were in a 1950s sitcom.

"That's right," he said, though Saskia would have bet good money that he didn't know what they were talking about.

"It's summer, you've been gone way too much for a girl your age. So, before you see him again, you're going to invite him over for dinner."

Saskia opened her mouth, but she knew that expression on her mother's face too well. She wasn't grounded; she was too good for that. But her heart hammered hard. What was she supposed to do? Invite Patrick over?

"Yeah, sure," she said lightly, and scampered up to her room.

Obviously, Patrick himself was out of the question. But staging a breakup would be more trouble than it was worth, because what was she supposed to say when she kept disappearing on Wednesdays and Sundays? It might take her mother a month or two to notice, but she eventually would.

She opened the school directory, and there he was, right on the first page. Josh Asher. One of the boys she'd imagined when she'd first lied to her parents. The boy from Lexi's party.

She picked up her phone, started dialing. She felt stupid, this was too fucking stupid. But what did she care what he thought of her? Though the kids at school would crucify her if they found out about this. Frozen, she closed her eyes.

He wouldn't tell. She didn't know much about Josh, but she felt certain of this.

"Uh, hi, is Josh there? This is Saskia Kreis."

The jostling of the receiver against a table, the hollering for him—it was so domestic, benign, that it thawed her a little. And then, his voice, mild and curious.

"Hello?"

"Josh? It's Saskia Kreis. Look, I have a . . . weird situation. And I was wondering if you could help me out."

"You had me at *weird*."

And she smiled.

Somehow, for some reason, he agreed to do it. That Saturday afternoon, she snuck him in the side door and up to her tower for a debriefing. It *was* weird, but he was game, he was going along with it.

"So, you were in California, then Spain, then Italy—" Under the hanging bulb, his face was scrunched up like he was studying for a test. She appreciated his earnestness. It kept the potential rumor from floating around in her mind. *And then she took him up to this* attic . . .

Other than Lexi and Patrick, she'd never brought anybody up to the attic before.

"No. California, Italy, Spain. But they're not going to test you on that, honestly. It'll be more . . . what I'm like. Silly things I do. My favorite color."

His eyebrows shot up. She sighed.

"I'm intense. I tap out music when I'm nervous. I get random nose-bleeds. And blue."

"Blue?"

"Navy blue. Like the edge of the lake in a storm."

She offered him a hundred bucks, but he wouldn't take it. *Good karma*, he said. She didn't believe in karma, but she didn't have much choice, then, either. And at five minutes to seven, she rustled him back down the servants' stairs and out the back so he could walk around to ring the front bell.

He was the perfect choice, she thought as her father opened the door. Framed there between the elves' hanging feet, his face had the perfect amount of intelligence and guilelessness. And he kept it up throughout dinner, as they made their way through the quail and the asparagus and the lemon tarts: laughing the exact right amount at Mike's jokes, listening to Evie's stories with an interest that bordered on—but never crossed over into—awe. And the whole time, casting looks at Saskia. Little grins, once a wink, all of them meant for her yet visible enough that her parents would catch them.

He's done this before. For real, she realized halfway through the meal. *He's been to a girlfriend's house.*

She didn't know what to do with the bitter tang of envy this realization produced in her.

And at the end of the evening, when she was allowed to walk him to the door on her own, she kissed his cheek, slipping a fifty into his palm.

"Sas—"

"No—" She held up her hands. "You were a wonderful actor. You earned it." She contemplated telling him that only her parents, Patrick, and Lexi called her *Sas* but refrained; it seemed too mean.

His face twisted into an impish grin. "All right, then. How about I use it to take you out sometime, then? For real?"

For a moment, the possibility of that future flashed in front of her. Not unpleasant.

But . . . Patrick. Always Patrick.

She wished she had someone she could bring home to her parents for real.

"I don't think so. But thank you," she added quickly.

He nodded. She thought he was going to say something as he turned away, but he stayed silent. Just shoved his hands in his pockets and walked down the drive.

"Happy now?" Saskia called to her parents as she bolted up the stairs.

"Delighted!" Evie called back.

"Ecstatic," said Mike.

February 2020

THE TEXT COMES EARLY IN THE MORNING, JUST AS she awakes.

Can I come by today around 6?

Why does Patrick want to come to the house?

Kelly got in touch with him—no, she'd never. Julia, then? Far more likely. He's heard something from Gary, or Sheila let something slip. . . .

But what is Saskia going to do, say no?

She descends the back staircase, where she can hear her father shuffling around in the kitchen.

"Dad?" she calls. "What are you up to today?"

"I'm going out with some old friends for a beer at five," he replies. "We'll probably have dinner after. You'll be okay on your own?"

She says yes to both men.

The day passes excruciatingly until she sits at the piano, runs her hands over the keys. Enough music and she'll get lost in the movements, lost in the notes, and this trembling will go out of her fingers. She'll be the heroine once more, ready to face him—

What is this that she's playing? (This used to happen to her sometimes, her hands seem to, quite literally, have a mind of their own.) It's a symphony—yes, that's it, she can hear the jagged sounds of an orchestra rising around her. Something slightly schmaltzy, balletic—Cinderella at the ball, transposed badly for solo piano.

And she thinks: Maybe this is an opportunity.

Forget about what Patrick wants. Forget about what his agenda is. Who is to say that she can't achieve hers at the same time? And it's so simple, really, what she needs. Just two sentences. The first: *I lied.*

He wants the house. Wants it for himself. She knows it, she knows there's no progressive-liberal artistic haven in his plans, that there never was. But no matter what Tara says about having established disposition with the phone and the photos, she wants another way, in case she chooses not to use them.

But it's more than that. She wants to nail him to the wall with his own words.

The second sentence she needs: *You were fifteen.*

She sat up all night with her yearbook photos, with pictures plucked from her mother's archives, with her album cover, with the postcard. She was younger than sixteen in the photos, she knows it. She had to be older than fourteen, though; she'd had bangs that year. She can trace the outgrowth of her bangs from fourteen to sixteen, when they were fully integrated with the rest of her hair, but it's impossible to tell exactly how long they were in the photos, as her hair is brushed back from her forehead.

But no bangs. Bangs would have stuck up.

I lied. You were fifteen.

That's all.

She lifts her hands from the ivory keys and sets her voice recording app on automatic, so it'll be triggered by their conversation. Capture it all.

Patrick in prison with a sentence longer than her life. Maybe even his money, *his* house, belonging to her (she has to call that lawyer Tara recommended, Christine, she really should; Monday, she resolves). His words twisted against him for the first time in his life, his silver tongue turned to clay.

By her.

But is she enough?

She can't help thinking about one of the first times James came over to her apartment. They hadn't slept together yet, had only danced around it with what they called a "friendship" that started after he kissed her, that first night, in the alley behind the dive bar where they'd met. But it was pretty clear to Sas what was going to happen that afternoon. Her heart clogged her throat, she couldn't breathe; she took one of the Xanax the doctor kept prescribing *just in case*. And then another, and pretty soon she'd taken four.

By the time he came over, everything was a blur. But the snippets she does remember still haunt her. *I'm not sure I'm even capable of love. Do you know what made me choose you? No danger.*

Why, she wonders, is she thinking about this now?

And then her eyes land on the liquor cabinet.

Just a few pills, she thinks as she runs upstairs to get them. Just a few pills to get him to open up, to lower his inhibitions. A few pills, just like he used to give her. What's good for the goose is good for the gander, after all. But she finds herself mashing up ten with the kitchen mortar and pestle, because he's a big man, and who knows how much he'll drink? Besides, it's not like it's going to hurt him.

As she's mixing the powder into the whiskey, she notices the grime on top of the cabinet. The dust on the baseboards behind. The smeared shoe scuffs left over from the memorial service. The filth of it shames her.

She goes through the kitchen to the cleaner's closet (turns out she did know where the vacuum was; her father owes her $15). Pulls it out, as well as the mop and bucket. Soft cloths, furniture polish. One hour, two, she's scrubbing, she's polishing. It takes so long. It's just so much *house*.

It's 5:45 and she hops into the shower, washing everything but her hair. Fresh clothes on, back downstairs, back to the piano.

She waits.

The grandmother clock chimes quarter past six.

He's late. For a second, hope zings through her: maybe he won't come.

But the only thing worse than him coming is him not coming.

With her index finger, Saskia presses into the final chord of the movement she was playing earlier. It rings out, pure. Wholesome. And for a single second, she lets the notes vibrate through her; her skin seems to throb with them.

And then the doorbell rings.

PATRICK TAKES HER HAND AND IT IS LIKE THE first time, it is like every time: her perfect fourteen-year-old skin against his tanned, calloused hands, when she'd stared down at him reaching for her and in the second when he'd taken hold thought: Yes, it has finally happened. We are equal. I am a person.

"I'm so glad you could see me," he says. His bass voice resonates through the hall, through her.

She inhales, deep, looking at the broad set of his shoulders, the cocksure tilt of his head. She can still turn back; this doesn't have to happen, she tells herself.

But it does, and so she can't.

She squares herself in an approximation of his posture.

And then Saskia smiles. "Come on in."

He wipes the soles of his Timberland boots carefully on the doormat.

"Want a drink?" she says, and though he'd never balked at a drink before, she suddenly wonders how much of that was for her benefit. She had craved how the buzz of alcohol in her brain quieted it. "There's an eighteen-year-old Johnnie Walker that we cracked open last night," she says, casting a sly glance up at him.

He always loved it when she'd look at him like that.

She pours with steady hands, his Johnnie Walker and her Bombay Sapphire gin and tonic, explaining as she does so that she only drinks brown liquor after dinner these days. He looks bemused at this, perched in one of the winged armchairs as if it were a throne, and she feels stupid for a moment but brushes it aside. The important thing is getting his drink inside him.

He's already taken off his coat, thrown it over the arm of the sofa. She picks it up, takes it into the hallway closet as he cradles the crystal tumbler between his large palms. A quick skim of the coat's silhouette with her fingertips tells her the one thing she needs to know: his phone's in there. He's not recording her. She gives thanks to the god of Boomers for letting them separate so easily from their devices and goes back in to him.

She waits for him to say any of the things she's imagined: *I've heard that you've been digging into my past.* Or: *I got a call from Julia yesterday.* Or even, dare she hope: *I've been thinking over what happened between us, and I want you to know. It was wrong.*

"Well," he says, rolling his glass between his hands, "I guess you're probably wondering why I'm here."

"Of course."

"Look. This house . . . it's a lot, right? It's huge."

"Sure," she says, matching his mildness.

Patrick downs the rest of his drink, holds out his glass to her for a refill. Did he use to do that? She smooths the affront away and turns back to the bar.

"I've been thinking about our conversation the other day. And you know, Sas, I think I was just refusing to see the truth." She makes herself look mildly interested. "I think . . . well, you get to a certain age, and you look at all you've done, and you think: This cannot be all my life is worth. You know? And that's why it meant something to your mother, thinking about the arts center. Well. It really meant something to me. But I just don't think it's going to be possible."

She fights to keep the smile from her face. He doesn't want the house. But—the inner smile freezes—what about the photos? Is she now just supposed to pretend that they never happened? Pretend that whatever sacrifice her mother made had just never happened?

"And this house—this huge, wonderful house. You know, I do understand how important it's always been to you. So, I thought, well. Give them a chance to buy me out." He's holding his palms open to the ceiling as she turns back, and she forces herself to be gentle as she places the tumbler in his right hand. "I wouldn't ask anything close to what it's worth. Say—say, one-point-nine."

She tilts her head. "Because that's about what it's worth once you subtract the cost of the part Dad owns, the work, and the lien?"

He nods and throws back his whiskey. "Just to be fair." And he looks at her with expectant, bright eyes as he settles back against the red velvet cushions.

One point nine million dollars. It's close to the total valuation of their assets that she added up the other day. The piano. The artwork. The antiques. The royalties for the next couple of years.

How many times is she going to be asked to give up everything she has, only to keep everything she'd been born with?

She wants her fresh start. She wants freedom; she wants the Elf House safe in the hands of some anonymous, rich couple with a bunch of kids and a penchant for DIY. She wants her own life, her real life, to start.

It's funny, though; after days of thinking about $3 million, $1.9 million seems so little to her now.

So little.

But also, so wrong. She's not going to give everything up. She can't do it. She can't do it again.

"That's incredibly generous," she makes herself say. "You're right. This house means so much to us." Should she have said that? But she's not telling him anything he doesn't already know. "Let me talk things over with Dad."

Her honeyed voice is so curdling, she thinks for a panicked second that she's given it all away. But he must see her as a completely different person from the one he'd loved, because he gives a quick, satisfied nod and starts to get to his feet.

For him to leave now would be intolerable.

And the words come out without a thought.

"Before you go. Will you let me show you something? I know it might not be possible, now, but I always imagined this would be the perfect studio space." She lets her voice go as plaintive as it once did, as young and as yearning. It feels so fake, it's as if she's telling him that they'll always have Paris, and yet he sets his tumbler down with a decisive thud and rises to his feet. Responding to the echo of the girl he'd known.

"Sure," he says. And then, with barely repressed pleasure: "Sure."

"Come on, then."

He's following her: through the foyer, up the stairs, around the corner, through the dark hallway with the burned-out bulb she's been meaning to replace.

She opens the tower door and he smiles at her. "I've been here before," he says, and then he's actually climbing the stairs. She steps back to let him pass, marveling.

He's not following her anymore. He's leading her.

AT THE TOP OF THE STAIRS, PATRICK TWISTS HIS head from side to side, as though he could activate his night vision in the windowless room if he focuses hard enough. Behind him, Saskia flips the light switch and the lone bulb buzzes on.

And there she is. Her body, her body and the others, spread out over the bare mattresses, leftovers from two nights before, when she'd spread them out to choose a candidate for Tara.

His gaze dances around them. Over Saskia's breasts, her jawline, the soft and sharp parts of her. Over the others.

"You found them," he says with soft admiration.

Imagining him coming to the Elf House this afternoon, she had braced herself for his shock. His anger. His mockery. Anything except this—love, there's no other word for it, and the tart jealousy that tightens her body in response. That's me, she tries to reason with herself. I can't be jealous of me.

But it doesn't go away, the feeling.

She watches him looking at her, and the same sensation she experienced on 9/11 washes over her, like a spell freezing her into place: the realization that history is happening, that something so awful, so unforeseeable, has just transpired, and any illusions she once had about stepping into the role of the hero—heroine—are just that. Illusions.

But she isn't eighteen, staring at an exploding skyline from her favorite café all the way down on Lafayette Street. Not anymore.

"Do you know how old I was in those photos?"

He looks at her with canny eyes. Shakes his head. And it ignites something in her, the rage she's kept stoked in simmering coals flying into life.

She takes a breath.

He's not playing by her script, but maybe it doesn't matter.

"I was fifteen," she says.

His eyes are lit from behind as he studies his work. "Hmm?"

She reaches into her pocket, lets her hand rest on her phone.

"I was a child. Look at these pictures, Patrick. I was a child."

She watches as he gathers himself in, shoulders straightening as he turns, almost reluctantly, back to her. *Say it*, she dares him silently. *Say it into the recording.*

"I don't know, Sas. Why would you even think that these *are* you? This one," pointing to Julia's torso, or what she thinks is Julia's torso. "This one's definitely not. And besides, come on. Do these really look like children?" he says, pointing to her black-and-white breast.

"I'm fifteen!" she explodes, grabbing a picture. She's lying on her side, naked, staring somewhere out beyond the photographer, out into space. "In this photo, I'm fifteen. And how can you look at this and say that's not me? How could you dare?"

Almost as if he senses the phone in her pocket, capturing his voice like the Sea Witch stealing the Little Mermaid's, almost as if he knows, he tilts his head. *Prove it*, the gesture says. Instead he replies, "That's impossible. You were eighteen, Sas. We both know that."

She can't stand that expression and lets the photo drop, drift slowly to the floor. "I know that you know exactly what this is. It's child pornography. Do you not feel bad about that? Do you not feel even a little bit guilty for taking advantage of me?"

He sticks his hands in his pockets, rolls back from the balls of his feet to his heels. "Sas, I really don't know what you're talking about. I mean, I've always worked to push the limits of artistic forms—"

"Bullshit, Patrick. You took pornographic photos of a child, and then you blackmailed my mother and it's wrong. It's wrong on every level—"

He breaks the staring contest he's having with the photos and, almost with a cringe, turns back to Saskia.

"Your mother was a collector." The corner of his mouth lifts. "And a dear friend."

"And so, what? You demanded a *house* in exchange for a mother keeping nude photos of her teenage daughter from ever seeing the light of day?" Saskia runs to the CD player and starts the *Appassionata* booming at them, loud and angry. "Listen to this. Listen to *her*. I was fifteen when I recorded this. Listen to her and remember. You won't tell her that what we did was wrong?"

"But all I did was take your photo," he says. His words have slowed down. That wasn't the intended effect. She wanted the pills to loosen his inhibitions, to yank the lever that would pull him from whatever track he'd let himself ride along for decades, force him over onto hers, where a new, terrible reality had taken hold. But all they seem to have done is make him double down into his own story, only slower.

His face tilts toward the photos. He looks almost as sad as she feels, and something in her chest cracks open, softens, in the split second before she notices something else on his face, too. Something in the slightly moistened lips, in the strange hopefulness of the eyes.

Longing. It's longing.

"Saskia?" he says, not turning away from the picture. His voice sounds like it's underwater. "Was there something in the whiskey? Xanax, maybe?"

He takes a step back, legs half bending, half crumpling, as he finds a seat on the damp pile of mattresses. She savors her own cleverness, even as a chill runs through her, as she wonders how he knows what Xanax in whiskey would feel like. Has he also taste-tested a concoction designed to make a visitor more pliable than they might otherwise be?

She's suddenly struck by a visceral memory of his large, rough hand pressing a pill into her palm. This had always been a part of it.

She watches him blink up at her, now. Watches his breath come shallow, stiff.

"You've been bad," she says, harsh, and she doesn't know where the words are coming from until he looks up at her with an expression that is part baffled, part aroused, and she realizes it is a reversal of one of the games they used to play.

"I've been—"

"I think you need a time-out."

"A time—"

It's satisfying, this. Almost a litany.

"Yes," she says. "A time-out. To think about what you've done. We'll see if you feel like telling me my *real* age in a few hours."

It is only after she navigates her way down the steep, uneven stairs, two feet on each one in the semidark, only after she has closed the attic door behind her and turned the key, only after that key is safe in her pocket, that her heartbeat evens again, perfect as a metronome.

It's not what she thought she'd do.

But it's what she's done.

AN UNFAMILIAR RINGTONE SOUNDS OUT FROM downstairs.

"Dad?" she calls. "Wolfie?" No thumping paws answer her, and she weaves through the hallway, descends the main staircase carefully, almost as carefully as she came down from the tower.

How long will it take for Patrick to crack? An hour, two? Up there with her fifteen-year-old self on the mattress, booming at him from the stereo. She pauses, holding her breath, but the soundproofers had done their job thoroughly—not a note leaks through.

The ringing has started up again, though.

As she descends the front stairs, it becomes clear that the ringing is coming from Patrick's coat pocket, and the realization zaps through her: he's not a doll she can just lock away. He has a life, a context, and that involves other people. People with whom he might have appointments, people he's supposed to be meeting this evening. Tomorrow— Oh, fuck, he's definitely going to crack before tomorrow, right?

Well, she's done it now. She's officially thinking like a criminal.

This is okay. This is going to be fine. She'll let him out in a few hours, just as soon as he admits to what he did.

What he did. Fucking *hell*, she forgot to grill him about the house. She needs him to say that, too: needs him to say that he lied.

Saskia dips her hand into his coat pocket but yanks it out before she actually touches the telephone. She's listened to too many true crime podcasts, she scolds herself as she fishes into her own coat for her gloves. And yet it can't hurt.

As her father's headlights round the drive, Saskia's already donning her jacket and boots, already slipping Patrick's phone into her pocket. She'll go down the beach path to the marina, just the way he'd have walked it. And then—oops—phone in the water, phone and its geolocation skills utterly spoiled by the lake seeping through its silicone and metal innards.

She darts out the back door, letting the wind slam the screen behind her.

Chapter 22

The first thing you need to know about Puss in Boots is that Puss was a girl. The second was that she had a wild and willful intelligence. She could solve a problem in a heartbeat, did crosswords with a pen, and was reading Schopenhauer before her tenth birthday. I don't know why people focused on the boots so much. They were all right, as far as boots go. But the way she dressed was far from the most important thing about her.

—FAIRY TALES FOR LITTLE FEMINISTS:
PUSS IN BOOTS, EVELYN HARPER KREIS

November 1999

SASKIA WAS SEVENTEEN.

"Holy shit," Mike said, staring at the SAT score report. "Sas, you sure that you're the one who took this test?"

She giggled. The perfect 800 in math had been as much a surprise to her as to anyone else. Certainly it would be to Mr. Fletcher, who'd squeaked her by in trig last semester with a B minus.

"It's wonderful, honey," Evie said, brushing her lips on the top of Saskia's head. "But this English score—"

Saskia grimaced. A 550. Yeah.

"Don't you get two hundred points just for writing your name on the test?"

Saskia groaned and flipped the paper over. "Mom. It's not like it even matters, okay? Nobody gives a shit about this stuff except you."

Evie rinsed her coffee mug under a tap hissing water so forcefully, it sounded mad.

"It'll matter to colleges," she said.

"It would if I was applying," Saskia called, louder than she needed to.

"If you were applying. Christ. Mike, you see—"

But Mike was shaking his head, holding up his hands as he left the room. "You two work it out."

Saskia knew, by now, how to work things out. She went up behind Evie, put her chin on her shoulder.

"And what did you even get on the SATs?" she said. "I bet you can't remember, because all art schools cared about was your portfolio. And all music schools care about are auditions."

Evie smirked and twisted around, tucking a loose hair behind Saskia's ear.

"Should we go get your winter formal dress after your lessons tomorrow?" Saskia blinked.

"Isn't Josh going to take you to the winter formal?"

Saskia's lips were suddenly very itchy. She bit down, gnawing on the bottom one.

"Um, that's not really Josh's thing."

"Oh." Evie's bob shimmied around her face. "Well, maybe you could just go with some girlfriends? Just for the experience? I hate to think of you missing out on all of these rites of passage. You're only young once, you know?"

What girlfriends? she wanted to snap. But she didn't have to actually go, she could just say that she was going. She could stuff the dress in the trunk of her car, could spend an extra four or five hours over at Patrick's—

She squeezed her mother's hand.

"Sure. Let's go tomorrow."

February 2020

SASKIA LIES IN BED THE NEXT MORNING, STARING at the midwinter sun flickering against the white lace canopy. She woke with guilt like an avocado pit at the root of her stomach. It is all too apparent that this is not a viable long-term solution, keeping Patrick in the attic. She'd just been too quick to fly off the handle, and wasn't her mother always saying that about her?

She should probably feed him, shouldn't she. Or at least bring up some water. And they could have another talk. She won't forget to bring up the Elf House this time. If Patrick could at least admit to the arrangement he made with her mother—*there's* disposition, right there. No teenage Saskia would need to be splayed before the court; no adult Saskia would have to see the pity in the jury's eyes. Just say it, Patrick. Just fucking say it: *I lied.*

It would be a start, even if it wouldn't be enough.

It would never be enough.

Descending the back stairs, though, she hears the low rumble of voices rising from the kitchen. She pauses, pulling her multicolored silk kimono closer around her. With the fuzzy slippers, she looks straight out of *Grey Gardens*. But though she can't hear the words, Mike's voice rises in laughter, and there's a familiarity in the conversation's cadence. She takes the risk and goes down.

"Sas!" Her father is sitting in front of an enormous breakfast spread at the counter: a pot of coffee, mugs, creamer, and sugar. Plates full of croissants, doughnuts, assorted pastries. His arms spreading wide, he looks like a dragon offering access to his hoard. "Join us for breakfast, won't you?"

"Oh—"

The two men turn to her. Both around her father's age, though the years are heavier on their faces; Mike looks about ten years younger than he actually is.

"This is Dennis," Mike says, and the redhead with a washed-out orange coloring that makes him appear the same color as his beige sweater nods at her. "And Richie." The other guy with white hair and a retro mustache gives her a strangely old-fashioned salute, two fingers from the forehead.

She can tell by her father's voice that she's supposed to know who Dennis and Richie are, so she smiles, nods, and takes the stool next to his. Wolfie shoves over, wiggling his tail as he tries to direct her attention, and her scraps, down to the floor. She runs an absentminded hand over his head.

"It's nice to meet you."

"Guys, this is my daughter, Saskia."

"I think we got that much, Mikey. Doesn't give us much credit as detectives, does he, Rich?" But the redhead's eyes are smiling, his voice the broadest Wisconsin she's ever heard, straight through the nose. She notices even as her heartbeat starts to tremble in her limbs, as her fingers freeze in Wolfie's fur.

"Detectives?" she says brightly.

One night! she wants to scream. *He's only been here for one night!*

The imaginary courtroom and the imaginary jury that have been haunting her all morning—yeah, they'd been preceded by an imaginary police search, of course. But that officer had been faceless, nameless, had been a stand-in for someone she'd never really thought she'd meet. These two are overwhelming in their specificity. She can't stop looking at the large pores on Dennis's nose, tiny black dots like on her mother's tomato pincushion. Can't stop looking at Richie's torn cuticles, the places where the blood has rushed to the surface of his chewed-up fingers.

She's always been good at decoding permutations and combinations, and she sees them converging on this moment, now. This is a nexus in the web; this is a moment that will produce all future moments, this, here, now, sun shining bright through the archways, this moment will be the one she looks back on later, the one she realizes ruined or saved her, the one—

Saskia represses a shiver as her father hands her a mug of coffee.

"Sure, kid. You remember—we were all at Washington High together. These guys joined the force together when they came back from the service. And with everything that's going on with the house and all, I thought it'd be good to get some details on the guy. There's something not right with him, something not right about *any* of this. I've been saying it—"

The cops are shaking their heads.

"Motherfucker," Dennis says under his breath.

"Real piece of work," from Richie.

There are police. In her house. Discussing the man trapped in her attic.

Shouldn't they be retired by now, if they're her father's age? He's over seventy, sure, but his job isn't anything like being a police officer.

"Patrick?" The gravity in the room shifts as her voice cuts through them, chirpy. Three pairs of eyes are on her now, and she licks her lips, trying to moisten her dry mouth. "Gosh, what are you trying to find out about him?"

The cops look at Mike, but her father's looking at her. "Anything," he says, and his calm, low words are like a battle cry. "Everything."

Richie, though, is happy to elaborate.

"Guy's just a real creep. Nothing official, but we talked to the provost down at UWM on Friday. Three girls in his classes brought harassment complaints about him to the dean, three years in a row, 2012, 2013, 2014, and they all got shunted on up to the provost's office, and they all ended up withdrawing the complaints once he got moved on over to Development. There's something not right with a guy like that."

Saskia seizes it: an opportunity.

"I *knew* that he manipulated Mom. I just knew it. No way that arts center stuff was for real."

The squiggly vein on her father's forehead appears as he tenses his jaw. She's blown apart his carefully modulated information drip. The detectives, to their credit, don't say a word. They just watch. Wait.

"Evie," Mike says finally. "She left this guy . . . well, she left him a fairly generous bequest."

Dennis blows his cheeks out like an enormous red squirrel. "Shit."

"But better than . . ." Richie says, gesturing vaguely in Saskia's direction with a fat hand.

Two identical navy gazes latch on to him.

"Better than what?" Mike says in a sepulchral tone.

Dennis nudges the other cop. "Well, our first thought was that maybe your daughter was currently involved with the guy." The cops chortle, but neither Mike nor Saskia is amused. "Hey. You'd be surprised to find out how many fathers want us to peek into the new boyfriend's past."

Richie bites into a chocolate croissant. "Fathers of daughters," he says. "They're a special breed."

A few dismissed charges. Would a judge allow them in as evidence? She'll have to ask Tara. Or, better, Christine. Fuck, she needs to send that email. Eleven days left.

In the meantime, Saskia can't bear up under scrutiny, either.

"Thanks so much for looking into this," she says, grabbing an almond croissant and refilling her coffee as she stands to go. "But, unfortunately, I can't imagine you're going to find anything that would be useful for us. What, like he had a pattern of scamming ladies out of their property? I think we'd have heard by now."

Her father's gaze is as hot as a dragon's as she climbs back up the stairs. The second she's around the corner, too far away to be seen, she picks up into a run. Runs all the way to her bedside table, then to the tower with the key in hand.

She has to let him out. She can't wait any longer.

She'll play it off as a joke. Then she'll take him out the side door—and she'll . . .

But no, she realizes as the tower door swings open with a creak. No, she can't let him out. Not yet. Because in what world will Patrick go quietly?

Who would *stay* quietly, for that matter?

She relocks the door, trots back to her room, and drops two Xanax into the coffee. Waits a minute, swirling it in her hand like a beaker, and adds two more. He just needs to stay quiet until the cops leave. That's all.

The dusty attic smells like a close room in the summer, when the windows have been closed for rain and you've slept slightly too long, waking in the muggy fug of it. Not even a day, and already he's permeating every cubic inch of the space.

He's only half-awake as she hands him the croissant and coffee. He doesn't take his eyes off of her as he sits up, back against the wall.

"Saskia," Patrick says carefully, "what are you doing?"

She doesn't drop his gaze, either, as she points at the pile of photos at his feet.

"How old am I?" she asks. She wonders at how measured her voice is, how cool. She never knew about this part of herself.

His eyes follow her finger, raise unwillingly toward her face again.

"Eighteen," he says hoarsely.

She stares at him, waiting for him to break; but neither of them moves.

"Was there ever a plan for the arts center?"

He closes his eyes.

"Yes."

"Okay."

And then she's skittering down the stairs, slamming the door behind her and jamming the key in as fast as she can.

Why can't she do it? Why can't she fucking let him go?

Because it's too late, she realizes as she drops the key back into the drawer of her bedside table. Because she's already climbed up the playground slide, and there's a line of kids waiting impatiently on the ladder behind her.

There's only one way down.

SASKIA DOES RUN OUT THE SIDE DOOR LATER THAT morning. But the cops are long gone by then; she just doesn't want to pass her father in the study. She's headed for her mother's studio.

It's only once she's sitting at the desk, sunlight dappling the cottage around her, that she realizes: she's living her mother's life.

In the Elf House. Writing her book. Playing her Scrabble side. She hasn't boxed in a month, hasn't so much as jumped rope. She's said goodbye to her best friend and her boyfriend (such as *he* was); she's hanging out with Georgia, she's—

She puts her head in her palms.

Well, she's not exactly like her mother.

She has, after all, trapped Patrick in the attic.

It's enough to make her sit up straight and start writing.

Her Persephone, though, doesn't want to do what the original did. She doesn't want to wait, a damsel to be rescued, for the shitty deal her mother is capable of negotiating. While the Demeter scenes are easy enough to craft—she's written two of them so far, Demeter trapped in a haunted castle, Demeter searching through caves—Persephone's just sitting there. Playing nice with Hades.

But what if she didn't?

What if she took what was his, instead?

She grabs her phone and sees she missed a message:

Christine had a cancellation tomorrow. I say we take it. 2:30 work for you?

She's not entirely sure what day it is anymore. She has to check the phone's calendar to verify: still eleven days to the hearing. Still time.

Can't do tomorrow; let's touch base next week? How's the affidavit coming?

A long time for the three dots to resolve. And then: *It's in your in-box. Let me know if I have the go-ahead to file.* What was the potential message Tara never sent? A failed girl-power call to arms, she's sure. She's grateful Tara changed course. There's something extremely decent about Tara, despite the pity.

Lexi picks up on the first ring, just like she always used to do on the house phone.

"Sorry to call—"

"Nah, it's like old times. What's up?"

"Okay, so. Mom's book. Here's what I'm thinking: Persephone kills Hades, and then *she* takes over as Queen of the Underworld."

"No." Lexi's response is quick, final.

"No, it's perfect. It's like all of Mom's other stories. The princess— that's Persephone, here—she takes action. She reaches her goal. She vanquishes the villain, she—"

"Yeah, I mean, it totally works *narratively*," Lexi says. "But it doesn't make any sense in the world of the Greek myths. I mean, Hades is a god. He's immortal."

"Yeah, okay," Saskia says, flopping back in her chair. A frustrated noise rises from the back of her throat. "Ugh. I just . . ."

"What?"

"I just really wanted to kill him, though," she says, staring out at the trees.

Chapter 23

February 2000

SASKIA WAS SEVENTEEN, AND BY THAT WINTER, the magic of skipping class was gone. Not only did she have her own driver's license now, as well as her own car, but junior year was harder than sophomore year, just like the adults had threatened. Every missed class meant an extra hour of staring in bafflement at her textbooks late into the night. Every extra hour was an hour she spent alone, an hour without Patrick, an hour in which his texts rained down, gratifying yet increasingly annoying: *I miss you. I'm thinking about you. Are you almost done?* Every extra hour was an hour she spent away from the piano, an hour in which she could feel the muscles of her hands tightening, weakening. Atrophying.

But after putting Lexi off for days, Saskia finally agreed to meet during a morning free period. She should have been in the library, working on an English paper due at the end of the week. But instead, Saskia sat across from Lexi in the diner booth, two mugs of black coffee, the cheapest thing on the menu, between them.

"How are things with Josh P.?" Lexi asked, lighting a cigarette.

Saskia gave a weak smile. "Good. Fine. You know."

Lexi stared at her, the hard look in her eyes making something in Saskia shrink back. It was so foreign, so *adult*.

"Give it up, Sas," Lexi said. "I know there's no Josh P."

The air in the diner was vibrating, twitching against her skin. There was no Josh P. What else did Lexi know?

Saskia lifted the mug to her mouth. The coffee was too hot, thin and scalding.

She tried one of her mother's phrases. "Why do you say that?"

Lexi's eyes rolled. "Because. I talked to Becca the other day, and she said the only Joshes are the ones I already knew. There's no Josh P."

Saskia's mouth went dry, despite the coffee. Dry and burned.

"Okay," Lexi said with a sigh. "But there's obviously someone. So, who is it? Why did you lie to me? Is it a teacher? Is it, like, really bad?"

Outside, a snow plow garbled its way down the street, pushing the new snow over the grayed and dingy remnants of the old.

Saskia took a deep breath. "It's—"

But she couldn't bring herself to say it.

Three years now. Three years, it had been him and her. Nobody else. The only two people who knew about the golden cords of energy between them. About what they meant to each other. About the future they'd imagined, the present they owned, about his hand on the side of her cheek, caressing—

"It's nobody," she said, and closed her eyes. "I made him up to seem cool."

"Bullshit." The flint of Lexi's words made Saskia jump. "Bullshit!" Lexi said again, bending forward. "Nobody lies about a boyfriend to seem cool to their parents. Unless, I mean—are you gay?"

Saskia toyed with the idea of this new lie for a moment. But she knew Lexi would never keep that from her mother. And it would trickle up and over, and within a day, two max, her parents would be purchasing books about helping their child come out of the closet.

But she hated keeping this secret from Lexi. She hadn't known it before, but she knew it then, in that moment: when she'd chosen Patrick, she'd chosen not to have a lot of other things. Maybe a million other things.

It was worth it. Wasn't it?

"No," she said. "I just don't want to talk about it."

Lexi thrust herself back in the booth, wrapping her arms over her chest. "Who even are you anymore? You're, like—I mean it, I don't even know who you are anymore, Sas. You're, like, not even a teenager. You're like a grown-up."

Lexi meant the words as an insult, Saskia could hear the barely contained rage in the flat tones of her voice. And yet they lit something inside her. She *wasn't* a teenager, not like the others. She wasn't listening to Jessica Simpson or the Backstreet Boys, she was listening to Bach and Mozart. She wasn't dating some kid named Josh, she was dating a grown man, a man with passion and purpose. Each realization pinging down into the pit of her stomach, filling it with a trickling pride.

She raised her eyebrows.

"I know," she said. "I'm not a teenager. I'm a real person."

And everything seemed to drain out of Lexi as she looked back.

"But I'm a real person, too," she said.

The next time Lexi texted, Saskia didn't answer. And eventually, Lexi went away.

February 2020

JOSH IS VERY MUCH THE TYPE TO ARRIVE EARLY for a date. Saskia already knows this, but she's so busy trying on her mother's earrings that when the doorbell rings that Monday, Mike gets to it before she does.

"Shit shit shit," she mutters to herself as she runs down the stairs, shoving her phone into an old black clutch, stumbling in Evie's heels. There's her father, squaring off in front of the door like John Wayne in some old western. Boomer dads—they love that shit.

"Josh!" she cries, too loudly and too excitedly, too much, just enough to break off whatever conversation they've been having. "Hi!"

And then it's the three of them at the door. Both men are looking at her expectantly, and she leans over to kiss Josh's cheek, then swoops over to the closet.

"Okay!" she calls, shrugging her mother's camel coat on too quickly, getting tangled. "Back soon."

"Curfew's at ten," her father says, and Josh chuckles politely. Saskia rolls her eyes. She never had a curfew.

Heels crunching against the gravel, she can't help casting a glance over her shoulder as they leave the house. It's just hit her: What if Patrick thinks things through and tries the door? The floor's soundproofed, sure. Maybe even the stairs, she's not positive. If he starts pounding the door, though—

"You look great," Josh says as she opens the passenger door.

"Do I?" she says, genuinely caught by surprise.

"You do. Just like you did back at school."

She shakes her head. "I wasn't big on makeup or jewelry back then."

"No, it's not that. It's something . . ." He stops. "Something else."

They pull onto Lake Drive and fall into easy, simple conversation about the weather. *All of these backs and forths, heat waves and blizzards . . . and they say climate change isn't real!* It's a rote, routine sort of conversation, and she doesn't have to pay too much attention. In the meantime, at the back of her brain: Patrick. She's leaving Patrick alone in the house with her father.

But it's okay, she tells herself. She's ensured that he's too far gone to try messing with the door.

For their dinner, Josh has chosen Beans & Barley. Not a vegan restaurant, not even a vegetarian restaurant, but a Milwaukee institutional holdover from the 1970s: a health food restaurant. The ceiling arches high above, thirty feet at least, the wall behind Josh's back sheer glass. Yet it's a paper-napkin kind of place: a relief. Josh, with a quick glance to check in with her, orders a bottle of pinot grigio. When it arrives, he tastes it dutifully, nods. Is he a wine guy? She's never dated a wine guy. One sip and it's like she can hear a Klaxon sounding: *Maybe this guy isn't for you.*

But her radar is fucked up, she's known that for a long time. It sucks to not be able to trust your own instincts. His quiet earnestness, she reminds herself. His intelligence. His deep, hidden intensity. Those are qualities she likes, that she could like.

There's a reason she's here.

Although she can't think of anything to say. The one thing that brought them back together, her mother's will, is the one thing they're not allowed to discuss. The one thing she wants to talk about, Patrick, is the one thing she's not allowed to disclose to anyone.

"So. University School, huh? You seem to have fonder memories of it than I do," she says, and it's someone else's voice coming out of her. Fond?

But as soon as it's out there, she realizes that she really is interested in knowing what it was like for Josh—and, okay, she's interested in seeing herself through his eyes.

Josh's earnestness serves him well. "I'm not sure. It felt like hell at the time. Looking back, though—the stakes were lower, you know? Or, if not lower . . . I don't know, things were spelled out. The path was clear. I guess I do miss that."

"Things were spelled out?"

The waitress is hovering next to them, and she skims the menu quickly as Josh orders salmon. With a smile, she orders the grilled chicken platter. Look at her. So healthy, after days of leftover sandwiches and frozen pizzas. She feels like she's glowing with the virtue of it.

"I don't know," he says, returning his gaze to her, palms up and helpless. "I don't—I was just talking, that didn't actually mean anything."

He grins, and they're back where they started: the conversational void.

She opens her mouth. Closes it.

Reconsiders.

Well, why the hell not? She's on a real live date with a man, which is something she never thought she'd do. She trapped another one in the tower. Maybe her instincts are getting better.

"So," she says, twirling the stem of her wineglass. "I mean, I know there's only so much you can tell me," looking up at him. "But—I can't stop wondering."

He has a shy smile, a guarded smile. "What's that?"

"How on earth did you become Mom's executor?"

"Ah." His face is still pleasant, but it's professional now, too. "Pretty simple, really. Your mother came by the office last summer to see Paul, and she recognized me. We grabbed a coffee. After that, she had the will . . . she had the will revised."

Saskia laughs. "Back when we were in high school—you remember—?" She can't make herself say *pretending to be my boyfriend*, but he doesn't make her, just nods with a grin. "Well, she *loved* you. She asked me about you for years afterward."

"What did you say?" he asks.

"Oh, I had a whole life made up for you," she says as the waitress sets their food down on the table. "Funny, I haven't thought of any of this for years. Um, let's see. I think you became an architect. And you got married a few years ago." She'd told her mother it was to a man just to get her off of her fucking back—but no need to tell Josh that now.

He's thinking, fuzzy eyebrows drawn slightly together.

"Were you invited to the wedding?" he says finally, and the two of them laugh.

"I was," she says, tipping her glass to him, "but I declined to go. Out of respect, you know, for your new partner."

"How kind of you."

Silence again, but not uncomfortable now. Strange how telling someone something personal, intimate, could make things easier between you. That's never happened to her before.

Over the tiny votive candle, she sees his eyes fixed gently, darkly, on her.

"Josh?" she says. "I'm— So, I talked it over with my father, and I've been making some arrangements, and—"

He is watching, patiently waiting.

"I'm going to stay in Milwaukee," she says.

"Are you?" The delight as he leans forward in the booth. "I didn't want to ask, I figured you'd be here through probate, at least, but—Sas. That's great fucking news!"

"Is it?" she says, though she can't keep the smile off of her own face. And holds in a gasp as he brushes his fingers over her palm, so lightly it's as though it's not happening at all.

"It is," he says softly. "Because I think we might really have something here."

She stares at him, but he just stares back. There is a world where men say these kinds of things to women. It exists. And, somehow, she's ended up in it.

After they split a piece of carrot cake, they walk briskly into the wedge-shaped parking lot. The night is chilled charcoal and streetlight yellow. The renovated library, slick polished gray nothing, is lit up across the street; old-timey Milwaukee taverns crowd up around it with their brick façades and neon signs. She pulls out her phone; two hours, passed in a heartbeat. Her own pounds through her as she slides it back into her pocket.

"Thanks for dinner," she says, the rest of her chicken boxed up and swinging in a bag from her wrist, ready for Wolfie to scarf down. "You really didn't have to pay."

"It was fun," Josh says. And as he leans toward her, she's wondering how his lips will feel, if she'll be able to taste the wine that must still be on his tongue.

His mouth brushes against hers and she almost cries out.

The soft lips. The light touch.

The ghost of Patrick will live on forever. In each first kiss, in every caress.

He marked her. He owns her.

Saskia pulls away first, and Josh squeezes her shoulder with a surprisingly strong hand.

They're quiet on the way back to the house. And it's not until Josh's Prius rounds the drive, as she hears the familiar barking greeting her at the door, when she watches his taillights flicker back on, recede into the distance, that she realizes. Patrick may own her in one sense, yes.

But in a much realer one, she owns him.

IN THE AQUARIUM-BLUE DARK, SASKIA OPENS THE door. Wolfie's yapping his head off, but he immediately quiets as she sets the box before him, as he attacks the chicken with gusto.

It's ten, and her father will be in bed, if not asleep. And Patrick?

Surely he must be ready to talk by now. She lugs a six-pack of Poland Spring from the kitchen up the stairs with her, Wolfie circling her heels. As she puts the key in the lock, she turns to him.

"Wolfie, *stay*," she hisses, and the dog gives her an annoyed glance but sits just outside the door. After kicking the water inside the stairwell, she locks the door behind her and slides the key carefully back in her pocket. Four hours since his last Xanax, it's unlikely Patrick's at full strength; still, why risk it?

But though the bulb is lit, though she can hear its buzz from the bottom of the stairs, he's fast asleep. She drops the water bottles on the ground, just lets them fall, but it doesn't make a difference: he's out. He always slept through the night like this, like a machine that had been flipped off.

Well. She can come back in the morning. She'll have to.

Saskia turns to go, her hand on the light switch, when he turns with a groan and she catches a glimpse of his sleeping face.

For the first time in twenty years: his sleeping face.

The night has erased his wrinkles. If she doesn't look at the silvery hair, it could be the Patrick she'd known all those years ago. Sleeping Patrick still has an angelic look to him. The dark sweep of his lashes sweet against his cheeks, which have been given a new roundness by his slack, relaxed jaw.

She reaches down and pinches one, like Grandmother Harper always used to do to her. He doesn't respond, and she lets her fingers draw closer until his skin, his flesh, is caught between the fingernails of her thumb and index finger.

He grumbles, and she draws back. In the flickering light, she takes a minute to admire her handiwork: the perfect crescent moons.

Chapter 24

Odysseus looked at Penelope frantically, then back at the Sirens.

"You must do it, my love!" he cried. "You must strap me to the mast so that I can ignore their song. If not, I shall be compelled to throw myself overboard and give myself up to them! It is just too irresistible!"

Penelope crossed her arms over her chest.

"I don't know," she said. "If you're so weak you need to be strapped to the mast, maybe I should just let the Sirens have you."

—*Fairy Tales for Little Feminists:*
Penelope and Odysseus, Evelyn Harper Kreis

June 2000

SASKIA WAS SEVENTEEN, AND SHE'D LONG BEEN taking advantage of the weekends when her parents were out of town. When Mike was playing in Akron or Syracuse or Miami, when Evie decided she needed a break from her stories and her students and went with him. She and Patrick had their own private getaway, extending far beyond the attic. Though at first she'd kept him there, where he could be neither seen nor heard by anyone popping home an hour (or a day) too early, he'd soon expanded his kingdom to her bedroom. To the kitchen, running down in his boxers to get them beer. To the yards, letting the screen door flap shut behind him as they walked hand in hand down to the cliffs. To the conservatory, pressing her bare back against the sticky gloss of the piano lacquer—

She couldn't get that last one out of her head, the next day on the beach. They'd had sex against the piano. Out of everything they'd done, that shocked her the most. Pleased her the most. It must have been those pills, whatever he had last night—she'd never have desecrated the piano like that, normally.

And now, in her rainbow bikini and a pink paisley wrap she was using as a sarong, she was letting the memory fill her up like helium, giggling and running around him like a puppy. The game was to try to surprise him with a kiss, it didn't matter where, his neck or his throat or his mouth (though she rarely managed the last, too hard to hit a moving target).

He was so handsome in his swim trunks and a green polo shirt. She caught the nape of his neck with her lips, his rough dark hair brushing against her lips.

"Almost—" And he laughed, grabbing her around her belly so she doubled over with laughter, the back side of her body pressed into him.

She was wriggling out of his grip when suddenly his hands fell. Frozen. "Knock it off."

She darted up, brushed her lips against his ear.

His arm knocked her back. And for the first time in anger, golden eyes blazing, he stared at her.

"I said knock it the fuck off, Saskia."

Sadness and shame roiling in her gut, until her eyes followed his retreating back, those tan calves, the slim ankles narrowing into his Top-Siders, and she saw them.

Beyond him. The two blue uniforms.

The quick, dark nod he gave them as she caught up.

"How you doing."

The nods they gave him back. "Nice day," one offered. It was Wisconsin, after all.

And his smile, quick and trustworthy. "Good to get the kids out of the house."

Sadness dissipating, Saskia turned her face to the waves.

She forgot sometimes that she was a secret.

But she'd never felt like a filthy secret before.

This wasn't just the delicious shared privacy of don't-tell-your-parents, this wasn't just liberal, *Manhattan*-style role-play. She was something that could ruin his life. She was something that he didn't want to hide just for fun, she was something that he had to hide or else.

And yet somehow, she learned to let it go.

February 2020

SASKIA HAD PLANNED ON GETTING UP EARLY AND going running with her dad the next day, but she wakes up later than she meant to. She's not hungover, though there is a hard mineral quality to her blood, like last night's sulfite-heavy wine is slowing its flow through her veins. She tries to summon the energy to make herself eggs, something with protein.

But before she can descend to the kitchen, a heavy thump comes from the end of the hall.

Another.

A third.

Seems he figured out that the door isn't soundproofed after all.

Peeking out the window on her way downstairs, she sees the garage door is open; the car isn't there. Mike must have returned from his run and already gone back out, taking Wolfie with him. It's useful that they're both out of the house, but where have they gone?

The thumps have redoubled. She grabs the last of the Poland Spring, a bunch of Kind bars (coconut—he hates coconut, convenient) from the kitchen.

Thump.

She's standing outside the attic door. "Okay, I'm here," she calls, louder than she needs to. "But you're insane if you think I'm coming in while you're by the door."

A pause, and the steps creak. She presses her ear to the wood, its varnish so degraded it's almost sticky to the touch. When she's convinced he's backed away, she unlocks the door, turning to lock it again the second she's on the other side.

He's sitting on the edge of the bed, looking at her through narrowed eyes as she drops the water, the Kind bars, onto the floor at his feet.

"Saskia, what are you *doing*?" She purses her lips. "You've snapped. You've truly and completely snapped."

She bites her lip, screwing up her face. It is a long time before she answers him. She's enjoying the way his eyes flit around her, above her, below her.

"Do you really think," she finally says, "you should make me mad right now?"

His gaze settles on hers.

"Saskia," he says, and his expression is pleading. As though those eyes could do anything to her anymore; he has such a limited bag of tricks, it's almost a little . . . well, tragic. "Let me go."

"All right," she says. "Just tell me two things. Was it real, the arts center? And how old was I in those photos?"

And his eyes turn frantic.

"It was *real*. And . . . sixteen, seventeen, eighteen—what difference does it make? What the hell difference does it make?"

She stares at him.

"I wouldn't have taken them if you were under eighteen," he finally says. He's on his feet now. She doesn't like it, the way her body instinctually softens at his approach, the way her eyes stay magnetized on his.

Her gaze hardens.

"I know what I looked like at eighteen, Patrick. There are other photographs from when I was eighteen. And there are other photographs from when I was fifteen."

He shakes his head. "You're crazy—"

"When has it ever," she says slowly, "*ever* been a good idea to call a woman crazy?"

For a second, they stare at each other. And then, whippet quick, he darts behind her toward the stairs.

Shouldn't have done it, Patrick; Saskia's trained for this, Saskia's the predator now. Smooth as cream, she whirls around and punches his sternum.

As he lies on the floor wheezing, she takes her time descending the stairs. Then she whips out the key and releases herself.

It's only a moment, of course, before he's pounding against the door again. Her back against it, she lets his movements vibrate through her body as she leans her head back, closes her eyes.

"You fucking bitch! Just open the goddamn door!"

"Patrick," she says, "you know what you have to say to get out. Until then, I suggest you shut the fuck up and think about what you've done."

THAT NIGHT, METAL SCRABBLE BOX CHILL UNDER her arm, Saskia pads into the study in her slippered feet. Mike looks so cozy there, the green glass of the lampshade suffusing the room with a kind of authoritative glow. He looks up from his book: *The Collapse of the Third Republic.*

"Up for a game?" she asks.

He twists his mouth, considering.

"Sure," he says finally. "I'll set up if you'll get the drinks."

By the time she returns with an open bottle of red wine and two glasses from her grandmother's wedding set, the board's out. He's pulled an A, so he goes first.

"So, what was with the cops the other day? What do you actually think they'd be able to find on Patrick?"

"They're not just cops. They're friends," he says, the firm note in his voice discouraging argument. "Good guys. And they have resources at their disposal that we don't. Think about it, Sas. They can strike fear into him the way we never could. And no matter what else happens, I still want that. I want him to be scared."

Strike fear. She wonders what he means, wonders what Dennis and Richie are capable of doing. To a suspect-who-isn't-a-suspect, to a bad man not yet charged with anything.

She wouldn't want to be on the receiving end of it, that's for sure.

She fights back images of taking her naked photos into the station, into the hands of men exactly like them. Fights back the prospect of years spent dealing with men like that.

"Yeah, but this Wild West, gathering your posse . . . I don't know. I just think, if you can get them to lay off a bit . . . that might be a good thing. We don't want to mess up the probate case by messing with him too much."

Hypocrite, hypocrite, her blood pulses at her.

He presses his thin lips together. Starts plucking letters, laying them flat on the board.

"I was thinking less of westerns and more of film noir," he says.

COMEDIC. She jots down the fourteen points in their notebook.

"But it's not a movie," she says, making herself cut the sentence off there. Fighting the urge to say, *But Daddy, I have him in the attic!* "We have a lawyer we're paying to do things right. *Legally.* Tara's on top of things, Dad! She sent me the draft affidavit the other day—" With a silent prayer to the lawyer to forgive her for not mentioning the numerous earlier drafts she'd completed, for not replying to the latest version yet. "And the hearing is in nine days."

Nine days, her heartbeat says. *Nine days.*

"How's the affidavit looking?" he asks.

She shakes her head, cursing herself for her cowardice. Because what's her endgame? If she wants to get Patrick on child pornography, her father is going to have to know eventually. And at this point, it seems like they don't have a real shot at challenging the will without showing the photos.

If only Patrick would just fucking say it.

I lied. You were fifteen.

"It's still messy," she says, and sets down her tiles. JEZEBEL. He eyes the word.

"No proper names."

"Is that a challenge?" Reaching for the dictionary.

"Use it in a sentence."

"*She's such a jezebel.*"

He waves a hand. "Take it."

Behind him, the windows rattle. And it occurs to her. Dennis and Richie—they've talked to the provost at UWM. They're already treating this like official business (though who the fuck knows what they'd do if they actually got their hands on Patrick—she's sure it would make his attic confinement look like child's play). How long until someone points them to the art museum? How long until they sit down at the café with Sheila?

How long until Sheila tells them: *There were some lovely nudes that Kintner wanted to include as well, but Evie Kreis threw a fit.*

"Please, Dad," she says, trying to catch his eye. But he's not looking at her, he's staring down at his tiles. "Call off your dogs. Let me and Tara—"

But he clears his throat, cutting her off. She falls silent as he wriggles his eyebrows. "Well, look at that—" He lays down the letters as he says the word. PRODIGY.

Bending over the table: "Will you, though?"

"Saskia," he says, exasperation edging his voice as he finally meets her gaze. "Play the game."

Chastened, she pulls back.

"Did you know that *prodigy* and *prodigal* have different roots?" he says absently, sliding his new tiles around. "*Prodigy*'s like *prodigious*, it comes from *prodigium*. Like an omen. Or a monster. But *prodigal* comes from *prodigus*: wasteful."

"Huh. I did know that, actually."

She'd looked it up once. What makes a prodigy? A wild and unexpected talent; yes, she'd had that. Youth; yes, she'd had that, too. But it turned out that the thing that truly makes a prodigy had been beyond her the whole time: ease.

She's staring into the middle distance, snaps back to the game at her father's voice.

"Sas. Look. I need my guys on this. I need to know that I'm doing *something*. I hate . . . seeing you beaten down by all this will business, this legacy stuff." He's searching her face for any sign of emotion, reaction. "Thinking this is your life now, that this is what your life looks like."

"What should my life look like, then?"

His gray brows jump. "Anything else! Going into the Symphony. Teaching at a university. Hell, becoming a mathematician—"

They peak early, too, she almost says.

"You just have so many talents, Sas. I'd like to see you—use them. Hustle, you know?" FLESHLY, he puts down. She does get out the dictionary on that, but he's right. It's a word.

"Yeah, I know." He looks up in annoyance at the perfunctory tone, but she is hustling—he has no idea how much she's hustling. "But this is something I've thought about a lot over the last few years. It's different for men and women, you know. Men get judged on what they might do in the future, on their potential. But women, it's always about what they've done, who they've been, and always in terms of whether they're meeting expectations that they had no part in designing. It's never about who they could be on their own terms. And the older I get, the more I realize that

I'm being judged entirely on my past." She swallows. "I guess it's just . . . *Why* do we have to use our talents? Like, why can't they just be something that we have? For ourselves."

She's not sure that her words mean anything, less sure still that they mean what she wants them to.

"Well, I think the easy answer there would be that we owe it to the world."

The world. The world of global warming and recession after recession and dictatorial fascists and structural misogyny and racism and everything the fuck else?

MORAL, she plays. "The world's a dumpster fire," she says lightly. "I opted out years ago."

Her father stares at her with their matching eyes.

"Yeah, okay," he says finally. "But did you, though?"

Chapter 25

"So you want me to cook. And clean. And generally look after you and the cottage. And in exchange, I get to . . . stay here with you?" Snow White said.

The dwarves looked at each other.

"Yeah," Grumpy said. "You got a problem with that?"

"Actually, yes," Snow White said, grabbing a paper and pencil from the desk and sitting down. "What we really need is an equitable division of domestic labor."

The dwarves blinked at her.

"Well, go ahead. Sit down," she said. There was some muttering, it must be admitted, but eventually all seven of the men pulled up their chairs.

Snow White cleared her throat. "I officially declare this commune's first governing meeting open."

—*Fairy Tales for Little Feminists:*
Snow White, Evelyn Harper Kreis

November 2000

SASKIA WAS EIGHTEEN. SHE'D BEEN LISTENING for it all day, and finally she heard the crunch of gravel, her parents' low laughter, and she jumped from the bench, bolted to the side door. It was autumn and the air was full of burning leaves, and in the moment before her parents reached her, she closed her eyes to smell the tang.

"Sas!" Evie said. Her eyes flickered wide with surprise; Saskia wasn't usually home on Sunday afternoons, was usually at the university or the conservatory or "Josh's."

"What's up, kiddo?"

She grabbed Mike's wrist and pulled him into the house, to the conservatory. Breathless, she dropped his hand and waited.

Mike's head twisted to the side.

"What is it?" Evie came up behind them, following their gaze to the piano. "Is something wrong?"

"It's new, honey," Mike said, setting a hand on her shoulder. "Sas bought a new piano."

Saskia broke into a grin as she ran to the bench.

"Isn't it wonderful? It's a 1923 Steinway. The resonance on this thing! Just listen—" She ran her hand down over the bass keys. "And yet there's a brilliance—" Up on the treble. "And the weight of the keys—well, it wouldn't mean anything to you guys, but they've got this gravity to them, it's really something—" She turned to them, bright eyes unseeing. "Isn't it incredible? It's so amazing that all this *sound* is produced by just wood and metal and glue! Some felt," she added. "And ivory, of course."

"Who . . . who let you buy that?"

Saskia's eyebrows jumped into delight.

"I went to the Steinway Gallery and tested out a few pianos. This was the best one on the floor, I did my research." A lot of research. "And turns out: when you have money, people let you buy things," she added, sarcasm lacing her otherwise gleeful tone.

Mike was peering into the piano's innards, while Evie clutched the side of it, palm leaving a greasy smudge against the black. Saskia opened her mouth, started to tell her, No, *please, don't touch—*

"Saskia," Evie said, "that was your college money."

Saskia looked down at the keyboard. Rolled her right hand into a quick arpeggio.

"No," she said. "It was my contest winnings. It was my album deal. It was my performance stipends, and it was *mine*. Besides, there's still plenty left over, stop freaking out. Anyways"—looking up, fierce, eyes fire—"I'm not going to college."

Evie's fingers tightened against the ridge, skin pulling against the lacquer with a squeak.

"Not *college* college, maybe. But surely music school—Juilliard or Manhattan—"

"But why, though? Why can't I just . . . keep doing what I'm doing? Tour more. Record more. People go to those schools to become like me, Mom. But I'm already there. I'm already me. Why can't I just keep on doing it?"

Evie smacked her hand against the gloss. "Because those names mean something, Saskia! Jesus Christ, you think anyone's going to be lining up to hear you once you're a bit older? You think there's anything at all novel, interesting, in a talented musician in her twenties? You have to keep honing your craft—"

"I can do that with Carrie—"

"You cannot. Jesus fucking Christ, Saskia, you've been better than that woman since you were about twelve."

Mike's hand on Evie's shoulder again, firm this time. "Evie—"

She shook him off. "No. No, Mike! This is just like the Saab, just like her to buy a stupid, *vintage* thing that will take specialist repair after specialist repair, spending willy-nilly because she thinks it looks cool—and how are you ever going to move this thing?" Whirling back to Saskia. "Great pianists are based on the coasts. Are you going to drive this out to New York yourself, pulling it in a trailer behind that Saab?"

Saskia played an A, long and resonant and vibrating through her. She matched her voice to it. "No. I'm going to stay in Milwaukee. I don't need to go to the coasts. But even if I did move"—she kept that A steady through her mother's indignant snort—"I'd just pay someone else to take it."

Evie bent over the music stand. "With what money?" she said. "Not with ours, I'll tell you that. You know what it costs to move a piano?"

It burned in Saskia's chest. Why were they having an argument about who would hypothetically pay for a hypothetical move to New York City? She sought her father's eyes, but he was murmuring soothing notes as her mother tried to twist him off. "Yours?" Saskia said, her voice low. "Your money? You must be joking. As far as I can tell, the only money around here is mine."

"Whoa, whoa," Mike said, holding up a hand.

"And we haven't laid a finger on it," Evie cried. "We've kept it *all* for you. We haven't spent a cent of it, not on your lessons, not on your school—yes, that's right, Saskia, somebody has to pay for that school, even when you don't go, which seems to be always—all so that you could have a future. So that you would never have to worry. So that even if you had nothing, you would always have an education." She paused, catching her breath. "But you're Saskia fucking Kreis," she said, her eyes closing briefly. "And you're going to do what you're going to do."

Mike cast an apologetic look over his shoulder as he followed Evie out of the room—he'd be back, the look said.

Saskia put both hands on the keyboard and rolled through the arpeggios.

They burned in her, though, her mother's words.

The money had been hers.

Hers alone.

February 2020

WHEN THE DOORBELL RINGS THE NEXT AFTER-noon, Saskia scrambles down to get it, Wolfie barking at her heels. Her startle reflex is on high alert, her heart beating wild.

"I got it!" she calls to her father as he approaches through the archway behind the stairs. She's not sure who it is—all of the possibilities seem terrifying—but she wants to be the one to head them off.

But when she opens the door, it's just Josh.

He grins bashfully as he sees her. She takes a step out into the cold to kiss him before remembering that her father's right behind them, and what she'd intended as a quick brush against the lips turns into an awkward bump.

"I'm sorry to just drop by, but I found this in my car and thought you might need it," he says, holding up Evie's black clutch.

"Oh, shit! Yeah, thanks. I'm not a real girl, I didn't even realize I'd left without it."

He smiles, then dives behind her as the door creaks open. He's on his knees then, rubbing Wolfie's head with a kind hand.

"Hey, buddy! Oh, hey!" as Wolfie slobbers down his cheeks. Worst watchdog ever. "Is it—Johann?"

She frowns. "Johann. The dog we had in high school, Johann?"

He nods, catches another lick from the dog with a laugh.

"Josh, that was twenty years ago. How long do you think dogs live?"

"I don't know," Josh says sheepishly, getting to his feet. "We never had one."

She laughs. "No, Johann died years ago."

"That's too bad," he says, brushing off his pants. "Dogs should live forever."

Saskia bends down to give Wolfie a rough kiss.

"Josh!" Saskia's father is joining the circus now, reaching out to clamp Josh on the shoulder. "Good to see you." Watch how smooth he is.

"Good to see you too, sir."

"Mike, please. Sas, aren't you going to invite your guest in?"

Josh in the Elf House again. What if now's the time that Patrick chooses to revolt? What if he floods the toilet? Throws his body against the door? Becomes *known* to Josh—

"Of course," she says, grabbing the cuff of Josh's coat and pulling him in. "We'll be out back by the firepit."

"Sas," her father says as she leads Josh in, as she watches him peer upward at the glory and the decay of the Elf House. "It's freezing."

"Hence the fire."

She directs Josh out back and throws the kettle onto the stove, catching her breath as it boils. Through the wavy glass of the mullioned windows, he's strolling around the yard, his hands in his pockets. She loves the broadness of his shoulders. I get to touch him, she thinks, the knowledge running through her with a zing.

He takes the mugs from her as she throws wood into the pit, pyramids it, and crumples newspaper at its base.

"You're a real Girl Scout," he says as the flames burst into life.

"I told you, I'm not a real girl at all," she says, laughing, taking one of the mugs back. He sips his, eyes widening at the kick of it.

"What *is* this?"

"Mom's secret recipe," she says with a wink.

He takes another sip.

"Swiss Miss and Captain Morgan?"

She shrugs. "Any kind of rum will do."

She's not sure how it happens, but somehow he maneuvers it so that they're sitting on the bench together, and his arm is wrapping around her. Funny: in her mind, he's still a gawky teenage boy. But he's had twenty years of dating, twenty years of practicing this.

He's not so much younger than Patrick was, back when.

But Patrick's not here, she reminds herself, staring into the flames against the lavender twilight, feeling the blood rise to her cheeks. She's suddenly very aware of the tower rising over them. Well, he's here. He's not *here*.

"So, the bag's not actually the only reason I came by," Josh says, and his voice is lower than before, less playful.

"Oh, no?" If she turns to look at him, their faces will be uncomfortably close together. There won't be anywhere for her to hide her reactions. She watches the fire.

"No. I've—I've actually stepped down as executor. I'm asking the court to name someone else, though I know this judge; she'll likely ask me to nominate somebody, and I can give them the name of someone at the firm. Someone great." She doesn't say anything right away—doesn't know *what* to say. But he feels her body stiffen. Turns out there was nowhere to hide, anyway. Not with his arm around her.

"It's just that . . . seeing you in this house. Thinking I have to give it to someone else—I'm having *feelings*," he says with a short laugh. "And it's turning into a conflict of interest."

She whirls her face to his as the flames crackle. The scents weave their way around the two of them, overwhelming. Pine sap with the sharp edge of snow, burning wood, hot chocolate laced with something stronger. Christmas, it feels like Christmas. It feels like long ago.

"You mean you could just decide to give it to us?"

His eyes crinkle.

"No. Of course not. I'm legally bound to do what's in the will. But that's the problem—I didn't want to. It's just so right seeing you here. It just—" He looks up at the house, glowing with otherworldly light in the falling dark, and there is a look of reverence on his face. "It just fits."

Maybe he truly did understand this place. The ghosts rising up around her, claiming her as their own.

"I don't know anymore," she says. "I really don't. There's a heaviness to it, you know? Like I'm being hammered into my place in the historical line. Like I'm nothing more than the next iteration of *Harper*, whatever that is. And the whole time, it's like Mom's around every corner, just reaching for me—"

She sees the pity in his eyes and shuts up, downs the rest of the cocoa. She's not explaining it right. And she can't say the next part, which is that nothing in the house truly belongs to her, anyway. The piano, once. The piano had. The piano still does, she supposes. But it's only in the tower where she feels like herself.

She hops to her feet. "I'm so glad you came by," she says, taking his hands and pulling him up. And she is, but she's gladder, now, to imagine him going. She needs to go and listen at the bottom of the stairs. She needs to make sure she is still safe. She needs a lot of things, none of which she can do with Josh here.

"Of course." They start walking toward the house. "I don't want to come on too strong here, but—are you free tomorrow night?"

Interesting. She's never had a relationship that wasn't some variation on her and Patrick's Wednesday and Sunday afternoons, limited by its own secrets.

"Three nights in one week?" she says, and laughs.

He kisses her laughing mouth—and for a fraction of a second, it's fully him. They are the only two people in the embrace. Josh's lips are on her lips, Josh's chilled hands on her neck, in her hair. Her leg twisting around his.

She pulls away, breathless, and they grin silently at each other.

"Dad, Josh's leaving!" she calls as they walk back inside, pausing in front of the den. The local news is blaring, loud, and he's reaching with the remote to mute it when:

Breaking news this evening—

She has vague memories of the headlines of her childhood flashing on the screen when she was little. The Gulf War, satanic abuse, missing children, Jeffrey Dahmer's murders on the other side of town.

We have a silver alert to share with you.

And Mike startles up, pushing to the edge of the sofa as Saskia and Josh come in to see what's disturbed him. There, on screen: a photo of Patrick, grinning in the darkroom as he stands next to a tray of liquid, pictures hung up to dry behind him.

This is sixty-year-old Patrick Kintner. He was last seen on the University

*of Wisconsin–Milwaukee campus on the morning of February eighth. If you
see him, you're asked to call Milwaukee police.*

Her father has turned to her now, his dark blue eyes pinned on hers.
Beside her, she feels Josh's gaze, too, darting between her and her father.
For a second, she'd forgotten he was there. He feels, suddenly, very far
away.

And finally, tonight, breaking news in the Democratic primaries—
The screen goes dark.

"Saskia," her father says, "what do you know about this?"

Her heart unclenches. *What do you know.* Not, *What did you do.* She
can almost hear the whirring of his mind behind the placid, pleasant face.

She swallows. Then frowns, trying to look as affronted as the teenage
Saskia once had been by almost everything.

"Don't look at me," she says. "I'm right here."

BACK IN HER ROOM, HER HEARTBEAT IS THRUM-
ming in her eardrums. Already she's missed a series of calls from Tara.

Saskia takes a deep breath. Finds the Wisconsin voice in her head,
adjusts herself to its tone, its volume.

"Oh my God, Tara, did you hear?"

"Yeah, holy shit. I mean—yeah, holy shit." Tara sounds a few drinks in.
All the better. Saskia swallows.

"I mean, I know he had problems. The man's a mess. You don't think
he—he *did* something to himself?" It's a new tack, it literally just came to
her.

Tara bites. "Who knows? Guys like this, once the jig is up . . . I mean,
look at Epstein . . ." She trails off. "Yeah, it seems not impossible."

Saskia pulls her knees to her chest.

"So, then . . . what does this mean? For our case?"

"It depends," Tara says, and her heart sinks. "Sorry. First things first, if
there's evidence that he ran off there could be a default judgment for you
and your father. Once you actually file the paperwork. But if there isn't
evidence that he ran away . . . we're looking at another stay."

"Until he's found?"

"Or declared legally dead. But just in case you're thinking that this solves everything—it really doesn't, Saskia. If you don't contest the will, the petition to administer will be granted and he'll still legally inherit the house. And then if he's eventually declared legally dead, it'll go to his heirs."

Who, Saskia wonders with a sinking heart, would that even be? No children, no siblings, and both parents dead since his early twenties.

"Another mess," she says.

"Well, yeah. I'll talk with Josh, see if he still wants to send an appraiser over, or if he's going to be chasing Patrick down."

"Didn't you hear? Josh's not the executor anymore. We're . . ." She's not sure she's ever said this phrase before, takes a deep breath. "We're actually dating. Or something."

"Too cute," Tara says. "Love that for the two of you. Do you know who'll be taking over?"

"Someone else from the firm. What happens if that person doesn't find him?"

"Well, they'll put the property into a trust, in case Patrick shows up demanding it." A pause. "That's if you don't choose to continue with challenging the will, of course."

"How long?" She's going too fast now, she should be pretending to ruminate or something. Oh well, in for a penny. "How long does the property have to remain in a trust? And could we stay in it, in the meantime?"

"Seven years before he's declared legally dead. And I don't see any problem with you staying there in the meantime. We'd have to run it by the new executor, of course."

She disconnects the call, staring shakily into the flames jumping in her fireplace.

Seven years.

It's such a long time.

Chapter 26

And as Cinderella fled, she felt a joy rise up in her with every step. It was wonderful, this running. The closest a human being could get to flying; the way it used every muscle in her body, the way she felt her blood pumping through her veins, like she was finally fully alive.

How she loved it.

—*FAIRY TALES FOR LITTLE FEMINISTS:*
CINDERELLA, EVELYN HARPER KREIS

March 2001

SASKIA WAS EIGHTEEN, AND SHE HAD MASTERED exactly two ways of using her body: for the piano, and with Patrick. Both of which had been pleasures for so long that her memory had erased the initial pain. And she had mastered him now, mastered him like a tricky concerto: a finger there, a breath here. In contrast, the burning grind of running felt intolerable, an indignity so painful she couldn't imagine why people willingly inflicted it on themselves.

But when she'd unwrapped the New Balance trainers yesterday, when she'd seen the veiled delight in her father's face as she held them up, the gray sneakers the women's equivalent of his, she knew she couldn't say no. How long had it been since he'd given her a gift just because? How long since she'd seen that kind of excitement in his face?

They were running together, and she was doing everything in her power to keep in front of her breath, when he said, "We could make Juilliard work, you know."

Saskia gagged. Stopped short to bend over.

"Fuck it—Dad—I know it could work." She swallowed, but her mouth was dry. "It was never—a question of money. I have enough."

She did: $160,000 left in her account. But that wasn't the point.

"Tell me this, then," he said as she righted herself. "Do you not want to go because it was your mother's idea? Or because you don't think you could hack it?"

She stared at him, blood pulsing through her eyeballs.

"It wasn't Mom's *idea*," she said. "It was her fucking evil plan. Her forged signature on the apps. Her using my record as an audition tape. The record from forever ago." And it had worked, too, right up to the point where Saskia had opened the acceptance packet and torn it into tiny pieces, there at the dinner table.

"But you're in. And it just seems like the perfect opportunity, Sas—to mix music and the real world, to actually live. My years in New York? They were some of the best years of my life. Until I met your mother," he corrected quickly. "Until we had you."

"Getting in wasn't the point. I'm not going to college. I'm—" Visions of her musical scores scattered across Patrick's floor. The thought of waking up next to that dark, tousled head every day. His sleepy eyes in the morning—

"Was it the razor blade story?"

"The—"

"At that dinner party last month? I told the story about how when I was at Juilliard, the piano students would put razor blades between the keys—"

Slicing open the finger pads of whoever came next, like a knife through ripe grapes. She stifled another gag.

"I just thought—if it was the competitiveness—"

She shook her head. "You know I don't give a shit about any of that. Not the ruthlessness, not the pain. Even if they did get my fingers, which they wouldn't." She'd caught her breath. "Don't you remember when I was learning to walk, and I fell down the cliff path? Just tumbling and tumbling over the concrete, down and down, and when you finally caught up, I just shook myself off, propped myself back onto my feet." She laughed. "I'm tough. I never even cried, you said."

It was a long moment before her father spoke.

"I'm not sure it's a good thing," he said finally. "Not to feel pain."

Her cheeks pulsed with the blood, the frustration pounding through her.

"You think I don't feel it?" she cried, louder than she meant to. "I fucking feel it. I just don't let it rule me."

He didn't know what to say, he just wanted this to be over. She wanted it never to have started, but now that it had, she had to see it through.

"Get this through your head," she said, wrapping her arms over her chest. "And tell Mom, too. I don't need an institution to become the best in the world. I don't need anything. I just need to get—to get back—"

To get back the magic, she'd almost said.

She'd never admitted it out loud.

But the past four years, the magic had been draining out of her, had faded, had faltered. She was still a virtuoso, but she would never again be a prodigy.

And she didn't know how to articulate the difference, what it felt like in her hands and in her heart and in her head. All she knew was that the magic had been *here,* she needed to find it *here, here* was where she'd lost it. Once she left for New York, it might be gone for good, forever and ever.

But her father didn't believe in magic. He believed only in effort. In work.

She couldn't read his face as he turned away.

"You're going to do what you need to do," he said simply.

There was the pounding of his feet, away from her, like a heartbeat. And then she was walking home alone, sweat chilling on her arms, becoming ice under her skin.

February 2020

IS SHE ESCAPING PATRICK, OR IS SHE A REAL WRITER now? Or does it make a difference, is she doing both? There was a strange thaw last night, and now, heading out to the studio, Saskia's boots keep sticking in the mud left from the melting snow. Wolfie, trotting at her side, is perfectly happy, slipping and sliding through it.

She needs an idea. Something more than what she has, which is nothing. But last night, in the half-life between waking and sleeping, she remembered a spiral notebook shoved atop the safe. She hadn't gone through it, had been too distracted by the photos. But her mother had kept a notebook for brainstorming each and every one of her princesses. Maybe she'll reach out from beyond the grave now with her wisdom. Maybe she can help Saskia solve this.

Wolfie's paws leave prints, weaving circles and spirals around the studio as he sniffs, pokes, explores. Finally, he finds a rawhide shoved way in back of the trash can and settles at the foot of the stairs to chew it with relish. Saskia grabs the notebook and flips it open with similar gusto.

Her mother's handwriting is beautiful. She hasn't seen it in so long, not in years, and suddenly the sheer discipline of it overwhelms her. Evie could have accomplished just as much with a scrawl, with block printing—and yet until the last, she never failed to produce beautiful penmanship.

The first entries are dated from June 2018, well before any of this mess started. The notes, as beautifully written as they are, are just scraps and fragments, half sentences and words dotted across the page.

2019. Her mother had found out about her in June 2019.

She doesn't know why, but Saskia finds herself flipping forward. Past sketches of the characters, past her own eyes staring out from Persephone's face. Past a Demeter who looks surprisingly like her mother. Past and past and past:

7/04/2019. Beneath the date, circled in purple marker:

Dedication: For Saskia.

She puts both palms on the desk, feet on the floor, to ground herself to the earth. But the bracing hurts, in her muscles and her bones. It is only after she tells herself, grudgingly, *You can cry,* that the hurt passes. As does the urge to cry.

She was always a contrary thing.

But she came out here to finish the book, and she's not leaving until she knows how.

Beneath her mother's notes about the dedication, a question:

What can Demeter give to save her daughter?

Then:

History is a nightmare from which I am trying to awake.

The rest of the page is blank.

The question burns bright in Saskia's chest. Sometimes a princess *does* need saving. Her mother finally admitted it. The sentence below makes no sense in context, though it sounds vaguely familiar. Though it resonates quick in her blood.

Saskia closes her eyes. What did her mother have to give her? To save her? Ambition. Opportunity. Privilege. Love.

But what did her mother think she had to give?

The Elf House. Or her stories.

The only two commodities she owned that the world actually wanted. And so when it had come to Patrick, when it had come to saving her own daughter, she'd had to pick. Which to save, which to spurn.

So, why not the princesses? Because those stories, faulty and flawed as they were . . . those stories were inescapable. The stories were already in her head, the stories were burned in her brain, the stories would stay with her forever. Evie owned them already; they owned her, too.

But more than that. They were her creation. Her product. Something she had made.

Just as Saskia was.

Beyond that: Money. Opportunity. Those were two things the Elf House would never give her. Instead, the Elf House would suck up every free cent and then some, until she'd sold off everything of any value to her.

And so, in the end, Evie had chosen the princesses as the more valuable of the two. The princesses that Sas had so derided, so despised, over the years. They were the asset that could now give Saskia a future. They were the ones opening the door to more money—and with it, more potential, more power. The Elf House was a drain, a sinkhole, the past. The princesses were the future.

She never would have believed it, as a girl. As a young woman. That the princesses would come to save her.

That, after everything: she'd gotten the better deal.

Opening her eyes, Saskia turns the page. There, only one sentence: *She can't move forward while the eyes of the past track her.*

She can't see how it applies to the story. And though she was never that literary, she suspects it's not even about the book. It's about her mother's choice.

Saskia stares out the window into the middle distance as Wolfie rolls over with a groan. The Elf House—in a way, it was like its very own Underworld. With earlier versions of you haunting every hall. Everything she was, everything she'd been, distorted and contorted and turned into a story that made sense between these walls.

And Saskia grabs the laptop and begins to type.

This time, she's not inventing anymore. She knows what Demeter did as certainly as she knows what her mother had done.

She gave herself up to save her daughter.

It was the only way to set her free.

Chapter 27

And the girl turned the doorknob in the forbidden room, watching in horror as it swung open to reveal body after body. All of the wives he'd had before.

"No way," the girl said when she was done screaming. "I'm out of here." And she went into town to raise a mob against her husband. Give him his own surprise.

—*Fairy Tales for Little Feminists:*
Bluebeard, Evelyn Harper Kreis

June 2001

SASKIA WAS EIGHTEEN, AND PATRICK HAD TEXTED her. *We need to talk*, it said, and she did not yet know the meaning of the words. She thought they meant that they had to talk about their future, about what it would mean that she'd given up Juilliard for him; about when she could break the news to her parents that she'd be moving into his apartment; hell, even about how they'd get the piano from her parents' house to his.

Was he going to propose?

She did not yet know.

And so she told him where to meet her, and she showed up at the cliff's edge that evening, her parents' absence an opening of their cage. The cage that wouldn't need to hold them much longer, now. She was already eighteen. She'd been eighteen for seven months. They'd been so careful for so very long, and it was time, now. Time to get their reward.

He was already there when she arrived, and she came up behind him on soft cat feet, wrapped already tanned arms around his shoulders, buried her face in his hair. She loved his hair, still. All the love stories in the world and nobody ever told you that it was like this years later, that there would still be a thrill to it, a thrill and a comfort at the same time—

He squirmed away, and as she blinked blankly at him, he patted the ground beside him. A clump of dirt broke off from the edge and fell, scattering, down to the beach below.

Beside him, she looked at him, into his face, waiting for him to kiss her. But he wasn't kissing her, he wasn't even looking at her.

"What's up?" she said.

"Saskia," he said, and he took her hands between his. Those same hands, after all this time. She absently ran her fingers around the fourth finger of his left hand; how long until she'd slide a ring on it, how long until that? "Saskia, knowing you has been one of the great privileges of my life."

She pulled her hands out of his, sliding them out slow.

"Okay," she said.

He saw the wariness on her face, and he gave a sad smile. She knew this smile. This smile of, *No, we can't leave the apartment together*, this smile of, *No, I don't think we should tell anyone yet*.

"Patrick?" she said, her voice rising, wavering in vibrato.

"Yeah," he said, and he turned out to look at the lake. "It's just—there's so much out there for you, Sas. And this talk of Juilliard—"

"But I don't want Juilliard," she said, the phrase now as familiar to her as her own name. "I want you."

He pressed his lips together. His skin reflected the fluorescent pinks and oranges of the sunset.

"You should want Juilliard," he said finally.

And the spiraling, the winnowing down of her future that had happened in that moment. They weren't going to spend the rest of their lives together. They weren't going to New York, or Paris, or Tokyo together. They weren't going to do anything together, anymore.

"Fuck it, it's not about Juilliard. Don't baby me. What did I do?"

She was scanning her memory, thinking back. Refusing pills— but she'd been doing that since last year, since she'd quit in an effort to clarify her playing once again, to bring back the magic. Being too clingy—but he texted first, he always texted first, even now she still waited for him to do it. Doing—being—her brain sputtered, came up with nothing.

"You didn't—"

Her small voice cut him off. "What did I do wrong?"

The waves breaking on the beach, the summer night so warm and humid it was almost fuzzy around them. The eternity stretching between them as she awaited his reply.

"It's nothing you did, exactly. It's a quality—a hard quality—I don't know how to describe it." And his two fingers, one under each of her eyes. "It's something in here."

And that, she had no response to.

His voice was soft as he turned to go. "I'll never forget you, Sas. You need to know that."

In what universe had she ever imagined he would forget her? In what universe had that ever even been a possibility? Their lives had been twined together, wrapping around each other like the roots of two trees planted too close. But the chain saw, the tools he'd used to uproot her—in the end, all it took was a handful of words.

And just like that, it was over.

February 2020

THE NEXT DAY IS BRIGHT, WHITE, AND COLD: PERFECT Wisconsin winter weather. When Saskia gets back from her run late that afternoon, Mike's out getting groceries, he's left a note on the kitchen counter. *At Whole Foods—D.* Saskia doesn't waste her time; she rushes to the piano. They've become precious, these few hours alone when she can practice. She's taken to working her way through the Horowitz catalog. When she was little, reviewers often compared her to him. And, now that she's grown up, their hands are startlingly similar. You don't need long fingers to play the piano well, but if you're playing the Romantics, like Saskia does, like Horowitz did—it helps.

She's stretching and flexing her fingers, trying to calm her racing heart into something like a steady rhythm. It's its own internal metronome, the heart, keeping pace and time. She takes a deep breath, tries to slow it. Why is she so wound up today?

The truth is: her playing doesn't have to be secret anymore.

None of it does.

She could tell her father.

The thought zaps warmth into her limbs. She wants him to know that she's playing again, that the pieces that were once the romantic howlings of a preteen are richer, now. Deeper.

She lays her fingertips against the cool ivory and begins.

It's *Danse Macabre* today. She loves Saint-Saëns; there's so much between the notes, the fiendish little twists and flourishes he demands. A pounding to the bass line that's like the thrum of blood in her ears when she descends from her tower every night after depositing Patrick's food and water. She runs through it once, but it's off. Weak.

Her hands hover above the keys, twitching with the momentum of the notes. One repetition done, not yet ready to start the next.

The car pulls into the driveway, she can hear its failing muffler.

And in that moment, in that moment before the car door opens, Saskia makes a choice.

She's playing again when he comes in, the door clattering behind him. "Hello, the house." Her father's voice, warm and round. He's heard that she's playing, and it's made him happy.

"I'm *playing*."

And he's in the doorway, Wolfie at his heels; she hears, though she does not look up to see, the dog's paws clacking over the slick wooden floors.

"*Danse Macabre?*"

She nods, gaze stuck on the page. "The Horowitz arrangement."

"It's nice," he says.

Above them, a dull thump. Another. Each one like a sack of flour being flung against the floor.

She forces herself to swallow, running through the arpeggios. As good a time as any. She'll never get a better opportunity.

"What the hell—"

"Oh," she says, rushing the ending, trying to finish the repetition. But it goes faster and faster and she can barely think and move at the same time, let alone think and move and talk, and then the words just come out: *whack*. "That's just Patrick."

"Patrick?"

"Yeah," she says, and she doesn't want to see his reaction, she can't look at him, she's too scared. "He's locked up in the attic. It's stupid," she says, and suddenly she stops, lacing her fingers together, twisting them. Maybe it's simpler than she's been making it. Maybe, at her core, the only true thing is how much she loves her father. The father she knew before and the father he is now; the man who has loved her without complication every day of her life. Silence like water filling the room as she looks at him, into her own blue eyes. "But I kind of hoped he'd be dead by now."

SHE TELLS HER FATHER EVERYTHING. SHE DOESN'T think she's going to, when they sit down in front of the conservatory fire; she thinks she will tell him just enough. But just enough requires everything, from her relationship with Patrick to their breakup, from the photos to the piano, from Evie's discovery to her decision.

"She set us free," Saskia says. "She set us free from the debts and the memories and the pain. She knew it, even when we didn't. History is a nightmare, and she's woken us up."

But what if everything isn't enough, she thinks as she finally stops talking, lets the silence fall. When she'd imagined telling her father, the aftermath had split into an infinite web of possibilities. He might smash a mirror. Might call Paul, get legal advice. Might phone the cops, turn her in right away. Might storm upstairs and free Patrick himself. As she watches her father push to his feet decisively, she realizes that in every scenario, she imagined him *doing* something. He's not capable of non-action.

"Dad? Where are you going?"

He's already halfway to the foyer.

"Getting my rifle."

"You have a rifle?"

"The elephant gun. In the other attic," he says, marching up the stairs. "You're forgetting, Sas. I have a tower, too."

She grabs his arm, but before she can say anything, the thumping redoubles; she can almost hear Patrick's exhausted wheezes between each hurl of his body against the door.

"Stop it!" she screams. "I already told my dad, okay? He knows that you're in there."

And her father turns back with—what is that on his face? It's been so long since she's seen it, she almost doesn't recognize it: pride. Pride, that she's used him as a threat.

It reminds her so much of what she used to feel, when she heard her parents bragging about what she could do. She realizes with a start that she hasn't felt proud of herself in a very long time.

"Dad," she says. "Let's go for a run. You always say that running helps clear the mind."

"Bullets," he mutters, twisting out of her grip.

"Dad," she says again. "Listen to me. You need to burn off some of this rage—"

And he whirls around, facing her, eyes on fire. "I'm not leaving that fucker in my house alone. You got that? Not for one more goddamn second."

There's the sound of cracking plaster next to the dumbwaiter and he reels back, clutching his fist. The place where he punched the wall is caved in, paint spiderwebbing around it. His hand, his cellist's hand. "I'm going to *murder* this guy."

She cuts him off before he can throw another punch, holding up a palm.

"Not your call, Dad," she says. Calm but fierce. "It's mine."

For a long moment, their eyes meet.

"Come on," she says, taking his hand and pulling him down the hall. Into Evie's fairy-tale dream of a young girl's room, a room that now feels barren and bereft without her childhood possessions.

He doesn't seem to know what to do with himself, paces in front of her fire. She watches him, hypnotized, until he stops, reaching toward the violin over the fireplace.

"Beautiful things," he says, his hand tracing a delicate finger along its edge. It comes away painted in dust. "I found them in the attic of my parents' house when I was a kid. I always thought"—turning back, sitting back down—"that they're the reason I became a musician in the first place."

"But you couldn't play them."

"No, of course not. But they made me feel connected, somehow, to something bigger. To my ancestors, yeah. But also, in a way, to history. To the larger story of humanity."

It hurts, with a dull pang. It's been so long since she felt connected to anyone or anything. To anything but this fucking house.

He's pacing the room, shoving his hands down deep into his pockets. "So, that fucker is the reason why you quit music?"

Catching their reflection in the dark of the window, she winces. "I don't think it's that simple. It was a time in my life when I felt . . . I don't know." She's already told him everything. And she still can't fucking say it.

"What are you going to do with him?" His tone is so even that it sends goose bumps up her arms.

She swallows, looks away.

"I don't . . . I don't know. I don't know what I *can* do with him. At first, I thought I'd take him to court, but that was before I locked him in the attic," she says sheepishly. "I really didn't mean to do it, it just kind of— happened."

Outside, the wind is rising. It's going to be a cruel night.

"Sas," her father says, "why did you really quit piano?"

Her heartbeat is irregular in her chest, a fucked-up metronome.

"I told you—"

"I know what you told me. But also, seeing you here, now. I don't believe it," he says, "I see how fierce you are, and I think that that's not it. You never cared about being like other people. If anything, the opposite's true."

She looks at the violin. Years above the fireplace have dulled its patina, have cracked its surface. It's duller now than when she was a teenager. Time. It's so thick in this house it's like something physical in the air, like you could reach out and gather it with curling fingers into the palm of your hand.

Saskia swallows, her gaze dropping to the fire.

"You know what it's like, there. You practice. You go to your lessons, your groups, and your seminars. You practice and you practice and you practice. It sounded like heaven. In some ways, it was heaven. But it didn't feel that way at the time."

In her peripheral vision, her father is nodding, and she turns to look at him. In his eyes are everything: patience, love, curiosity, acceptance.

"And all of the other kids were as talented as I was. And one or two of them—yeah. One or two of them were even better than me. But still, we were just dozens of talented kids in front of a group of teachers who'd seen hundreds, thousands, of equally talented kids pass before them, year after year. But where did those kids all go? It just hit me all of a sudden: I could see the years stretching in front of me, and with each passing one, I'd become slightly less exceptional. And I couldn't bear it."

Her father's face is open. Pained. "What do you mean?"

"I wasn't special anymore," she said softly. "I was losing my youth, I'd already lost Patrick. Without being a prodigy. Without him. It was all just . . . intolerable."

After a long moment, he speaks.

"I'm sorry," he says, staring at the violin. "I'm sorry. We had no idea, you know. No idea how to raise a child with your talents. Not in this world."

With each word, her throat tightens a centimeter more. She looks at him and nods. She can't offer him absolution, but she does hear him. She can give him that.

"I don't know what I'm going to do with Patrick, Dad," she says, and her voice is husky, low as her mother's. "But I'll promise you this. You'll be the very first one to know."

He looks at her, their eyes fierce and wild.

"Okay, kiddo," he says. He understands what she's capable of, now. "But whatever you decide, do it soon. The hearing's just six days off."

She flops back in her chair. No longer a Fury, no longer Lady Justice with her sword and her scales and her eyes that burn. Just a frustrated adolescent, annoyed at the world again.

"Ugh," she says. "Dad, I *know*."

Chapter 28

And in the blink of an eye, the Beast had turned into a handsome prince. His golden hair gleamed in the sun as he turned to Beauty and took her hands in his.

"Beauty. You have freed me from the spell of the wicked enchantress—"

But Beauty had already pulled her hand back and was holding it up.

"Wait a minute. Wait just a minute. People don't just poof! change."

The Beast looked at her quizzically.

"But I did," he said. "I have changed. With your love—"

"Who said anything about love?" Beauty cried. "For months, you have treated me with nothing but abuse. You threatened my family, you have treated me as nothing more than a servant. No," she said, even as her hand crept toward him. "No, I don't think so—"

And with a single stroke, she had pulled a dagger from his belt and struck it through his heart.

"But—" The Beast gasped as he stared at her hand. And then he fell to his knees, and he would say nothing ever again. For the Beast was dead.

"Now," Beauty said, turning back to the castle. "About that library . . ."

—*Fairy Tales for Little Feminists:
Beauty and the Beast*, Evelyn Harper Kreis

June 2001

SASKIA WAS EIGHTEEN, AND SHE STUMBLED BACK up to the house, barefoot in the dark, Van Morrison still booming through the headphones around her neck. But the second she cracked open the front door and Johann barked, she knew she was caught. Sure enough, a moment later: the soft sound of her mother's slippers on the plush stair runner, the floor-length silk robe flowing around her body. Approaching the stinking, blurred Saskia in the dark.

"Saskia Joan Kreis. Have you been smoking?"

And Saskia was so startled that she couldn't even think of a lie. Four years straight of lying, but it was like a fairy's gift, a spell that had dissipated the second Patrick had walked away from her, two weeks earlier.

"Yeah," she said, and braced for impact.

But her mother simply sighed and turned down the hallway toward the den.

Saskia stood, Coke bottle in hand, reeking of rum and nicotine. Was she supposed to follow? Or was that the whole conversation? Neither Mike nor Evie had ever ascribed to the yelling school of parenting. They were just disappointed in her. That was her punishment.

And yet something in Saskia wanted more. She deserved more. She followed her mother to the den, where Evie had already poured herself a glass of wine.

"So, what? Are we going to have a talk?"

Evie peered up over the gold rim of the glass. "Do you need a talk?"

"I mean—"

"You know why I'm disappointed?"

"Because of the smoking? The drinking?" Saskia taunted, holding up the bottle. But Evie shook her head.

"It's not the drinking," she said, exhaustion in her voice. "It's not even the smoking, though God knows it won't help your endurance at the piano. It's the waste. It's the goddamn waste." She took a sip of her wine. "I did not get you this far for you to stop here."

Saskia wrapped her arms around her ribs. "I got me this far," she said haughtily, but as soon as she heard the words, she doubted them.

Evie rolled her eyes, and then she was on her feet. "No. You know what? I'm more than disappointed, Sas. I won't fucking—I won't stand for it. I don't care what you do, but you're not going to spend the rest of your life fucking around and then crawling back into this house. Do you hear me? The world is so much bigger than that and, goddamn it, you are going out there. You are going to have adventures, and you are going to have experiences, and you are . . ." She trailed off, folding back on the sofa in an elegant pile. "Going to be happy, goddamn it," she finished weakly, running her tongue over her purpling lips.

The beast in Saskia rose, had been waiting for just this kind of fight. "What, Mom? Like the girls in your stories?"

Evie looked at her, eyes flashing. "Yeah. Just like the goddamn fairy princesses."

The princesses. The princesses who would always beat her, the princesses who would always win. The princesses who weren't real in such important ways; ways her mother had always refused to see.

"But your princesses . . . they never have to give anything up, Mom! The old stories weren't perfect, but they were realer—they were truer in a way. In actual fairy tales, no matter who you are, a princess or a witch or a mermaid or a dwarf, you can have what you want only when you sacrifice something. There are limits. There are restrictions. There's a—balance to those stories, just like in the real world. But your stories don't have that."

"Yes, and I wrote a better world. What's the matter with that?"

"Because—because," Saskia said. "Because it's a lie! When bad shit happens, it doesn't automatically make you stronger. You don't come out of it with superpowers. You might just come out—broken," she said, her voice fading to almost nothing. "It's a lie, Mom. You're selling little girls a lie."

"You know my books so well, yet you've learned nothing from them, Saskia. Of course they have to give something up. The difference is, the thing they never sacrifice is *themselves*." Her mother's eyes are flashing. "So, what I want to know, since you're so much smarter than the princesses: How did you let yourself get like this—like *this*—over a boy?"

A boy. Saskia laughed, despite herself, and felt the fight drain out of her. A boy.

But her mother was staring at her expectantly, still waiting for an answer. Her mother, who saw what Saskia had become. What Saskia herself had tried to ignore.

The hands that didn't fly the way they used to. The body that didn't move as it once had. The prodigy who was no longer a prodigy, who was just a woman, now—a woman and not a woman, something and nothing, a girl who had made a choice years ago and watched her world narrow and narrow without realizing it wouldn't ever be that wide again.

"I don't know," Saskia said finally. "I honestly don't know."

"Well, then, fairy princess," Evie said, bending forward to rest her elbows on her thighs. "How are you going to fix it?"

Saskia had followed her mother for a fight but, really, all she had wanted were answers.

"Juilliard?" she said softly. Maybe her mother had been right all along. Maybe her dad was, too. Maybe it would be fun.

But Evie had drained her glass and was already on her feet, turning out the light.

"Fuck it. Do whatever you want."

How long did Saskia stand there, in the dark archway? Long enough for her mother's footsteps to recede. Long enough for the emptiness of the house to rear up once again.

She accepted her offer of admission the next day.

February 2020

JOSH, IT TURNS OUT, LIVES IN SHOREWOOD.

"Don't you think that's kind of strange?" she blurted out. She'd imagined him in some loft down in the Third Ward, some bungalow in Bay View. Not a suburban house. Not a cottage like Patrick's.

"Strange?"

"Yeah," she said, "like . . . why would a single man in his thirties want to live in the suburbs?"

"Saskia," he said patiently, "it's my mother's old house. The house I grew up in. You might even recognize it from my old bus stop. Maybe that's strange in its own, Norman Bates kind of way—"

"No," she said. "No, you're right. Who's Norman Bates?"

She realized that she liked the idea that he was living in his past, just as she was. But now, locked together on his couch, she thinks of his wide, clear sixteen-year-old face as he'd lied to her mother. She thinks about him at Lexi's party, watching her hands play against her thigh in the bonfire's light. She thinks about him in his valedictorian's robes, scanning the crowd and pausing, just for a second, when his eyes found hers.

What would it be like, to be with someone who hadn't known her in the past? Oh, sure, James hadn't. Tim hadn't. None of the New York guys had. But that had felt different, somehow; she'd never trusted them the way she trusted Josh. For the first time she wonders whether she could have that trust, that intimacy, away from her history. Could anyone who hadn't known her as a prodigy actually love her?

Josh's mouth brushes her jawline, red wine breath hot on her face, startling her back to the moment, and she realizes she's frozen. To compensate, she gives a slight groan and his breath quickens. Men are so easy.

Patrick had loved her beyond her talent. That was the story she had told herself for years. And that was true, to an extent. He'd loved her for reasons separate from her talent, but just as equally out of her control. Her youth. Her innocence. Her naïveté. All of which he'd taken, gobbling down, leaving her bare as the orchard tree branches in January.

He's gentle, Josh. As gentle as she would have expected. It's a rare quality, though not one she much appreciates. She's more of a grabber herself. If she were paying more attention, she'd probably take his hand, clamp it onto her breast. As it is, he traces the curve of her hip with the backs of his fingers and she pretends that her shiver is one of pleasure rather than a response to the tickling.

But fuck, Patrick is in the forefront of her mind now. As ever. As always. His presence doesn't take away the pleasure altogether, but it does diminish it somewhat. Poising her on the knife's edge between her body and her brain and her history.

A lot of girls probably had their first orgasm earlier than Saskia did. She doesn't know, she's never asked any other women, but it wouldn't surprise her. Patrick had been her first kiss at fourteen, her first fuck at fifteen. He fucked her for a year before she came from it alone.

Until she was sixteen, she hadn't been aware that girls—women— could even have orgasms from penetration. Sex was already more involved than she'd thought it would be; Evie had been vague in her explanations. She couldn't be accused of any crime by the sex-positive feminists, but neither could she be credited with actually imparting any information of real value.

His hands climb higher, brush against her breast. She thinks: *Josh. I'm with Josh.*

Josh pauses against her mouth, breath coming short. She smiles into him, runs her hand along the side of his jaw. He has a wonderful jaw, all angles, and for a moment, that's it: there they are, the two of them together. But then he slides his mouth to her neck and she's half-gone again.

What had Patrick done that night she first came? With his mouth on her neck, her breath had caught as his palm skimmed her nipple, lighter than he'd ever touched her.

Josh's hand is under her shirt now and she moans as he pinches her nipple. There, yes, play with me.

She'd raised her hips, that was it. Gasped.

And Josh's breath is getting ragged—

She can feel the slap of that skin against hers. The force of his lips on her mouth. The heat of the place where they met, the slippery, wet darkness (she didn't know any of the clichés then, wasn't thinking in words then, either)—

Patrick—I'm—

Ah, fuck—

When you choose one thing, you're choosing not to have so much more.

"Josh—" she says, and he pulls back abruptly with a shy smile. That smile. It hurts her.

"Everything okay?" Josh asks.

"Yeah, of course. I just think—I should be getting home."

But though he sits back, he doesn't get up. Instead, he looks at her, studying her face.

"I'm sorry—did I do something wrong?"

Fuck. She's going to have to do this now.

"No—no. It's just—this is all a lot for me, Josh. There's so much going on, and it's just—it's too much, I think. For tonight, at least."

"Shit, I'm sorry—I shouldn't have—we can take things slower, of course—"

"No, it's not that, I wanted to, I just—"

His eyes have a strange intensity in the diffracted orange light from the streetlamps, leaking in through the windows.

"What do you want? Tell me what I can do."

Their bodies seem inescapable, filling up all of the space in the small living room, sucking in all of the available air.

"I think I might just need some space, Josh. To spend some time apart. It's not you, it's really not."

He can fill in the rest of the sentence as well as she could.

There's no air at all in the long moment before he speaks; or there's too much air, she's not sure; she's aware of how close they are, equally aware that she could just go to the front door, leap out into the night, start running.

Josh closes his eyes. "Yeah, of course," he says, with such kindness that it's all she can do to stop herself taking it all back. But before she can, she feels a hard layer of glass rising up around her, the living version of Snow White's coffin, and she just swallows, nods.

She gathers her clothes, her things, as he punctuates the silence with little grace notes of anxiousness—*You're sure everything's okay? There's nothing I can do?*—and she deflects, defends. She wants to end this as soon as possible. All of a sudden, all she wants is to get back home; to be absorbed, once more, in the Elf House.

Maybe that was why Evie had chosen to give her the stories, instead. Had decided to get rid of it for her. Because there is deceptive comfort in a house like that; the comfort of being a Harper, the comfort of a long, privileged family line. And yet it simultaneously stifles you, effaces the rest of you, everything else you are. You become part of it; it is never just part of you.

You could drown yourself in a legacy like that.

She reaches for the doorknob.

"For what it's worth," Josh says, "I'm glad I got to know you as an adult. Beyond the myth of Saskia Kreis."

Her hand hovering in midair, she pauses. There's something final in his tone.

"What do you mean by that?"

But it's too late now. He's looking beyond her, a crooked smile on his face.

"Nothing," he says, and he's staring out into the dark. "Nothing."

THE ELF HOUSE IS FLOODLIT, CHIAROSCURO IN the dark. She can't see her tower from the car, but she does catch a shadow passing behind the living room curtains, and something unclenches in her chest. Her father's downstairs. She pads upstairs to her room, suddenly full of a bone-deep exhaustion, hoping he won't hear her.

But Mike is standing in the hall between her bedroom and the tower door. Frozen, with Wolfie sitting patiently at his feet.

She breaks the spell.

"Dad?"

He looks over at her. "Sas. I was just coming up to ask—want to go for a run in the morning?"

"Sure, yeah. Sorry, I was out with Josh, I thought I'd said." He nods, shoves his hands into his jeans pockets. "It's weird, I thought I saw you in the living room from outside—there was this shadow behind the curtains—"

"I dunno, kiddo. I've been up here." Her father looks at her, grins. "Maybe it was a ghost."

Chapter 29

Demeter scoured the Earth for her daughter. She ran into witches and princes, merchants and sailors, farmers and weavers, and yet nobody, nobody could tell her where Persephone had gone. It was nearly fall; the harvest was coming in, the wheat fields full of ripe, plump gold. And yet none of it mattered, because Persephone was lost to her forever.

—DEMETER AND PERSEPHONE,
EVELYN HARPER KREIS (UNFINISHED MANUSCRIPT)

September 2001

SASKIA WAS EIGHTEEN, AND THE SUMMER HAD emptied her of everything she'd been. By the time she was ready to leave for Juilliard at the beginning of September, she felt like she was almost nothing at all. The airport, which had always felt like neutral territory, betrayed her by being filled with memories: the time they came back from Italy with that mirror; the trip to Los Angeles when both she and Mike played with the Symphony; the flight to New York when she got her first period.

In her own estimation, when she cut right down to the bone: relatively, she'd been a better pianist at thirteen. Maybe she'd even been a better pianist at twelve. She didn't know what she was, now, at eighteen. She was talented, yes, but she was no longer so talented that she stood out from the other talented students her age. She was pretty, yes, but she was no longer cute, she was no longer adorable, she was no longer surprising and striking. She was intelligent, yes, but she was no longer precocious.

She was no longer remarkable.

And it all felt like she was no longer herself. No longer Saskia.

Evie had spent the last month buying extra-long sheets and huge boxes of Tampax at Target, enough to fill an entire suitcase. That suitcase, cream colored and hard shelled and embossed with her own initials, SJK, a gift from Mike, who was currently in Tokyo with the Symphony. Who had wrapped her gruffly in his arms and pretended not to notice the tears in her eyes before he left.

And then they were at the gate, the two of them. Saskia and Evie. Together.

"Well," Evie said, and suddenly the only thing in the world Saskia wanted was for her mother to leave. She was so tired, and she wanted to put on her sunglasses and sit facing the tarmac and listen to Joni Mitchell whirring on her Discman, the CD that Patrick had given her years ago . . . *something's lost, but something's gained / In living every day.* She wanted to cry where nobody could see her, and she wanted to get on the plane empty and dry and wrung out.

But then her mother was clutching at her, sobs shaking her body with greater and greater force until Saskia could not tell anymore which of them was crying.

"I'm going to miss you so much," her mother said when she finally caught her breath. She spoke into Saskia's ear, and the low buzzing of it tickled, and Saskia tried to pull away but her mother clutched her upper arms and she couldn't get the distance between them that she wanted.

"Sas, I know the last few months have been hard for you. I know they have been. But I want you to know, too, how proud I am of you. You're so resilient, you know that? You're like me. Life knocks you down and you just—somehow, you just bounce."

The hands relaxed in Saskia's flesh. And it was an unfamiliar feeling, the cry that came ripping out of her. Something she had not felt in years and years. Maybe ever.

"Mom, I'm so tired," she said, her words wet between tears. "I'm tired. I don't want to bounce anymore."

And her mother pulled back. She put the back of her hand against Saskia's left cheek, then her right. Wiping the tears away.

"But you will. Because— Oh, darling. There's so much more to go."

And maybe.

Maybe there was.

Maybe there is.

Maybe Saskia will play again at Carnegie Hall. Maybe she will record one, two, four more albums. Maybe she moves to Prague, Vienna, Berlin. Maybe she learns how to read poetry. Maybe maybe maybe, and as her mother kisses her cheek, Saskia feels herself propelled, on the balls of her feet. Like she is pushing the floor away.

Like she's bouncing.

And Evie leaves.

And Saskia does sit facing the tarmac. And she does press *play*, and Joni Mitchell does spin on. And the wide Midwestern sky is bright blue and wide as the earth. And maybe something is lost. Maybe something is gained. In living every day.

And she wonders what comes next.

February 2020

SHE WEARS THE HOUSE HEAVY AROUND HER THAT night. The wallpaper wavers with ancient stories, ancestors' visages flicker in and out of mirrors, of windows: peripheral and forever uncatchable. The decades thick in the air, 1870s, 1970s. Evie's bare child-feet pounding through the halls, her own immediately behind them.

This place is so fucking haunted, she thinks as she runs a hand over her marble mantelpiece, flames licking high from the fireplace below.

Because if you lived here, that was all you really did, that was all you really were, pressed between its hallways like flowers in the pages of an old book. You were a Harper, you lived in the Elf House. The house turned everyone into stories, fixed them in time, fixed them in mirrors. Dour Georg. Flighty Emilia. Poor Cecilia, poor Annabelle. Playful Constance. Ambitious Frederick. Creative Evelyn.

Prodigy Saskia.

Maybe it's not haunted so much as it's haunting.

You couldn't escape the stories. They were fixed, carved into the panels of the walls. But maybe, she thinks, maybe she could turn them into numbers. She can play with numbers; manipulate them, mold them. Thirteen bedrooms, seven baths. Two towers, twins. Fourteen thousand square feet. $50,000 in property taxes. $100,000 foundation. $120,000, $2,900,000—

No good. You could turn it into music, maybe. It was already halfway to music. The metronome, the chime of the grandmother clock. The dripping of the tap in the Gold Room's claw-footed bath that no plumber could ever fix. The bright bell of the door, the hiss of the kettle, the bark of the dog—

At the top of the stairs, she catches Wolfie, curled up on the window seat. He looks more like a wolf than ever when he folds his body into a ball like that. He stares at her with watchful, curious eyes and she collapses down beside him, runs her fingers through his fur.

She wishes she could be like him. Forever in the moment, never looking forward or back. Each day a fresh start, each day an unknown adventure. Each walk exciting, each meal a gift—

Was that a thump?

She freezes, Wolfie's fur caught between her fingers.

It was. It was a thump.

Saskia drags herself grudgingly up to her bedroom and grabs her key, takes out her phone, presses *record* with a heavy hand.

"Get back," she hisses at the tower door, and waits for the footsteps to retreat.

But when she's spiraled her way upstairs, Patrick's sitting, composed, on the edge of the mattresses.

"What?" she says.

"Saskia," he says, and his eyes are clearer than they've been since he got up there. Clear gold around the center. "Saskia, I'm sorry. No, it was never my intention to give the house to the university. And those pictures—" The pictures surrounding him, now, the pictures spread around his body. He hangs his head. "You were fifteen."

Everything she wanted.

It *is* what she wanted. Isn't it? It's what she's been demanding, been begging for in the only way she knows how.

And her heart lies like a stone, caught heavy somewhere in the bones of her pelvis.

The cops, the recordings, the trail she's surely, unknowingly, left—Prodigy Saskia.

Prodigy Saskia isn't worried about the trail of evidence at all.

Prodigy Saskia is thinking about him in jail. She's thinking about a check for $100,000 with his name in the corner, his signature on the bottom. She's thinking about the ten, twenty years of life he has left, spent in a cage, and it isn't enough.

It isn't enough, it was never going to be enough for her. She wants him up here, she wants him to suffer, she wants to watch him die, slowly, over and over again, because everything she is, everything she was, everything she has always been—

"Fifteen," she cries. "I was fucking *fifteen*." She scrambles around him, grabbing photo after photo, cradling them in her arms like a pile of wood, like a bundle of laundry, like a baby.

"I know," he says, holding his hands up. "I know."

"I was a child, and you ruined me, you pinned me into place as this person, this teenager who thought she was a woman, and once you've been that person, you can't ever stop being that person, you can't ever let her go because she's all you have—" She's pacing, wild-eyed, clutching the photos ever closer, ever tighter, and her voice breaks. "She's all you are anymore."

"I'm sorry," he mutters again.

"Are you? You are? Sorry, then. Sorry for fucking *what*?"

In the beam of her gaze, he crumbles. He scrambles back along the mattresses, toward the wall.

"I don't know!" he cries as his head thumps against it. "You want the truth? That's it. I don't fucking know! We were in love, then we weren't. What's so bad—"

"I was fourteen when we started!" she screeches. "I was fourteen, I was a child."

He's hiding his face in his hands. "You were a woman to me."

"I was— What if I'd been twelve, Patrick? What if I'd been ten? Six?"

His voice is muffled, and yet he can't stop himself from saying it. "But you weren't."

"How," she says, her voice curdling into something calm, sour. "I don't know how to make you see what you did."

He lets his hands slide down his cheeks.

"Sas," he says, and she knows this voice now, the unfamiliar panic is gone. She hears the condescension, the cajoling. "Will you just admit it? You're not mad because of our relationship. You're mad because we broke up. And you never got over it."

She mirrors his tone back to him. On her, it's a nursery school teacher's voice, it's nasal, it's delicious. "Let's just pretend that I *am* mad. That I never got over it. Because why did you break up with me?" she says. She says it like a liturgy, like a call-and-response. She knows the answer. She's known the answer for a long time, even if she didn't want to admit it to herself. "It wasn't because of Juilliard, it wasn't because you were worried about me 'missing out' on having a 'college experience.' It's because I grew up. Because I got old. But, Patrick, tell me." And she lets the photos fall, bends over the bed, propping herself up on her knuckles, as she hisses it into his face. "What was I supposed to do instead?"

He shakes his head. Just once. Side-to-side motion and something catches in his throat, she can hear it in his breath.

"I loved you—I did love you. I loved you more than I think you'll ever realize. Ever know."

She can't breathe.

"That wasn't love," she manages through her teeth.

And his expression is one of pure—bafflement.

"I have these dreams. You're there, and Kelly, and Julia—" And the names come spilling out, each a stone weighing her to the earth. "And in the dreams, you're seventeen. All of you. Seventeen, and you're so full of—promise, of hope. Everything is exciting, nothing has been ruined."

She closes her eyes.

"And then I wake up," he continues. "I wake up and you're all gone and that's all you ever are. Just gone."

He looks at her.

Her mouth and eyes feel unbearably wet in skin that is too dry, Wisconsin winter skin. It's like he's cast a spell and she can feel the folds of her skin where it's wrinkled, she can feel the sag of her small breasts down, ever down. She can feel the places where already her body has gone loose, already started to fall apart.

What if she had never grown up? What if there was a version of her life in which Saskia Kreis, seventeen-year-old ingenue, had been driving back from a late night turned into an early morning at the beach. A version in which a truck had T-boned the already old Saab. A version in which, Malibu pounding through her system, she'd driven over the edge of St. Mary's Hill. A version in which she'd sat beside Lexi on the cliff and gestured too broadly, tumbled down onto the sand below. A version in which she'd been frozen forever in that perfect moment.

She never would have seen the towers falling, crumbling to the earth. She never would have run through Lake Park at sunrise, felt the pain and the pleasure coursing through her veins. She never would have truly known her father—not as he is now, not with his faults and his ferocity revealed in equal measure. Never would have known the joy of a knockout, the shame of losing. The grace of her body as she moves through the ring. All of the awful and mundane and agonizing events of her life; she'd never have lived them. The idea of their loss does something inside her chest, clamping a fist around them, pulling them closer. *Those are my memories. Mine. Me.*

But she looks into his eyes, then. He is watching her. And he is— fascinated. Scared. Unsure.

She is so tired of him having feelings about her.

She is so tired of being perceived.

"You were fif—"

"Don't say it," she says, her voice hoarse as she picks up the pictures. "Don't you dare fucking say it."

And the pulse, racing through the vein in his temple.

"But you said . . ." He clears his throat. "You said that once I admitted it . . . Sas. You said I could go."

She looks at him. Cowering before her. Frightened.

Still, always, trapped in his own story. Never so much as trying to see hers.

"I know what I said," she says softly.

You could turn him into music, she thinks as she turns the key behind her, clutching the slippery photos close to her breast. The wheeze of his breath when he runs. The low chime of his laughter. The moan of him when he's hit in the sternum or when he comes.

You could turn him into numbers. Sixty years old. A hundred and fifty thousand dollars a year. Three museum collections. Five years until retirement. Two boats. Five, six, seven girls.

You could turn him into stories—but no, she can't. Because he's already turned her into one. Patrick has as many stories as the house, but in all of them she is who he wants her to be, she is who he saw her as, she is pure potential; she is everything and nothing, but all of it bounded by the limits of his vision, by the limits of his own imagination.

Yet at the end of the day—she remembers the feeling of her fist going into his chest. At the end of the day, he is muscle and blood and bone. At the end of the day, he is just a man.

Patrick and the Elf House. They have one thing in common, at least. They exist in the physical realm.

And Saskia—Saskia has spent her whole life existing in abstract worlds. Of music, of numbers. Of illusions. Boxing was the only place where her body had broken through, merged with her mind. Her way of punching back, saying, *This right here*, this *is who I am*. Her way of saying, *This right here*, this *is my story*.

Hadn't that been what her mother had wanted for her the whole time? For her to take ownership, to lay claim to her life. She'd shown her with the princesses, she'd told her to fight for what she wanted. How hard she'd tried, to hammer it into Saskia's head: that this is her story. Hers alone. That she is the only one who can write it. The only one who gets to.

And after all. What is a fairy tale, anyway, but a ghost story about the living? About taking care of unfinished business, while you still have time.

She closes her eyes and sends a silent prayer of thanks to her mother. It is, she realizes, the first time she has ever thanked her.

Maybe a clean slate isn't about having nothing to lose, she thinks as she shoves the photos back into the holes of the violin. Maybe it's about channeling the energy that you'd let leak into the past, turning it around. Pointing it to the future.

And for the first time in a long time, the story she's telling herself feels true.

Wolfie at her heels, she treads in slippered feet down to the basement. The cobwebs are thick as lace, dust gathered in balls in the corners. The scratching of mice, scampering in the walls.

It takes her only a minute. She was a genius, you know. It takes only a minute, and then she goes upstairs to get her father.

Epilogue

THE FIRE COLLAPSES TIME. IT MAKES HER SEE. Time is nothing but a story we've been telling ourselves, because in the moment of the fire, everything happens all at once. Evelyn Harper is being born, Evelyn Harper Kreis is dying. She has not yet existed, she has ceased to exist. Saskia is being born, Saskia is dying. She has not yet existed, she has ceased to exist. There is no Elf House, there is an Elf House, there is no Elf House again. There will always be an Elf House.

Saskia and Michael Kreis stand in the orchard. The lake behind them, the fire before them, their dog Wolfgang between them. A soft snow, becoming thicker and thicker, falling from above.

"Electrical engineering?" he says softly.

She doesn't look away from the flames, her blue eyes turned the color of honey in the glow.

"Double minor with piano studies," she says.

Later, she will wonder what happened to the body. He would have curled up, fists to chest; a boxer defending his corner. But the blizzard that night postpones the investigation. And in the meantime, if three men—one with red hair, one with silver, one with snow white—were spotted poking around the wreckage, well? They'll turn out to be city officials accompanying the owner to recover what could be recovered. (Which isn't much. But then, that was never the point.) Anyway, no body will ever be found.

Later, she will get an email from a k12.edu address that turns out to belong to an elementary school teacher. After a minute in which she debates opening it, she finds that there's no text, just a link to the *Journal Sentinel*. "UWM VP of Development Still at Large Amid Allegations of Sexual

Abuse." The joy that rings through her like a bell, despite the subheading: "School Denies Prior Knowledge."

Later, she will not hesitate to take the piano money from the insurance company, though *Demeter and Persephone* earns out its advance within the first year and the *Little Feminists* royalties keep flowing in. In the meantime, the antiques inside were worth almost as much as the house itself. She returns the $850,000 check to her father three times before he wires the money to her bank account, ending the debate.

Later, she will stay quiet as the court wonders: Did Kintner flee, or is he dead? Does the insurance money from the Elf House rightfully belong to Michael Kreis or Patrick Kintner's estate? Kintner's continued mortgage payments argue for flight. And so, the judge says, he ran. Nobody thinks to ask: Who first taught him how to create online passwords, two decades ago?

Later, Saskia Kreis will finally get her clean slate. Nothing like a couple million and an electrical fire for a good slate cleaning.

But in the moment, none of that has happened yet.

In the moment, the Elf House burns.

She watches the bay window overlooking the lake. And in the second before the glass explodes, she can swear she sees a blond woman. Smiling, then turning palely away.

"It's time now," her father is saying to her. "It's time to go."

She follows him through the woods. And yet, she watches. Because he's right, of course. He's always right. And here they are together, and that is what matters. Them, and time.

She stares at the conflagration as sirens cut through the cotton-wool silence of the blizzard. But still she doesn't look away. She couldn't. She can't give it up, can't risk losing this moment.

No longer the spectacle herself.

There's so much in life to watch. How has she never seen it before?

She watches the Elf House burn.

She watches a death.

She watches the light. The light, as it plays tricks across time.

Acknowledgments

MY DEEP GRATITUDE TO:

First of all, the unbelievably talented editorial team who worked on this book: Sarah Cantin and Sallie Lotz. I was already incredibly lucky to work with them on one book; this second one was a dream come true. Without their sensitive and intelligent guidance, I don't think *The Ingenue* would ever have come together half as well. They truly deserve their places in the pantheon of editorial greats!

Every writer should be so lucky as to have an advocate as passionate, enthusiastic, and whip-smart as Sarah Phair. I'm so grateful to have her at my side—thank you for all of your wonderful work. Here's to many more Paris adventures to come!

Special thanks to my sister, Liana Kapelke-Dale, who whipped out her law degree to do the legal research for this book. Without her, every explanation would be "because . . . law." After this trial by fire, she has no interest in doing this for others, but she has an amazing poetry collection, *Seeking the Pink*, that you should check out! All mistakes remain my own.

The people at St. Martin's Press are truly exceptional. My profound thanks for the outstanding work that Kejana Ayala, Katie Bassel, Brant Janeway, Erica Martirano, Kelly Moran, and others have done on behalf of my writing. I'm so grateful to the sales team, as well, for getting my books in front of as many people as possible! Meanwhile, Danielle Christopher's designs never fail to delight me, and I'm thrilled she designed this cover. Finally, Sona Vogel is a genius whose eagle eye once again faced incredible challenges—and twisted chronologies!—and whose copyediting skills once again proved victorious.

I'm very grateful to all of the writers who have helped me—whether that's in workshopping my stories, promoting them, or just providing a shoulder to cry on! With that in mind, here's to DWG: Albert Alla, Peter-Adrian Altini, Peter Brown, Amanda Dennis, Nina-Marie Gardner, Sophie Hardach, Rafael Herrero, Matt Jones, Corinne LaBalme, Samuel Leader, Ferdia Lennon, Reine Arcache Melvin, Spencer Matheson, Mark Mayer, Dina Nayeri, Chris Newens, Helen Cusack O'Keefe, Tasha Ong, Anna Polonyi, Alberto Rigettini, Jonathan Schiffman, and Nafkote Tamirat. A special shout-out to Chris and Ferdia for not pushing me off of my chair into the campfire last summer— I would have deserved it.

The larger writing community has also been incredibly supportive. I'd particularly like to thank Daniel Goldin at the Boswell Book Company, my home bookstore (its previous incarnation makes a cameo here). I'm also grateful to Andrea Bartz, Ella Berman, Cathy Marie Buchanan, Christina Clancy, Laurie Elizabeth Flynn, Araminta Hall, Emily Layden, and Ellen O'Connell Whittet, all of whom showed such incredible support and generosity during my first book. Go buy theirs, they're all amazing! Similarly, I am so grateful to Layne Fargo, Pamela Klinger-Horn, and Ashley Winstead for their early support of this book.

I wrote this novel during a time when I couldn't get home to see my family. While they do not appear in these pages, they were constantly on my mind: Steve Kapelke, Kathleen Dale, Liana Kapelke-Dale, Jessi LeClair, Dave LeClair, Alden and Alex LeClair, Phil Kapelke, Joan Cushing, Paul Cushing, and Tom and Kevin Cushing. And, always, for Elliot.

Kate Sekules's wonderful memoir, *The Boxer's Heart: A Woman Fighting*, helped me understand Saskia just that much more. I'd also like to thank Tim Knox, photographer and author of the article "The Women Boxers of Gleason's Gym," published in *The Guardian*, who also helped open up this fascinating world to me. And, of course, the boxers interviewed there themselves: Carolyn DiCarlo, Ronica Jeffrey, Heather Hardy, Keisher "Fire" McLeod, Sonya Lamonakis, Renee Rickenbacker, Melissa St. Vil, Jessica Young, Natasha Lemaitre, Fiona Beswick, C'Lynne O'Brien, Hannah Benson, Gabriella Gulfin, Jenna Gaglioti, and Alicia "Slick" Ashley. I am particularly grateful to Ms. DiCarlo's quote in that article for introducing me to the boxing-world truth—that it's about not getting hit.

And, finally, to all of my friends, but particularly to Sarah Dosmann, my original companion in going "down to Downer," and Jess Pan, with whom I've explored the world since.